Wicked Creatures

Wicked Creatures

An Anthology of the
New England Horror Writers

Edited by

Scott T. Goudsward
Daniel G. Keohane
David Price

Interior Layout and Design by Daniel G. Keohane
Published in October 2021 by NEHW Press, a division of Wicked Creative, LLC
ISBN 978-0-9981854-5-3
www.newenglandhorror.org
Printed in the United States of America

Other Anthologies of the
New England Horror Writers

Wicked Women
Edited by Trisha J. Wooldridge
and Scott T. Goudsward

Wicked Weird
Edited by Amber Fallon,
Scott T. Goudsward and David Price

Wicked Haunted
Edited by Scott T. Goudsward,
Daniel G. Keohane and David Price

Wicked Witches
Edited by Scott T. Goudsward,
Daniel G. Keohane and David Price

Wicked Tales
Edited by Scott T. Goudsward,
Daniel G. Keohane and David Price

Wicked Seasons
Edited by Stacey Longo

Epitaphs
Edited by Tracy L. Carbone

For Lisa Mannetti

Table of Contents

Massive Entity-17 Bernardo Carpio

by K. H. Vaughan

"Who is that? Manbun?" Tasha says.

"Fucking Manbun," Vinh says.

"Who?" Boog says.

"Manbun," Tasha says.

"Fucking Manbun," Vinh says.

"I hate fucking Manbun," Boog says.

"The fuck's he doing?" I say.

We watch through sniper scopes as Manbun navigates his way through the rubble to the base of Bernardo Carpio. Bernardo does not notice him anymore than we notice the skin mites on our faces. Shit, Bernardo hasn't even moved as far as anyone can tell in ten years, not since he pulled himself out of the ocean and planted himself in Providence, looming over the wreckage of his passage like a mountain transported to the city. Manbun is with another crew working out of the East Side. There's nothing on the schedule today, so he's freelancing. We scan around and find some of his people scattered at a distance, watching.

Bernardo sheds black dust like copy machine toner. We still don't know what it is. Manbun is in it up to his knees as he approaches and it swirls around him, almost insubstantial. The area has been mostly cleared of obstacles; he's on a well-established approach. Tasha tries to radio it in, but there's too much interference today, so we can either hump back to a hardline or wait and see. Whatever he's doing, no one wants to miss this. Manbun walks back and forth at the base of Bernardo's tail, sizing up the situation, then starts to climb.

"He's not even hooking up," Boog says. "He's doing a free solo."

"Fucking Manbun," Vinh mutters.

There are years of pitons and cams in the lower reaches of Bernardo. His strange, shark-like skin; interlocking denticles the size of manhole covers until the boney armor across the chest and shoulders above. Manbun is past the graffiti line at the base and isn't hooking on yet. Maybe he will higher up. It's over twelve-hundred feet to the top. Three times the height of the Superman building which, miraculously, is still standing in his shadow. We figure out that his crew is positioned to get different angles on his climb, and they're recording. Jerk is trying to grow his brand.

This is going to be a while, so we settle in on the west-side edge of the break in the I-195 bridge, which Bernardo broke off when he came up the river into downtown. As word gets out, other people come to watch the climb, scavengers, military, locals who refused to clear the evacuation zone. They line up on the roofs of buildings and the highway on the south and west sides. On the bridge, people bring lawn chairs, grills and coolers. Around noon, the Colonel shows up, watches through field glasses for a few minutes, grunts, and walks back down the ramp to his car. He's probably annoyed, but he knows that after all the stuff we've done to Bernardo, this isn't going to be the thing that wakes him up.

So, me, Vinh, Boog, and Tasha eat burgers and drink beer while we spend the day on Bernardo Carpio surveillance. It's like an old-school cook-out. Manbun is about a third of the way up. People share their theories on why kaiju walked out of the ocean all over the world to just go dormant within a few miles of the shore. Why now? Why these cities? Which ones would win in a fight? It's nice. Normally we just sit and watch him as he sits, unmoving, in the ruins. All the buildings crushed by his passage, and the entire area compacted beneath his massive weight. From this angle I can see his profile—the main and secondary eyes, antennae, the edges of his lobster-like mouth. There's evidence that these parts move, but it's too slow for the naked eye to see. Things like this shouldn't exist. The physics of a living organism of this size are impossible. But he's there and doesn't care about our understanding of physics any more than he seems to care about anything else we do.

There is a collective gasp and I get my binoculars up just in time to catch the end of Manbun's fall. The fine black toner dust evacuates from the point of impact as he hits, the way powder snow gets blown around by trucks on a highway. He lands badly, femurs punching up through his knee and thigh, head flattening against the concrete in a red gout. The dust swirls like black smoke for a moment, then settles back in place, covering it all. The party breaks up. There is nothing left to see.

* * *

Massive Entity-17 Bernardo Carpio is one of the original twenty-six that walked onto land ten years ago. The rest came piecemeal. I think there are forty-three now, but it's hard to know what sources to trust anymore. Most of them landed at cities, but not all of them. When ours came ashore one of the man-on-the-street eyewitnesses was a Filipino sailor on a ship loading scrap metal at Port of Providence. He yelled "Bernardo Carpio" at the news camera and it became a meme. I guess it's from a Filipino myth about a giant who causes earthquakes. The Colonel—John Bermudez, U.S. Army—was stationed at the DEVCOM Soldier Center in Natick before being sent here to oversee operations on "Seventeen." It's mostly MPs guarding the perimeter and the research scientists and techs. I don't know what his degree is in, but he speaks fluent science with the nerds. The nerds talk to him and then he hands out gigs to the crews. Place instruments, collect samples, escort scientists in when they want a closer look. The evacuation zone is about a three-mile radius, so essentially all the city except for squatters. Probably 300K displaced, which isn't much compared to Manilla or New York, but still, the whole core of the state.

The Colonel had Manbun's crew arrested, confiscated their footage, and stripped their credentials. He locked down the Zone for a week and kicked them out of housing after he was done with them. No volunteers to get the body, so he picked us. We drive in on the Army's version of a landscaper's truck. Boog's at the wheel since you can't trust the nav system near Bernardo. Boog was just discharged after four tours in Afghanistan when the kaiju arrived. He could have re-upped, but he prefers being a private contractor. The pay isn't great, but you can walk away if you want to. He still shakes when we drive by a garbage bag on the roadside sometimes.

You can see Bernado the entire ride in, but it doesn't seem real to me until we get to the debris fields around Davol Square and the old power plant. Then he just looms over you. Maybe eighty percent of everything inside I-95 and the river is gone, either knocked down when he arrived or collapsed with the subsidence over the next couple of years. As you get closer, he doesn't seem to get any bigger.

We have to walk the last hundred yards through the black dust in the mountain's shadow. So, we carry the super duty transport bag and shovels to the base of Bernardo and fan at the dust.

"Jesus, can you believe this shit?" Vinh says, staring up the flank of the kaiju. "I mean, what are we even doing out here? Metal salvage, I understand, but all this testing and observation? Do we know anything useful about our boy here yet?"

"And if we do, does it even matter?" Tasha says. "What are we gonna do, kill it? You think cleaning up Manbun is bad, what happens if we ice this thing? I know I'm not scooping up a quarter million metric tons of rotting kaiju."

"Could be worse," I say. "He starts walking around, they'll probably have us following him to clean up his shits."

"Oh, man. I hope you guys brought an umbrella in case his bladder lets go," Boog says. "That'll be like Niagara Falls."

"Umbrella," Tasha laughs.

It's weird, getting used to this thing. It's been so long you just accept it, just like you accept the entire world economy is completely wrecked because some of the biggest container ports and financial centers all got donked up. I was going to be a freshman at Classical when this started. That's like a whole lifetime ago. Bernardo ain't going nowhere though.

"What we need," Vinh says, "is to build mechs and beat their asses. Get some Gundam or Mecha Samurai action up in here."

"That's science fiction," I say.

"So is this," Vinh says, pointing up at Bernardo.

"Found him," Boog says.

The body is not as flat as I expected, except for the head. The skin on his stomach is ruptured, with some tissue poking out, pink with yellow fat globules. But we can tell his structure is just wrecked. He's a bag of fragments now. We lay out the bag next to him and unzip it, size up the job. On the plus side, he was wearing a climbing harness—I figure he was going to rope back down once he got as far as he could. We talk it over, grab the harness at the shoulders and hips and lift. Everything sags unnaturally. Parts of his brain fall out in soggy clumps. We drop him in and use the shovels to collect whatever loose scraps we can. Then we zip the inner liner and the outer shell and hump him back to the truck. No one has anything to say on the way back to base, and after we get the job order signed, we sit in the cafeteria and just stare.

Fucking Manbun.

* * *

"Yo, this is stupid," Vinh says.

"You gotta narrow that down some, Vinh," Tasha says.

We're sprawled in what was a student lounge on the culinary school campus near the edge of the Zone. There are plenty of empty buildings to squat in, but staying in authorized housing has perks like steady electricity and hot water, and being on-hand if new missions or information come down from the Colonel. He doesn't spend a lot of time deliberating what crew gets what gig; if he sees you first, and you aren't on his shit-list that day, you're up.

"This whole thing," Vinh says. "Living right up under Bernardo like this. Poking at him every day. Damn. Dude's a fucking menace. And what do we do? Scrape him for barnacles and shit. Kaiju pose challenges. What Kaiju Are You quizzes? Memes."

"What kaiju *are* you," I say.

"Big Pappa Cauã. Obviously," Vinh says and flexes with his arms like the monster frozen in Rio. "But that ain't the point."

"What do you want us to do?" I say. "Still have to eat. People live on earthquake faults, volcanoes. This isn't any different. It's like climate change or the pandemic—it just moves so slowly you don't notice until suddenly it's a disaster."

"And when he moves?" Vinh says.

"Run the other way," Boog says. "We can't hurt him. They tried bunker busters, MOABs. The Russians dropped a thermobaric on Baba Yaga at Murmansk, and it didn't do squat. No one wants to be the first to go nuclear, but if Rahab wakes up in Tel Aviv, the IDF ain't gonna wait for it to reach Jerusalem."

"Hold up, hold up," Tasha says, hand in the air. We freeze. Gunfire. A few pops, the chatter of automatic weapons. Probably M-4s and a SAW. Sounds close to Bernardo. Tasha goes to the window and looks with binoculars.

"What's up?" I say.

"He ain't moving," Tasha says. "Probably unauthorized looters. Maybe protesters."

"Or those religious freaks. Kaiju cultists," Vinh says.

"Hey, if God walks out of the sea, who am I to argue?" I say.

"They got AKs," Boog says. "You hear that? *Bap-bap-bap-bap-bap-bap-bap*. Like being in Kabul all over again. Shit, Imma catch some bad dreams off that tonight."

The PA system chirps, and the Big Voice says campus is in lockdown and blackout protocol. We go out on the balcony and watch the tracer fire run back and forth, ricochet off into the sky. Soldiers scramble below, getting into trucks and Humvees, and a convoy of vehicles heads toward downtown. We aren't supposed to carry weapons, although we have knives and a handgun each.

"What the hell's an authorized looter?" Vinh says.

"We are," Tasha says. "We got ID cards and lanyards and everything."

There's an explosion. Maybe an RPG. And in the middle of it, Bernardo Carpio stands silently, ignoring the occasional stray round that hits him.

"Shit, I'm going up to the roof," Tasha says. "Can't see anything from here."

* * *

I follow her up. Boog and Vinh go back to playing FIFA on the PlayStation.

"Can't see much better from up here," I say.

"No, but it's easier to hear if it's getting closer," she says. "This shit can shift fast. We're only a couple minutes away if it moves."

The roof of the dormitory is flat with a short concrete lip. I walk to the street side of the building. I doubt the shooting downtown is a diversion so they can attack here, but there are a lot of scientists on campus. They bombed the CDC at the start of the COVID-22 pandemic, so it's possible. There's an Abrams at the gate, though. Kaiju don't care about tanks, but guys with AKs still do.

All the houses are dark for blocks. You look south or west and you can see where the lights come on again. Across the Bay it doesn't look like anything changed at all. But a couple miles north is a mountain, oblivious to the firefight around his feet.

"You think they'll start dropping nukes if they move again?" I say.

"Probably," Tasha says. "I'd bet money they've got a bomb with Bernardo's name on it right now. Only question is how big."

The apartment I lived in with my Mom growing up is in the dark zone. I watched all the monster movies growing up. All the original Toho and Daiei films, the knockoffs and remakes. Every giant insect movie from the 50s. I never figured it would be like this.

But it is.

* * *

The warning sirens go off. One of the loneliest and most desolate sounds I know. Every once in a while, the Pentagon tests something out on Bernardo. We wake up to a PowerPoint presentation and go on standby. Today, they are going to drop a tungsten spear the size of a phone pole on him from space. Twenty-four thousand pounds at over seven-thousand meters per second. A Rod from God. The Lance of Longinus. They say that we are at a safe distance because although the kinetic energy is like a nuke, it's focal. But that assumes they hit the target.

We watch the sky. Drones circle in the distance. The siren dies except for the echo. There is a voice on a speaker counting down. We watch the high gray sheet of altocumulus clouds stretched like bunched cotton batting at around twenty-three thousand feet. Bernado stands passively, as he has done for ten years. We hold our breath, each of us, alone.

A fiery streak punches a perfect circle in the clouds, like an angel expelled from Heaven. There is no time to react before it strikes.

Bernardo is almost instantly enveloped in a plume of dust, and then the earth shakes violently. Then the sound. The sonic boom and the sound of the air being torn to shreds. The thunderous impact.

Bernardo Carpio screams.

It is a horrible cry of pain, rumbling from the deepest abyss. Primordial. A sound from before there were humans, or the small, frightened creatures that eventually became humans.

Bernardo staggers and falls. A spray of blood coats the Superman Building from top to bottom. It takes forever for him to land. Massive shape turning, blood from the entry wound in the shoulder and the exit wound tearing down through the abdomen and inside of the thigh. A massive torrent of crimson fills the depression where he has stood for ten years. He tilts, his left arms hanging uselessly and the two on the opposite side grasping with their three stubby fingers for some purchase in the empty air. He turns on his back, smashing the Convention Center, the Omni hotel, I-95 and part of the Mall. Buildings shake and compromised structures all around give way. The sound dies, and the dust settles. But the blood continues in a deluge through the streets to inundate downtown.

* * *

There are aftershocks and more building collapses for days. They say the Lance is buried at least a hundred yards in the ground beneath the basin now. The bleeding goes to a trickle and eventually stops, but the debris berms we built around downtown contain the lake. There's an oily slick from all the chemicals and grease left from the city. I don't know how to describe a rainbow sheen over blood. It's slowly finding the working storm drains and oozing its way through the barriers into the river. People come in small groups to be baptized in the crimson river down where the hurricane barrier used to be. The Colonel leaves them be as long as they don't get any closer, and we don't get as many people trying to get into the danger zone this way. I caught striped bass and bluefin there when I was a kid. We see the pilgrims when we travel in and out of the site. They enter the water in white robes and come out pink. They wave when we drive past. There are always a few zealots who will brave the machine guns to drown themselves in the pure blood of Bernardo, but it's not so bad anymore.

The roads we cleared are now hazards again, so they've got demolition crews pulling debris out and marking safe pathways. There are slabs, statues, signs, all encrusted with gore and dust, as landmarks for our passage. We wade up to our waists in hazmat suits, guiding rubber rafts with coolers for tissue samples. Look for internal tissue, nervous system in particular, they say. Get it on ice and bring it back for analysis. They tell us there isn't any exposure risk from the blood itself. Probably lying to us about that.

"This ain't gonna be no different from burn pits," Boog says. "They say it's cool, but in a few years it's gonna be all respiratory problems and cancers. Bet you a hundred bucks I pick up an autoimmune disorder or some shit off of this."

People have no idea how much toxic shit is around them. A city's worth of cleaning supplies, fuel, air conditioner fluid, asbestos. Fiberglass, PCBs, Dioxin. Sewerage. All mashed up and spilled all over the Zone. Now floating in a lake of blood. I develop a chronic rash. Vinh can't stop coughing. It isn't long before we all have tears in our suits and are patching them with duct tape. It doesn't work well, and we shower the blood off at the end of every day. Once we get to that point, we don't bother with the hoods. The smell isn't any worse, and at least we can breathe. At least it's cold weather. The flies would be unbearable if it was summer.

His eyes look dead like a shark's. But they always have, all six of them. It's strange to see him lying on the ground, ripped open. His torso is completely ruptured, and you can see massive organs hanging there, although they don't obviously match up with anything we have. Strange lobes and spirals, enormous veiny sacs and elongated masses suspended in rubbery membranes. Even these internal tissues are hard to injure. We use pneumatic tools with diamond cutting edges just to extract shavings. Once, a crew pierced some sort of bladder and they were dissolved by the caustic fluid in seconds. They are trying to build a scaffold so we can get to the head. I think the scientists want us to tunnel through the mouth and try to find an artery or soft part of the skull so we can sample his brain.

That's gonna wait, though. With the crew getting melted, they want us to steer clear of the tear in his abdomen for now. They send us to pick over the area where Bernardo was standing originally under the assumption that we'll be able to find tissue shredded from the Lance. The area hasn't been cleared by the engineers, so they tell us to be careful.

"I'm just saying that if they can move all the debris from 9-11, they can clean up this mess," Tasha says. "Cut him up, put the pieces on barges and dump him in the ocean."

"You want giant shark monsters?" Boog says. "Cause that's how you get giant shark monsters."

"Giant shark monsters would be better," I say. "They stay in the water."

"Shit, you never watched classic horror movies, did you?" Vinh says. "*Sharktopus. Sharktopus versus Whalewolf.*"

"Man, you are not helping my anxiety with that," Boog says. "Shit! Something just touched my leg."

We pause. There is no wind and we stand in blood up to our waists in our torn yellow suits. The blood has begun to coagulate with gooey gelatinous strands and lumps of hardening fibroids floating throughout. They stick to the exposed rubble like jellyfish stranded after the tide. Rusty brown stains mark the high tide of his exsanguination. The clots stick like pine tar. At the edges, a leathery skin has formed, like the skin on pudding in the fridge, but a foot thick. Minutes pass. Maybe an hour's worth.

"Anyone else got anything?" Tasha says. We are close to Washington Park and the Superman building. A lot of open space.

"Nothing?" she says.

We look at each other, paralyzed.

"You guys really think there's little shark monsters in here? Come on," she says. "This is like the worst public swimming pool on the planet, right? It's fucking gross. But no monsters. So let's get some samples and get paid."

It's enough to get us moving again. You can get used to anything. In the shadow of the Superman building, we find scraps. Shreds of grey meaty tissue the length of a person, strange fatty globules floating in the blood.

"Here we go," I say. "Sashimi. Or is it tartare?"

"If it comes out of the ocean, it's sashimi," Tasha says.

"Think about it," Boog says. "Someone is going to go down in history as the first person to eat kaiju. That is gonna be their claim to fame. And they'll be internet famous and get content deals and everything. Unless it kills them."

"Still be famous though, right?" Vinh says.

"Fuck, yeah," Boog says.

We take a collection of the interesting bits that will fit in the coolers. It's nasty work, and everyone is pissed off by the time we are ready to wrap up. We're ready to call it when a massive sticky clot the size of a RIPTA bus sloughs off the side of the Superman building and splashes down nearby. We are covered, wiping the gore from our eyes and spitting it out of our mouths. The blood is oily, fishy, nasty. I puke before I can stop myself and it floats on the dull red surface of the lake.

"Goddammit," Boog says. He's shaking. He unleashes a violent stream of profanity, beating the blood slick with his fists, and thrashes down the street away from us, screaming curses in at least three languages that he's picked up from his tours overseas. And, as sympathetic as we are, we can't help but laugh. We're just as soaked and freaked out too. It's just so ridiculous, watching him wade through blood up to his armpits, screaming absolute murder and splashing around like a toddler in a bath. He grabs hold of a signpost and starts pulling on it—there's nothing loose to throw, and we cheer him on, yelling and hooting until his blood-slick hands slip and he falls backwards and goes under. He does not come up right away.

"Stop fucking around, Boog," Tasha says.

He stays under. We work our way over to the area he fell until we find the edge of a hole with our feet. Vinh takes a deep breath and goes under. Comes back up, gasping.

"I can't find him," he says. "It's deep, the hole down there."

After a while it's clear he isn't coming back, so we get the raft and make our way back out to report in.

* * *

The Colonel doesn't have divers to retrieve the body. They put a steel road plate over the hole so no one else falls in. If Boog had anyone to notify, we don't know about them. People don't talk about those things around here. We get rotated out towards the edge where the lake isn't as deep. About a week later there's a partial building collapse and Tasha ends up with a piece of rebar through her shoulder. Doesn't hit anything vital, but it's bad. They put her in the infirmary, and pump her through a cocktail of most everything they can think of that will kill viruses, bacteria and fungi. She'll probably need kidneys and a liver just from the drugs if she doesn't go into cardiac failure first. She looks pale and jaundiced.

"How you doing," I say.

"A little ibuprofen and I'll be good to go," she says.

"You never said what branch you served in. I mean, you're obviously ex-military."

"The Corp. I re-upped once, but decided that I wasn't cut out for officer training. Wanted to try something different."

"USMC. When you absolutely, positively need to fuck a target up overnight."

"Semper Fi." she says. "You want to hear something funny? I dated a Coast Guard sailor for a minute. His entire job was changing light bulbs on buoys, if you believe that shit."

"Some people fuck shit up. Some people change lightbulbs."

She laughs, which leads to a painful bout of coughing. Her veins are a blue roadmap everywhere I can see her skin.

"So it's you and Vinh, now, huh?" she says when it passes. "You got to be careful out there. Maybe bring in a couple new hands to the crew. Might even be time to get out. I mean, our boy is decaying and that blood lake is getting more toxic. They're gonna start finding bacteria from other dimensions before this is done."

"I don't know what else to do. I didn't even finish high school. Not a lot of work in the post-kaiju economy. Giant goddamn motherfuckers just wrecked everything. I don't want to go to one of those relocation camps. Hey, you hear about the helicopter crash? News helo got too close, and the electronics failed. Full of foreign press. Came down hard in the Bay. More people died just being stupid since he showed up than got killed when he walked out of the ocean."

"Well, ain't that the way? Look, all I'm saying is, this is going south. The Colonel will keep sending you guys out doing stupid shit until he runs out of guys. I know you get paid and work is scarce, but you need an exit strategy, alright?"

* * *

Pilgrims in robes wave to us as we drive in. They seem to think we are special because we walk in his blood all day while they only get the runoff in the River. There are thousands every day and the Colonel doesn't have much choice but to give them access to the River. He brought in big pumps to drain the lake out into the Bay, but it isn't making much of a difference as far as I can see. They take over both sides of the Bay. MP's shoot one every once in a while to keep them out of the Zone, but I'm thinking that won't be enough before too long. The cultists wave and smile. It terrifies me.

* * *

Me and Vinh are set up on the I-195 bridge by the edge on overwatch again. Bernardo lies unmoving, as he has been for weeks now. They've been building scaffolding around him. I wouldn't want to be right on top of him these days. Whatever he's made of doesn't decay as fast as regular animals, but he's definitely ripe at this point. The stench of the gigantic carcass and the thick crusty blood lake is oppressive. You get used to it, but it soaks into everything. It's sunny out, so I put my chair back as far as it will go and put my feet up on a crate. I take my shirt off to get some sun on my rash. The cream they gave me didn't seem to do anything, but we've had a week out of the lake and it's scabbing over. We have a radio, which still doesn't work well near Bernardo, but one of the Spanish stations fades in and out, so we've got a little music at least.

I take a scan with the binoculars. The workers erecting the scaffolding look like insects. They've been making progress, though. Maybe they'll put an enormous tent over him when they are done. Maybe they'll bury him in a concrete tomb like Chernobyl. Or maybe they'll figure out how to carve him up and truck away the bits little by little.

"Aw man," Vinh says, digging around in his mouth with his fingers. "Look at this." He pulls out a molar and holds it up, then chucks the bloody tooth over the broken edge of the bridge into the River. "How much longer we got?" he says. I look at my watch.

"Three hours," I say.

"Long three hours," Vinh says. "These days are getting long."

"I was talking to Tasha before they sent her to the hospital," I say. "Or hospice? I don't remember which. She said we should think about getting out. I don't know what I'd do, but this just keeps getting worse."

"You know, I got a cousin in Minnesota. Nothing bigger than a moose or a bear for a thousand miles. Probably ain't no work out there either, but this shit ain't worth it and he's just getting nastier."

"That sounds good. I've got a little saved even after room and board on campus."

"Same," Vinh says, nodding. "Maybe we should cash out our scrip for dollars. Probably have enough for a couple bus tickets between the two of us. Or it's gonna be warm enough for a while we could hitchhike or jump a train. Sleep rough. That way we'd have a stake when we get to Minneapolis."

We talk for a while, throwing ideas for the future back and forth. It is the beginning of a plan. The beginning of a future.

There is a metallic bang, and we pick up our binoculars. One of the huge cantilevered cranes groans and tilts. Six-hundred feet tall, it has been the largest thing on the skyline since Bernardo fell, and now it is falling next to him. The main boom of the V frame buckles and it describes a languid arc in the sky as it comes down, cables flailing, scaffolding collapsing beneath and then it is down across the remains of the highway. The sound of its impact arrives a few seconds after, rolling over us like a bomb blast. The scaffolding around Bernardo collapses like a house of cards as section after section comes down. An immense cloud of dust rises above it all. Soon after, the warning siren sounds.

"Jesus Christ," I say. "There were a ton of guys down there."

"Could have been us, easy," Vinh says.

"Jesus," I say. "Jesus."

There is movement in the dust. A vast, impossible shape.

Bernardo Carpio rises. His eyes are clouded like old fish in the market, and his gut is torn open. A slurry of rot slides from the cavity and viscous brown fluid leaks from his mouth and nostrils. His two left arms hang uselessly, dangling from connective tissue and strings of muscle. He stands, pus and blackened sludge running down his legs. He reaches across with his two good arms to tear the useless ones from his body and tosses them casually onto College Hill. We hear the sirens of first responders heading to the scene. The pilgrims chant in jubilation.

The Spanish music on the radio is interrupted by the emergency broadcast signal.

All around the world, the giants have begun to move again.

The Mumble Man

by James A. Moore

You walk around the neighborhood, sooner or later you're going to meet all kinds. Three houses down from my front door is a couple who look like they walked right out of an ad for a dating site. He's buff, has dark hair and a million-dollar smile. She's blonde-haired, blue-eyed, with just the right number of freckles, a half dozen dimples and a body designed solely for wet dreams. I call them Ken and Barbie, but never to their faces. That would be hurtful and rude. Across the street is the cat lady. I don't know if she actually has cats, but she looks like the type: older than Moses, stooped at the shoulders, white hair and glasses, a slightly confused look on her face, and she almost never goes out.

Next to the cat lady is Wellington House, an old brownstone that has been converted into six incredibly small apartments held by different college kids. There're two stoners, the girls I think of as the Sad Saturday Twins—a little heavy and getting heavier: they never leave on Saturday nights and their too loud conversations have an edge of tragedy that hurts my soul—Louis Temple, one of my best buds, and lastly the upstairs neighbor that Louis calls the Shadow. Dude is always in a floppy, wide brimmed fedora and only comes out at night. He'd maybe be a figure of mystery, but I've walked past him a few times. He's short, he's nerdy and he'd probably wet himself if anyone ever spoke to him. Nervous doesn't begin to touch it.

They are the periphery of my world. I see them every day, or close enough that it doesn't matter, and they are stable and steady. Even the ones I don't know by name are like cornerstones to my current existence, and not having them around would mess with my mental equilibrium. I like my world in balance.

We all take pride in the little zone we've made for ourselves. Despite the high crime only one block over, almost nothing ever happens on our street, in our tiny zone of comfort.

The graffiti came along and changed everything.

First was just the name, spray painted on alley walls and even on the side of the apartment building: "Mumble Man." It sounded like a bad name for a character from a comic book. I think Dick Tracy even had an enemy with that name, or something like it. I saw it the first time and I was just a little pissed, because it's a good neighborhood and we don't usually get graffiti. Mostly the little Italian lady right down the street, Mrs. Tuscoli—at the edge of my known universe, but seldom a part of it—comes out and sweeps the sidewalks in front of her place and in a few minutes someone else will come out on my end of the street—sometimes even me—and do the same and the next thing you know, the street and sidewalks are neat and everyone is happy. So, no, not really a lot of gang tags around here and even if there were, who the hell calls themselves the Mumble Man?

So, it was one of those things you have to accept in the city—some asshole somewhere is tagging buildings. The little Italian lady? She whitewashed the side of her home and most of us followed suit. She leads by example. I like her.

A week or so went by and I stopped thinking about it. The paint was gone, the memory faded.

It should have been nothing more than a memory, really, but the tags came back, only modified. Now it was "Look out for the Mumble Man." I invested in some paint remover the first time I saw it, and I got rid of the tag that some prick had put on my front door. Not funny and not cute. I was pissed about it if you want to know the truth. I work, I come home to my nice neighborhood and I expect peace. Instead I had some dick trying to ruin what was mine and I did not like it at all.

Louis popped by with a sixpack of his favorite micro-brewed specialty beer around the same time I finished removing the tag. Louis likes to experiment with the local pubs. If they have a new flavor of beer, he's got a twenty to spend on it. I don't think he's ever run across a microbrew he couldn't befriend. Except the stuff that I buy. Those he'll hate on general principles. That's okay. These days he buys the beer and I buy the pizza. It works out.

He frowned as he watched me working on removing the last vestiges of paint.

"The fuck?"

"The 'Mumble Man' struck again." I shook my head and tried not to look as pissed off as I was. I'm pretty sure I failed.

"Wish I'd seen someone, bro."

"That's two of us. I ever catch this prick, I'm gonna change the shape of his skull."

"Graphic." Louis faked a wince. We were on the varsity football team together. We had both changed the shapes of a few skulls in our time, but only when it was deserved.

Louis nodded and held out the beer. There was a scarecrow with a jack o' lantern face and a scythe on the bottles and on the container holding the bottles. Halloween was coming on fast. Maybe the only thing Louis liked better than his beers, and women, was Halloween.

"DaVinci's okay with you?"

"Yeah. Just leave off the anchovies this time."

"That beer have pumpkin spice in it?" There was maybe an edge of accusation in my voice.

"No." There was definitely a defeated sort of guilty tone in his response. He knew what he'd done.

"Then you won't get anchovies on your pizza. Call it a lesson learned."

Louis smiled. He looked like he was just getting ready for puberty whenever he smiled.

I gathered my rags, paper towels, and paint thinner, then opened the door to the apartment. The smell of cinnamon and clove wafted through the threshold and tried to deodorize the whole neighborhood. Louis wrinkled his nose and walked in after me.

"For a guy that doesn't like pumpkin spice your house sure smells like a bakery."

"My 'house' smells like something other than dirty underwear and socks, which is more than I can say for your place." Part of me wanted to correct him for calling my place a house, but I chose not to be a dick about it.

"Dude. I washed all of my clothes."

"Yeah? Was that this year or last?"

"Like, maybe August?"

"I do not understand why Sarah stays with you."

"Because I know the way around a woman's body, bro." He smiled as he spoke. I rolled my eyes. In truth, Sarah would have agreed with him. Not that it mattered. The two of us chose not to talk too often. It was better for Louis that way. I liked Sarah maybe a little too much. She maybe felt the same way about me. The one time we hung out without Louis around we wound up in a heavy petting session. We agreed never to talk to Louis about it. We also agreed to never put ourselves in that situation again.

We settled on the two recliners placed directly in front of the TV and I called DaVinci's, ordering a pizza with the works and double cheese, hold the anchovies. That was the real reason we normally got together at my place. I had a better TV.

While I was talking on the phone, I heard Louis say, "You fucking kidding me?" I looked his way as he got out of his seat and moved to the closest window. He was still there when I hung up, so I stood and joined him.

Without a word he pointed to the little old Italian lady's apartment building. There, very clearly visible, was a black form painted on the whitewashed brick wall. Under that shape were the scrawled words, "Beware the Mumble Man."

I studied the painting. It stood around seven feet in height and it was a long, drawn out form in a heavy coat and what looked like ragged blue jeans. Someone had taken the time to illustrate the Mumble Man with crude detail, from the boots on the feet to the jeans, the overcoat and the messy long hair around the face. In the drawing you could clearly see the eyes. They glared out hatefully past the hands that covered the mouth and nose of the spray-painted illustration. The eyes were buttons, easily two inches around for each of them, complete with four holes to tie the thread in place, but they glared just the same. A pool of shadows showed on the wall, creating a very convincing illusion of a man casting his shadow against the Italian lady's apartment building. If a man had been standing in that spot, the shadow he cast would have fallen exactly that way at that time of the afternoon.

"When the hell did that get painted?" Louis' voice carried a note of exasperation. Like me, he was tired of the tags and paintings.

I shook my head. All I could say with any certainty was that the cleverly designed street art had not been there when I was cleaning my door. I'd have seen it, as that was the direction Louis came from.

Someone had painted the entire thing in less than five or six minutes.

We went outside and looked at the painting up close. The sun was still up, and the light was hitting the tag full on. The brick wall was warm to the touch. My skin shivered into goosebumps as my fingers moved over the dark paint.

The paint was completely dry. The paint thinner was still damp on my door, but the paint on a massive illustration that was less than five minutes old was completely dry.

Impossible.

Up close I could see the texture of the cloth on the painting. It looked as if someone had spray painted the entire thing. There were faint wisps of the black that could not be deliberate, but rather a side effect of the aerosol forcing the stuff from the can. I looked at it closely, examined it as carefully as I could while trying to absorb the fact that the entire illustration simply shouldn't have been there and completely dry.

While I was puzzling out the mystery of the dried tag, Mrs. Tuscoli came outside and let out a low moan. A moment later she went back inside the building, grumbling in her native tongue. Louis looked my way and shrugged, but when she came back out with a can of whitewash and a brush, he was the first to offer to help her. In a matter of minutes, he was painting over the bottom of the image and I was covering the top, while the lady whose home had been violated ran around the both of us, smiling and nodding.

Mrs. Tuscoli tried to offer us money, but we shook our heads. Sometimes you just have to do the neighborly thing.

By the time we'd finished, the pizza delivery girl from DaVinci's had come to my apartment. Her name was Tina, and we got along well enough. As Louis always put it, she "gave good flirt." She was cute, she knew it, and she knew how to use it. I always tipped her well.

Except that time Mrs. Tuscoli was faster on the draw. Tina had to come over to where we were finishing up the whitewashing job, to get paid, and before I could reach for my wallet the little old neighbor of mine was handing the girl money and talking to her in rapid fire Italian.

Tina smiled and said, "Leonora here insisted on paying for you. She says you're 'good boys.'"

I smiled and asked her to thank Leonora. She did, and the little old lady smiled back, looking as beautiful as any woman ever had in that moment. It's amazing how much difference a smile can make.

A couple of minutes later we took the pizza back to my place. Just me and Louis, but I have to admit that after the conversation I was seriously considering asking Tina for a date the next time she had the day off. She kind of melted when she saw that we'd been helping Leonora, and her usual flirting became a more comfortable thing, more intimate if that makes any sense. I guess maybe she looked at the two of us as people instead of customers. That's the only way I can put it.

Louis stayed long enough to eat half a pizza, catch a movie with me, and knock back half the beers. Then he moved out into the night and headed for his apartment.

I didn't think about the Mumble Man or any of the street tags until the next morning, when I stepped out onto the sidewalk in front of my apartment and looked around as I did damn near every day. The sun was out but muted by clouds that promised rain before the day was over. My eyes were immediately drawn to the left, to the apartment building where Leonora, my little old Italian friend, was being lifted into the back of an ambulance. The door to her apartment was open. The sheet that covered her hid away her face from the world, more a shroud than a way to keep her warm.

That thought sent a chill through me.

On the wall of her apartment building, the shape of the Mumble Man had bled halfway through the whitewash, a ghostly reminder of the tag that some street "artist" had put up for all to see.

That sent a deeper shiver through my body.

Within a couple of hours, the news was out. According to the Sad Saturday Sisters, Leonora died of a heart attack. One of her friends had come by to take her shopping and called the police when Leonora didn't answer. Perfectly natural, right? It didn't feel that way though. I looked at that shadow form creeping through the paint we'd covered it with, and I couldn't get the notion out of my head that she was a victim of the Mumble Man.

Absolutely irrational, of course. It was just graffiti. Just some asshole tagging the neighborhood. I made myself a promise that if I saw the guy doing it, I was going to kick his ass and worry about calling the cops later. I also promised myself I'd paint over the damned thing again.

Louis beat me to it. I'd planned on going out when everything was calmer and covering up that damned painting. I wanted it gone. The thing was like a personal insult to Leonora's memory and I thought she would have wanted us to get rid of it. By the time I was ready to get out of the apartment and hit the local hardware store for the necessary supplies, Louis was halfway done with the job.

Instead I went to Hardigan's Liquor, bought a case of that beer he liked so much and told him this time it was on me. I even ordered us Chinese food from the place he liked. Though, truth be told, he really only liked that place because the hostess was hot. He was committed to Sarah, but that didn't mean he didn't look.

We ate in silence, mostly, and toasted Leonora's memory. She was a quiet part of our world and she'd been taken too soon. Twenty minutes after we'd finished eating, Louis looked at me and said, "I can't take that fucking painting. I mean it, Dan. I feel like that shit is haunting the street."

"We covered it up, Louis. And we'll keep our eyes open."

He shook his head. "There were two pictures of the Mumble Man today."

"What?"

He let out an exasperated half-laugh. "Why do you think I was ready with the paint, dude?"

I shrugged. There was nothing I could think to say. So, of course, Louis explained. "Bitch painted the same thing on the wall of my building. The side facing away from you, so I can see you not knowing. I finished covering it up and was going inside when I saw the one from yesterday."

Not gonna lie. I felt my blood pressure swing to the high side.

"I see him, I'm gonna hurt him." I barely recognized my own voice.

Louis nodded silently and killed off his third beer.

"He isn't worth going to jail for."

I nodded and reached for my second beer. Then I set it aside. No reason to get buzzed if all I was going to do was get pissed off.

Half an hour of shooting the breeze passed quickly and then, when Louis headed for his place, I asked him to show me the spot where his building had been tagged. It wasn't much to see, really. He'd already painted over the offensive work. All that was left was a faint image that tried to bleed through.

It was enough to see that this one was different. There was still a warning to "Beware the Mumble Man," but the picture above was different. The same basics. I could just make out the coat and shaggy hair, the boots. But this time the stance was changed. The shape was in profile for the most part, hands clenched at sides into angry fists. The head was turned to look at the viewer, but if there were any features to the face, the paint had hidden them too well to discern.

"It looks different." Louis spoke softly, but I heard him. I turned in his direction and saw the frown on his face.

"What are you talking about?"

He shook his head. "My imagination, I mean, obviously, but I thought he was facing differently when I painted over him. He was more casual, you know? Leaning against the wall with his arms crossed."

"Too many beers, dude." I said the words automatically, but I didn't feel them. The thought that the damned thing might have shifted positions was unsettling. Impossible, but no less disturbing.

Louis went home to change for his date with Sarah, and I lamented the fact that Sarah was with him and not me, if only because I wasn't with anyone at that time. I gave a lot more thought to asking Tina out.

Later, when I was drifting to sleep for the night, the thought occurred to me that the image was angered by being painted over. And maybe that was why it had killed Leonora.

I didn't get much sleep that night. The notion that the street art was alive and angry wouldn't leave me alone.

The morning found my little neighborhood surrounded by cop cars, fire engines and an ambulance. It seemed like overkill, which made me nervous. I walked outside of my apartment and squinted against the sunlight. Deana, one of the Sad Saturday Sisters, saw me and came running. Her face was tear-streaked, and her eyes were swollen from crying.

It only took a minute to find out that Louis was murdered while I was sleeping. It wasn't an accident. It wasn't an unexpected aneurysm. No heart attack for my best buddy. He was murdered. The Sad Saturday Sisters had found the door to his place kicked in, and called the cops immediately.

Whoever killed Louis did it with extreme prejudice. Eventually it came out that the cause of death was strangulation, but his hands had been shredded, likely by someone stomping down with heavy-treaded boots. Whoever murdered him stomped until bones were broken and skin was pulped away.

Louis died badly. If Leonora's death bothered me, Louis's haunted my day. I wandered around my neighborhood with my eyes looking everywhere and basically seeing nothing. I cried a bit as I walked along, and I saw people I knew and nodded to them, but everything I did, every interaction I had, was me working on autopilot. I couldn't get past the notion that the Mumble Man was angry about being painted over.

I didn't want to get over it. I wanted to revel in it. I wanted him angry. Scary and stupid as that sounds, I wanted the Mumble Man to be easily riled, because angry people make mistakes and I needed him making mistakes if I was going to catch him.

Somewhere along the way, and I knew it in my head even if my heart saw things differently, I had started equating the street artist with his or her creation. The Mumble Man was alive to me. A foolish notion and I knew it, but one that I couldn't escape.

I was walking back to my apartment, heading right past Ken and Barbie's place when I saw the image of the Mumble Man painted on their front door. This time he was just a head and shoulders, head thrown back in what I knew had to be a throaty laugh. His eyes were half closed, with smile lines, his brows were heavily shadowed over his obscene button eyes. His lips were open and showed bared teeth behind a joyous smile. Thread had apparently sealed his mouth at one point but now the remnants floated around the open grin. There was nothing otherwise malignant about the artwork. It was an expression of happiness that should have been a pleasure to see under most circumstances: a smile breaking free of its restraints, I suppose. It would have been in most cases, but with Louis still freshly dead and my mind locked on the way he was killed, that street tag was an outrage and the words "Beware the Mumble Man" only added insult to injury.

The way he was positioned, he was looking directly at me from my angle of approach perfectly at eye level with me. That is to say he was taller than me, but his button eyes looked down in my direction. I didn't think that was a coincidence then, and I don't think it now, either. It was deliberate. I'm certain of it. Dear God, I hated him at that moment. Had I seen the artist painting him, I would have committed violent murder.

He was laughing at my pain. I knew it in my heart.

I don't know what I would have done if I hadn't been interrupted by Sarah. I heard her call my name and I looked in the direction of her voice to see her coming my way. I'm ashamed to say I hadn't spared a second for my best friend's girlfriend. I had been far too focused on my own grief to consider her or her feelings. That made me a petty bastard in my own eyes. But when I saw her I started crying again. Lost in guilt and grief. She cried too, even as she ran over and hugged me.

All of my rage dissipated. All of my fury and bluster meant nothing in comparison to the sorrow. I don't know that I've ever cried that hard in my life. Sarah held onto me and I clutched at her, two people caught in a storm of misery. We stayed that way long enough for both of us to get through the crying jags, united in our loss. We held each other without saying much of anything, and then we went back to my apartment to drink a few too many beers and talk about who would be heartless enough to hurt one of the kindest people either of us had ever met.

I didn't mention the street art or the artist. She hadn't noticed the laughing image of the Mumble Man, who even then had his damned warning written under him. Eventually, Sarah left for her place, and I let her go even though there was a part of me that wanted her to stay, that wanted to explore the possible chemistry between us. I know that sounds horrible. I do. But part of me wanted to know what we would have been if Louis hadn't found her first. If they hadn't been so damned compatible.

Instead of acting on that impulse, I wished her a good night and reminded her that she had my number if she needed anything. Then I took my can of paint thinner and a few rags, and I meticulously and slowly wiped the latest incarnation of the Mumble Man from Ken and Barbie's door. It wasn't my place to do so, and I didn't give the least bit of a damn about that fact. I wanted him gone, pure and simple.

Barbie—whose real name, I soon learned, was Sophie—thanked me for cleaning her door, and when she learned that I knew Louis she offered her condolences. It's a small world when you all occupy a neighborhood together, but sometimes not as small as you think. Years in the same neighborhood and that was the first time we ever spoke to each other, aside from an occasional hello.

When I was done with my task of erasing the latest tag, I wandered back to my place and settled in for the night. I turned on the TV and started watching a documentary on graffiti artists, of all things. The director tried to make them look like unsung heroes, but with the smell of paint thinner still on my hands, and the growing dread of the next tag lingering in the back of my mind, he failed to get his point across. To me they were vandals, pure and simple.

My disdain of the Mumble Man's creator was rapidly swinging toward hatred, and I was okay with that.

I fell asleep with thoughts of street art run amok and disturbing dreams of Sarah running through my mind. In my dreams we rutted like animals, while the Mumble Man watched on and laughed to himself. Somewhere in the distance, I heard Louis weeping as I screwed his girlfriend. Somewhere nearby Tina and Leonora talked in Italian and I strained to understand their words.

When I woke up, the sun was peering through the window and damned near blinding me. The blinds rattled and shook with the wind, and a cool breeze blew through the open window that I'd have sworn was closed the night before.

I squinted against the glare and stumbled my way to the safety and darkness of my kitchen, lamenting the way my back was doing its best to imitate a question mark. I promised myself I'd never sleep sitting up again, and got myself a cup of coffee.

The night's dreams were still lingering inside my mind, and I felt a disturbing blend of guilt and mystery as I thought of Louis and Sarah.

I dared my living room and reached for the window shade, ready to block the sun's overpowering glare. I saw shadows on the wall and was puzzled by them until I managed to pull the shades and block the worst light. It was only a few seconds for my eyes to adjust.

It was only a moment longer before I saw the Mumble Man painted on the apartment wall. He stood as tall as could be, just at seven feet in height, and his button eyes glared at me, with a deep and abiding dislike. His feet were planted firmly on the edge of the wall and the paint from his appearance bled into the thin rug I'd put over the hardwood floors.

Scared? I let out a squeal of fear and backed up as I dropped my coffee mug. Scalding fluids spilled down my calf and foot, the pain only adding to my sudden fright. The thick ceramic mug broke all over the floor and I kept backing up until my backside tapped the wall next to the kitchen entrance.

The artist had painted the mouth open again, but this time it was in a snarl, and tight lines of fresh string kept the Mumble Man's lips close together. A crude painting? Where had I ever gotten that idea. The features were unsettling in their detail. As much as the figure looked like an angry man, it looked like an old school zombie.

Through my fright at the unexpected image came the knowledge that someone had broken into my apartment and painted that form while I was sleeping only a few feet away. I ignored the pain in my foot and walked closer to the image. Freshly shattered ceramic bit at the web between my toes and I noticed it, but did not care. I was too fixated on the painting, on touching it to make sure it was real. I could smell fresh paint and something else that I couldn't identify. I could see the image. I touched the dried paint and shook my head even as my skin crawled.

I don't like to think I'm a coward. I prefer to think I just needed to collect myself. It was too much, really, having someone inside my apartment felt like a violation. Part of me wanted to rage and roar and fight. Part of me wanted to back away and regroup for lack of a better way to put it.

I found a reason to visit my folks, if only for a few days. All it took was a phone call to work, where I claimed a family emergency, and a call to my mom to let her know I was coming. Then it was a few hours of driving and I was in a different, calmer world.

Call me a coward if you want to. I needed to get the hell away before I let my imagination take over. I stayed at home and drank beers with my dad while we watched football. We ate out and cooked burgers on the grill, and I relaxed like I hadn't since I'd graduated college four years earlier.

I was safe and comfortable for the first time since the graffiti started. I called Sarah every day to see how she was doing, and we promised to get together once I got back to town. I thought about Tina every day, too, and considered whether or not I was going to ask her out. I also felt an absurd guilt over that notion when I thought about Sarah.

On the evening of the seventh day, my old man came home from work and broke with his usual routine. Instead of coming inside, he began puttering around in the garage. I went outside when I noticed, because my father is decidedly a creature of habit. I found him with several rags draped over a handled bucket.

"What's up?" I asked him without giving the notion any thought, already planning to help with whatever fix up needed doing. It was the least I could do, right?

Instead of speaking he pointed to the exterior of the garage. I had to walk around the side of the house to see the words, "The Mumble Man," scrawled there. My flesh crawled.

"It's a damned shame, Dan." His voice was calm enough, but he had an expression of disappointment on his face the likes of which I hadn't seen since I failed eighth grade algebra. My father shook his head and used an old church key he pulled from his utility knife to open the paint can he pulled from inside his bucket. "I never thought I'd see this sort of crap in the neighborhood."

I couldn't find the words to answer him.

Carving Grace

by Kristi Petersen Schoonover

It's been said in my town that if you're happy, the Wailing Women will come for you.

It'd be easy to not put much stock in that, save for the long faces that haunt the aisles of the grocery store, the library, and the pews at Sunday services. There's a gloom that shrouds Timber Inlet, a melancholy that trundles down the alleys between the centuries-old saltboxes like a sea fog.

Every street passes the garden where the Wailing Women wait. They're made of wood, not unlike the figureheads of ships, except they're never looking out to sea; they're staring at *you*. No matter where you are in the town center, their backs are never turned.

Strangers comment on how lovely they are, and to an outsider, I suppose they would be. They're as colorful and exaggerated as carousel horses and come from a multitude of eras. A girlish blonde is carved in a Robin's egg frock that reminds me of my illustrated copy of *Little Women*. A bobbed brunette is etched in what's clearly a flapper dress, and in the sunlight, her salmon-colored diamonds sparkle. The dour one is the most elegant, her corseted emerald gown so real-looking I expect it to flutter in the breeze.

There's one, though, whose attention comforts me. Her straight jet hair plunges down the back of her flowered blouse, to the waist of her bell-bottomed jeans. Her expression is frank, but I swear I can see the hint of a satisfied smile, a glint in her atrophied eye that says *It's okay, I got what I wanted.*

I don't mind when that one watches me because that one, I've been told, is my mother.

* * *

At night, the Wailing Women comb the neighborhoods in search of happy souls. The streets echo with shrieks and moans, and there's a sound as they creep past the shuttered windows, the sound of creaking boards and labored breath. Everyone I know sleeps through it. I can't. I'm always in a shallow doze, haunted by an uncertain memory of it close by, a mournful cry, a shadow on the wall.

"You didn't sleep well *again*, Gracie?" Vendi, my boss at the TI Whaling Museum Gift Shop—*Here Be Treasure*—has been watching me struggle with compass-inspired jewelry. Each piece is wrapped individually, and the plastic's strong, so I need a steak knife from the Four Winds Café to get them open.

"You're going to have to do something about that. It makes you weak and it makes me worried." Her r's are rolled, and her w's are v's.

It's a reprimand. Although she speaks softly and everything sounds like she's asking a question, Vendi's strong stock. She's originally from Vestmannaeyjar in Iceland, the village that beat the lava of Eldfell volcano by pumping sea water on it for weeks. Everyone knows she's the only townswoman unafraid to show cheer, so she's always good for a smile. Everyone also knows not to ask why, after working so hard to save her village, she came here. There's a sharpness in her eyes.

"These are pretty." She holds a large gold compass on an eighteen-inch chain against her slim fingers. "They are going to sell nicely."

I point to a stack of glass blocks against a mural of an antique nautical map of the coast. "I was going to use one of the treasure chests and sort of drape them around in between the map posters. I can . . . put the bracelets and rings in the fake clamshells, and then we have those decorative faux pearls, too."

"No, the last time you displayed, the wine glasses got broken. I'm glad you weren't hurt? But this seems like not the thing for you today. There's a workman here. He's come to create the figurehead for the *Northern Cross*." She sets the necklace in my "unwrapped" pile and winks, then nods and gracefully points out the store's paned window overlooking the wharf.

A man in a pea coat stands before the nineteenth century whaling ship the museum's been restoring.

"He's cold," she says. "Bring him chowder?"

The tourists keep us alive, but strangers aren't welcome at night for obvious reasons—it's why there's no lodging on the island; they day trip it on the ferry from Rutterbank. Even then, we don't like them here for more than a weekend at most. After that, they start asking about everyone's sorrowful pall—especially mine. I've had a hole in my heart since full-on awareness, a hole that makes me darker and lonelier than the others, a hole I don't discuss. But on occasion, a stranger is a necessary albatross. Once the *Northern Cross* has her figurehead, she can open as a walk-through exhibit.

I also know better than to disappoint Vendi. I've been taught to have respect for my elders, but she also saved me when Mom—of whom I only have fragmented glimpses, the vague scent of daisies, and a beat-up paperback copy of *Happiness is a Choice*—left. "Sure." I shrug into my coat and head toward the restaurant.

Vendi isn't finished. "You tell Ellouise it needs to be *fresh* chowder! Not yesterday's scraps! She has been doing that lately. I cannot imagine why? But it isn't nice."

Vendi forgets that sometimes it's yesterday's scraps that keep us going.

* * *

The *Northern Cross* has always been here, if not on the off-limits beach where it wrecked, then here in port, where it was rebuilt but never put to sea again. It sat—maintained, but more doleful with each passing decade—as it watched the sunset of whaling, the abandonment of the industry, and the establishment and long tenure of the museum.

The water has a chop to it, and the waves make a soft *thunkshhh* sound as they lap against the *Cross'* hull.

Mr. Pea Coat is sketching, his charcoal moving on his artist's book like a figure skater on the ice. His unruly, longish hair is shiny black like a magpie, and his five o'clock shadow errs on the side of devil-may-care.

I'm captivated. "What are you . . . drawing?"

"Not sure yet." He looks up at the hulk, then at me. His eyes are a piercing, glacier blue. "You don't, by chance, remember anything about this ship's figurehead."

No one—alive, anyway—knows what it looked like. "It rotted . . . *years* . . . before I was born."

"It didn't rot." He lowers his sketchbook and motions me closer. "I'll show you. Match my line of sight."

It's a little close, but I lean in. The smell of him, like acorns and wood shavings, overwhelms the salty April air.

With his charcoal pencil, he points at a block above the forepeak. "It was poised on that pedestal. See that white spot?"

I make out something that, from here, looks like seagull droppings.

"Those are naked toes from a right foot. It's a clean break. It was deliberately *shorn* from that ship."

My hand brushes against his pea coat. The wool is rough and feels like the bristles of a wet brush, but there's a strange comfort in it. "Why?"

"The practice started with animal heads. Sacrifices to the Gods for protection. Later, sailors painted eyes right on the hulls. Eventually, they combined the two. Figureheads were supposed to keep a lookout, but if they failed, and a ship wrecked? When it was recovered, they'd lop the figure's head off. So no other ship would carry a bad talisman. In this case? Somebody lopped *all* of it off."

A ternery wings across the inlet, its calls reminiscent of caged monkey cries.

"I apologize for the lecture," he says.

"No! It was . . . it means you're passionate." I'm flushed.

"You need me for something?"

I motion to the picnic table. "I brought you . . . chowder . . . and our homemade rosemary raisin bread."

He smiles. "Little early for lunch."

"Uh . . . the . . . gift shop . . . maven? She said you . . . looked cold."

He flipped his sketchbook closed. "Do I?"

"Well . . . it's . . . raw, yeah."

"You always talk like that?"

I feel the same electricity I did in high school when the boy I liked had slipped a card in my locker. "Like what?"

"In ellipses?"

An embarrassed smile blooms on my cheeks. "No, I just . . . "

"It's okay. Means you're a careful person. I like that. What's your name?"

"Grace."

"I'm Dirk." He gives me a serious nod. "My bones could use warming."

We settle at the table. The breeze chills my hands. I ram them in my pockets.

He eyes the serving for one. "Not joining me."

I always skip breakfast. "I've had plenty. Ellouise makes the best chowder south of Nova Scotia."

"Spent plenty o' time in towns that romance their chowder. I'll judge." He grabs the spoon. "Quite a collection of figureheads you have on the town green. Was thinking about checking them out."

"No!"

His first bite stops just short of his mouth.

"I mean . . . that's a . . . special place."

"There you go. Ellipses again."

"We don't really want strangers going there."

"I understand." He tastes the chowder, swallows. "Maybe after some time, I won't be a stranger, and you can take me."

I don't know how to respond to that, so instead, I get up. "I need to get back to work. Nice to meet you."

"A little too much dill, but you might be right." He yells after me.

"About what?"

"The chowder."

A strange warmth courses through me.

That night, for the first time, I don't hear the Wailing Women's creaking or wheezy breath; the cry and shadow memory recedes. I'm haunted instead by the sound of Dirk's voice and the scent of wood shavings, and I fall into a sleep so deep that, in the morning, I don't hear my alarm.

* * *

It'd be easier if we could leave Timber Inlet, but we all know what happens if we do. There are stories of greatest loves succumbing to debilitating illness, gifted athletes struck down by maiming, beloved children growing into serial murderers.

If you find true happiness, it's better to stay, and at night, shutter the windows and lock the doors.

Eventually, though, they get you.

When I was little and when the museum first opened, its snack bar was called the *Chowder Chantey*. It was barely a seaside shack, albeit with the most clam-loaded stuffies and the strongest cocktails for tourists who needed lube to get their families through the outdated planetarium show. Then my friend Ellouise went away to culinary school. Like the rest of us, she knew she couldn't live her dream *out there*. She moved the snack bar into the same building with *Here Be Treasure*, expanded the kitchen, upscaled the menu, added tables with shell-inspired centerpieces and called it *Four Winds*.

But her dreams are bigger, and she's been fighting with the town elders to make them come true.

Today, when I arrive to get Dirk's soup and bread like I've been doing every day for the past month, she's kneading dough, her unruly blackbird hair tied up in a flamingo bandana. She's an orchidaceous person—always in bright colors as varied as a pandemonium of parrots. She brushes the back of her hand across her cheek, leaving a smear of flour, and leans conspiratorially over the counter.

"I need to tell you something, but gimmie a sec!"

Around here, when people have good news, they whisper.

She throws the dough baby in the glass-doored cooler behind her, then comes around the corner and seizes my hand; hers is slippery as she tugs me into the walk-in. "Come 'ere, come 'ere, come 'ere!"

I've only seen her this excited twice in our lives: when she'd been accepted to culinary, and before that her ninth birthday, when her mother had finally gotten her the tiny chocolate cookie baking set she'd been eyeing for her dollhouse.

A chill settles into my bones, but it's not from the walk-in.

She bounces on her toes. "I did it! The council approved a renovation, and we're going to not only turn this place into a five-star, we'll open it up for catering events, like weddings! Daytime only, of course, but can you *imagine*!" She squeals and throws her arms around me. She smells like baking yeast and rosemary.

I force a smile. "That's great!"

She frowns. "You can't be more ecstatic than that?"

There's a silence between us, a heaviness that hangs in the air. There is no sound but the rattling of the walk-in's fan, the tittering of a metal piece inside that's long been out of place.

"Ellouise—"

She nods. "I know. I'll be careful. I have every intention of seeing this through to the end. Those bitches are gonna have to go some." She grabs a tub labeled RAISINS and leads me out, hipping the cumbersome door closed with a *thud-switch*. "And anyway, *you* might wanna get prepared *yourself*."

I blush. "What do you mean?"

She rolls her eyes, plops the tub on the counter. "I've seen the way you glow! The only person who's fooled around here." She plunges a ladle in the chowder pot, fills two cups, and sets them on a tray with four packages of crackers and two slices of still-warm bread. "Is you."

That night, the Wailers creak and groan and scream down my street. They come closer than usual, and one of them stops. She breathes heavy.

Then she lets out an ear-piercing cry of agony, making me aware that she knows, too.

* * *

Those who are content think of happiness as a state of being. For those who ache with longing, happiness is a place. A place where even asphalt is vibrant and litter is beautiful. A place at which we never seem to arrive. So death holds promise, perhaps because that place is waiting for us on the other side.

My place is next to Dirk. Where he planes and carves as he tells tales about his work, tales about the world outside of Timber Inlet, tales about myself that even I haven't heard yet. Where he works me on the woodshop floor, on a sawdusted blanket beneath the centuries-old beams, and anywhere he touches triggers a tingle that spreads into previously unknown corners of my body. Where my life out there is either fever dream or has never happened at all, and I'm not Grace, but an elegant winged creature, free and lovely and destined for monumental things.

We spend only the afternoons; he needs to catch the last ferry back to Rutterbank before sundown. But at night, when I hear Wailers, I imagine him holding me, imagine his autumn smell and downy chest hair against my cheek; imagine the sound of his heartbeat overtaking the Wailers' too-close breathing, and I could swear the hole in me is full.

* * *

The woodshop is a long, two-hundred-year-old building that once housed a cordage company. I didn't know the names of its curiosities, but now I know thicknessers, planes, saws, gouges, chisels, mallets, sanders, cutting tools, resins in colorful clay pots. It's become familiar, except for today. The air, stenching of mothballs and dog feces, is nearly impossible to breathe.

"Mask up! On the wall there!" Dirk yells.

He's never made me do this. I fit one over my face, but the odor is pervasive.

A massive chunk of wood, wider and taller than a person, looms in the middle of the work area.

Dirk balances on a ladder next to it. "Sorry it stinks." He pushes a plane and flicks his wrist. A curled scraping drops to the floor. "She's made of Camphor Laurel. Wanted to be more authentic—oak or yellow pine—but we want her to last. Some of the original woods're vulnerable to dry rot, and the insides turn to shredded wheat. Camphor's still got issues, but it's more resistant."

The thing's blank face is unsettling. There are just angles where the chin should be, a rough elongated block for a nose, two jutting parallelograms on either side of her brow that might be hair. There's a loose shape of something like clothing, perhaps a dress.

She reminds me of someone.

"Breathing the dust in's a bad idea—if your throat starts burning, you go outside immediately, okay?" He sets his plane on the ladder's shelf and monkeys down. "But camphor's easier to shape. She'll finish faster."

I'm disappointed; I haven't considered the day he's going to leave—even though I know he has to. "Are you . . . in that much of a rush?"

He wipes his hands on one of his old T-shirt rags. "No, actually." He comes close to me, takes my small hands in his. "You're beautiful."

I blush.

"And I'm ready for a break. What's say we get out of here?"

"And . . . go where?"

"Come on," he says.

At his pick-up truck, he opens the passenger door and a large covered picnic basket is in my seat. "What's that?"

"That." He seizes the handle, sets it in the truck's bed. "Is a little lunch I had your friend Ellouise put together for us."

He drives to the opposite side of town and turns down a weed-choked road that I know leads to the beach.

He pats my leg. "What's the matter? You look white."

"We're . . . " I give him my best undisturbed smile. "Not supposed to come here. It's off-limits."

He chuckles. "Who's going to stop us?"

We traipse through the dunes; the yellow beach heather and salt grass rustles in the breeze, and the roar of the surf gets louder. Sandpipers scatter as Dirk shakes out and spreads the blanket on the sand.

I sense we're being watched.

He settles down and unrolls a tablecloth. "We have wine, some kind of baked brie. We have a coupla roast beef sandwiches on that awesome bread . . . "

I hear the shuffle of melamine plates and the *clink* of inexpensive silverware, but I'm too stunned by where I am. I envision what it all might have looked like, as though it's happening in front of me. The *Northern Cross'* captain, during his lonely nights at the helm, would stand as far out on the forecastle as he could and talk to his figurehead. Eventually, he fell deeply in love with her, a force so powerful it gave her life. But when she revealed herself, he was terrified and repulsed. Brokenhearted, she slayed the crew, ran the ship aground, and became the first Wailing Woman.

She was undoubtedly the founder of the garden, but no one knows which one she is.

He offers me a glass of wine, but I don't take it.

"What's up? Are you not hungry?"

"No, it's just . . . this is really sweet of you, but…"

He leans over and kisses me. He tastes like grapes and alcohol. "My ellipses girl." He sets the goblet on top of the basket. "I'll just cut to the chase, then." He pulls off his sneakers and socks. "I've been thinking. The Rutterbank cottage is sweet. Ferry ride back and forth? Not so much. Especially when I wanna see you." He thrusts his bare feet deep in the sand. It makes a crater. "There's nowhere to rent in town."

A beetle wanders over. It slips into the crater and lands on its back.

I can tell Dirk's hemming and hawing.

"The museum has plenty of work for me. They're more than happy to keep me on. Keep the place from falling apart. I can do restoration on just about anything, and some of those old buildings you got there—they need a lot of work."

Oh, no. I want this. I want this so. *Much.*

And I can't have it. Wailers are already closer than I'd like. "You can't move here."

The beetle can't turn itself over. It flails its tiny legs.

Dirk stops, stares at me, quiet and blinking. "But, I thought—"

"It's . . . complicated, Dirk." I reach down and turn the beetle over. He takes a moment to get the feel of the sand under his legs, then he starts to climb out of the gully. Only to get halfway up, slide back down, and land on his back again.

"I thought maybe we could get a place of our own. Together. I love you, Grace."

I want to scream *I love you too and yes!* to a saltbox in town with a yard full of Virginia rose and sea lavender and wild raisin. I turn and grip his hands. They're rough and warm and I want them everywhere on me, and I lean in to kiss him and then comes the horror: We'll have to have our saltbox hemmed in by a gated picket fence to help put distance between us and....

I am just like that beetle.

Flailing.

I scramble to my feet, and I bolt. I hear Dirk yell, but it's stolen by the wind. I clamber up and over the dunes, and I don't stop running until I reach the museum.

* * *

I slam the door to the shop so hard the shell and bottle wind chimes tinkle like shattering glass.

Vendi stands with a crate in her arms. "First you are late because you don't sleep well for weeks? Now it is your new thing to be a whirling dervish?"

It comes out *virling derwish,* but I can't defend myself. My head calliopes with joy, terror, excitement, grief. My heart thrums. I gasp for air. "He . . . Dirk told me he loved me . . . and . . . I ran away!"

Vendi's annoyed look shifts to concern. "You can talk to me." She jerks her head. "While we put the candles together."

I'm slow to move, but trail her to the back room. It smells like lemon cleaner and brewing coffee.

She sets the crate on the long oak table, walks to the coffee pot and fills two mugs.

"Now." Vendi slides me a mug, then eases herself into the chair across from me. It creaks in a sound like Wailers make. "Why would you do that?"

I sip the coffee. It burns going down. "Because I think he makes me happy?"

She nods. "Mmmm." She reaches for the crate, nabs foil labels that read MIDNIGHT BEACH and depict laughing people, faces orange from the glow of a campfire as they roast marshmallows. Behind them, the moon glitters on the ocean's surface.

I wonder if that's what our off-limits beach looks like at night.

"And it's a bad thing to be happy?" She lifts tumblers from their hay-lined nests and sets them between us.

The smell of smoked vanilla, wet beach sand, and driftwood is dizzying. I peel a label off the sheet. "We know what happens to people when they're happy here, Vendi."

Vendi draws a deep breath; she still has a label stuck to her fingers as she considers me disapprovingly. Then she averts her gaze, applies the label, and presses a lid on the jar.

It seals with a *thwuck*.

"What is it?" I ask.

She gets up and goes to the narrow window that overlooks the *Northern Cross*. "Do you know why you don't know how your mother ended up in the garden?"

I shake my head. "No one knows?"

"*I* know." She folded her arms. "Your mother was my first friend when I came here. After Eldfell. My husband was the only man who died—he was crushed under our roof, trying to get to our baby."

The news stuns me. "I'm . . . I'm sorry."

"I'm not done talking." In her moment of silence, a seagull cries outside. "I wouldn't be able to stand a life with happy people. A university friend in Reykjavík thought Timber Inlet was a legend, but discovered it was real. So I came. Your mother lived next door. And she was, after a time, in a similar situation. Only it was that she was pregnant with you."

I don't think I'm ready to hear this. I press a label onto the candle and it's crooked.

"She wanted you more than anything in the world. More than she wanted even your father."

I've never known who my father was. I've always assumed he was out there, somewhere. "What happened to him?"

She shrugs, comes back to the table. "He left when he found out what goes on here." She picks up a label sheet and peels one off. "You were six months old when Wailers took your mother. We'd decided to pass the long night making shell jewelry, and I'd forgotten the glue. So I went home to get it. Out the window, I saw a Wailer at your mother's door. I hid, waited until I saw it move on. Then I went. Your mother opened the door, and . . . " A shiver shot up Vendi's back. "She was one of them."

In my mind's eye, I see my mother as she is now, in the garden. I know she prowls the streets with the others, but I've pushed the thought away.

Until now.

Vendi sets the candle down. I think she's going to reassuringly pat my hand, but she doesn't. "There were marks on the front door. Marks from their painted eyes, all around the peephole. Your mother must have looked through it to see if it was me."

The only way Wailers can get you is to look you dead in the eye for several seconds. I've heard stories of them holding down their victims, forcing their eyelids open or slicing them off with their splintered nails.

"You've been with me ever since." She presses another label on. "But your mother . . . she would've wanted better for you. She would've wanted you to *fight*."

I think of the saltbox of my dreams. The flowers, the golden afternoons, the cozy winter nights.

Wailers beating on the door.

The screaming just beyond the wall.

In Timber Inlet, it's better to dream about love than to have it.

"If I let him go," I say, "I'll be *safe*."

She eyes me. "That what you want? To be like me?"

The air is heavy with sorrow. The front door wind chimes signal a customer.

"One always takes a risk to be happy. You were worth that risk to your mom." She rises from her chair and heads back towards the shop. She stops in the doorway. "You have to ask yourself if Dirk is worth that risk, but I will tell you now—he thinks *you're* worth it."

I hear her ask if she can help whoever it is as I stare at the lot of finished candles. The happy campers roasting marshmallows mock me with their hearts that don't have holes.

I ask myself why Dirk and I *couldn't* have that saltbox in town with a fenced-in yard full of Virginia rose and sea lavender and wild raisin.

Then, the next day, Ellouise is missing.

* * *

When a woman disappears, the first place we check is the garden.

I don't have to.

I want, instead, to see how it happened.

Ellouise's Ricketts Street Cape Cod, flanked by unmanicured red chokeberry and beach plum, appears secure: the first-floor shutters are closed and latched; the front door is locked, perhaps still bolted from the inside.

The back of the house is a different story. The shutter covering the kitchen's over-sink octagonal window has been shorn off, but it's clear Wailers actually entered, because the interior screen door is half disconnected and buckled, its mesh drooping like peeled banana skin. The outer door isn't right. It yaws open, undamaged. Not even scratched, no tell-tale paint marks.

I've heard that houses in Rutterbank have the screen doors on the outside and the solid on the in, but because Wailers can't penetrate wood, we do it opposite. I try to close the outer door, but it won't budge. I notice a thick caulking in between the interior edge and its frame, as though someone glued it.

As though someone wanted to ensure it'd never close again.

Inside's a minefield of her broken things: dishes, glassware, jars of tomato sauce and homemade jam. Her enormous butcher block island is the only furniture unscathed; the cabinets are scratched up, and the refrigerator is on its side, puddles of milk and orange juice stickying the tiles. There's a crowbar, a hammer, a fireplace poker, an ax—*what she used to defend herself?*—and she was, apparently, baking. A dough blob lolls on the floor, its butter melted and pooling in the grout. Rosemary sprigs, ripped from the overhead wooden beam where she dried them, litter the scene like hay. The air is rancid and thick with a strange heat—a metallic, suffocating heat, like something smoldering.

Her oven, its door agape, is on.

I close it up and turn it off.

Just beyond the kitchen, near the dining room table, is the smashed husk of her beloved childhood dollhouse. Scattered are thumb-sized furniture and accessories smaller than pennies: a Dutch oven, an abacus, the tiny chocolate cookie baking set, complete with its bamboo cutting board, cocoa powder, treats in the shapes of apples and pears.

I'm overwhelmed by despair. I've heard of this—a certain atmosphere where Wailers have attacked. That their third eyes have been left behind; that you aren't being watched, but being *penetrated;* that they've blackened you with sorrow, and you feel hopeless.

Everywhere I see Ellouise's ghost, and I know she won't ever come home. But I can't leave the place like this.

In the kitchen, I kick aside a double boiler, drag the trash can into the chaos, and settle on my knees.

"Shit. What *happened*?" It's Dirk. "My God, are you okay?"

"Fine, just . . . " It strikes me I don't have a rational explanation. "What are you doing here?" I wipe my teary eyes with the back of my hand.

"Vendi told me Ellouise . . . passed during the night."

For the first time since I've known him, he's talking in ellipses.

"Passed" and what this looks like right now are obviously on opposite ends of the spectrum, but to his credit he doesn't ask. "I came to say . . . I'm sorry."

I dump a piece of sharp orange stoneware in the garbage.

He hesitates, then steps over a toppled stack of baking pans. Glass crunches beneath his sneakers. "Look, can we talk?"

Clink. Shard of ashtray meets fragment of crystal vase. "About what?"

He crouches before me, sets a hand on my arm. "I've always wanted to keep moving. Always. But for the first time, I really wanna stay. With you. And I *know* you love me, Grace. I know you do. Sounds corny, but I see it when you look at me."

I want to tell him the truth, because his glacier blue eyes suddenly seem gray, and they say that sometimes that happens when your heart breaks, but I can't fix this. He doesn't understand. I lie. "I . . . don't."

I've hurt him. He quickly lets go and looks away, palms two jagged pieces of what was Ellouise's favorite platter. "I don't know what's going on here." I watch him focus on picking up ceramic splinters. He doesn't even seem to be careful about cutting his fingers. "But when you're ready to talk on it, we can."

I want to curl up against him and go to sleep. Right now. Forget all of this. "It's a long story."

A shattering sound as he throws more pieces in the bin and fixes me with a fierce gaze. "Then talk to me."

"It's . . . " I chuck in a piece of her Rooster-shaped butter dish. "You wouldn't believe it."

He reaches for my hair, tucks a loose strand back behind my ear. "Try me."

* * *

When I've finished, there's silence. After a time, he nods. "Makes a lot of sense."

"You believe me?"

"You forget. I've been a lot of places. Seen a lot of things. Heard a lot of tall tales. Question is, do you want to make a go of it?"

Yes, yes, yes. I look around Ellouise's disaster of a kitchen. *No, no no.* She took a risk. Now she's been reduced to memories and broken glass. "I just . . . I can't. Not . . . not right now."

He presses his lips together as though to say he should've known better. "Ellipses. I'll miss that."

I'm stabbed by regret.

He gets to his feet. "For what it's worth, I figured out what the

Northern Cross' original figurehead looked like. The lady in green in the middle of the garden? That's her. The toes are a match."

A chill shoots up my spine.

He turns to go through the busted screen door. A piece of paper is stuck to the back of his jeans.

"Dirk."

He pivots with a hopeful look.

"Something's on your pants."

He twists his body. "What the hell?" He pulls it off, hands it to me.

It's crinkled and stiff, sticky with dried orange juice, but I can still read it.

When I do, I'm punched in the gut.

It's a letter from the town elders. They reversed their decision for Ellouise's catering venue.

It's dated yesterday.

I glance up at the open back door.

She let them in.

I gasp.

Dirk steps forward in concern. "What does it say?"

"Ellouise, I—"

I hear a distant cry of agony.

Oh my God.

I've been so preoccupied I haven't noticed the change in the light. I rush to the octagonal window, pull back a torn curtain.

"What is it?" Dirk asks.

It's beyond sunset.

"What time is it?"

"Eight thirty or so. Why?"

Shit. "You missed the last ferry!"

An eagle-like scream fills the air. It's not like any of the Wailers I've heard before.

I wonder if it's Ellouise.

Dirk looks terrified and sweaty. He seizes my hand. "We have to go."

"We can't. They're already out there."

A piercing shriek.

I rush to Ellouise's front door. It's still bolted, the windows shuttered. "We have to shore up the kitchen! Somebody did something to the door. It won't close."

Dirk turns over the huge butcher block island, and everything on it—rolling pin, bowl of fruit, bill accordion—goes flying. I narrowly escape getting clocked by an empty wine bottle.

He grabs the legs, tries to up-end it onto its short edge. "Help me!"

We struggle, but drag and wrest it in place against the screen door. It doesn't fully cover.

"The cabinets!" He's breathless. "We'll rip off the doors, board over the openings!" He grips a door to try to break it free.

I spy the ax in the corner. I grab it. I shudder to think it may have been the last thing Ellouise held. I thrust it at him. "Here!"

The crying and wailing advances.

I clutch a crowbar and pry off doors as fast as I can. They separate with a great splinter against the intensifying groans and creaks from outside.

Wailers are close.

He hurls aside the ax, grabs the hammer. "Pass me nails!"

Nails! We didn't think of that! I'm frantic, yank open every drawer. Old phone books. Pens. Forks, knives, herb choppers. Tape, scissors, glue. Letter openers, nightlight bulbs, a blue box . . . NAILS.

Wailers shriek and moan and throw themselves against the house like rabid prisoners.

He braces the unsecured wood against the door frame with his left hand and wields the hammer to beat back a gnarled, knotted arm in the other. The Wailer shrieks like a shot animal.

I join him, eyes closed for fear of even a stolen glimpse at their painted eyes because I know what I will become. There is hissing and crying and my heart pounds and I can't get enough air, but I shut them out and hold up the nail box and he hammers and there is more creaking and moaning.

Finally, he hammers down the last cabinet door. It's far from perfect. The night's salty breeze whisks through the cracks.

But they can't get in.

I shake from shock. From fear. From exhaustion. I shiver in a cold it seems only I can feel.

I burst into tears.

He's with me in an instant. "It's all right, now." He pulls me against him. The smell of acorns and wood shavings is comforting. "They won't get to you as long as I'm here."

I trust him. I'm safe. I'm content. Even the Wailers outside fall silent. I open my eyes to look at him and over his shoulder, above the sink, I see a movement.

We forgot to cover the kitchen window.

An angry Wailer fixes her painted stare at me.

My love turns bitter in an instant. My mouth wells with the taste of low tide and rotten wood. The hole inside me floods with dark.

The last sound I hear before I bark over is Dirk's terrified scream.

* * *

Those who are content think of happiness as a state of being. For those who ache with longing, happiness is a place. A place we never seem to arrive, so death holds promise, because perhaps that place is waiting for us on the other side.

I will never get to the other side, because I am in the garden now.

What no one knows is how painful it is to walk at night. How my joints pop and grind every time I step. How the spring rain seeps in, and my legs swell and grow leaden. How the summer sun parches my bark so I constantly itch. How the winter ice splits me apart, searing like alcohol on open wounds.

But my soul is as tough as my body. If I am not allowed to be happy, neither is any other woman.

Each afternoon, Dirk ventures into the garden to see me. There is always one day every April on which the familiar weather, its certain smell of salt and sleeping greens, its certain grayish light, softens me. For a moment, I wish I could scream at him to stop mourning. To go. But when he does not, the moment passes and I am glad. Because if I cannot have him, no one else should.

I stand next to my mother. Her smile reminds me that at least I had happiness for a short time. That it is better to taste once than never. At sunset, before we roam, we trade glances, and she nods in empathy.

Then we step off into the night, looking to settle the score.

Birth of a Creature

by Cindy O'Quinn

The County—where I live
is haunted by the living dead.
Creatures from woods
made of rotting nature unfed.

Wood spirits carved in trees
reminders of primitive time
resurrected from disease.
People decay and forests breathe.

I walked without fear into the grove.
Maple, cedar, and pine,
creating incensed—green divine.
Building a forever graveyard home.

Men came with chains and saws
wielding weapons of destruction for all.
Felling trees to the forest floor,
opening the gates of mountain lore.

Letting loose the wood carved spirits
allowing them to take their revenge.
Axemen died and the woods were fed
tainted flesh from those who bled.

The forest was satiated—until a young deer ate
the bloodstained herbage left as bait.
A new monster did a legend create.
Nature called her name . . . Wendigo.

So little did man ever really know.

Silver Leaves and Moth Wings

by David Bernard

Momma passed on back in 1899, and Daddy said it was a blessing because she didn't live long enough to see the town die. Old Man Whipple had died, and his idiot son was mismanaging the coal mine before his daddy was cold in the West Virginia clay. When the Coal & Coke Railway connected Elkins to Charleston and bypassed Critchley's Corner by a good thirty miles, it was the final nail in the coffin. The mine was already drying up, and the new shafts were just hitting shale. Whipple Junior kept ordering deeper test pits until Shaft 12 collapsed and killed fifteen men.

Soon after that, Junior lost the mine, and everything else, to the bank in Wheeling. He then went and hanged himself, saving the miners the trouble of forming a lynch mob. The bank didn't want a spent mine so, all these years later, I'm still not sure who owns it and don't much care.

Most of the miners moved on after the last cave-in and headed down to Gassaway. The rest left when the bank seized the Whipple estate. Even if the mines weren't hiring in Gassaway, it was on the C&C Rail, and mines further down the line would be hiring. By '05, Critchley's Corner was mostly a ghost town. Only a handful of farmers like my daddy remained, too stubborn to pull up stakes and move away from a town that wasn't much more than a failing general store, a practically abandoned church, and a Main Street of empty buildings.

Reverend Elias had taken to walking up on Pine Meadow Hill around the old mine. He said it was therapeutic, but Daddy suspected he was looking for Toby Braden's still. The good Reverend was a bit of imbiber since his wife died of fever. Then his sons were killed in the Shaft 5 cave-in We weren't sure if he was looking to save Toby from both Hell and the T-men or just in search of a local source to ease his "affliction."

We all knew Toby was cooking mash somewhere up around there because the 'shine was always a little murky looking from the coal dust, no matter how many times Toby filtered it. The land around the mine was a dead wasteland; Pine Meadow Hill hadn't had pine trees or meadows in the thirty years since Old Man Whipple found coal. The hill had been stripped of trees to make access easier. Erosion did the rest. The coal dust swirled around constantly and got into everything – including Toby's moonshine.

One day, the Reverend stopped by the farm talking about a man with moth wings flying over a forest of silver trees on Pine Meadow Hill. Daddy figured he'd finally found the still and loaded up. Trouble was that Toby's 'shine glued the coal dust to your teeth if you drank any amount of it, and the Reverend's were still pearly white. Daddy decided he'd better humor him and nodded and agreed to take a look up on the hill after chores. Then Daddy sent me over to Doc Hallen's to tell him the Reverend had finally cracked from liquor and grief.

Doc Hallen looked puzzled when I told him. He had just had a visit from old widow Haimer, complaining about a giant transparent moth who sat in an invisible pine tree that had appeared in her parlor during her morning Bible reading. Doc told me his first reckoning was some sort of hallucination. The poor folk in town gathered coal from the discard piles of low-grade coal dumped along the Whipple mine road. When they burned it, it released arsenic. But the poor folks were long gone, and even I knew arsenic poisoning didn't cause hallucinations. Besides, Widow Haimer and Reverend Elias weren't quite poor enough to be scavenging coal. Doc wondered if gas was leaking from the mine, but I wondered if living in a dead town could cause insanity. More importantly—was it contagious?

In a town as small as Critchley's Corner, word spread fast. Harry Clark claimed he was abandoning his farm because he got a job in Selbyville, but everyone knew it was because his wife claimed she was chased out of the barn by a flying man with glowing eyes.

I went by the Clark farm at sunset a week or two after they packed up, and I noticed the buildings looked like they had been abandoned for months. The shingles and clapboards were falling off both the barn and the farmhouse—far too fast for only being empty a few weeks. What made it really weird, the damage was the type you saw out in the woods, where vines climbed up abandoned buildings and forced apart clapboards and let the weather in. There were no vines, just moths.

The moths started to appear everywhere. I'd lived here all my life and never saw that many. To be honest, there wasn't much wildlife or insects left in the area – the coal dust long ago choked out the insects, and the animals moved into the mountains where there were still trees and plants. Daddy says he hasn't seen a raccoon or squirrel around Critchley's Corner in twenty-five years. He had enough work keeping the farm stock alive without wasting time deer hunting, especially since no one had bagged one since he could recall. Seeing the Clark house in such a sad state was a little creepy, but the moths gave me hope – maybe life could come back to the land now that the mine was closed.

Reverend Elias stopped by a few days later and said he had found Toby Braden, dead, up on Pine Meadow Hill. Toby had fallen in an old test pit and appeared to have strangled himself on a vine while trying to get out. Daddy reminded the Reverend there weren't any vines up on the hill on account of Old Man Whipple poisoning the ground. The Reverend looked at us oddly and said Whipple hadn't done a very good job, then – the plants were starting to come back.

Widow Haimer died the next day. She had never been quite right after seeing the giant transparent moth in the invisible pine tree. When Reverend Elias went to call, he found her collapsed in the parlor with an axe in her hand. Doc Hallen said she died of slow apoplexy, causing her to become confused and pick up the axe when she meant to pick up her Bible. I don't think he believed that any more than the rest of us. But as attending physician, he had to put something on the death certificate. He figured the State wouldn't appreciate "died trying to cut down an invisible tree" as the cause of death.

Folks kept seeing the giant moth, but at a distance. Ben Price was convinced the bankers were trying to scare folks out of town with a man-shaped airship on account that there might still be coal in the ground. Of course, Ben Price also thought Theodore Roosevelt and Kaiser Wilhelm were conspiring to give Earth to the moon men. We really didn't consider Ben the most reliable source of current events. One day, someone noticed the Civil War cannon was missing from the town square. We knew it had to be him. We rushed up Pine Meadow Hill before the damn fool tried to fire the cannon and blew himself into a million pieces.

We headed up the old mine road, expecting to hear the cannon explode any moment. About halfway up the hill, we heard the scream. Pieces of Ben Price started falling out of the sky. When his head bounced toward Reverend Elias, he fell to his knees, retching too hard to pray. Teddie Brown and Cam Baldwin eagerly volunteered to stay behind and tend to him. Daddy, Doc Hallen, and I continued up to the summit. The cannon was still in one piece. Whatever happened to Ben was not because of that.

We found most of him. I think Doc listed his cause of death as a "hunting accident." We didn't know what he thought he was hunting, but the State never asked that sort of question.

Cam Baldwin thought maybe a bear got Ben. The rest of the town knew it was the moth man—there hadn't been a bear sighting since the mine opened, and I'm pretty sure bear attacks never resulted in a rain of body parts. I suppose if I was a moth man and someone pointed a cannon at me, I might not take it too kindly either.

There was some talk of forming a hunting party to track it down.

Problem was, there weren't more than eight or nine men left in the Corner. That included me, Reverend Elias, and Pegleg Harley—not exactly a fear-inspiring group of monster hunters. Plus, I'd never seen the creature, although one night at twilight, I swear that for a split second I saw a silvery pine tree poking through the roof of Widow Haimer's house.

A week after we buried Ben Price, Doc stopped by and mentioned that he went by the Clark farm and the barn had collapsed. That was downright unnatural since Harry Clark built it himself only four or five years ago, and Harry was a damn fine carpenter. My father went to take a look at it himself and said the wood in the barn looked solid except for the main roof beam, which looked like something big had smashed down on it, which brought down the summer and winter beams. Naturally, the town blamed the moth man. Daddy said it looked more like Widow Haimer's invisible tree toppled over and landed on the roof. I *think* he was joking.

It took another two months before I finally saw the moth man. I was putting the cow in the barn at sunset and happened to look up. There he was, gliding around Pine Meadow Hill. He didn't seem scary to me; in fact, he looked downright peaceful, almost a natural part of the land. Made me wish I could fly, maybe far enough to escape this dying town, or just far enough to never taste coal dust again.

Then came the Sunday when Reverend Elias didn't show up at church. Everyone assumed he was passed out drunk in the parsonage. His drinking had gotten worse since Ben Price's head landed next to him. He wasn't in the parsonage or anywhere else a man of the cloth would pass out drunk. They finally found him up on the hill by the mine entrance clutching a crucifix in one hand and a bottle in the other. He was crushed to death, as if a tree had fallen on him. That was the end of Critchley's Corner. Mountain folk aren't that easy to scare, but Daddy and I were the only ones left within a week.

We saw the moth man a lot after that – always flying around Pine Meadow Hill. We walked up there one night after chores, just to take a look. The plants had started creeping onto the dead land, and we spooked a deer. I'm not sure who was more surprised – Daddy or that buck. I was thrilled. Life was returning. When the moon came out from behind the clouds, we were suddenly surrounded by trees, transparent and shimmering silver in the moonlight. Daddy thought it was the ghost of the forest that used to be there, but I knew it wasn't – it was the moth man, planting hope. We were seeing the future, not the past.

Within six months, the forest had completely reclaimed Critchley's Corner and was making good progress up Pine Meadow Hill. I guess without people around to keep messing things up, the land just recovers faster. Now, the only other folks living in Critchley's Corner are deer, raccoons, squirrels, and the occasion possum. Frankly, they're the best neighbors I've ever had.

Daddy died last year, and that pretty much leaves me as the only human resident of Critchley's Corner. Of course, there is no Critchley's Corner, just a healthy old-growth pine forest and a dirt road leading to our farm. Daddy taught me to respect the land, and maybe that's why our house and barn are still in one piece.

I let most of the fields go back to seed – why plant more than you need when there's no one else to buy the surplus? It's a little lonely, but I don't mind most days. I still see the moth man once in a while, and I've come to believe he's tending his forest just like I tend my crops.

At night, I go to sleep staring out the window, watching the moon dance off the silver leaves of a big elm tree that mostly isn't there, dreaming of flying across the mountain on giant wings.

Wood You Love?
by Rob Smales

She had long since given up on men. There had been many, but they never stayed, never lasted, and left her brokenhearted every time. But time was something she had much of, and always, her heart healed. And what lives within the heart with love? Hope. So again, like all the other times before, she went out into the world looking for love—for a man who would love her back, and stay.

It was a small town, set high in the mountains, with only one road in and one road out, and she found the places men congregated: places of food, places of music, places where they might find women. She went to where the men herded thickest, one of the places of music and women, and slipped among them, slight and lithe, her diaphanous white dress shimmering against her tawny skin in the fading light of evening.

The music pounded at her ears, a rhythmic beat strong enough to echo in her stomach and make her skin thrum. In the lighted central square, women danced to the invasive beat. They danced alone, they danced with other women, they danced with the few men who'd joined them on the wooden floor, writhing and grinding in a manner so suggestive she might have called it scandalous, had she cared about such things. In the shadows outside the light, more men watched, with staring eyes and thickened breath. The air, heated and damp with the working of so many bodies, was filled with the scent of the barley, and the hops, and the grape. And of the sex thing—of the unfulfilled *desire* for the sex thing—so strong she could taste it.

It was the taste of sweat and desperation. She was in the right place.

She stood, bare toes on the edge of the wood-floored square, half in the light, half in darkness, pondering whether to join the dance. She wondered if this was the way of men and women now, if she was expected to put herself on display. Before her mind could be made, heat enveloped her upper arm in a firm grip: a hand so large as to wrap entirely around, thumb far overlapping fingers. With the hand came a surge in the scent, that musky smell that said *I want I want I want.* She turned at the hand's urging, into the scent, to find a man. Larger than the rest, tall and broad, though thick through the middle, the man wore his need like a cloak of mist. She was smallish, fine boned, and he blocked her view of half the room as he hulked closer, raising his voice to be heard.

"I ain't seen you around before."

His teeth were discolored, and some were absent, and the breath buoying his words was far from sweet but it mattered not; what was *inside* the outer shell, *that* was what mattered.

His words had been shouted over the music. Hers were murmured under it. "I have never been here before." He had no trouble hearing.

"You wanna dance?"

She looked to the dancers. "I've no idea. I've never danced to . . ." She gestured, indicating the music with fingers that could feel the pulse of it in the air. ". . . this."

"Wanna get out of here?"

"If you like."

He led her through the throng, gripping her hand tightly, both of them wrapped in the aura of his need; it grew palpable, and she imagined it preceding him, thrusting people aside with his wanting of her. They made it as far as his truck before his need took over and he was on her, hands no longer firm, but rough, mouth no longer speaking, but slobbering. She let him do as he wanted, shoving and pinning, parting and panting. They did the sex thing there in the oiled dirt parking lot, and it was over quickly, as she'd known it would be.

He asked where he could take her, but she had nowhere to be but where she was. This place was not her home, and she'd arrived this evening. He brought her to his home, a shack out on the edge of town, the last structure before the thick, mountain tree line. Her heart leapt. Often, after the sex thing was done, men had gone away, or faded immediately into sleep. That seemed the way of things. But he was keeping her with him—*wanted* her with him. Could he be the one who'd stay? Would it be safe to share her heart?

They did the sex thing again. It took longer this time. She didn't mind. She was patient. She had to be.

Then, with her there in his home, he slept.

* * *

In the morning, it rained. She stood in front of the shack, spreading her limbs wide to catch the water, flowing over skin as she dug her naked brown toes into the mud and grass, tasting the clean spring-storm air.

"Hey! What the hell are you doing?"

He took her arm again, much harder than he had when she'd straddled the light and shadows in the place of music and women, and spun her around. He wore short pants and nothing else, thick middle jiggling, panting and rosy with either exertion or emotion. Or both.

"I am greeting the rain." She smiled. "I am feeling the day."

His fleshy face darkened. "Well, I don't want you out here like this! Like *that*!" He pointed. She looked down. She'd put on her light white dress before coming out, but it was soaked through and plastered to her body, clearly showing everything beneath.

He loomed.

"I don't want you out here, giving everybody a free show of what's mine. Understand?"

Jerking her arm, he sent her stumbling across the cool, slippery grass toward his front door. He followed, rumbled words about "knowing what's good for you" and not wanting "to have to teach you a lesson."

It had only been a single night—they had only done the sex thing twice—yet here he was, practically throwing her into his home and calling her *his*! *I think he may be one who'll stay*, she thought. *My heart might be safe with him!* And deep down, within the very root of her, she sang.

They did the sex thing again.

* * *

The next morning he dressed and grabbed his keys.

"Gotta go to work. Keep this glorious roof over your head, right?"

But she didn't want this roof over her head. Not for long. The walls were close, the ceiling low, the air a miasma of man smells, of old food and older excrement, of body odor and bad teeth. The windows were small and dirty, blocking out more sunlight then they let in.

"I'll come with you."

"No, stupid, you can't come with me."

"Then I will go out to the—"

He slapped her.

She let him.

He struck her again. And again. And in the heat of that close little cave, she smelled his need once more growing to a taste. He struck her a fourth time—and then he was on her, as he had been in the truck, pressing her to the floor and parting her legs, his free hand fumbling with his trousers. He was on her and he was in her, and she understood.

She was small, he large, and he thought that mattered. She knew he was mistaken, that all of *this* was an outside thing, while it was the inside that mattered, that made someone what they were. She didn't care about the outside. She wanted a man who would love her. She wanted a man who would *stay.*

When he'd finished and buttoned his trousers, he leaned down to take her face in his hand, digging hard into her cheeks with powerful fingers and a thick thumb.

"You don't go anywhere. You're staying here with me." He grinned. "You got no one else, and you know it. *I* know it. New in town, and you don't know *nobody.* I'm giving you a roof, ain't I? You were lucky, the night you run into me."

He leaned closer.

"But I'm *from* here. I *know* people. They'll take *my* side. I come home from work and you're not here, I'll find you. Betcha *ass* I'll find you. Ain't nobody gonna help, or hide you from me. You're here with me until I say so."

Her cheeks and jaw flexed against his grip. "Would you love me?"

He stared into her silent eyes and grinned a sudden, brown grin. "Sure I love you, baby. And I'm gonna keep you with me for *ever.*"

He thrust her face away, hitched up his pants, and was gone.

She rose from the floor, took up her dress—it was growing tattered—and clutched it to her breast as she spun a quick pirouette. He'd said he wanted to be with her forever! That he'd chase her if she left and hunt her if she ran.

I hope you do, she thought, twirling again. *You might be the one. I might share my heart. But you need a test, to see if you mean what you say.*

* * *

His truck rounded the last bend before the shack; she waited just off the road, a few steps from the trees, her dress, though tattered, white as fresh snow against the browns and greens of the forest behind her. The vehicle rolled to a stop and he climbed out.

"And where do you think you're going?"

She pointed into the trees. "That way."

"No, you're not."

"Yes." She smiled. "I am."

"Oh, shit." He wiped a hand down his face. Put his hands on his hips. "Even after this morning, you need a lesson, huh? And boy, oh boy, are you gonna get one."

And though there was anger in his voice—she knew enough of men to recognize that—there was a small smile on his face, his lips upturned in anticipation. The breeze carried over the pheromones of his need (*I want I want I want*), and she knew he had remembered that morning in his head and was now planning to do far worse and anticipating the *after.* Because he was one of *those* men.

They would see.

"Catch me if you can." Flipping the back of her dress like a doe flagging its tail, she scampered into the trees.

"Son of a *bitch*!" He was after her like rolling thunder, beating his way across the tarmac and then into the wood in his hard-soled boots. She ran a bit, weaving through the trees, then stopped, making sure he saw her.

"Oh, I am gonna *beat* your ass!"

With another flip of the dress, she was off again. Her fleet, bare feet made no sound. She left not a sign, flowing over and under and through and around, barely touching a leaf as she passed, perfectly in tune with her surroundings, feeling almost at home. Almost *home*. The urge to slip out of the dress, to leave it behind so she might better feel those slight leafy touches, the wood-scented air cool against her skin, was strong, but she could not.

She needed this bit of cloth, this thing of men, for the white showed well in the forest. It made it easier to give him the occasional glimpse, spotted through the trees or on the rise ahead, to keep him moving in the right direction. For an hour, as men counted time, he followed, crashing through the forest as most men did, going through when he should have gone over, over when he should have gone around, and all the time panting and gasping and grunting. She heard him easily from a quarter mile away as he swung his arms, paddling the underbrush aside, swimming across the forest floor, muttering words between hissing breaths.

" . . . Run from . . . *me*? Show her . . . not . . . leaving . . . she's *never* . . . getting away . . . from me . . . *fuck!*"

And when the breeze carried his scent, his *I want I want I want* was no longer there. He'd run so far, he'd left it behind, shed in his efforts to keep up. There was anger in his sweat, and a need, but not the need for sex.

A simple need for her.

He's the one!

A final glance back, a last flash of the white where he could see, and she slipped into the glade.

Home.

The great oak's branches spread wide over the clearing, reaching for the surrounding trees even as they stretched for the sky. The great canopy rustled in greeting, though there was no wind.

From behind, a frantic, breathy roar. "I'm coming to *get* you!"

Soon, she thought, tugging the dress up and off and laying it against the wide trunk, *we will have each other*. Then, naked skin as brown as bark, she ran to the tree line and stood quite still.

Bursting through the trees, he lumbered right past her, eyes only for the bright white prize. He snorted like a bull, out of breath and unseeing as he glared about the glade before he marched over to snatch the dress. Saw the hollow in the great trunk that had lain hidden beneath it, gaping like a sideways open mouth. Bent to peer in.

"Are you in there?"

"Yes," said the oak.

"And no," said she, pushing his great backside *very* hard.

It was a tight fit. He almost didn't make it. The hollow was only so big, and he was quite a large man, and he struggled and fought, but with some judicious shoving—he howled when his shoulder broke with a thick pop (she was *much* stronger than she looked)—she got him inside her bark, inside her wood, all the way in deep.

All the way to her heart.

Screaming, wailing at the pain, he managed to turn himself in the hollow to face the sun and air—and her, outside, patiently watching.

"You bitch—I'm gonna fucking *kill* you! I—"

He tried to work himself out to her, mindful of his shoulder, but found the opening too small. Smaller, in fact, than it had been when he'd gone in.

"What is this?"

She was happy to explain. Joyous, in fact. "This is us."

"What are you talking about? Get me out of here!"

"But this is what we both desire." The split in the oak's skin shrank a bit, right before his eyes, which grew wide. His mouth opened and closed, though no sound emerged. "I am sharing my heart with you, and you will be with me forever."

* * *

It went slowly. It had to. Too quickly and he would die, and that little thing inside that made him *him* would be gone. And she wanted him. Just as he wanted her.

Forever.

The hollow closed slowly to frame his face—allowing him light and air, for he still had need—as her cambium grew and flowed around him, supporting him, holding him still. Letting her work. He begged food and water for the first days, until her growing sapwood made its way through the fabric of his jeans and began sending creepers and tendrils, slow but steady, in through existing openings and canals, rootling along his rectum and urethra.

Then he stopped begging and began to scream.

She let him. The shoulder, his thirst, his hunger, these were things of his outside, and she knew it was what was inside him that counted. *He* was inside of *her*, and soon, so soon as she counted time, *she* would be inside of *him*. The thought made her so happy she danced, leaping and twirling to the unrhythm of the wind, to the rustling of her leaves, to the song he sang as he gave voice to their love.

The sun and moon played tag across the sky again and again as her sapwood made its way up through his bowels to share her water, surging and pushing and growing, in and around and *through*, his blood mixing with her sap while he wept and screamed. He gibbered and begged as, for weeks, her plenum burrowed through his skin, bringing nutrients up from her roots and down from her crown. He no longer slept, for trees do not sleep. He no longer ate, for her plenum supplied. He no longer drank, for her sapwood supplied.

When he no longer had need of a mouth, her bark grew to cover it. Thus, he did not scream when a new twig—his first!—grew slowly out through the center of his left eye.

That was, however, when that little spark departed. He could not die—like her, he would live with the oak until *it* died—but that thing inside that had made him *him* was gone. Somehow, like all the others, he had gone.

Heartbroken, she turned her back on the world of men, finished with them forever.

Again.

Until . . .

Dryads brown as the leaf
Move in the gloom of the glade;
When meadows are grey with the morn
Dim night in the wood has delayed.
~Sigfried Sassoon, "Dryads"

Dragon's Scales
by Victoria Dalpe

Be careful what you wish for. We've all heard the saying, right? Wish wrong on a gnarly old monkey's paw and your dead son comes back a rotting zombie. You make one bad wish and your life is ruined. It happened to me, in fact. The fucked-up part? It was a child's wish. What horrible world do we live that would distort and punish a desperate child and her family for one silly wish?

I digress. If I start rambling right at the start, I'll never get this story out. Let's try to keep this straightforward. You wanted my story, you wanted to know why I look this way, why I live this way. You're too polite to ask of course. All you asked was about this house, but I can see it all over your face. Let's start with the house.

Well, for starters, it's haunted.

Personally, I never understood the fascination with haunted houses. You'd think people would just burn them down. Salt the earth, move on. Who wants to read stories or watch movies about haunted places? It's ghoulish. No one ever wants to live in a house filled with terror, abuse, tragedy, and domestic violence. Aren't those the elements that create a haunted house?

This house, my house, is a cursed place. Marked. Worse still the ghost is my grandmother, a woman I adored in life. I'm even more sure that it was my fault.

Of course, if you'd asked my father, when he was alive, he would say I was being ridiculous, or worse crazy, and liked to tell stories. If you asked my mother, before dementia made a mess of her mind, she would have said I had an overactive imagination and that my grief, my *guilty conscience*, presented itself as a haunting. My sister, had she lived and not tumbled down the stairs and broken her neck at the age of ten, would have told you there was definitely a ghost in our house, one that thinned the air and made it hard to breathe, a ghost that made it cold, impossibly cold. A ghost that kept you too scared to sleep, or eat, or think. A ghost that made you clumsy on the stairs.

After grandmother died, I could never get warm. I felt like the ghost froze the marrow inside my bones. It was a raw, teeth-chattering cold that made it impossible to sleep, to think, to do anything. I can remember so many blisteringly hot summer nights where I would lay in bed, bundled and shaking, knowing that it was over ninety degrees. My brother, had he not jammed a gun in his mouth to escape, would have told you the same. That the ghost was real, the ghost was relentless. He would take it further, tell you how it didn't matter if you ran away, the ghost followed. Like a disease or a rash. There's no running away from a rash, it's on you, it's in you. A haunting is like that, deeply personal. My brother ran, but the ghost followed. He would drink and do drugs to hide, but even in a blanked-out stupor, the ghost followed.

I know how this sounds. You don't survive as long as I have, haunted and alone, in this place, without staring in a mirror and questioning your sanity. If I'm being honest (and really why shouldn't I be?), I wish I was crazy. At least then they could give me drugs and a cozy hospital room. At least I wouldn't be forced to think about the ghost and what it means about the consequences of our actions and the afterlife. And of a fucking kid's wish.

* * *

I should go back a bit. I'm telling the story all wrong.

My grandmother's name was Shannon O'Doyle, the only child of Irish immigrants. She was a lovely woman with fair hair and blue eyes and freckles. She was a bit rough around the edges, but she loved deeply. She was loyal, kind, and a hard worker. She married young and had three kids. Her husband, my grandfather, was something of a brute and she endured many nights of drunken fights and fists. She sheltered the children as best she could. The night he crashed his car and died a quarter mile from home, my grandmother breathed a sigh of relief. Both because he would never come home and because she kept a sizable insurance policy on him that he was unaware of. Her joke was that he was a better father dead than alive. The insurance money allowed her to move them to a better neighborhood and helped cover the costs of being a single mother. Her eldest daughter, Cheryl, was my mother. My mother was very close to her mother. After my little sister was born, we moved in with my grandmother in her big old house.

My grandmother and I were the most similar. We looked alike, shared the same laugh, and both ran rough around the edges. Two peas in a pod. We got each other's jokes and were known to be a little harsh to others. Every day after school we would watch our soap operas and eat little snacks on TV trays. We took long walks, went swimming in the community pool, and loved to look for treasures at antique stores. I knew my siblings were jealous of our relationship, as my grandmother was a bristly woman who didn't give her attention and affection to just anyone.

The woman wore a locket, a simple thing, and in it, she claimed, was a scale of a dragon she'd seen once as a child in the field behind her house. She said when the dragon saw her, it flew away. Running to the spot it had been she saw something shining—a scale off the dragon's back. She would occasionally open the locket for me. Inside, delicate and iridescent, was a dragonfly's wing.

She was not a woman known for flights of fantasy. I always wondered if my grandmother told this story to entertain us. Surely, she knew it was just a dragonfly wing. Still, she wore that locket nearly every day, kept it close to her heart. It was warm from her skin in my memory of opening it the first time. How wondrous that she'd seen a dragon and had proof! She warned us that it was a secret. Dragons were very private by nature and did not like to be talked about. If I ever hoped to spy one myself I had to keep their secret.

When I was twelve, I was an awkward thing, as most are, gangly, pimply, with hair and skin that always looks oily no matter how much I washed. I was teased and, outside of my family, had no friends. It was during this hard time that my grandmother got sick. Cancer. She wasn't much for doctors and so by the time we convinced her to go, she was gray-skinned, thin, and quite far gone. Inoperable. They started chemo but the prognosis wasn't positive. I was devastated. She'd gone from bigger-than-life to a dried-out husk in a matter of months. I would sit by her bed, trying to be strong, hating to cry in front of her, and always failing.

"I don't want you to leave me. I'll be all alone."

"You won't my girl. You have your family; you will make friends; you will find your place. It won't always feel this hard."

"I want more time."

"I don't have it. I can't eat; I can't sleep. I wouldn't wish this on my worst enemy. It's like I'm stuck here watching you all live your lives while I waste away. It's torture. Like hell on earth."

"What can I do?"

"You can help me . . . in a very special way. It will be our secret, like the dragon's scale." Saying this, she clasped her locket tight, unaware of doing it. So small and thin, her body was little more than bones and gristle. How I hated the world at that moment, the world that could take something so cherished, a best friend and confidant, and kill them this way. *Why me?* I thought selfishly, *Why do I have to suffer?* Why did she? She'd never hurt anyone, tried to live a just life. Why punish and ravage her body? Why take everything?

Even then, at twelve, I hoped there wasn't a god because if there was, I would hate him so. She wanted my help to take her medicine. All of her medicine. I looked at the orange cylinders with white caps; there were so many. Hard to believe anyone could take so much medicine and not get better. Or worse.

"You want me to help you kill yourself?" I said in a small voice. The scene, her lying in bed surrounded by medicine in a dim room that smelled of death and despair, and me, her gawky granddaughter with red-rimmed eyes and braids.

"I'm already dead, on borrowed time. I'm suffering. You remember when Hank got old, full of tumors? What did your dad do?"

"Took him to the vet. He was . . . suffering. Mom said it was 'cruel' to leave him like that."

"Right. It's cruel to leave me like this."

"I don't want to go to jail."

"Oh honey, you won't, just open all these bottles up and slide them close to me, then go on out and do whatever it is you do when you aren't sitting here with me with a face like a slapped ass." I wiped my tears. I didn't want to. I also couldn't forget Hank, whining on the floor, diarrhea leaking from him as he dragged lame back legs. It was horrible. The world was horrible.

I looked back after doing what she asked. My grandmother was smiling, sadly and looking at me.

"Thanks kid, you know I hate mushy stuff, but I love you. Probably love you more than anyone else in my life."

"Ditto." I choked out.

"Now go, go on a bike ride, make a friend, get in trouble. Have a life."

* * *

I don't remember where I went the rest of that day. I think I just wandered around outside, maybe walked down the old logging trail across from my grandmother's farm house. However I got there, I eventually found myself in a field, the late summer grasses coming to my waist. Under a cloudless blue sky, the only sound was the *swish* of wind running through the grass. A few feet away something glinted in the sunlight. I moved toward it, attracted to the sparkle like a crow. There, clinging to a stalk of tall gold grass was a huge dragonfly. It didn't move as I approached. How beautiful it was. Its body alternated between emerald green and a vibrant electric blue, wings a complex gridwork like a rainbow mosaic, or stained glass. It was a magical animal, so alien and so lovely. I thought of my grandmother dying in her bedroom, clutching her dragonfly wing in that old locket. The insect raised its wings, preparing to take off, but as it lifted my hand shot out and I grabbed it. It fought me and tried to wriggle free, but I held it tight, looking at it all the closer.

At that moment I felt very sad and very cruel. I wanted something to hurt, hurt like I did. I wanted to trade its little life for my grandmother's. One death for another. I yanked its wings off. It died so she could stay with me. Forever. A life for a life. That was my wish: *Make her stay.* Before my eyes its beauty curdled, replaced with my shame. I was tempted to drop the wings, hide the evidence and run away. But that felt disrespectful and the poor little animal would have died for nothing.

I'm not a monster. I was just a sad kid who'd been asked to assist her beloved grandmother committing suicide. I carried the wings, cupped carefully in my hands, all the way home. An ambulance idled in the driveway. When my mother saw me, she came running.

"Oh Celia, I've been looking for you. *She died.* Your grandmother died. I'm so sorry." She pulled me into an embrace. She wasn't supposed to die. I killed the dragonfly. A life for a life. I'd made a wish. All of that kept running through my head, like it mattered or I had that kind of power. I let my mother hug me and weep, all the while focused on protecting the dragonfly wings in my hand.

* * *

I didn't believe in magic, or God, or ghosts, or dragons. I wasn't a fanciful child and tended to trust a combination of my eyes and gut. For that reason, I would have said I did not believe in ghosts. Remember the ghosts? I started way back talking about ghosts, but needed to set the scene, right? Lonely girl, middle child of three, an older brother, a younger sister, and two parents. Left in my grandmother's big old farmhouse on the edge of the woods.

My grandmother's death changed the tone of the household from the moment the ambulance pulled out of the drive without the lights on. It was an unspoken secret that she'd killed herself. My brother David had found her, not breathing and covered in sick with pill bottles all over. Everyone knew my grandmother's arthritis and overall weakness made it impossible for her to open the pill bottles on her own. When Mother asked about it, her eyes bloodshot, we both knew the truth.

"Did you open up the bottles for her? You can tell me."

"I wasn't in the house when it happened; I don't know what you are talking about." I kept my chin up, but she'd been my mother for twelve years and I was a punk kid. She couldn't get me to admit it, but suspected I'd helped her mother kill herself and hated me for it. "She trusted you, she confided in you. Someone helped her. Was it you? You won't be in trouble, I promise, I just want to know." She pushed, her voice shaky.

"I went for a walk in the woods. I wasn't in the house. I don't know." She slid my grandmother's locket across the table to me. It sat between us for a moment, like a telltale heart. I gathered it in my hand and stroked the cool metal, trying to warm it. She watched me hold it, lips tight.

"It would be a horrible burden to carry a secret like that, for the rest of your life. You sure you don't want to confess?"

"There's nothing to confess." I stood up, holding the locket. For the first time, it was cold to touch. I took it to my room and carefully added the other wings inside. Then I slung it over my neck. While I doubted the chain could hold fragrance, I swore I could smell her perfume at that moment.

That night I lay in my bed, fighting sleep and watching the shadow of branches stretch across the ceiling. My body was tired but my mind refused to calm, running like a gerbil on a wheel. In that murky place between sleep and waking, I felt eyes on me. That goosebump-causing sensation of being watched. My eyes shot to the doorway I'd left open only an inch, a habit since childhood. There, peeking through the crack, was a person, little more than a dark shape. A wet eye in the scant light. My blood chilled watching the figure watching me. Too short to be my parents, and I knew it wasn't my siblings. There was no one else in the house. I squeezed my eyes shut, heart frantic in my chest. When I reopened them, the figure was still there, watching me from the seam in the door.

"You're not funny." I said, trying to sound brave, and failing. My voice was high and warbled. Gathering what little false bravado I could, I slid out of bed and marched the few feet to the doorway and yanked it open. No one there. The hallway was long, my room at the end. There was nowhere to go. The motion-activated night light in the hallway blinked on. I talked myself into believing it to be an eerie dream. Anyone else would have tripped the motion light. There had been no one watching from the crack. If I smelled a whiff of my grandmother's perfume in the doorway, that was coincidence as I was wearing the locket.

* * *

From that night on, I was watched. Wherever the shadow was thick, a closet left slightly ajar, a dark corner behind a chair or curtain, it watched. I took to closing everything tight, stuffing suitcases beneath my bed, and filling empty spaces everywhere. It didn't matter, the ghost always fit and there was always enough room to watch. It was a shadow stretched along my ceiling, a quick movement behind my reflection. It watched and, while giving no outward indication, it judged.

With time I could make out more of its shape, and that shape was my grandmother. The ghost was small and hunched, with messy hair and judging eyes. There was no fondness or familiarity. Just a thing, a shade that watched me with such disappointment and possibly hate, if a thing like that could feel.

We talk ourselves into and out of a lot of things. We want a world we understand. To merely exist, playing a game with no clear rules or outcomes, would drive us all mad. So, we try to create a reality we can live with. Some of us have a god with a checklist of good deeds. Others have science. Each of us works hard to design a world we can exist in without running off into the woods screaming. From that first night, the ghost in my house worked hard to crack my family's beliefs. At first, I thought she was only watching me, but as the days went on, I could see the wear and tear on each of my family members. The dark circles, the wan complexions, the shaky hands and spacy expressions. No one in our home was getting enough rest.

"There's something bad in the house." My sister finally said over a bowl of artificially-colored cereal. "I've been having bad dreams."

"Yeah." My brother said, eyes never leaving his comic book, "I feel like someone is in the house, spying on me all the time. It's creepy."

"I saw her once, you know, got a really good look," my sister said, her voice barely above a whisper. "It looked like--"

"Enough!" My mother yelled, her voice cracking and startling all of us, "Enough of this talk, there is no such thing as ghosts and you are all just grieving grandma's loss." She stormed out of the room.

"Grandma. It was grandma." My sister said, her dark-circled eyes meeting mine. "Didn't she love us? Why would she be trying to scare me?"

"She died in the house. Maybe that's all it takes." I refused to admit that I made a wish. A wish that she would stay with me, forever.

"Killing yourself is a sin. Maybe this is her limbo or hell or whatever. For what she did." My brother looked at me with an expression that was twin to my mother's. Hateful. He blamed me. I shrugged and cleared my plate.

"Maybe it's nothing and we are all crazy," I said, avoiding their eyes. How I wished that were true, but even then, in the bright light of morning, I could see a crouching shape watching us from the corner. Never far away.

* * *

Time passed and nothing changed. The ghost was there all the time. I got in the habit of talking to it, hoping that maybe it would remember who it was and talk back. That she would be my grandmother again. It never responded, besides the feverish and hateful stare.

"What do you want?! Do you want an apology? I didn't know! Maybe if I hadn't killed a stupid bug and wished you to stay, you'd be in heaven. *Or* maybe if you hadn't killed yourself, huh? You think about that? That maybe this isn't my fault but yours. *And* if that is true then this isn't fair, you are terrorizing your family!" It was then that my mother opened my door in a rush, her face pale.

"Who are you talking to?" She looked into the corner where the dark smudge ghost of my grandmother stood and judged.

"Who do you think? She's standing right there!" My mother looked at where I pointed and did nothing. I added, "Tell me you can see her? She's right there plain as day, like always!" I was crying then. My mother wiped her eyes and shook her head. She thought I'd gone mad. No doubt the guilt had poisoned my mind.

The next day I was sent to a professional who took notes, tutted, and did not believe me. While I was there, talking to this *professional*, my sister ran down the hallway screaming in fear and fell down the stairs, breaking her neck.

The loss of my sister rippled. My parents' marriage was first; my father decided to move out. I begged him to take me with, in part to flee the house and my mother's endless hatred toward me. She blamed me for the death of her mother and now her youngest child. My father said no, better to stay together. And he left. Down the dusty trail for new wives and fresh starts. What he found though, after years of poor sleeping and abusing sleeping pills, was death, thought to be an accidental overdose.

We carried on, year by year, thinner and paler, lessening with each day. The ghost filled the house, growing larger as we shrunk down. Perhaps she was a vampire. I remembered folktales about suicides coming back as the undead. Maybe she was growing fatter on our souls. My brother had gotten heavy into drugs and was gone for long periods of time. The last time, before he left and never returned, I asked him why he came home at all. "Doesn't matter where I go. She follows." He said it while staring out the window at the overgrown fields. "Doesn't matter where or how fucked up I get, she follows. She gets in my dreams."

"What does she do to you in your dreams?" I was afraid of the answer, as I hadn't yet dreamed of her, but I saw her all the time. Even then, I whispered the question and leaned close, for she was at the bottom of the stairs watching me through the rails.

He laughed. It was an ugly, manic sound, "Nothing! She just fucking stares at me, all the time. She just watches me. She watches me take a piss, she watches me sleep, she watches me snort heroin. She just fucking watches." Then he was gone and a little later he was dead. He got hold of a pistol.

It was just mom and me after that and she barely spoke to me, a broken and sad woman who had watched her entire life unravel. Her mind couldn't handle it and bit by bit became a stranger to herself. She wandered the halls, she looked at photos and recognized no one. The mercy in this was that she'd forgotten who I was. So, she stopped hating me.

Meanwhile, I had honed myself into a machine, one that ate enough to survive, who went to school, who did enough homework to pass and slept best I could. Then I worked, a mindless job in the factory in town, which brought in just enough to keep the lights on and food on the table. Years passed. The ghost never let up, and was tall enough now that she had to stoop, hunched shoulders fitting into the corners where the ceiling and wall met. Eventually, my mother went into a home and I was left in the house alone. Just the two of us. Just like I wanted all those years ago.

That brings us to now. To why I am here in this old house on the edge of the world. Why I look the way I do and why I wear this old locket. See, I made a wish, long ago when I was young and selfish and believed in the power of love. I wanted my love to transcend death and I guess in a way it did. She's always with me, always, can't you see her? She's just there over your shoulder. Hard to miss her, big as she is now. Hell, she's half the room. Look at those judgy black eyes, big as dinner plates. Hungry but never fed, hateful. I wonder if, when I am gone, I will just be added to her mass, absorbed, and she will just grow bigger. Or perhaps I'll be cursed to stand beside her, waiting and watching silently myself. Or maybe nothing will happen. Best case, maybe I will die and that will break the curse and she will be free and I will be free. Maybe a big storm will blast through this valley, demolish this old house and all our trinkets and we will just vanish. Like we never existed.

That's my wish now.

This Night Has A Chill

by Katherine Silva

I heard Max's droning voice through the haze of gin as I fidgeted with my empty cigarette box. He was talking about his and Effie's plans for the rest of the night. Leece was drinking it up. This promotion was important to her; she needed to feign interest in whatever her boss had to say. Or maybe she was actually interested. All I could tell was that it was fucking cold standing out in the wintry night and I would kill for a smoke.

I'd tried to stay attentive during the two-hour long discourse about competitive marketing strategies for their company, all while they slurped down oysters and gargled with hundred-dollar bottles of champagne. Before dinner, I'd agreed to Leece's plan: I wouldn't say much. I wouldn't talk about how I thought she'd deserved the promotion a long time ago; I wouldn't mention the nights Leece stayed at the office until dawn devising the company's next crucial advertising campaign. I would keep my sarcasm to a minimum.

I lost the battle somewhere between the salmon tartare and the zucchini-tomato verrines. But rather than let my annoyance slip out in a perfectly timed quip about how Effie's hair resembled a steel wool scrubber sponge, I sucked down the rest of my Singapore Sling and ordered a second. Then, a third.

Effie laughed next to me, her high-pitched tittering chasing up into the blackness above, like a hyena in heat. I pulled my coat closer, fingers crinkling the empty box in my jacket pocket. Damn, if only I'd remembered to replace it. It had been a breakneck day though.

I'd come off a double at the hospital, my only motivation to move being that I thought I'd have the night to recharge. A polar vortex had swept through our region a couple nights ago and left dozens of the homeless and disenfranchised people of Toronto exposed to the elements. I'd seen patients with superficial and deep frostbite, exacerbated chest infections and asthma, and hypothermia.

The last patient I'd tended to was a young girl, barely ten, named Ally who had disappeared at the playground. Police had found her a half mile away near the bay. Ally claimed she'd followed a caribou there. It was obviously a lie: we don't have caribou in the city except the zoo. Maybe she'd seen a deer or moose? Even then, the story didn't make much sense after she reached the lake. Ally claimed the caribou had changed shape, turned into a woman and tried to carry her away. She always was scary-looking, had long fingernails and red eyes. The girl hid in a sewer drain until she'd passed out and the authorities found her.

Once out of her cold wet clothes, we set Ally up with oxygen and a saline drip. She was going to be okay. Her mother's red rimmed, tear specked eyes haunted my thoughts as I took the metro home. Someone had nearly kidnapped her daughter, someone perceived as a monster in Ally's eyes. I didn't have kids of my own, but I was unsettled by the idea that there was someone out there who had traumatized a little girl, had nearly killed her. Toronto was one of the safest cities in the world. The thought of a child predator on the loose had people on edge.

The single stop on my way back to the apartment was for boxed wine, cigarettes, and a TV dinner of Salisbury steak and mashed potato. Two steps through the front door, I found Leece in her black shift dress, the one I'd only seen her wear once or twice, and those clunky wedges her sister had bought her that had never left the closet.

"Please, babe," she'd pleaded, even as my shoulders slumped and all desire to continue existing in this world diminished. "It's one night. This is the promotion we've wanted!"

A proverbial "you've" should have replaced the "we've". I'd watched Leece struggle to gain any footholds in that company for the last three years despite the break-neck pace she worked at and the number of times her ideas had been used by the company execs to rake in the cash. A dinner like this was her chance to show them the woman I already knew she was.

With no argument, I slithered out of my scrubs, showered, and donned a form-flattering, above-the-knee, navy sweater dress. I dumped my essentials from my shoulder bag into a clutch, forgetting my cigarettes, and off we went.

"Babe, are you listening?"

I turned toward Leece. The seriousness in her face sobered me but only a little. Her mascara had left dots over her eyelids. I opened my mouth to tell her.

"Oh my god," she said, taking a step back and waving her hand briefly in front of her nose. "You're wasted."

I glanced over at Max and Effie. They were giving their ticket to the valet to have their car brought around. Out of earshot.

"Seriously, Kirima?"

I sighed. "Did you get it? Was all of this worth it?"

A disgust curled her lip. "Is that what you've been thinking the whole night?"

My brain screamed for the taste of menthol, that cool breath of calm to quiet my head. I shivered. Damn this dress. Damn this cold.

"Never mind," Leece mumbled, reaching into her purse. She slapped a wad of cash into my hand. "Take a taxi home. I'm going to stay out for a bit."

I frowned. "It's almost midnight."

"Max and Effie are going to Delusions. It's that new club over on Eighth and Fernald? They want me to come, too. Said we'd talk about the promotion there."

I was too distracted by the thought of a smoke to be completely hurt by the prospect I was being dumped; the feeling of the bills in my hand flipped a switch somewhere in my head. "Did Max actually use those words?"

Leece didn't say anything. I knew he hadn't. She was embellishing, as she often did when she got her hopes too high about something.

The nearby glare of fluorescent lights pulled my attention away from the conversation. A convenience store sat in a concrete lot across the street. They'd have cigarettes.

"I'll see you later."

I turned to see Leece walking away from me toward Max and Effie as the valet returned with their black Lincoln Corsair. Her back was stiff, her strides short. She was pissed.

They piled into the car and drove off, the blur of their taillights fading in the gloom.

She'd left me. My lip shook as I crunched the cigarette box into oblivion in my pocket. I couldn't believe Leece cared more about mollifying those two power-hungry assholes than coming home with me…

A blast of metal music from a passing car pulled me out of my thoughts and made me realize that I'd been staring at a figure in the shadows between the brownstone apartment complex and the gas station.

Or . . . not. I squinted. There wasn't anyone there after all.

"God, I need to sober up," I said to myself. I stumbled to the crosswalk, thumbed the button for the HAWK beacon to light up, and waited diligently, my eyes glued to the red hand signal. Cars zoomed past, cacophonies of music, horns, and conversation drone over the gales of icy wind. The numbers counted down to the bright pedestrian walking graphic. I crossed the four lanes of traffic with a group of twenty-somethings in puffy jackets and wide brimmed hats, the golden lights and Vivaldi of the restaurant behind me paling in the neon glow of the Shell gas station. The S had burned out leaving only HELL in bright red.

I chuckled at the irony. It certainly felt like Hell had frozen over.

My gaze lingered on the group I'd crossed with, and to the shape I thought I saw out of the corner of my eye. A newspaper vending machine, bright yellow and not even tall enough to be a person. It wasn't what I thought I'd seen.

I yanked open the door to the gas station, the stench of petrol and old pizza assaulting my senses. There was only one other patron inside besides me, a truck driver getting some coffee from one of the dispensers in the back. One of the lights flickered on and off in the far corner and day-old hot dogs lazily sizzled inside a mini-rotisserie on the counter. I found my way to the coolers and grabbed a bottle of water, then stepped up to the counter to buy cigarettes. The attendant was a five-foot, rail thin guy with coke bottle glasses, a twitchy eye, and a stained striped shirt.

"Just the water?" he asked as I set my bottle on the counter.

"A pack of Bihan, Mentholated."

He pulled a blue box from the rainbow of cartons behind him and tossed it onto the counter. "Eighteen forty-seven. Stuff can kill ya, ya know?"

I handed him a twenty. "Thanks, Crack Waldo."

He opened the drawer with a CHING, slotted the bill, pulled my change and flung it on the counter. The change bounced off the plastic and onto the floor. I stamped my boot down on a quarter but lost the rest as they rolled away.

The truck driver behind me had scooped them up and carefully handed them over to me as I righted myself. "Thanks," I said before flashing an evil eye at the cashier and pushing out into the cold once more.

Popping the water bottle under one arm, I immediately tore the clear plastic away from the cigarette carton, flipped it open with my thumb and slid a caramel and white cancer-stick into my hand. I cursed as I tucked it between my lips and searched for my lighter. I'd left that behind, too, in the sweater I'd worn at the end of my shift at the hospital. I turned to reenter the Hell station, but immediately thought better of it. Crack Waldo was staring at me from behind the counter even as he finished ringing out the truck driver. I could bum a light off of someone else. No use in wasting my money on another cheap lighter that I'd no doubt eventually misplace.

I hoofed it up the sidewalk, passing the darkened alleyway between the brownstone and the gas station. Looking into its depths provided no clearer sights of lingering figures, only a new blast of wintry air, this time with sand. I wiped at the grit in my eye as I continued on toward the lighted bus stop ahead.

An old lady sat on the bench in the shelter, a ratty olive coat her only protection against the night's cruel temperatures. Her insulated boots were torn in places and her purple sweatpants were pilled but otherwise, probably warmer than my lack of any pants. I decided better than to sit on the cold bench but hovered nearby and checked the bus schedule. There was one more coming through before it stopped running for the evening. Bus fare was cheaper than a taxi any day and as much as I wanted to use all of Leece's cash just to spite her, I decided it was safer to keep some of it to grab coffee and breakfast sandwiches for us tomorrow morning.

"You got a light?" I asked the old lady.

She looked up at me and quietly shook her head.

Fuck. I pulled the cigarette from my lips again and stuffed it into my pocket.

I opened my water bottle and took a long swig. Tomorrow morning, Leece was going to wake up and feel miserable, whether it was from lack of sleep or the fact that she'd spent her entire evening out gunning for a promotion that wasn't going to happen. Max and Effie had seemed more like the people who enjoyed entertainment, good conversation, and a diversion from their usual gig every once and a while. Tonight, our company had been the diversion, but that was it.

I'd go out and pick us up some everything bagels with sausage, egg, and sriracha; her favorite. We'd talk over coffee and she would apologize for leaving me on the street like that. We'd talk about how any business would kill to have someone with her talents and success. Maybe she would finally see that she was too good for this place anymore.

The rumbling of the bus brought my head up as it careened around the corner to the right and chugged up to the bus stop. The old lady struggled on quaking knees into a standing position and shouldered her bag. Again, I thought I saw something move out of the corner of my vision, again from the alley. It had to have been litter, something being swept up into the air by the wind. The brakes squealed as the bus stilled in front of us and the door folded open. The old woman climbed on and with hesitance, I followed. I didn't have a pass ticket on me but the driver took one look at my ten bucks and let me pick out a seat.

The city bus line used a fleet that had been in service for the last twenty years. Still rolling with over two hundred thousand miles on the engines, lots of other things on the busses had deteriorated to the point of no return. This one had no working interior lights and some of the vinyl on the seats had worn through to the foam cushions. I chose one of those seats unintentionally near the front of the bus.

Across the aisle, a couple of tourists glanced nervously at the road ahead, clutching their bags to them. This probably wasn't what they'd had in mind when they were promised an "airport shuttle" to their hotel. The bus doors folded shut and the huge vehicle thundered to life .

I was already lost in thoughts of what I was going to do as soon as I got home: out of the dress and into some flannel pj's; a long luxurious smoke on the fire escape outside the kitchen; a huge bowl of that blackberry chocolate chip ice cream and re-watching the first series of *The IT Crowd.*

Somewhere in this daydream, I noticed that the bus was colder than it had been outside. I glanced around, searching for an open window or more appropriately, a hole somewhere, but didn't notice anything in the dim lighting. "Hey!" I finally called to the bus driver. "Does this rig have heat? I'm freezing over here."

The driver barely paid me any attention, a small wave of his hand as though a fly had swooped too close to his face and then, nothing.

Frigging falling apart piece of shit. I buttoned the top button of my jacket and pushed my head a little further down into it like a bird burrowing into a nest.

I noticed a dark shape in the very back corner seat of the bus. I blinked and squinted to see it clearer. I hadn't noticed anyone there when I'd gotten on. No matter how I focused my eyes, I couldn't discern any features in the shadows. Whoever it was sat with their knees primly pulled together, feet tucked under the seat, back ramrod straight. A hat or hood shielded their face.

The ride back to my apartment downtown took all of ten minutes. I found myself unable to stop glancing at the mysterious rider. I'd sneak peeks every thirty seconds or so, half expecting them to blip out of existence, like my weird "sightings" on the street earlier. This person hadn't vanished, though. They just sat there, as stiff as a board, staring straight ahead.

While the drink was beginning to wear off and the dull thump of a headache replaced it, the very intoxicated part of me imagined throwing my bottle of water at the shadowy rider. I wondered if they'd have any reaction. So far, they hadn't moved at all, not even a turn of the head or shift of feet.

The ride wasn't the smoothest; the driver flew over potholes and took turns as though trying to drift a racecar in the Indy 500. A few times, I expected the bus might tip over and from the terrified expressions of the couple and the old lady, I wasn't the only one. But that dark figure on the back of the bus? Nothing. Barely phased. Then, again, I couldn't see their face. Or maybe they rode this bus all the time and were used to its driver's insane antics.

I got off at my stop and hiked a block to the apartment building. Inside, I ditched my coat, the warmth like being inside a woodstove.

Our apartment was small, but clean. Well, I tried to keep it clean. Leece's days off were like a tornado sweeping through a small town. I turned on the lights and kicked off my boots in our cluttered entrance hall. Padding down to the bedroom, I yanked off the dress and slipped on pajamas. Within moments of being in comfortable clothing, my bed was so much more promising than a bowl of ice cream and a cigarette. I resisted the urge to collapse onto the lush white comforter and instead shoved my feet into my shearling slippers.

Our kitchen was my favorite room, peppered by red and yellow accents. True to most of Leece's days at home alone, she'd left a full sink for me to clean and the egg carton was out on the counter.

I took a deep breath and focused on my necessity for a smoke. The window between the sink and the oven led out to the fire escape. We'd decorated the window with Christmas lights a few months ago, and their golden bloom brought the last of my anxiety about work and Leece down. I retrieved the new cigarettes from my jacket, found a spare lighter on the butcherblock island and shimmied the window open.

Arctic air purged my solace almost immediately, but my need for nicotine far outweighed my discomfort. I lit up and took a deep pull before letting the smoke seep from my mouth. As I leaned out the open window, I watched the smoke ripple up into the night and sighed.

Finally.

I took another long drag and gazed down at the street. Someone stood on the fire escape one level below me gazing out at the city. They were dressed in dark clothing, a hood drawn up over their head. I couldn't see their face and through the rusted metal of the fire escape, I couldn't tell their exact build or height.

It's a coincidence, I told myself, even as I realized I'd held onto the smoke from my last cigarette for too long. I coughed hard, feeling bile travel up my throat. The noise was like an explosion. I instantly swallowed down any further noises, my throat burning.

I'd expected the figure to look up at me, to at least be curious about the noise. No. They stayed still, like a store mannequin almost.

I retreated back inside the apartment, shutting the window and dropping my half-spent cigarette into the sink. It fizzled in one of the water-filled bowls.

The apartment was frigid. I checked the thermostat next to the fridge and twitched the dial up a few degrees. Then, I noticed the water bottle that I'd abandoned upon arrival on the kitchen counter. A crisp layer of ice skimmed the top of the liquid.

The hell . . . I bumped the temperature up again, until the dial was at seventy-six.

Bed: that's all I needed right then. I was still out of it, my head reeling with imaginings after the day's grueling shift at the hospital and too many cocktails. I needed to sleep and wake up to a brand-new day: to sunshine and soberness.

I left the kitchen, flicked off the lights and moved to the bedroom. Snuggling down deep into the silky sheets, I didn't remember my head hitting the pillow before I was out.

* * *

I fluttered back into consciousness, immediately realizing that something wasn't right. Vapor pillowed in the air as I breathed out and I shook in my bed despite having gone to sleep warm. I listened for the rhythmic sound of my clock and was rewarded with only silence. I sat up. In the pale light that tracked in through the tiny window of our room, I noticed a glint of frost on almost every surface: the walls, yesterday's clothes on the rug, the television. The glass on the window was feathered over in intricate fractals by ice.

Had the building lost power? I struggled to get out of bed and immediately regretted it. I dropped a hand down to the floor in search of my slippers. They, too, were incased in ice and crunched like fresh snow under a boot when I tried to grab them. Even my cell phone was dead, the battery likely drained by the cold.

Forcing myself up out of bed, I nearly shrieked when my feet hit the frosted carpet. I went for the light switch only to be granted a blip of light before the bulb shattered in the fixture overhead.

I need to get out of here. I left the bedroom and started to the front door, my eyes glued to my usually cozy apartment and the sparkling rime on every surface. As I passed the kitchen, there was movement out of the corner of my eye. What I saw made me flinch so hard that I bumped into the wall behind me.

A dark figure stood in my kitchen near the stove, facing me. Like before, clothed in black and a wide deep hood pulled up over their head. Their eyes glowed red in the pocket of darkness where their face was. Even stranger, those eyes were one on top of another on the left side of the face. There wasn't a pupil, nothing to distinguish a gaze or a modicum of humanity. Just red, sideways eyes.

I couldn't make myself utter a word. I couldn't scream. The worst parts of my brain started filling in the features on the face that I couldn't see, perhaps a mouth that ran parallel to those eyes, racing up the right side of its face in a slash of feral shark-like teeth and gums.

And then it opened its mouth and I was right. The teeth looked human and that made it all the worse. I wanted to tilt my head so that I was looking at the face the way it was supposed to be. Or maybe I wanted *it* to tilt *its* head the right way.

"*Child...*"

The word scraped through the air as if being dragged over sharp rocks. I flattened further against the wall. "What?"

The eyes widened and its ugly mouth parted once more. "*Child!*"

"I don't have any," I muttered, my eyes glancing at the door to the apartment hallway. I hadn't deadbolted it last night, leaving that for Leece to do. Is this how it had gotten in?

No.

The kitchen window. I hadn't locked it. It must have been on the fire escape, came in that way even though the window was closed behind the creature now.

"*Child!*" it rasped. "*Child...*"

"I don't have any!" I said again, slower and louder.

Even as I said it, I remembered my shift at the hospital, the teary gaze of Ally's mother, of the little bedridden girl I'd helped intubate. The story the little girl had told. A monstrous woman with red eyes...

I looked down, for the first time noticing the long talons that extended from the creature's fingers, glinting in the dappled moonlight from the frozen windows. "Ally," I said.

The creature blinked slowly, the talons twitching slightly at the name.

It wanted the girl that it had lost. For some reason, it knew that I was responsible for her care. I didn't know how, couldn't understand why this thing had latched onto me. Why couldn't it have found one of the other doctors or nurses attending her? Why did it have to follow me home?

"She's in the hospital," I said. "She's safe."

The last word induced a snarl from the creature. The side-mouth opened and the teeth inside gnashed together hideously.

My feet were going numb from the frozen carpet and shivers racked my body. I needed to make a break for it, before this thing took out its frustration on me.

"*Get child.*" The creature raised its needle like claws as if in challenge, its eyes boring holes through me.

The command made me shiver harder. I was being given an ultimatum.

I turned and raced to the door. My hand slid over the frozen metal of the knob, struggling to gain purchase. I used both, wrenching it to the side and fell into the lit corridor. My vision fogged, hot air closing over me like a blanket. I stumbled over my own feet as I ran down the hall, not looking back . I screamed as I reached the end of the hall and banged on my neighbor's door. "Let me in! Open the door!"

As my fingers scrabbled at the door, I looked over my shoulder. Nothing emerged from my apartment. No creature. No needle-like claws wrapping around the doorjamb, no twisted face and ghoulish red eyes peering out from the darkened front hall.

The apartment door in front of me opened and I practically leapt into the confused older man's arms, wailing and blubbering.

* * *

The police were baffled by the scene in my apartment. The building manager couldn't explain why the water heaters in my apartment alone had stopped working. Why it was only ten degrees Fahrenheit inside while the rest of the building stayed warm. There was no sign of forced entry, no sign that there had been anyone but me in the kitchen that night. The police chalked up my hysteria to an alcohol-induced nightmare. I was told I could sleep on the couch at my neighbors' (Beverly and Bill's) apartment until the landlord could hire someone to fix the heating.

I was graciously allowed Beverly's cellphone to call Leece, but the call went straight to voicemail. It was after three in the morning and as much as I hated the idea that Leece still might be out partying with Max and Effie, I figured she had crashed at their place.

I didn't sleep the rest of the night. I was wired, twitching at every shadow. I kept the lights on in the living room while Beverly and Bill snored softly in their bedroom down the hall. I waited for the sun to rise for what felt like forever. I was rewarded with a gradual lightening to an overcast sky and snow. I thanked my neighbors for their hospitality once they woke and left.

Returning to my apartment left a fresh scar on my mind. The entire place was damp. The paint on the walls had run in places. Dark water stains ran across the ceiling in our bedroom and the living room. The apartment smelled like wet cotton. I managed to find a dry set of clothes deep in my bureau. My boots were wet, which didn't matter as my socks were soaked through. My jacket had fared better, a dampness in the sleeves the only thing uncomfortable about it.

Collecting my purse, I took the elevator down to the lobby and asked the building manager to call a taxi for me. My phone was still dead and upstairs.

I asked the driver to take me to the hospital. It was supposed to be my day off, but my encounter the previous night had me dying to make sure that Ally was still safe. I had told that creature where to find her last night, not even thinking at the time that my refusal might mean it would try to collect her on its own.

Snow cascaded from the sky in sheets and traffic ground to a halt about a half a mile from the hospital. I didn't remember seeing snow in the forecast, but the weather was rarely as predicted in Toronto. After inching along in traffic for what felt like hours, I paid the driver and climbed out, choosing to traverse the windswept streets to the hospital on my own time. Not even three blocks into walking, my boots were frozen, and my toes hurt inside them. I pushed through the pain, my thoughts locked on the monstrosity in my apartment last night. It had sought me out specifically, thinking that I would just take it to an innocent girl and let it…what? Kill her? Drink her blood? I wasn't entirely sure what that thing wanted with Ally, only that it wasn't good. Why try to kidnap a child in the first place unless it was to do something horrible?

I reached the hospital at quarter to nine. The emergency doors slid open and let me spill into the white, warm building. The receptionist gave me a blank stare and I returned it, my brain fighting the cold in my extremities, the panic of what I'd find, and the confusion of where my girlfriend had ended up last night.

Finding the locker room, I quickly changed out of my boots and into my clogs and a fresh, dry change of clothes. I kept them here in case of emergencies; this counted. Then, I set about finding Ally's room. The last I'd seen, she'd had a bed in the ER, but after she'd stabilized, the nurses probably moved her to one of the patient rooms upstairs.

The smell of antiseptic in the halls brought me back to life a little. I checked in at the nurse's station on level one, which at the time was unoccupied. I logged in and checked the patient registry. Sure enough, they'd moved Ally up to level three, the children's ward, pending a morning exam from the doctor.

I searched on the web for the thing I encountered last night.

It didn't take long to find it; I wish it had. A simple search of "sideways face ice monster" brought up an artist's rendering of the thing I'd seen in my kitchen last night, although not exact.

"The Ijiraq…" I read out loud, scanning the cryptology website where I'd found the image. A shape-shifting creature that kidnaps children.

"Gesundheit," someone said from behind me.

I jerked back. Denise, one of my fellow nurses set a clipboard down on the desk beside me. "You're not supposed to be here today," she said, dropping into the chair across from me. "Just couldn't stay away, huh?"

I reflexively backed out of the website and got to my feet. "Just checking in on my patient from yesterday. Had a hard time sleeping without thinking about her."

Denise clucked. "You mean Ally Gerard? The doctor's been up to see her already. Once her mom gets here, she can head home."

I blinked. "Her mom didn't stay overnight?"

Denise wasn't even looking at me, instead choosing to scribble at something on her clipboard. "Don't think so. She might have had to go to work. Imagine: poor woman can't take a day off to attend to her own child without being docked for pay."

Ally was all alone.

I backed out of the nurses' station and bypassed the elevator, heading directly for the stairs. I took them two at a time, not passing anyone on my way up. My footsteps echoed up the stairwell, reminding me just how alone I was. I had no plan for if that thing was there. All I knew was that it was daytime: there were more people on duty now than there were a few hours ago. As long as this creature hadn't slipped in between the incident at my apartment and now, Ally was probably safe.

That thought died as I opened the stairwell doors and found myself in an ice-coated corridor.

Fuck.

The silence was penetrated by the sound of whimpering. I crept down the hall toward the sound, trying not to make noise. Where were the on-call nurses? Why was there no one making the rounds? As I approached the nurses' station, I realized why. Cassidy was on the floor, eyes wide and staring at the ceiling. Five puncture wounds in her abdomen bled across the linoleum floor. I'd only met her the other day. She'd just moved here from Quebec.

Around the corner was another body: a male nurse I recognized from around the hospital though I struggled to remember his name. One of his eyes was missing, his lips parted in what may have been his last scream.

All of this had happened between two bustling floors, filled with doctors and nurses and other patients, as though it was lost in time. No one had any idea this had happened. As though the Ijiraq had somehow carved out the third floor from the rest of the building and put it up on a high shelf where no one could see it or reach it.

Except me.

I popped my head in the nearest patient door. The bed was empty, the sheets ruffled as though the patient walked out in the middle of the night. The next few were the same. All of the children being cared for in this ward were missing.

The crying around the corner intensified. I scanned the area, searching for some kind of weapon, anything that I could use to protect Ally. There was a surgical cart sitting outside of one of the rooms, the tray on top glistening with shining silver implements. I picked up a trocar, the handle swallowed in my grip as I stepped toward the last room opposite the nurses' station and peered in.

Ally was sitting up in her bed, hugging herself. Her black hair was tossed about her quaking shoulders and her blanket had fallen to the floor. Hurried breaths puffed out of her nose and frozen tears dotted her cheeks. Standing next to the door, concealed in half-shadow, I recognized the cutting red gaze of the Ijiraq, the long talons. Something seemed different though. The snow-filled window brightened the room and features I hadn't seen in the darkness of my apartment last night. What humanity it had seemed to possess was all but gone, replaced by long nimble limbs that resembled an elk. I stopped. Or a caribou. Course fur coated its arms and legs and the curvature of antlers wreathed its face.

Its face. I could see its face finally.

In the full light, all that I could discern was that it had no nose and that the eyes and mouth were indeed framed sideways on its face. The mouth opened and closed to reveal its normal incisors, and a long blood-red tongue that every so often lashed out to run over those teeth. It was the shape of the face that caught me though, the shape of the chin and ears on either side that sent me reeling, fighting for some recognition of normal, everyday existence.

"Leece?"

The thing's head jerked up to me.

I didn't understand, even as I dropped the trocar on the ground and found tears welling up in my eyes. Why did this thing have Leece's face? It couldn't be her. That couldn't be possible.

Her face rearranged into the one I thought I knew, the one that had been devouring expensive hors d'oeuvres last night. The one that I fell asleep next to, that I kissed and ate breakfast sandwiches with. But it seemed so horribly wrong now, framed on the body of a monster, on a neck too long for its contorted body.

"I'm getting promoted," Leece said, her voice twisted and gravelly.

The sentence hit me like a train and I doubled over. Did that mean what I thought it meant? "Th-this? This was the promotion?"

Something in her throat clicked. Her eyes resumed their red depth, their emptiness as she cocked her ungainly head to the side and said, "All those nights I spent at the office . . . You never once suspected?"

My feet felt numb as I digested each word. "How long have you been—"

Leece chuckled. It was an ugly noise, like mud bubbling in a vat. "I *really* wanted that job . . . Max and Effie were so encouraging once they saw what I could really do."

Even as the sorrow ravaged through me, my anger smoldered. "So, it was all a ruse? You lied to me the whole time."

She used one of her long talons to flip a piece of her auburn hair back. "I was going to tell you. I was just waiting for the right time."

"So, you decided to threaten me in our apartment last night?"

Leece rose up, towering over me, her body morphing in the pale light back to the elk-human behemoth that I'd seen when I'd entered. "You knew where the child was. I had to find her. That was my final test. Then, I could become an Ijiraq and cross over like Max and Effie. Here I am. I'm ready to earn my promotion."

I glanced at Ally. She was crying harder now, her face red and so, so terrified. I felt my chest swell with rage as I moved between Leece and the girl. I crouched down and picked up the trocar where I'd dropped it. "You crazy, sadistic bitch," I said. "No."

Leece shrieked and lunged toward me. Her enormous body crashed into mine, careening us back into the cabinet against the far wall. Barbs jabbed into my shoulders and hip as I fell. Swinging my hand up, I forced the trocar into the side of Leece's face, between her two bottomless blood-burning eyes. The skin gave beneath the force of my hand and as we collapsed in a pile on the floor, Ally's shrieking broke over the room like an alarm.

I lay on the floor, Leece's weight like boulders on top of me, her putrid stare burning through me as her face stopped twitching and stilled. I slid out from under her and picked myself up. Bloodied slashes from Leece's talons raked across my chest. Breathing felt like a struggle. I glanced at Ally who quickly leapt from the bed and grabbed hold of me, like a gosling clinging to its mother's back.

Leece was dead.

Max and Effie were still out there.

Even as I picked up Alley and held her to me, I realized that I'd overlooked something, something that I should have realized immediately entering the children's ward. If Max and Effie had taken Leece away last night, it couldn't have been them following me. They couldn't have been who I saw across the street in the alley, who I saw on the bus heading home, who I saw on the fire escape before going to bed.

There were more of them. So many more of them.

Toronto was no longer safe.

And I was the only one who knew what had to be done.

Burning Bright
by Errick Nunnally

The Marine leading Alice burst open. What remained of him crumpled next to her. He'd been guiding her through what was left of a residential block. Bullets had stitched a line straight up from his thigh and into his face, splattering her with a potent reminder of both his sudden death and war. They thought they'd been moving *away* from the melee.

The explosion followed shortly thereafter—which was why she was squatting behind the largest piece of rubble within spitting distance. Alice used every muscle in her torso to force her stiff flak jacket to bend. She cradled her camera, blinking hard to get the debris out of her eyes, praying it wasn't blood.

Her hearing slowly returned, amplifying the nightmare. She was in the midst of a fierce firefight that was soon, she knew, going to become a running gun battle.

"No," she muttered to herself, "this is going to become a *fucking* running gun battle." Her voice quavered and she ground grit between her teeth. There would be no choice. She steeled herself for running, blinking back fear and tamping down the trembling in her body.

I am not a girl, she thought, *I am a goddamn survivor. I am woman incarnate.*

She remembered what her ex-Army cousin had told her about firefights and how to behave amongst the enlisted. He'd spoken passionately, occasionally reaching down to scratch one or both of the remaining stumps of his legs.

Rounds whined overhead, pinging off the rubble in front of her. Shards of concrete cut her face. She raised one hand to protect her eyes and used the other to protect her camera.

Why are they shooting at me, for Christ's sake?

She screamed, "journalist!" several times in Arabic to no effect. The platoon's lieutenant scooted in her direction.

With any luck, they're shooting at him.

It was a guilty thought as she automatically snapped a few photos. An honest thought, too, but guilty nonetheless. He shouted orders and the Marines returned a more organized and steady gunfire. Where was the platoon's gunnery sergeant? He was the one usually shouting orders when the situation became sketchy.

Alice used the brief respite to search for her goggles. Her hand brushed a sharp bit sticking out of the Kevlar on her chest.

Best money I ever spent.

She found the bulky goggles in her camera bag and dragged them over her head. When she'd tried to keep them on her helmet, it unbalanced the pot which had a tendency to drop onto the bridge of her nose. Snapped in place on her face, she was reminded how stifling these were.

Great, I'll be able to see exactly how I'm going to die. Wonderful.

Daring a low glance around her chunk of sanctuary, she saw a blur of orange and black. For an absurd moment, Alice thought she'd seen a tiger. She'd seen militias wear odd clothing before in Africa and didn't give it another thought.

The assignment on the border of Nigeria had been a wild goose chase, seeking stolen SAMs. This time, they were chasing chemical agents, a rumored biological weapon. The photos she'd seen of the testing, the visual evidence . . . She'd never forget how, even in death, the victims appeared to be screaming.

Alice glanced again, but this time with her camera, snapping a few wild shots. The lieutenant thumped down into the grit in front of her. There wasn't enough room for him to huddle against the scant protection, so he simply hugged dirt.

"What are you doing, Ms. Poren? Put that camera down and listen up!"

Lieutenant Logden always pronounced her name carefully with a gentleman's southern manner, enunciating both the first and second half of the word. There had been at least one incident where one of the Marines had called her "Ms. Porn."

The goof on her name made absolutely no sense to Alice. According to most standards, she was plain, to put it mildly, a hair under five foot, four inches tall with flat brown eyes and sun-ravaged skin. She'd cut her thick brown hair short—well above shoulder length—for this assignment and she thought it made her nose look even bigger above the thin strokes of her lips. She wasn't normally the center of men's attention.

This wasn't her first time in a war zone, either, but it had never been as hot as it was at this moment. Pelted by tiny debris, she pretended to fumble with stuffing the camera into her pack while the Lieutenant shouted his plan at her.

"We are going to pull back to that structure there." Logden indicated a blown out two-story building whose walls were intact. "We are surrounded, support is en route, we have to hold out for about ten or fifteen mikes." Sweat poured down his young face, leaving grimy streaks that disappeared into his collar. Alice wondered where he was getting all that precious water from.

Fifteen minutes may as well be a year in a firefight. She nodded, then remembered that a verbal response was required, "Yes, sir, let me know when to move!"

"Right now, Ms. Poren!" He surged up, put a hand on the nape of her flak jacket, and heaved. They both lurched to their feet and the Marines' return fire increased. Logden had planned their escape route and zig-zagged inside the relative safety of a surrounding cone of concentrated fire.

Panting hard, running bent, Alice swung her camera left and right, over her shoulder and straight ahead. Snapping shots as steadily as she could, praying that the auto-focus would keep up, and paying most attention to where she was putting her feet. The inevitable stumble that happened to fleeing girls in movies was not what she needed right now.

I am a fucking surviving machine, she thought hard at herself, *I will survive this because I can survive anything.*

Two violent thumps threw plumes of dust and debris into the air and pelted them anew with bits of sand and mortar. A cloud of black smoke obscured the view all around them—she couldn't see anything but the lieutenant's back and her own two hands. Until this assignment, she'd had no idea that a cloud of fine grit could be so painful. Another deafening blast followed and the air left her lungs. Something sharp smacked against her chest.

Lieutenant Logden pirouetted sideways, out from underneath his helmet. He'd moved so suddenly and in such a perpendicular direction that she'd only glimpsed a blur that had struck him and spun her around.

Her chin bit rock as she kept her camera from smashing on the ground. The palm of her other hand stung, scraping across the war debris. Her hearing was muffled again by explosions. She lay flat on her belly, panting hard, spitting sand, and trying to recover her senses to determine which way to haul ass when a massive paw thumped down next to her head. Then another. The second paw had blood, and something else, caught in the claws.

Alice's mind seized. A tiger in a war zone was a distinct impossibility, insane on every level to every one of her thoughts. Then she felt hot breath on the back of her neck and, regardless of her muffled hearing, could feel the big cat's rumble of a growl on her back. Alice didn't know much of anything about tigers, but she did know that, pound for pound, they were the most deadly land predators on the planet.

Fear laced her body from the back of her head and down her spine. Her feet were suddenly freezing in her desert boots, fingertips went numb. She dared not move.

The beast abruptly clamped moist teeth on the back of her flak jacket, a hair's breadth from her neck—right where Logden had taken a grip—and hoisted her off the ground. With a jolt, they were moving fast. She struggled to get her legs going quickly enough that they weren't scraping across the ground. No tiger should be this big. This was some kind of prehistoric monster, a nightmare come to life, but the beast's hot blasts of breath on the back of her neck continuously reminded her of reality as it now stood.

Alice needed a plan to get loose and draw the attention of the Marines. Other than gravel and sand zipping by her face, she could see nothing. No radio, her phone was tucked away in the bag strapped to her side. The way the tiger held her by the stiff, Kevlar vest, pinned her arms up at odd angles. The helmet on her head forced the goggles to bite hard into the bridge of her nose. So, she did the only thing she'd trained herself to do without thinking: she kept taking pictures.

Alice could still move her wrist and elbow. She spun the camera at every angle manageable and snapped shots. When they found her masticated body—if they ever found it—there'd be proof that, to the end, she was a photojournalist through and through.

And the victim of a giant fucking tiger.

Alice was certain that if something were to be found down at her gooey center, the monster cat would certainly get to it soon enough.

The kitty-carry continued to the outskirts of what was left of the town. Alice began to struggle in earnest. Being dragged from "civilization" was too much for her. She shouted and flailed and kicked, even tried to use her camera to bash the beast in the nose. It just grunted and kept going.

The sun, low on the horizon, reflected her spirits. She could feel the slide into a painful depression coming: too tired to cry, exhausted from the constant adrenaline and physical punishment dealt by explosions and near misses. Alice despaired. When she let go of her camera, the strap around her wrist held for several more meters of jostling.

When the strap found its way to her fingers, wrist slick with sweat, she convulsed and grabbed it. It was at this point that Alice's tears found release because she was absolutely certain that not only was she doomed, but she'd lost her mind. It was a gentle cry, more of a sigh of submission and fatigue. Not the kind of sobbing that a full crackup might bring on.

The tiger continued onward. She had no real sense as to which direction they were going other than southward. If anyone saw them, they'd be able to make out something moving, but not what it might be. There was too much dirt being blown into the sky, and twilight was the worst time of the day for human eyes.

Fear, fatigue, and depression all passed as the animal continued to jostle her as it loped forward with her in its jaws. Frustrated, and wanting to avoid hysteria, she began talking to the cat.

"What are you doing; why did you take me?"

The steady rhythm of the cat's snuffing continued.

"Can't we take a break or something? I think I'm gonna puke, you're making me sick…"

The tiger grunted in the back of its throat again, sounding hungry to her. Then it stopped and released Alice. She crumpled to the ground, her pack twisted around her and some of her gear skittered out onto the rapidly cooling ground. She remembered the show she put on for Logden.

Must have left the pack open.

Oh, God . . . Logden.

She sat on the desert floor and shivered. Outside of the big cat's proximity, it was decidedly colder. She didn't want to look up or even move for fear of drawing its attention again. Escape was what she wanted, but she had no idea where they were or what direction to go. Wandering around the desert was a sure death. Just as sure as staying with this animal.

She looked up, tilting the helmet back off of her goggles. The tiger was barely two feet in front of her, waiting. She licked her chapped lips and slowly started to collect the things that had dropped off of her. The cat growled, low and deep. Then it batted at a back-up canteen, bending to gnaw on the plastic container. Alice watched as its impossibly large teeth dug a groove in the hard plastic.

I'm going to need that water. Her next thought rang hollow in her mind: *If I'm going to survive.* She screwed up some resolve and was reminded of her earlier mantra: *I am a surviving machine.*

The tiger lifted its head and seemed to take little notice of her. She was reminded how house cats could seem bored and indifferent one moment and flip the switch to vicious. It dipped its head forward and growled again, ending in a kind of slothful pant. She slowly reached out and took the canteen, eyes locked on the space below the cat's eyes; on the business part.

Her hand closed on the cool surface and the beast's mouth snapped shut, golden eyes turning on her. Alice froze and waited, studiously avoiding its eyes, muscles clamped down against shuddering. It resumed panting and she drew the canteen slowly towards her. From the canteen, a precious sip, she didn't know when she'd have water next. Being held hostage by a gigantic tiger, water was the least of her problems.

"I'm going to be breakfast for monster kittens." She muttered to herself, voice trembling, unable to formulate a plan of escape. The cat was easily four feet at the shoulder, maybe more. Remembering how her family's pet feline could leap to the top of the refrigerator in one hop, she held little hope that she could outrun the thing. Even if she had somewhere to go.

Alice sighed and readjusted her gear, taking off the helmet and goggles. She ran fingers through her coarse hair and regarded the tiger: it was huge and beautiful in profile. Muscles rippled everywhere beneath its coat. It was fascinating to observe until the animal turned its gaze in her direction. It sat with its tongue lolling, knowing she couldn't escape its reach. She wondered what it might be thinking—if tigers even thought. It absently licked its paw and groomed its face.

"Well. Here we are." Her voice only trembled a little. She took a deep breath and steadied herself. Camera still in her hand, she raised it and snapped one shot, bathing the animal in a brilliant flash of light.

The tiger roared, full throated, bristling at her.

"Oh, shit, I'm sorry, I'm sorry, I'm sorry! Don't kill me!" Alice stumbled backwards onto her ass and raised one of her two ineffectual hands towards the tiger. It sat back, rumbling in the back of its throat, licking its paw. She could see what was left of the firefight in the air behind the tiger. A lone flare popped over the combat zone and drifted down, illuminating the area. Then the shooting started again, firecracker pops in the distance as two helicopters advanced on the ruined town, streaks of brilliant white lines caressed the ground here and there, explosions flared with mesmerizing sparks and smoke. Concussive sounds followed; they were far enough away that sound traveled across the desert a beat behind what she saw.

She sighed, torn between the idea of being shot at or toyed with by a gigantic tiger. The smell of gunfire floated on the wind. A bright whistling sound caught her attention. The animal's head swiveled towards it, alert. The sound was coming from above the combat. There was a dull flash followed by the muffled thump of an explosion. The cat growled low and threatening in its throat. Some kind of pellucid mist headed in their direction, blown across the town by the wind, creeping across the flat desert floor.

Alice took a deep breath, steadying herself again, trying to determine what to do, when the animal sprang. She squealed and curled up, trying to shrink into the flak jacket, pulling the helmet tight to her head, hoping its claws wouldn't be able to rend the battle armor. It clamped down on her collar and hoisted her off the ground. They were on the move as quickly as the cat could manage without bumping her with its forepaws. At least she was warm again, but the jostling was none too gentle. She kept hands clasped securely to the helmet lest it batter the bridge of her nose. The camera swung wildly on her wrist, bruising her forearm.

They lumbered on into the night, leaving the unusual fog behind. As time passed, Alice began to realize how sore she really was, stiffening up as time passed, trying to keep her feet from dragging. The last battle had knocked her around hard and a spot below the collar bone was starting to itch. She began to cry again, small tears of frustration and not knowing.

The cat came to a ragged outcropping of rocks, a kind of anti-oasis, and dropped her on the ground. She unscrewed herself and readjusted her gear while trying to look around. There wasn't much to take in and there wasn't much light to see the nothing around them. She scratched at her breast and felt a needle-sharp pain.

"Ow! Dammit . . . "

The cat stood a couple of feet away watching her, tail twitching. She ran the heel of her palm roughly across her eyes and stretched her legs out, ass chilling on the cold, hard ground.

Fuck it, she thought, and scooped the helmet off of her head and shrugged out of the flak jacket. As the vest slid open, she felt a long scratch cut across her body from collar to shoulder and yelped again.

"Aaaah, for Christ's sake! What the hell?" Alice held the jacket up as close to her face as she could. There was something embedded in the Kevlar. She ran her finger around the inside and felt a sharp protrusion. Feeling around the outside, she found the embedded object and pulled it out. It must've been the impact she felt when she scrambled from the skirmish with Lt. Logden.

Feeling around inside her shirt, she sucked her teeth at a sharp pain, fingers coming away wet. The tiger lumbered forward and sniffed at the ground where she'd dropped the shrapnel. Then it yowled at her and gave her a determined push towards the rocky hill.

"Oh, God, what now?"

The tiger butted her again, but harder this time, opening its maw uncomfortably close to her face, fetid air burned hot from its throat, it sniffed of her deeply. She stumbled onto her back and the breath whooshed out of her as the big cat brought both paws down on her torso, snarling into her face.

"No, no, no . . . " she whimpered ineffectually, barely able to breathe. Her middle was wide open to attack, she expected to be gored and left dying.

The tiger hopped back, crushing her anew, leaving her breathless. She rolled over and had barely gotten to her feet when the first swipe spun her around. Dizzy, in the dirt, and with a fresh sheen of sweat on her, she scrambled forward toward the outcropping, scooping up her gear. The tiger butted her in the back, causing her to stumble.

"Okay, okay! This direction; I got it, I got it!" She shrugged back into her vest and pack.

Again, the tiger hammered her in the back and this time the impact was followed by a sudden stinging pressure in her thigh. She looked down at the cat's head, turned sideways in her perspective, its mouth clamped securely to her thigh. One massive paw wrapped around her right hip. She screamed loud and hard, hysterically pushing at the massive head, panicked. Primal chemicals pumped through her body's overtaxed glands, blurring her vision as she scrabbled to get away, screaming hoarsely and ineffectually. The tiger released her and she pitched away into the dirt, the biting of sharp rocks and debris a distant feeling as the hot pain of the animal bite seared her thigh.

Alternately grunting and crying with effort, she heaved herself to her feet feeling dizzy and weak, wanting nothing more than to escape. She took one step, threw her full weight on her wounded thigh, and immediately regretted it. New pain blazed electric paths along her muscles as she tripped over onto her knees and tumbled forward. Both of her hands remained clamped around her thigh, wet with blood. She rose up again, uncaring of where the tiger was, one bitter thought rang clear and bright in her mind: *Fuck you, animal, fuck you to hell; I am out of here.*

Alice stumbled forward and started climbing as quickly as she could, encouraged by an occasional growl close enough to make her bones vibrate. The puncture wound in her chest started to itch and burn with her efforts, echoing the fresher wound in her thigh. She wore the vest open and loose. Her helmet, hanging from the canteen behind her hip, swung awkwardly as she climbed.

Muscles straining and sweat slicking her forehead, arms and back, Alice reached an outcropping that was a small plateau. She rolled over the side and breathed deeply of the cool desert air, feeling dreamily free for a moment. The tiger startled her by leaping directly over her position and nimbly landing further in on the shelf.

"Jesus!" She rolled into a fatigued ball, expecting the worst, and looked up when the tiger made a grunting noise in the back of its throat.

The big cat dipped its head at a crevice in the rock and growled low at her. Dropping its head at the crevice again, it came towards her, circled and started pushing. She stumbled to her feet and made her way to the crack.

"Why won't you leave me alone or just kill me?" She hated the way her voice squeaked with fear when she spoke. Everything about her was screaming vulnerability, but she was in pain, she reasoned, and she deserved a little panic. Hot, dirty, bleeding and sore. She'd had enough.

"No! No caves! No!"

The tiger roared at full blast and reared up. She dropped to her hands and knees and scrambled away from the crack—there was no way was she going in there. In a motion too quick for her to follow, the cat batted her legs from under her, seized her shoulder painfully in its jaws. A dizzy, painful confusion of motion followed as it dragged her into the cave. The opening would have been comfortable if she'd crawled in alone. Being dragged by the cat, she scraped along the wall and floor of the cave, disoriented and bruised in the dark.

Just inside the cave mouth, she crashed into some kind of equipment and lost herself in a tumble with assorted metal and plastic objects. Released, she groped around her pockets for her penlight. She could hear the big cat breathing near the entrance, agitated.

Switching on the light, she swept the cave once and saw all kinds of human comfort items. Her light illuminated a large, battery-operated lamp. She grabbed it and lit the cave in a warm glow.

There was a cot set in the very back, with sheets, a blanket, and a pillow. A small nightstand next to it with several books underneath, a large water canteen next to that, and a fuel-burning lamp on top. She could see now that she'd crashed into a chest with several pieces of equipment stacked on top. The tiger paced by the entrance of the cave, near the chest. Next to the animal, a small, gas-powered generator and a jerrycan.

It was annoyed, pacing and huffing. Its path took it closer to the chest. Then it rammed into the small locker until it tipped over and the lid popped open. Amongst the items that spilled out was a first-aid kit. Alice hesitatingly took it. The tiger pushed at the back of the locker, growling and forcing the spilled contents towards her. She spotted a folded, green canvas pocket-case with military style letters stenciled in black.

Hoping for a weapon, Alice scooped the case up, keeping an eye on the tiger, and desperately pawed her way into it. Nestled inside were several glass vials, half of them full of a yellowish liquid, the rest clear, and with a folded sheaf of papers slid into an inner pocket. She noted that the glass containers were secure within their sheaths and sealed with some permanence before she gingerly closed the case and put it down. There was no way she wanted to mess with something as weird as that. The cat practically whined at the mess. Then it roared in the closed space and Alice screamed in response—not fear, but anger, raw and final:

"WHAT DO YOU WANT FROM ME!?"

The resulting silence made her think she'd been struck deaf. Then the cat blasted her again with a roar from the mouth of the cave. She scrambled backwards, clamping her hands over her ears, ignoring the pain from her wounds for a moment. Her back hit the cot and she scrambled onto it, clutching her wounded thigh, ineffectually trying not to use the muscle. She flopped there, teeth ground together, leg out straight, while a slow whine hissed from the back of her throat. A creeping, icy cold tickled her extremities and darkness crept in at the edges of her vision. *Stay calm, stay calm, stay calm*, she repeated in her mind. Shock wasn't going to help.

The big cat settled down for a beat before resuming its agitated pacing. After several long moments, she cracked the seal on the first-aid kit and got to work on what she could: cleaning her cuts and scratches, downing some pain-relievers, and bandaging the shoulder and thigh wounds. Cleaning the tiger's bite, she noted the four clean punctures weren't bleeding as badly as she'd feared, the tiger hadn't torn her open. The puckered holes shed blood mixed with the burning alcohol from the swabs she'd used. Spotting a small bedpan, she eventually relieved herself, painfully squatting over the bowl.

After eyeing the tiger for a bit longer, she took an inventory of the equipment in her camera bag, followed by her rucksack. Everything for a one-day patrol was accounted for.

Just one day.

If she couldn't get away from this predator soon…

No sense daydreaming about the impossible. Maybe it'd be best if she tried to figure out what was going on. She let her thoughts wander, trying to dissociate from her predicament and be objective. Her thigh throbbed, dragging her thoughts back to her most recent wound and where it had come from. She choked down more pain-relievers from the kit.

Maybe this was a trained animal? All kinds of institutions like circuses and zoos had been abandoned since the war began, maybe the animal's caretaker had escaped the conflict by coming into the hills and this cave, but why bring the goddamned cat? The logistics of caring for it would be well beyond what this desolate area could provide.

Alice was ill-equipped for this situation. She was a photojournalist and, in many ways, observed more of what was going on than anyone else. She took photos by instinct and those images spoke volumes. If she could escape, her camera would bear the evidence of her unexpected absence. Surely the Marines would've discovered that she was missing? Especially since their Lieutenant had been the one escorting her. He had to be dead. Hell, the whole platoon was probably dead. All of which amounted to the obvious conclusion: no one was coming for her. *Evidence.* She gingerly pulled the bandage from her thigh and snapped a few shots of the wound. Then did the same for the swollen and tender shrapnel puncture.

Alice adjusted her position on the cot at the far end of the cave. The big cat's ears twitched and it flopped down, its eyes closed. *God, so much like a gigantic house cat*, she thought, *and way more dangerous.* In a sudden frenzy, the tiger began licking its forepaws and grooming its face, then it settled back down with a huff.

Alice pulled her pack close and sorted the contents out again. Then she cleaned the camera. Sand had gotten into everything. She uncoupled the flash and tested the device by snapping photos of the gloomy cave and the animal snoozing at the entrance. She took a quick peek at her phone, dismayed that her assumptions were correct: she couldn't get a signal inside the hill and besides, the battery had run down while searching for a signal outside. Exhausted, she noted that the batteries in her camera were about gone as well—and those were the back-up set. She unhooked a portable charger from the side of her bag and cranked it for several minutes. It only had one port on it, so she glumly decided to trickle-charge her camera first.

The green canvas bag caught her eye and she opened it again, gingerly avoiding the vials and their ominous liquid. She extracted the papers tucked into the inner-pocket and unfolded them. Cheaply printed, they were in a few languages, including Arabic and English; warnings about handling the contents. Long paragraphs about how to manage the liquid, where it could be introduced, in which environmental situations it might be rendered ineffective. On and on the tiny text ran, dry instruction covering situation after situation. Words like *catalyst* and *suspension* and *vector* dotted the text. At the end, a separately printed list of names and locations for resupply and further instructions on the fluid's use entirely in Arabic. Her rudimentary experience with the written language was paying off.

She looked up and saw that the tiger was watching her—how long she didn't know. Its eyes sparkled; it lay unmoving, but entirely alert. A shrill burst of adrenalized fear sputtered up her spine as she realized for the first time that there are things afoot as deadly as the tiger and deserving of as much terror. She slipped the papers back into the pack and considered what she held. The realization passed as quickly as her trepidation. Exhausted, she laid her head down on the cot to think and…

She woke with a start; the tiger was gone.

Ambient sunlight created a swirling gloom inside the shallow cave. Alice bolted upright and immediately regretted the sudden move. All of her joints ached and the cuts she'd suffered the day before stung like acid. Doing her best to ignore the body-wide pains and the pressure on her bladder, she scooped up her pack, took a mouthful of water and headed to the cave mouth. Stopping short, she wondered if the tiger might be sitting just outside.

Alice flipped her camera on, brought the digital display to life and slowly maneuvered the device out of the crevice as a makeshift periscope. The camera was her second-most prized possession after her head and she wanted to keep them in that order.

No giant tigers outside. She flipped off the screen and tucked the camera away. With one deep breath, she scrambled out of the entrance, briefly hoping to shimmy over the edge and continue on her way. The bright sun gave her pause, however, even though her eyes adjusted. There was no hint on the horizon of the ruined town where she had the unforgettable experience of being caught in not just one, but two explosions. Flipping open her sunglasses and shoving them over her nose, she took a closer look. There was nothing in sight.

At the sound of rocks sliding, Alice yelped and spun around, losing her balance and tumbling onto her ass in a little puff of dirt, sunglasses slipping to the tip of her nose, a dull distant pain thrummed in her thigh.

The tiger sat on the ledge above her field of view, its coat and teeth brilliant in the bright sun. A light breeze ruffled its coat.

"— thefucknow!?" Alice noted the bright edge of panic in her voice and struggled to calm down. As abstractly dangerous as the tiger may have been, it hadn't killed her yet. She felt fear bubble back up in her throat when she noted that the brilliant white fur beneath its muzzle was marred by dried blood.

It hopped down from the ledge. She felt stupid for it, but Alice shuffled back when it stepped from the ledge.

She exhaled softly, "Okay, so I'm a hostage."

She felt a sharp pain in her chest, the jolt so sudden she started at the tiger. The wound where the shrapnel had cut her through the vest burned and her skin felt hotter than normal, prickly, unsettled. Her knees trembled. The tiger moved close, circling so that she had to enter the cave's mouth to keep a distance. Crouched, she noticed that the bite wound in her thigh, though fresher, felt better than the wound in her chest. She should have felt cooler out of the sun, but the heat built within her.

She shakily rose from all fours and crawled onto the cot. As the tiger watched from the entrance, Alice pulled her shirt open enough to peer at the chest wound. It had crusted over and the flesh around it was red and tender. Hot to the touch. She could feel a lightning shock of pain all the way through to her shoulder. It was starting to creep down her arm. She looked around, focusing on a parcel she hadn't noticed last night. She found food inside: figs, bread, some kind of yogurt—and four strawberries!

She grabbed a berry and bit into it greedily, savoring the pulpy juices. Mid-bite, Alice considered whose food this might be and where that person was now. She had a second fruit before she even realized she'd finished the first and decided to focus on her water to distract from the other two. The tiger hadn't made a move since entering the cave behind her. It sat growling, panting, and appearing as agitated as she'd remembered it from before.

Alice didn't wonder about it any longer. Distracted by food, she gobbled the final two strawberries and started in on the bread, ignoring the tangy yogurt. She couldn't stand figs, but ate them anyway and immediately regretted the entire meal. Her stomach heaved and a fresh sweat blossomed on her forehead, prickling across her scalp, trickling between her shoulder blades and breasts. Shrugging out of the blouse, she stripped off her trousers next and peeled the socks off of her feet. Then she awkwardly pulled the tank-top off, struggling through the stiffness in her muscles. The remaining garments came off in a numb haze. Alice sat slumping, hot and spent, on the cot, feeling the dread tingle of a mounting intestinal pressure.

Reflexively grabbing the bedpan, she vomited the contents of her last meal into it, absurdly regretting the loss of the strawberries while her nose hovered inches from two rounds of urine and one aggressive vomiting session. She wiped her lips and tried to lubricate her dry mouth with water. Her body burned, feeling like moisture was being sucked away from her, drawn out from every pore.

What the hell is making me this sick so quickly? She wondered.

When she glanced at her shoulder, her stomach lurched again. There were black and purple tendrils spreading from the wound. They hadn't been there before and the familiarity of the lines turned her stomach further. It didn't take long for her memories to produce an image. Amongst the evidence that was driving the mission of the Marines she'd been embedded with had been a photo of prisoners allegedly exposed to the synthetic contagion. The images had been a recent piece of the puzzle, the only visual confirmation of what the military was chasing. The photos were shared on the helicopter ride in, passed around the cabin as they wound low across the desert, heading for a town whose name none of them could pronounce.

They had been shriveled and laced with the same blackening lines that now spider-webbed from her wound. Eyes bloodshot and bulging, photos of silent screams. She realized with a nauseous wave, that she'd been poisoned by the shrapnel. Then the fog that had come later.

Oh, God, this is—the town—a biological attack! I'm dying! No one's at home waiting for me; my parents are gone; I don't even have a pet. All I have is an abrasive, legless cousin.

Screw it all. I'm alone and I got used to it a long time ago.

Alice's jaw locked, she struggled to form a word or some kind of gesture—anything purposeful as all of her muscles seized. She could hear the faint gurgle of her own breathing and the slowing thump of her heart. Her blood swam molten in her torso and collided with a tide of ice water rising from her legs. She was aware of the creeping weakness that pulled her into the dark and she rolled onto the floor of the cave, the canvas case of vials flopping onto the ground into her line of sight. She trembled violently, forced one more tiny breath into her lungs and felt her fingers and toes curl with a moist and muted popping. A wet crunching noise filled her ears, drowning out the base, hoarse howl that her raw throat was producing through her clenched teeth.

And then she was gone.

* * *

Alice awoke, clawing from the dark. She writhed, desperately trying to take in air. Why couldn't she breath?

Oh, yes, that's right, I died. Now I'm…being smothered?

She arched her back, scraping her shoulder on the rough floor, and pulling her face away from the blanket of heat. A wall of orange and black fur obscured her vision and she was wet with cooling sweat. Despite the excessive warmth, she felt…comfortable.

Rolling onto her back, pebbles and sand dug into her skin. The smell of tiger musk filled her nose. Alice rocked onto her elbow and gazed at the tiger resting on its belly watching her. The creature fairly glowed, the tips of its fur sparkled in the gloom of the setting sun cutting through the cave's mouth.

Alice gasped. She was naked. The entire experience of being alive broke away and she scrambled for some modesty. She couldn't remember what had happened. Yesterday? Earlier today? She'd lost time, there was no way of knowing how much. Casting about, she stumbled across her watch on top of her clothes.

Holy shit, it's been two days!

She was ravenous. After pulling on spare panties and bra, she still felt out of place within her own body. She couldn't shake the feeling and stopped getting dressed. A slow gaze down her body confirmed that the ugly cut above her right breast was gone, the four punctures on her thigh were closed, and none of her cuts and bruises were evident. Other than hunger, she felt fantastic. Her skin tingled with potential. All the tiny cuts from the past few days were gone. She continued to search her now unfamiliar body, moving inexorably down. Her knees still bore the scars from countless falls during her youth, but the effects were all impressively muted. The dime-sized mass of scar tissue she'd had on her left shin from a bike accident was nothing but a pale mark and—*oh, God.*

Her skin had been scrubbed clean; it was pristine and hummed with vigor. Her blood was no longer an innocuous thing, she sensed its flow, fully present in her body. Alice stared at the tiger filling the cave in front of her. She noted the fur around his jaws was thicker, mane-like and the cat's ears looked more like tablespoons than the half-circles she'd often seen on zoo cats.

Near her clothes she found another bundle similar to the one she'd eaten from earlier. Sure enough, it was full of the same foods—sans strawberries. This time she ate the figs without malice and choked down the yogurt. The food felt fine in her stomach, very different from her last meal. She peered again at the giant animal and something gnawed at the back of her head, tugged at her core.

The beast became a hazy explosion of color, radiating waves of orange and yellow, pink and red. Wisps of energy curled lazily from the edges of the cat's coat. She blinked rapidly, sure she was imagining everything that had happened and was happening now. Where there had been a tiger now sprawled an old man.

"Now, you see and hear." His voice rasped, low and soft; the deadly silence of the desert offering nothing.

"What?" Standing, her arms floating at her sides, she didn't know what to think, how to process this. For a sickening moment, she thought she may be dead and this was a cruel afterlife, a quantum trick. The man addressing her was nothing like the tiger. He was thin, ancient. Grey scraggly hair and leathery skin. He sat naked in the shadows with one knee pulled up modestly, his arms resting at his sides. He leaked weariness where she felt energized.

"I am sorry. This was never meant for you. I have shared the last of the Caspian line with you."

"I don't—I don't understand. How—?"

"You were going to die. You *were* dying. I *am* dying."

"I was—" Alice rocked on her heels and settled slowly to her knees. She'd been unconscious for two days and now the tiger had become a man. And was talking to her.

"You were in a coma. The virus affected the passing of the gift. It fought the process."

"Wait— 'shared'? What does that—?" Her mouth tingled and she fought thoughts of tiger fur and musk.

"There is not much time; you must accept this. I chose you to carry the message, not the gift, but you were dying. I had no choice and I'm not much longer for this world."

A horrible pressure in her jowls forced Alice to pitch forward, mouth agape. Her eyes swam with color—more color than she'd ever known.

"Every month, on this day, you will succumb and hunt and feed. For five days, you must be Caspian as I have been; no one near you will be as safe as you wish unless they too are Caspian. You must gain experience and discipline if you want to be close to anyone again."

She felt a sickening pull in her throat. Muscles, tendons and cartilage slid downward into her chest, her heart pounded. When she spoke through grit teeth, her voice was a desperate octave lower: "What did you do to me?"

"I gave you a second life, to replace the one you lost. Take the bag, expose the existence of this poison; this much your people owe us. What I have given you is a small wrong for the lives you may yet save. A sacrifice your culture is familiar with. No?

"I am the last. Entire villages wiped out, sprayed like weeds. My family. My friends. My life. Gone. I will die here, as well. Take the vials, put an end to this war. You will not see me again, both our country's fates rest with you."

The old man levered himself up and shuffled through the cave mouth. She feebly held up a hand. "Wait." Alice's voice gurgled, pitched low enough to be unrecognizable to her own ears. Her back bowed and in a final gasp, she became Caspian.

* * *

Alice brushed her teeth for a second time and scooped up her helmet with the other hand. The head protection was the last of her gear and it was definitely time to leave. She felt confident despite her situation and, for the first time in many years, she didn't feel the least bit vulnerable in her compact size. She did feel some revulsion from the hunt and worried her tongue around the imagined bits left caught in her teeth. The memories she'd gathered while changed wouldn't sync with her present state, it was as if she were accessing someone else's thoughts. Her feelings fluctuated between the horror of feeding and everything she'd learned about being human to date.

It had taken a few days to stop fighting her old instincts, an hour heading east to locate the ravaged town, minutes to locate one of the militia, and seconds to take him silently. They were bad men, one less was no loss to anyone. She took two more before she'd been sated.

Serves them right, she reasoned, as two sets of perceptions danced precipitously, challenging her sanity. *They blew me up. Twice.* Her head spun causing a nauseating moment, recalling the way a human male's head had popped liquidly in her mouth. The memories were hazy and *wrong*. Her eyes stung and she dragged the heel of her hand aggressively across them. *I am a survivor, dammit. Woman up.*

She had twenty-five days to expose the truth and get to safety. Moving due east at a brisk pace, she started out, leaving the cave forever, the bag of evidence strapped securely across her shoulder, right next to her camera.

The Quality of Mercy
by Richard Alan Scott

"As lately as 1892, an Exeter community exhumed a dead body and ceremoniously burnt its heart in order to prevent certain alleged visitations injurious to the public health and peace…" -The Shunned House

I have never been one to submit to superstition; I find all of it claptrap. I should have paid attention, however, on Friday, the thirteenth of October, 1911. It had been two months since I'd turned twenty-one. I'd have been wise on that day to keep my usual practice of remaining at home. I ventured forth, however, and the whole affair became a serious threat to my being.

I was unwell in the years after prematurely leaving Hope High School. I suffered from fatigue and lethargy and thought myself unworthy to be seen in pleasant society, having miserably failed at becoming whatever it was everyone expected me to become. There were also Mother's oft-repeated exhortations about my hideousness. I am bedeviled with the most prominent lantern jaw and walk in a very slump-shouldered manner.

"Perhaps it would be best for you not to walk the streets, permitting others to gawk at you," she once advised.

I did not disagree with her. I was all the better for being locked away. I preferred it that way, just as I liked to be awake through the night, and sleep in the daylight hours. I abhorred the glaring sunlight. Any Englishman knows that a white pallor is a sure sign of aristocracy.

That was why the request that came in late September from Backstreet, my editor at the *Providence Evening Bulletin*, was such a bother. He telephoned and asked me to edit the new edition of a book which had debuted in Europe over a decade before; *Dracula* by Mister Bram Stoker.

I rose early to walk to the newspaper's offices downtown and collect a copy of the work. *Why me?* was all I could think. I wrote a paltry Science column which ran one night a week. *The Bulletin* was evening sister to *The*

Providence Journal, the most prominent daily in my home state of Rhode Island. You'll recall we were one of the original colonies to succumb to the madness of rending ourselves from the glorious British Empire?

"Susie mentioned to me that you have interest in these sorts of . . . weird tales," the rotund Backstreet declared through the bushy blackness of a moustache. Ah, Mother, the meddlesome harridan. It irked her no end that I had left school, eschewed college, and thus far lived as she did, from Grandfather's endowment.

"I know of no one else who may fit the bill, so you're it. Write a foreword and check it for British drivel. Now get out," he barked, reinserting a well chewed stogie without pause.

I'd have preferred some sound British writing to the ranting of a boorish Irishman, but some extra dollars would be welcome. I accepted the unanticipated task.

Even more surprising was my enjoyment of the piece. Though lacking in technique, Stoker wove an addicting plot through the letters and diary entries of his characters. His Count Dracula was a formidable villain, and the novel had much to teach about overcoming the mythological creatures known as vampires. I could see why the public was taken with it but doubted it would have any lasting appeal.

I did hit upon a fantastic notion for the theme of my foreword. Rhode Island coincidentally had its own vampire legend. The most I knew was that the nasty business took place in the outlying township of Exeter. That remote country was a rumor-shrouded den of backwoods riffraff, and will always remain so. I was determined to educate myself wholly on the matter, and since it was a part of local lore, I could visit the site in question. I only needed someone with an automobile to convey me on my mission.

"You should simply hire a car, Howard." This first of Mother's suggestions was not to my taste at all. No, her next solution was preferable; an old school chum of hers was of all things Roman Catholic, and volunteered that a priest at her Cathedral, Father Bernard Reilly, was in possession of a Model-T Ford. I telephoned the Rectory and I must say he was quite amenable to doing me the kindness at no cost to myself.

"There is a restaurant beyond your destination, near the shore, that I've wanted to try for some time," he said in a barely comprehensible brogue. "Fridays are my only day to pursue leisurely activities I'm afraid, and, oh dear, this next one upon us is the thirteenth, very unlucky."

"Never fear, Father, I shall protect you from the winds of misfortune. That date would be altogether satisfactory for me. Shall we say tea at four o'clock?"

"You won't want an early start?" He was astonished at the hour for such an excursion, but I assured him it was quite normal for me.

He arrived at Angell Street, on the east side of Providence, promptly on the appointed day, and Mother wasted no time in humiliating me.

"Come in Father, come in," she exclaimed, and as the poor man moved to take her hand, Mother backed away. She didn't hold for physical pleasantries. I can't even say the last time she hugged or kissed me, the son who's been her sole companion for two decades.

"You must forgive my barbaric son, he's still in dressing gown and slippers."

"Please call me Bernie, Missus," the good Father replied. He was as tall as me and looked in age to be two score and ten, with a large pot belly.

"In that case, I'm Susie. Howard!" Mother shrieked.

"I'm right here, Mother," I said calmly, having slithered into the entry unnoticed. I rather enjoy doing that to people.

"Oh, for heaven's sake," Mother said, startled. "The boy is like a wraith, coming at you from dark corners. Tea, Bernie?"

"The boy is a tall man. Hello, Howard, nice to meet you," said Father Reilly, offering his hand. "And yes, I'd love some, Susie."

"Hello, Bernie," I said, shaking it. "I can't tell you how much I appreciate your driving me, and on your free day."

"It's no bother, Howard. I will enjoy getting out of the city for a while. My goodness," he suddenly interjected. "Your hand is cold as ice."

"Ah, yes, I'm always cold, even in high temperatures. No one knows why. My aunts say shaking my hand is like touching a corpse."

"Well that's a new one on me," said Bernie.

"Which reminds me, Howard, don't forget to feed Darkie while I'm at your aunt's," Mother nagged, handing Bernie a cup of Earl Grey.

"I wouldn't, Mother."

"Who?" said Bernie, aghast.

"My cat," I clarified, as Mother handed me my usual coffee, into which I poured the usual abundance of cream and eight spoonfuls of sugar. Bernie watched as if I were committing an act of suicide.

"Aren't you joining us, Susie?" he asked when Mother didn't sit.

"No, no. As you boys are settled, I'll be on my way. I'm off to my sister's for the weekend and I must catch the trolley." All this as she gathered the small valise she had packed and put her coat and hat on. "Howard, do telephone tonight so I know you're all right."

"I'll be fine, Mother, but yes I will telephone," I said, wondering when she might ever leave.

"I'm off, then. Enjoy your vampire hunt," she proffered nonchalantly and went out the front door.

"What did she say?" asked Bernie. He resembled a man finding out he had just joined a cult.

"I'll explain on the way," I said.

* * *

"Oh I'm very familiar with Mr. Stoker's book," Bernie said as we discussed my assignment on the ride to Exeter. "He's a Dublin man as I am, you see. Most religious people are schooled in the workings of Lucifer. We mortals are up against it; we surely are."

I have to admit I was enjoying our conversation. The priest was far more learned than I had imagined. The jostling of the car was playing chaos with my cranium. I massaged my forehead beneath my hat and held my kerchief to my mouth.

"Are you all right, Howard?" he asked with great sincerity. I liked him.

"It will pass; I have had a rough time these few years. I suffer from…"

"If you don't mind my saying, Howard," he interrupted. "You seem quite the strapping lad to me. I can't help but wonder if your mind is playing tricks, is all."

"No Bernie," I said shyly. "I don't mind. The thought had occurred to me. I've always been the nervous type. As a child, I had nightmares that these creatures, night-gaunts I called them, would fly to my room and carry me away."

"Night-gaunts is it?"

"Have you heard much of this Mercy Brown incident, Father?" I asked. "I found some old clippings that were general in nature."

"Well, yes. Even though it's a Baptist case," he said, "most of us that have been around at Saints Peter and Paul do know about it. Ghastly business, that. The poor girl was nineteen when she succumbed, and the abruptness of her departure, only a few years after her mother and sister went the same way, spurred on rumors of a family curse. It was believed that a vampire spirit inhabited one of the family members, and this fiend was leaving the grave by night to suck out the lifeblood of the living. When Mercy's brother Edwin became ill and his life drained away by the very same means, well. . ."

"That's when they exhumed the bodies," I added.

"Yes. Supposedly the mother and sister, Mary and Mary Olive, were in states of decomposition appropriate to their time of interment. Not Mercy, however. Though in the grave for months, her cheeks were rosy and the body had even moved position."

"This is where I can't believe what transpired." I went on. "The crowd, including members of Brown's own family, removed the heart of Mercy. It was said to be filled with fresh blood. They burnt it on a nearby rock, and-…"

"And, they even made Mercy's brother Edwin consume some of the ashes," Bernie chimed in. "It did him no good; he died soon after. No one in that town will go near that rock, much less touch it now."

"What if the family *were* cursed? What if the lot of them were vampires? There have been plenty enough mysterious deaths in those parts over the years."

Bernie laughed at this, thinking I was making sport.

"Now, Howard, much as my colleagues and I debate the issue, I don't think anyone actually believes those people died of anything more than consumption. You have quite the imagination, Mr. Lovecraft."

"And you're not like most priests I've known, Father Reilly."

We shared a laugh over that. We were close to the town in question, and dusk was arriving with us, at a quarter to six. I asked Bernie to take me directly to the old cemetery before he went off for his meal. This rendered him flummoxed.

"Surely you'll be joining me at the Inn, they are said to have the most deftly prepared seafood," he pleaded.

"To be frank, Father, while you partake of the God-damned stuff, I'll be conducting my research, and do please forgive my vulgarity." I don't often swear, but when I do, I save it for something abhorrent, such as anything pulled squirming from the sea.

Within moments, with my direction, he drove onto the dirt path adjacent to two white buildings on our left. One bore a sign reading Chestnut Hill Baptist Church. The cemetery lay before us. He chugged away, leaving me alone in the blessed silence of the dead.

I found Mercy Brown's stone fairly easily, as it was just to the left of the well-worn path down the center of the graveyard. It had her parents' name and her dates of birth and death. A bible inscription was already worn away by vandals in the two decades since her departure. A pleasant enough stone, but nothing to indicate anything ghoulish. I did a small rubbing of the words in graphite.

I read her mother's and siblings' stones then strolled along the grounds. I looked at the alleged spot of the organ burning, and not only risked touching the rock but also sitting upon it. I pulled out my journal and made some notes while I awaited Bernie.

Whatever daylight enabled my writing soon faded. I judged the time to be toward seven in the evening. The whole atmosphere of the place began to change. Some crows alit on stones very near to me, acting unwary of my human presence, cawing in communication to one another.

I put away my book and got up, feeling uncomfortable, as if their plaintive cries were a remonstration to vacate the premises. I was no longer welcome. Walking back along the path, I noticed a handful of people dressed all in black near Mercy's monument. I thought an evening service or club meeting would begin soon.

I didn't want to alarm them and resolved to introduce myself. A young woman from their ranks approached me. I turned my attention to the stone, savoring it, since I was about to be asked to leave.

"I'm most terribly sorry, I'm…" My courtesies trailed off. It was the oddest thing. She was gone, her group and the birds as well. I was solemnly alone, and a sickly, nervous feeling invaded my stomach. I questioned my own sanity.

At that precise instant, two headlamps pulled into the dirt drive. Bernie had returned. I moved toward him and my legs gave way; I stumbled to the ground. Bernie came running from the car.

"Howard, are you all right?" I could find no voice to answer. The most dreadful sense of doom rushed over me, perceptions of a dark abyss that none of us could fathom. I was over-wrought. Bernie put my arm around his neck and hoisted me.

"You poor man. Why, you're terrified. What on earth happened?" He walked me to the car and opened the door to settle me in the passenger seat.

I was trembling. My heart beat strenuously and my mouth was dry. I took out my kerchief to wipe my lip; I was sweating. I never sweat! I don't know what was more upsetting, the apparition or my reaction to it.

"Did you see anyone leaving here, just now, as you approached?" I asked him.

"No Howard, just you alone. What's going on?"

"Get us out of here, Bernie," I found myself saying. "Please take me away from here. I'm sorry I came. Something isn't right here; something definitely isn't right!"

"Why don't we go to the Inn where I dined and take a room," he opined. "It will save you the return trip, and your mother is not at home."

"Oh no, Bernie, no. I appreciate the thought, but neither god nor man can pry me from my own bed. I'll be better soon."

As he reversed the car, I couldn't help but look back at the pitch-black graveyard. There was a round, blue orb of light hovering over the area where Mercy was buried. I didn't bother alerting Bernie to its presence. I knew it was there expressly for me.

* * *

On the ride home, after I'd calmed, I could not shake the distinct feeling that we were being followed. There wasn't another soul on the road, and I felt silly looking behind us for the fifth time.

"Howard, what do you think you will find back there?" Bernie asked.

"Am I that obvious? I know that I'm letting my imagination play havoc again. I think Stoker's vile creations will get me."

"You don't have much faith in God, do you?"

The question was forward, and I answered honestly.

"No, Bernie, I don't. I'm content to live and serve as best I can, without reward at the end of the day. After all, we floated in the ether of oblivion before entering this world; I look forward to returning there, free of desires which may be unrequited. No, I would not relish immortality at all."

"But faith can be a great comfort in troubled times. The characters in your Mister Stoker's story were certainly lucky to have God on their side."

"But they are just that, Bernie; characters in a story. This is real life."

There was an awkward silence.

* * *

When I was safe and sound at home, back in robe and slippers, the dread remained palpable. I got some leftover soup from the icebox and heated it on the stove.

The cat was decidedly anxious and pulled one of his disappearing acts after he got his supper.

The house, and indeed the whole neighborhood, was deathly silent. I usually consider Mother's time away to be an oasis, but on this occasion I'd have been grateful for the company. After cleaning my dishes, I retired to my favorite easy chair to work on my essay for *Dracula*; the sooner to be rid of the foul tome. I thought of the anguish of those nineteenth century inhabitants of Exeter. It must have been inexorable for those Godly people to give in to their medieval fears and desecrate the graves of the Brown family. I also thought of the suffering of each of the Browns, as a spreading affliction rapidly devoured the health of each in turn.

There was the tinkling of glass just outside, and I knew from the change in light through the window that a streetlamp had been damaged.

I further knew deep in my heart that I had been foolhardy in continuing to ruminate on the Browns in my parlor that evening. I had summoned them.

Whispering voices began. I sat quaking in silence. I could hear women calling "Howard" to me in a most sensual manner, interspersed with a masculine "Lovecraft" at intervals. Only the events of the early part of the evening kept me from succumbing to the notion that I was insane. The languid calls were hypnotic. They unquestionably came from outside the house, yet had the illusory quality of swimming in my consciousness.

The next sound of glass shattering came from very near me. A large rock was thrown through a pane to my right. The shock of it hurtled me from my seat. I knew I had to act to retain any hope of survival and found myself spurred forward by this instinct.

I turned off the few lights I had been using. I ran swiftly about, bolting doors in the large house and locking every window. On one occasion, when I approached a kitchen window, a young male face was right there, hands against the glass, shouting "Lovey," a childhood nickname. It was so jarring that I jumped violently in reaction. It stood leering as I locked the window.

I had gotten a good look at my otherworldly adversary. His stark pallor was dimmer than my own, yet his lips were blood red and full. Most horrifying, I caught sight of the long and protruding canines as he railed at me. They filled me with horror. I imagined them capable of unutterable damage to human flesh.

Beyond that I didn't know what more I could do. I was surrounded.

There was a knock at the door, which again caused a spasmodic full body flinch. Any attempt I made at bravery was counteracted by my reactionary nerves. The banging became louder. I tried to ignore it, but it persisted.

I moved to the front door.

"I say, please go away," I began timidly. "I'm terribly sorry to have disturbed you, and you can count on my leaving you in peace from now on." Did the Un-dead react favorably to polite entreaty? I hoped as much.

"Open the door, Howard," came an impatient voice. "Howard, for heaven's sake. It's Bernie. Open up, quickly."

I was unconvinced for a moment. Could they disguise their voices? I tried to remember from the book.

"Open the God-damned door!" The brogue was unmistakable.

I turned or unbolted several locks on the solid oak then opened it a crack to peer out. Father Reilly was standing there with his arms full. I opened it further to allow him passage, and then quickly began bolting it.

"No," he said, stopping me from finishing the fortification. "I'll be of more use to you out there. I may be able to turn them away before they get to you."

He moved to the kitchen table, where he unburdened himself. He lay down two large milk bottles filled with water and a metal, covered bowl. He pulled several small crucifixes from his pockets and put them on the table as well.

"These bottles are filled with Holy Water," he said. "I blessed it myself. My housemates will have to go without milk for the weekend."

He put his thumb and forefinger on the knob atop the metal dish and lifted. It was full of small white cookies.

"Communion wafers," he said. "These, the water and crosses will only slow them down. We need some stakes."

I winced as he turned over one of Mother's kitchen chairs, took hold of a leg and began to put all his weight into kicking at it. He managed to break off all the legs. He left three lying on the floor and stuffed one in his belt.

"Oh," he said, as he pulled two folded purple stoles from his pocket. He put one around his neck and one around mine, saying, "In nomini Patri, et Fili, et Spiritus Sancti, amen," as he waved his hand about.

He then took out one of the wafers, and held it up before me.

"Corpus Christi," he said. When I opened my mouth to ask what to do, he shoved it in.

"Eat it all," he said, "but don't touch it with your teeth."

The brood outside began to call his name along with mine.

"Oh, Father, Fatherrr," they taunted, rather more hatefully than they had summoned me. The voices were so prominent in my head I became dizzy. I thought for a moment I may faint.

"Howard. Howard, listen to me!" Bernie reprimanded. He took me by both shoulders and shook me roughly. "You're going to have to bear up. I'm going to need you to dredge up any courage which may be in you and help me, do you understand?"

"Oh, Bernie," I said, pointing to the objects on the table, "I'm sorry, but I don't believe in any of these things."

"Well, for lack of better ideas, Howard, let's just give Stoker the benefit of the doubt, shall we?"

As if in response to that battle plan, several windows suddenly crashed in at once. A rock from over the sink hit the priest solidly in the back.

"Aaaarrrgh," he cried, bending his arm back there as he twirled, sucking in air.

"Bernie," I yelled, grabbing his elbow.

"I'm fine, Howard," he said quietly. "Now I want you to let me out. Then go upstairs and throw on all the lights, to illuminate them. Stay away from the windows, all right? These demons despise Christ the Risen Lord. I'm going out there and drive them away."

"You're a brave man, Father," I said. "I'll try not to let you down."

"I know you won't, Howard. I have faith in you." He locked my arm as I opened the door for him. I never went in for sentiment, but I felt a twinge at that moment.

He ran out, praying aloud.

I ran in the opposite direction, going upstairs to cast light upon them as Bernie had instructed.

Returning to the first floor, I looked out the front windows, and finally could see what we were dealing with. Father Reilly stood with his back to the house as he recited in a clear, commanding voice.

"I cast thee out, unclean spirits," he repeated over and over. He held a book in front of him with one hand, and the jagged chair leg behind his back with the other.

A thick fog was beginning to encircle the estate, as if the phantoms had brought it with them.

Before him on the lawn four people faced him. They laughed and sneered from a few yards away, held back by his words. They were dressed as they had been at the cemetery and the personalities were very distinct to me now.

I could recognize the mother, Mary Brown, by her weathered face, and her older daughter Mary Olive, nearly the spitting image but hanging back a bit, taking it all in. Young brother Edwin was the most hostile and animated, stepping forward toward Bernie with each taunt, and then retreating a few steps to laugh with his sisters. Lastly there was Mercy, the youngest and prettiest, but with a fire in her eyes that told me she was in charge, and the most dangerous. Without question, the roles in the family hierarchy had changed in these new incarnations.

I freely took the opportunity to gaze out the window. It occurred to me that one of them was staring directly into my eyes, as if seeing me in the clear light of day. Her eyes were glowing, penetrating mine, and an alluring smile curled on her lips. It was Mercy. A shudder passed through my very being, as if the shadow of death had fallen over me.

She nodded to her mother Mary, who charged at Bernie. He dropped the book and met her surge by pushing his spear into her. I could hear the wet gush as the wood cut through her body. As if by magic, Bernie was now holding not a middle-aged woman, but a dusty skeleton, which crumpled at his feet as he dropped it.

The other three were on him within seconds, and he couldn't brace himself to rear the weapon. I saw it fall to the ground as they bit into his neck at different places. I shall never forget the pathetic screams that came from him.

Something came over me as I watched the man who came to my aid getting mauled. There was a protective notion, and a rage that flushed over me, the like of which I'd never experienced.

"No, no," I screamed. "Over here, take me. Come in here and get *me*!"

"No, Howard, not that, anything but that, Howard," Bernie managed to cry out, and it dawned on me immediately what he meant. I'd forgotten Stoker's codicil that they had to be *invited* in. God-damn.

They dropped poor Bernie on the ground, blood spewing sickeningly from his neck, and came at the house. I saw Mary Olive disappear along the side, heading for the back yard.

I ran first in that direction also. On the way by the kitchen, I filled the pockets of my robe with hosts and crosses.

I stopped and waited quietly by the side of the only full window. Sure enough, an arm came through to grip the frame. I took out a crucifix and pressed it hard on the back of the hand. I was amazed at how efficiently it worked. It melted deep into the flesh as a hot knife into butter. The creature let out an inhuman shriek.

I grabbed her wrists and took the stole from around my neck. As she snapped at me, trying to bite my hands, I wrapped it around and through both her wrists, tying her firmly to the window lock. The cloth burned into her skin, and as she remained there helpless and moaning, I couldn't believe the ease with which I took up one of the wooden chair pieces from the floor and drove it into her heart. She folded in on herself over the shaft, and a rickety scaffold of bones shattered to the ground, the skull falling through the window and rolling at my feet. I felt very pleased with myself and marveled at my veracity. My reverie was ended when a war cry split the air behind me, and I fumbled with the stake. It bounced off the sill, into the back yard.

Mercy had come through a front window. I ran toward the parlor to waylay her. There was no time to procure another stake from the kitchen floor. I passed the fireplace and instead brandished a heavy brass poker. Running at full speed I wasted no time in impaling her. She smiled at me. The point of entry burst forth a flow of blood, but it didn't harm her in the least. She pulled the implement further into herself, inching toward me, laughing and baring her fangs. She was a hair from my face as she hissed like a challenged animal.

"Do you know why I followed you, Lovecraft?" Her voice was not wholly male or female.

"I thought you were one of us. Your skin, your temperature, your manner. And something . . . deeper." I held firm to the poker and pushed against her chest with all my strength to hold her back. I felt she could take me whenever she wanted. Her might made me despair utterly for a moment.

"Your thoughts are dark," she continued. "Dark as the night which you inhabit. It also inhabits you."

A black shape suddenly leapt to the top of a cupboard behind her, drawing her brief attention.

It was Darkie. You had to admire a cat's unexpected entrances. I've always thought them superior to dogs.

I put my foot on her leg and pulled the poker out. I began to beat her over the head. Each blow struck her skull solidly, and I could hear a nauseating crack. Her black bonnet fell forward and flew off. Blood clotted in her hair. She fell to the floor. I lifted the fireplace poker and brought it down, again and again. I let out my rage about the whole day, Father Bernie, this blasted assignment. I let out my anger at my wasted life full of wasted opportunity. She did not become a cadaver, but she certainly was no longer moving.

Someone jumped at me from behind, out of the kitchen. It was Edwin, opening his jaw to finish me. His arms wrapped around my upper torso and I held my neck back as far as I could. My arms were pinned at my side, and with a mild shake I dropped the poker. He was far from human. Just a snarling, mindless beast wanting desperately to feed. I managed to reach into a pocket, pulling forth a crucifix. With one gasp of power, I lifted my arm to push it into his face. As soon as he caught sight of it he backed away instinctively. I ran past him into the kitchen.

I couldn't get at the shards of wood on the floor, so I procured one of the "milk" bottles and pulled off the cardboard cap. It was awkward trying to control the stream from the bottle's mouth as I waved it up and down to project the liquid. He easily stayed far enough away. I grabbed the other bottle from the table. I ran near the sink, needing time to contemplate. I couldn't waste this water. I turned away from him momentarily.

"You know, your sister had a point. You are all so strong," I said, in hopes of distracting him. His head slanted like a puzzled dog as he crept in for the kill. "I really should join you," I continued. "She's correct, you know. I'm such a denizen of darkness; I'm more than halfway there."

He was so close I could hear his halted breaths. I whirled and threw the rest of the Holy Water into his face. I had poured it from the bottle to a soup pan from the drainer. This time I had a perfect trajectory and a wide splay of liquid. Every part of his visage became a boiling cauldron of agony, with fingers of smoke rising off him like volcanic spouts. As he threw his hands to his face I had ample time to fall to my knees, grasp a chair leg firmly, and thrust it directly through his chest. A lifeless corpse fell at my feet, wind from the broken windows blowing dust off its rotting bones.

I slumped down in anguished exhaustion. Then there was a rustling at the front of the house. I headed there.

I took a moment to nudge Mercy's lifeless body with my foot, then lined up my wooden shaft to finish the job securely.

"Howard." A loud whisper came from the parlor. I got up to peek, and as I rounded the short hall, I could see a head sticking only slightly into one of the windows. It couldn't see me.

"Oh, Howaaard," came its voice in sing-songy fashion. "Aren't you going to invite me in, Howard? We're friends are we not?"

My heart wept. It was poor Bernie of course.

He had become one of them.

In my soundless way I shuffled to the side of the window. I considered the stake in my hand, but instead reached into my pocket.

"We got them, Howard. You came through with flying colours lad. Now please help me out of this cold night air. I'm so cold, Howard."

What was it Father Reilly had said?

"Corpus Christi," I shouted.

"Wha-?" Bernie opened his mouth to speak. I popped some hosts between his fangs and pushed his head and chin together. He bawled a muffled screech and ran into the night, smoke billowing from his mouth as he disappeared into the thick fog. It grieved me that I had brought this upon him.

I returned to finish Mercy, but as I neared the bottom of the staircase, a figure darted at me from the hall. Mercy took hold of my arm like it was a child's, and shook it sideways, forcing me to drop the stake. I turned to run up the stairs, and wrenching out of her grasp made me cry out in pain. My escape attempt was futile. She had me by the ankles. I fell forward. I got my long hands around one of the banister spokes and grasped it for dear life. I felt her immense strength pulling at me. She laughed softly, but there wasn't much humor left in her.

"It's over, Lovecraft. Let go. I'm tired. Let me cut my losses and return to my coffin."

I tried to think. My grip was firm, but the old dowel began to split and loosen.

"You've watched your whole family die. Again," I said, trying to stall.

"They're nothing to me."

Evil, I thought. Subhuman. Surely I was more worthy than her.

It was pure serendipity. The rung came loose completely, and Mercy was tugging so hard that she fell backward with a firm grip on my legs. I tumbled blindly on top of her, and was able to pin her. I pressed the tip of the jagged wood to her breast first, then turned my body around. Her head was jammed against a wall at an awkward angle, further restricting the use of her arms to push off anywhere. I had her.

"Get off," she grunted. She tried a loud and horrifying roar to unnerve me, but I was resolute. I used all the weight of my gangly legs to secure my position.

"I could run you through. End this God-forsaken nightmare," I said.

She tried a different tack, crying like a child and pleading with me.

"It isn't my fault what I am, Mister Lovecraft," she sniveled. "I didn't ask to become this."

I ignored her.

"I feel strong," I bluffed. "I could wait a while and see what the sun does to you."

At this threat, her eyes widened with real fear.

"No, no," she cried. She tried to writhe but couldn't even accomplish that. I realized that the contents of my pockets were adding to my upper hand. Also, quite possibly I suppose, the one Bernie made me swallow.

"Let me go, Lovecraft," she said, returning to her former manner. All pretense of the naive girl discarded. "Spare me and I'll make a deal with you; I can make it considerably worth your while."

"What have you to offer me? An eternity of decrepit misery? No thank you."

"I hold power, Lovecraft, which you couldn't comprehend. As an immortal entity, I can tap into a wealth of knowledge."

She hit upon my weakness. All I truly ever wanted or cared about was further enlightenment.

"I could tell you things, Lovecraft," she continued. "There is a vast universe of esoteric wisdom unknown to mortals. There is a storehouse of magic and enough tales to quench your thirst for a lifetime. There are powerful forces and beings that wait in silence to rise up again, creatures older than time itself. The monster I have become is privy to all of this."

I thought long and hard. I knew this devil could, as in Eden, be persuasive. In truth my arms were getting tired.

The new incarnation I had become on this night had taken many risks, and I was about to take another.

"I'll show my good faith in our bargain by getting off you," I said with justifiable hesitation. "I will let you continue your existence. But you cannot seek retribution, do you understand? You must let me continue mine."

She nodded.

I got off her. She stood, and as if to put me at ease, backed several feet away. She curtsied.

"So you do retain some manners," I chided. "They burnt your heart years ago. I don't understand," I said.

"I don't know where they got the idea that would do me in," she answered. "I no more need a heart than a brain. I have no further use for them."

She perched on the window to leave.

"Wait. How will I reach you?" I asked sheepishly. This compact was no more ludicrous than the rest of the evening.

"I'll come to you some night when you're up," she said. "After I've fed to satisfaction, to be safe."

Not a hint of her remained as she receded before my eyes. There was not the slightest sound.

I looked around the battered house with all the blood and refuse strewn throughout. I had survived the most unholy battle of my life. Would I survive mother's return?

Mother. Too late to call, thankfully.

* * *

It would have sent me to Butler Sanitarium, where my mentally stricken father ended his days, so I shall never know how Backstreet, or anyone else, would have received this foreword to Stoker's saga of the Un-dead. **-H.P.L.**

Harvest
by Morgan Sylvia

Harvest never waited
Now it rots in the field
You wanted the wind
And she wanted the seas
But you never cared for her dreams
I know what you did
The night the moon turned red
I saw them
The ones you summoned from forgotten graves
I watched them raise her severed head up to the sky
The crows carried her ghost into the wind
The spiders took her eyes into the wood
We used to laugh at the tales
Those forgotten legends of old
But the stories were true
And those grey cold lords
With their purpled skin and rotted eyes
And their arachnid kin
The ones you brought back
They filled the boneyards with their hatred
Filled the summer wind with screams
As the forest withered around them
Those wretched yellow days emptied these hills
We saw the old lord trying to escape them
Let them chase him, you whispered to me
Let them tear the meat from his bones
He should die
And I believed you

They took him down as the sun rose
We stood watching from that old stone tower
A pale August morning drenched in blood
They tore him to pieces
In the time it took a vulture's shadow to cross him
I can still hear the wailing
I can still smell the gore
And you
You sang their praises
You spoke of absolution and transcendence
As they feasted on his last meal
When he was gone, they spoke to me
They showed me their truths
I remember it well
They crouched over his corpse
Their leader raised its bloody jaws and fixed me with its stare
Its eyes burned into me
Blood-black and bulging with devoured dreams
I heard the music start then
That was the moment I awakened
That was the moment I knew
Amber memories turned grey
Grey skies turned red
That night I walked with them
The spiders a living carpet around us
I burned your words on the bone fires
Just like she taught me
Your lies floated up to foul clouds in acrid smoke
They watched from twining shadows
They sang to the hunter's moon
They were never human at all, were they?
Those beautiful monstrosities
Nor were you
I remember the man you once were
Before the madness took you
But that is gone now
And those brighter days we spoke of
They will never come to pass
You sold those dreams to the spiders and the dead
In return, they peeled the thoughts from your mind
Sliced the flesh off your bones
But they never let you go
Nor will I

And now?
You lie rotting beneath the wheat we planted
Alone
As you should be
The ghosts of those you betrayed
The ones they vivisected by the pond
They are waiting for you
In waving blades of sharp pale grass
She stands with them as the skies darken
The storm is coming
And they are rising again
As will you
Before the tempest touches this poisoned soil
Your rotting eyes will open
And you will claw your way through black dirt with greenish, bloating fingers
You will stand with them
As you should
They will darken the horizon, those grey cold lords
With their purpled skin and rotted eyes
And their arachnid kin
They are calling
I can hear them
They are coming
I can smell them
The beautiful monstrosities lumbering off to the east
They will fall slouching and famished upon cities filled with fools
As forests wither and die around them
You've chained me to them
A spell I cannot break
But my way is different than yours
—my death
is different than yours
She taught me well
I welcomed the fangs
My death lifted me into the trees on ebony pincers
Where silver webs trapped my dreams
Now I scuttle forth with the others
Against a sickly pallid dawn
But all I taste in the blood of innocents
Is rage and ignorance
All I taste is rage
We hear the sacred song as our ears rot off

We see the secret colors as our eyes bulge and bleed
Our tongues burst open with sable words
We have it down now
—*father*
We have your ways in chains
Let us rage into the red hours
We bled
As you told us to
We died
As you told us to
And we rose
As you told us to
What was it we were forbidden?
Blood or bone or tears
Or just the chance of peace?
Who ever knew that you would be the one, led us into madness?
As the innocents smiled into the sun
Our forests are hung with spiderwebs and bloody entrails
Our golden fields reek of death
The rains fall into silence
And your precious harvests are rotting in the field
Let us dance into the dying of the old world
Let us bleed our broken dreams into the nest
Let us crawl forth, slathering and enraged
Putrid and perfect against the rolling waves of wheat
We saved the pain for you
And you will have nothing else
Not even righteousness
(the dead win no wars)
And in those last hours
As the yellow wind fills with screams
I stand
As witches do
And curse your final hours
Your harvests
Are rotting in the fields

Heart of Frankenstein
by Trisha J. Wooldridge

My creator, Victor Frankenstein, promised to make me a mate—an equal to love—in return for my promise that we two would retreat into wilderness far from mankind. He aborted that promise, so I broke mine. Instead, I vowed to unmake him through torment equitable to his transgressions upon me. *That* promise I fulfilled, but not with joy. I then made a new promise: I would surrender to the Arctic's icy prison, righteous judgment of my daemonly wickedness.

And I did for some time.

But Frankenstein's hubris damns me still. What he created was not life, for what is alive must certainly die. I waited, entombed in ice atop the world as Dante's Lucifer was frozen deep below Hell, for an end that never came.

Were there some Divine Creator, I concluded, His cruelty must be what drives mankind. Or perhaps there was no creator but mankind. Fearing insignificance, they designed gods to bless them with control over all, to assure them death was not merely the closing of an eye, a blink in time, nothing more.

If death were just the end of consciousness, if mankind were nothing special for their sentience, why should I be denied this final rest? What weight had any penitent promise I made?

And if some Divine Creator should hold me accountable for my sins? What worse suffering could He impose?

Nothing. *Nothing*, I thought then.

But am I not the inheritor of Frankenstein's sins, blessings, and consequences? He rationalized so eloquently. He inspired people to love him, to help in his unholy creation of me. Even enthralled in the deepest madness, his friends loved him enough to risk their lives in his quest to destroy me.

Let *me* tell you of love. And promises.

* * *

In this frozen wasteland, sunlight upon snow can create light more blinding than the deepest hour of the month-long night. Even on the cloudiest nights, I can see. When daylight expresses brilliant tyranny, I remain inside this outpost I—no, *we*—have claimed as home.

This painful illumination feeds my greater purpose, my promise to my beloved, so long as I keep the solar panels clean. I have mastered the collection and storage of energy. No longer slave to storm or god, I am as methodical in the science of power and electricity as I am—and my creator was—in the application of chemistry, anatomy, and surgery.

Power: My creator's notes say nothing of needing electricity to awaken me. Nothing! When he created me, there was little at his disposal to generate the charge I have found necessary in recreating his experiment.

This outpost was built for scientific study. Humankind regularly attempts to reclaim it. That each attempt fails with no survivors ensures the next attempt will bring new and better tools for my application. And hope for my eventual success.

What power has Hell without hope?

But I promised to speak of love, and I digress.

My beloved mate, my dear Ingrid who I rescued and recreated, has her own chamber during her dormancy. I would not keep her in the morgue with our human stock; she is *more* than they, as am I. She is not dead, and she is my wife. We cannot share a bed when she is in this fragile state. And even a fiend such as I would revile taking comfort in her body when she cannot respond.

It is to Ingrid's chamber I now go, for the power storage reserves are full. It takes nearly the entire year's daylight to reach this point. It has taken years to calculate the most efficient power surge for her awakening.

Last awakening, Ingrid and I shared two precious days and one sacred night, the longest duration since our original meeting. My hope—my *promise*—is that our time together never need cease.

Before I move my beloved, I examine her left shoulder and below her right knee. Gone are obvious stitches and Frankenstein's crude alchemical sealant; modern surgical thread and grafting create almost seamless transition, a complement, an *enhancement* to her already superior beauty. Assured of her body's structural integrity, I carry Ingrid to the main medical lab as a husband carries a newly-married wife over their home's threshold, as I shall bring her over the threshold between states of life.

Her flesh, though cold and hard as marble, is as smooth and fine as the artist's stone against the mummified swaths of my own skin that have not been replaced. My creator was thoughtless of my experience in this vessel; I have taken great pains to maintain the perfection of my beloved's body.

After laying her on the insulated table, I unbutton her dressing gown just enough to access the incision to the left of her sternum while maintaining her modesty. I open the incision and remove the preservatives I so carefully placed barely a year ago. Next I retrieve the heart treated with my most recent attempt at replicating my creator's formula.

Will this time be the last time I must do this? The hope on that question never dulls.

I connect the heart with the expertise of a surgeon who is *more than* human, one with nearly a century's practice, needing minimal rest and pause for sustenance.

Once her heart is meticulously secured, I apply the cathodes. I inhale and exhale slowly, anxiously, though my work is nothing short of perfection. I rebutton her dressing gown and kiss her on the forehead. She has said she feels my kiss in those moments between waking and sleeping; she says that kiss carries my love to her consciousness.

A bolt of lightning was the dramatic kiss that woke her from true death the first time. Today, I click a small switch between my thumb and forefinger. The facility's lights go out so quietly I hear her first gasp.

Though this compound has no windows, outside the sun is rises for this season-short day. I planned her awakening for this; her appreciation of poetry is equal to mine. LED candles create a romantic glow upon a timer's command.

I caress her face, stroking her golden curls as she returns to consciousness. When Frankenstein woke me into being, I met only terror and revulsion. She should experience only love.

She leans into my touch as her breathing evens. My beloved smiles and kisses my hand just before opening her eyes.

I do not flinch when she looks at me, though the definition and clarity of her sky-blue eyes have taken on the watery, glassiness of mine. I suspect it is a side effect of my creator's chemical compound; nothing else has deteriorated. Regardless of their appearance, she sees as well as I, better than any human, and I find her no less beautiful.

For her eyes hold the same love I carry in mine.

She clears her throat and tests her voice. Like mine, it has a rasping breathiness. She speaks in the song of an antique violin.

"You've done it again, beloved. You've done it again." She rewards my efforts with her lips upon mine, renewing our vows of nearly a century.

* * *

1944

My cursed existence would have me return to the lands of man when the world was at war. As insult upon injury, I would learn that not even a century's progression of war machines could end me.

Initially unaware of the battle-scarred landscape to the south, I first went to Scotland's Orkney Isle—where my creator had assembled, discarded, and interred my intended mate—to find and procure Frankenstein's tools and chemicals. In my vengeful stalking of Frankenstein, I had committed to memory all the man's correspondence. My mind held a narrated map of names and places where I might find more clues to solve the mystery of my unmaking. Mourning the unbirth of my intended partner, I decided that my remains should lay with hers. Feeling a semblance of peace, I continued my quest on mainland Europe.

I was incorrect to assume nothing could be more wretched than an awakened consciousness entrapped in ice. Worse still: A landmine rendered me limbless and helpless in the mud of human blood and excrement.

My supposition of the inherent cruelty of a Divine Creator, if such existed, changed only in realizing the *depth* of universal brutality. Yet my belief more readily accepted the *actuality* of Divine Consciousness; only a Divine Consciousness would write the sadistic irony that befell me.

To maintain sentience whilst trapped in a shattered and scattered body was horror enough, yet my head and torso had the fortune of being collected by what I can only conclude was an incarnation of my creator. Once more, the limbs of various corpses were attached to my body. This house of science, however, was also ornamented in Pagan runes and symbols I knew from literature. And observers! Adorned in dress suits and uniforms as if attending an elite theatre performance!

The deliciousness of their dissolving applause when I snapped the false creator's neck! The rapture of their hysteria when I turned on them!

Though I was then ignorant of the extent of their war crimes, a part of me I dare consider related to a soul *understood*: I was but a single showcase in a menagerie of depravity.

Of my actions that day, I regret only that some escaped my feral wrath.

After finding my bag of Frankenstein's work and tools—and adding to it those of this mad doctor—I fled that laboratory. In my travels, I obtained more durable clothing and a rucksack in which to carry my growing research. Commanders quickly learned the limit of their soldiers' courage and morale when bullets proved ineffective against a monster faster and stronger than any human.

I learned to dress my wounds and give myself blood transfusions when I sustained too much damage. When a building collapsed by bombs trapped my right arm, I severed it to escape and exchanged it for one from a soldier's corpse pinned under an overturned AGDZ. The success of that operation, and the greater utility of the new limb, led me to replace the rest of my extremities. The showman doctor who rebuilt me, while using fresher parts than Frankenstein had access to, had not collected the best specimens of humanity.

But I chose my battles carefully. I know not the extent humans feel pain, but I do suffer from it, and what intelligence would willingly endure such misery without the promise of death's final freedom?

I made my way to Ingolstadt, where Frankenstein first learned the secrets of my creation. From there, I sought the secrets of my utter and complete destruction. How and where I traveled, seeking artifacts of Frankenstein's academic Odyssey—over a century past—is of little matter. I obtained the knowledge to accomplish the events in my tale of love.

But not enough to evade the more damnable consequences.

* * *

As I serve my beloved Ingrid breakfast, she grabs my most-recently acquired hand with a gasp. "What's *this*?" The disgust upon her lips sends an unexpected twist through my stomach.

I yank away as if she struck me.

She softens at my reaction, but doesn't smile. "That *colored* flesh . . . It doesn't become you. Your hand should complement your status, your intelligence . . . your *greatness*."

I glance between the arm and her, flexing and fanning the long, dark fingers. I took it from the commander of the most recent attack upon our home. He'd distracted me from my protected position and destroyed my former forearm with a well-aimed explosive. As formidable an opponent as any human could be, he was a strong specimen that would make me stronger.

"Don't fret about it now, beloved," Ingrid says, offering me her celestial smile. "We've been parted too long. Let's eat. Later, I'll help you change that appendage for a more worthy one. Surely more human *offerings* have been sent to try and unseat us from our temple." She chuckles at her reference to our godlike state; I do not argue. She is Persephone to my Hades, and I endeavor to smite every pomegranate seed that keeps her from my company.

I return to the table, taking her hand in my paler one, and kiss her knuckles. With the same unnatural speed and grace, she pulls my hand to her lips and returns the affection. Warmth I experience no other time than with her, warmth that doesn't bring decomposition, dances up my arm and settles like a dove in my heart.

"You have advanced even in your cooking, my love." The bliss crossing her face heats me elsewhere than my heart, and I anticipate the ecstasy of later affections.

"In one of the invading human's electronic book collections, I found several volumes on food." I lower my eyes in the coy way she does when she wishes to impress me. "I wanted to make our time together even more satisfying to your senses."

"Mmmm . . . " She moans as she chews slowly, sensuously.

My desire for her as my wife grows physically uncomfortable and compelling. I stop eating that I might visually feast upon her.

Ingrid looks at me through her lashes as she swallows and smiles. "I appreciate your dedication to my pleasures. Have you also found research that prolongs the pleasure of my time with you?"

I admire the deep intellect behind her gaze. "I hope that I have. Do you feel any different with this awakening?"

Putting her utensils on her cleaned plate, Ingrid stretches her back against the chair so her well-formed breasts reach heavenward, still hard from death's chill or erect in expectation of what I hope is an immediate repose to our shared bed. It takes me a moment to attend to her spoken response: "I believe I do feel more vigor than I have before." She stands, stretching further. "We should test that, of course. Rigorously."

I need no further enticement to leave my unfinished meal and embrace her.

Ingrid stops me and pulls my sleeve past the seam attaching my new forearm. Touching only the paler flesh, she guides me not to the bedroom but to the morgue and its adjoining medical area.

"But first, my beloved, let's make sure all of you is aligned with your greatness."

* * *

1944

"Put your hands in the air." The voice was female and unafraid.

I complied out of curiosity. I'd just climbed down a hole through a demolished office building, seeking shelter from a snow storm. The woman could clearly see me; the rifle-click echoed an accurate aim. It had been . . . a very long time . . . since I had conversed with a woman. Longer since that interaction was not one of terror.

"Turn around."

With a sigh, I did so, prepared to rush and disarm her upon the immediate panic I expected. German troops were retreating from this village, which had been hollowed out by the prior evening's air raid. I had hoped for sheltered respite while I scavenged for more food and potable water.

She did not panic. Nor was her face overtaken with revulsion and abhorrence. The drawing of her brow and lips, the scrunching of her delicate nose just behind the rifle butt revealed only a mild disgust, wariness, and—most surprising—intrigue. "What are you?"

A shock of air burst from my nose and mouth. It took me a moment to recognize it as a laugh.

"You find that question funny?" she asked, unwavering in her grip on the rifle.

I studied my apparent captor. She knelt behind the remains of an auspicious-looking desk. Her head covering was that of a nurse, but she faced me as a soldier: unwitting that a gunshot would not slow me.

"I do." My voice croaked; I could not recall the last time I'd spoken aloud. For her part, she waited patiently, gun steady, while I collected myself and warmed up my vocal chords. I finally finished, "Find your question funny."

The rise of her golden eyebrows demanded further explanation.

The interaction excited me in a way I had not felt for longer than a human lifetime. I *wanted* to speak with her, to communicate with the mind behind those sharp, sky-blue eyes that saw a monster—a massive construct of corpses with drowned eyes—and demand he explain his very existence.

I tried to better enunciate: "I find your question funny because you face me and request the one answer I cannot provide to even myself."

She squinted at me. "What is your business here?"

"The damage to this structure led me to conclude, incorrectly I see now, that it would be uninhabited and, therefore, a safe place to rest until this snowstorm passes." I gestured to the hole where snow fell upon the rucksack I'd dropped in before I'd descended.

Her deepened consternation suggested my response was not what she'd expected. "You are not Wehrmacht. That uniform you wear isn't yours."

I looked from her to the uniform that barely held together against my largeness. "No," I said. "I took it from the last person who aimed their gun at me."

The rifle barrel quivered, accompanied by a poorly hidden gasp.

"I have no need of women's clothes, so if you reposition your rifle away from me, I won't come any nearer while I rest." Though I was loathe to leave her company, rifle or not, I also offered, "Or I could find another building for shelter before I continue my own journey."

The nurse did not reposition her rifle. "And just where might your own journey be taking you?"

"Scotland." Thrills danced up my spine as our conversation continued. "I return to the Orkney Isles specifically."

"And what's your business in Scotland? What's in the Orkney Isles?"

"Very little but hovels. And the body of one who was promised to me." Did I intend to be coy in my answer? I could not honestly say, but the thought of our interaction ending had grown nearly as painful as a bullet wound.

"I'm sure there's more than that." She spoke with a sneer, but that did not deter me.

"Oh yes, there is. But that is a very long story, and it is tiring to stand here with my arms in the air." That was my first lie to the woman. The effort engaged in complying with her initial words did not tire me in the least; it was just an aggravation. "Would it so inconvenience you to put down your weapon?"

"It *would* so inconvenience me to allow you space to assault me. And even if you've the honor to not attack a woman, I couldn't allow a potential spy to 'carry on with his journey' to Scotland or wherever you may truly be going."

"You think I am a spy?" I was delighted with her accusation; did she really assume I was some ugly, oversized agent for other parties in this war?

Had she just allowed me that measure of personhood?

"I don't know what you are but one who casually confesses to the murder of my countryman and theft of his belongings."

I took a step closer, studying her face.

Her eyes were clearly focused as she moved her finger from alongside the barrel to the trigger. "I will shoot you. You would not be the first man I killed, nor even the second or third."

"And you would not be the first woman I killed, nor the second or third either. But I truly do not want to harm you." Bored with my submissive charade, I lunged.

Her shot was immediate and accurate. The bullet went straight through me. Were I human, my death would have been instant. Instead, I stumbled, slowed indeed, reeling in pain as my torn heart pumped blackened blood and fluid down my front and my back.

How I live through such mortal wounds, my creator's notes never revealed. I would shortly fall into a torpor to heal; I would be weakened and pained until I transfused more blood, ate, and drank fresh water. I had but moments to kill her or convince her to not abuse me in my coming unconsciousness.

Now horror crossed her face. And . . . awe. As I barely held myself erect before her, she reached as if to caress my wound. "How is this possible?" she asked.

I had neither wit nor strength to answer. More pertinently, the last moments of consciousness revealed her choice to face me was not entirely of courage or intrigue. Her foot and calf were crushed beneath a pile of rubble, hidden—along with a corpse of a soldier, likely the original owner of the rifle she'd just shot me with—behind the massive, ornate desk.

My final observation, as I slumped upon that space between us, was that she not once looked upon *me* with fear.

* * *

Ingrid runs marble-pink fingers over my new forearm and hand, this one nearly as pale as hers. She kisses the seam, still visible for its recentness. Her breath is heavy from our lovemaking, ragged from the cries I urged from her being. I am trembling as I lie in our bed, not recovered enough to evaluate if she indeed has more vigor than usual.

"Have you ever found me with child while I am in torpor?" she asks.

"No," I answer. "I could not have hidden such an event." After we share our marriage bed, we have always done a thorough examination of her body, including ultrasounds and X-rays of her internal torso. We would have seen such a development.

She snuggles against me, unflinching as her perfect breasts, now supple and soft, press against my sallow, rough skin. "Have you ever studied my reproductive system while I . . . was not awake?"

I scowl. Does she think I might violate her so while she was indisposed?!

But her visage holds no accusation, only curiosity that flashes to surprise and offense. "Do you *not* wish to have children with me?"

"I do," I assure. "I only never considered examining you while you were not awake to know what I was doing."

"Why not?" When I do not answer—I cannot explain why I find such an act repulsive—she adds, "I do not feel pain when I am in that state. I would not suffer any study."

I am still speechless. That we might have children—that she would have my children—the very thought brings indescribable euphoria. Yet that is not how I feel.

"If my awakeness does not last this time, do so. See if there is decay or damage to my reproductive organs; ensure your revitalizing alchemy has preserved those parts. And if you find any deformation or imperfection . . . " My beloved makes a face as if ill. "Some of the missions to steal our home have included women, no? See if any have parts in better condition. And if so, give them to me." Then, she adds, "But only so long as the woman *is* a good specimen. Do not give me the womb of a colored woman or a Jew."

I nod and kiss her forehead, though I feel emotions foreign to love.

She settles against me once more. "We should populate our domain with the most perfect children."

* * *

1944

I awoke from torpor between the woman who shot me and the corpse of the soldier she likely also shot. Upon finding her sleeping form against mine, I defied the aching sluggishness of temporary rigor mortis to pull away. Far enough that I might see if she had violated me beyond the gunshot wound.

I only managed cursory examination when her soft and ragged moan yanked back my attention. She sat up with similar rigid pain and stared at me. Bruised rings underlined cerulean eyes, which had grown paler, and she squinted, revealing crinkles of dehydration. "You live," she croaked through parched lips.

"In a manner," I said after a pause to keep my speech from slurring. "I do not die, in any case."

Cringing as she attempted to swallow, the woman looked between the dead man and me. "You cannot die?"

I shook my head. My heart beat beneath a scar fresher than the papery yellow skin of my chest. I found no evidence of either harm or healing by the nurse's hand and was relieved at the absence of both. Pressed with the weight of her gaze and the question hanging between us, I replied, "I have thus far found that to be true. And that is my business in the Orkney Isles; I return there in hopes of finding and executing my demise."

Her eyes widened in a shade of horror I did not comprehend. "Why *ever* would you do such a thing?"

I had no answer for her, or rather, I had too many. Disarrayed by physical discomfort, I could not assemble my thoughts.

A wild fervor fueled her words. "You have what all mankind seeks, what they aspire to, what they'd sacrifice their own gods to attain, and you seek its *demise*?"

Unable to validate my decided course of action, I pushed myself to my feet and limped toward my snow-coated rucksack. "I need food and water, and so do you—"

Feral laughter clawed from her mouth and darted through the ruins like a swarm of bats exposed to sun. I glanced up and out the hole outside, not eager to face any soldiers potentially within earshot; I perceived no life besides my cackling companion.

After the last rabid chuckle fluttered from her lips, she said, "Oh, my strange friend, I am well beyond what food and water can repair. Does your undying nose function? Can you not smell the putrescence spoiling me? Unless your bag also carries the secret of your immortality, you would waste your supplies to share them with me."

Little did she know how closely her words brushed against truth. But I was intent on my hallowed destruction. I retrieved my sack and sat nearer to her.

I did smell putrescence; I had become accustomed to its ever-present stench in this damned warzone. But she was right; it was stronger here—and it did not come from the dead soldier. The cold air of winter's lingering days had slowed his decomposition.

I studied her crushed leg. Infection's yellow pus soaked the deflated pulp within her stocking. No doubt gangrene stained her flesh with active death. I wished otherwise, but I knew the pain she bore. Even as I admired her fortitude in such agony, I envied her ability to end it.

I nodded to the rifle she still clutched. "Are you out of bullets? Perhaps the pistol still in his holster is loaded."

The contempt in her glare hit like a blow. "If Death should defeat me, its victory will not come by my surrender." She drew the gun closer as if she feared I would take it and hasten her enemy's triumph.

I drank from a canteen I'd pulled from my bag. The thirst in her eyes pulled upon my reconstituted heart and, I confess, excited me with a sense of power. I held the canteen within her reach and said, "Did you not just tell me it was a waste to give you food or water? How is that not surrender?"

She loosened her hold on the rifle to snatch the canteen. A peculiar sensation flitted from where our fingers nearly touched. Upon draining my canteen dry, crystal sharpness returned to her eyes. "And you . . . You did not contradict my wondering if you carried the secret to your immortality along with food and water. Or did I miss it in my delirium?"

I pulled a second canteen from my bag, the last I had, drinking half before passing it to her. My heart pounded in anticipation of that momentary nearness, rewarded with an even stronger flight of energy from my fingertips to my chest. I required a moment to compose myself before responding, "I have known you for only a short time, but you strike me as one who misses very little, even in the throes of delirium."

"And you strike me as one who knows Death well enough to be wise enough not to discard the treasure of conquering mortality."

When she handed back the canteens, our fingers brushed. I was overtaken by a shiver of that phantom palpation—a thing I had never experienced in all my abject existence: pure pleasure. Once more, my sentience was taxed to reply to her more sober observation. My dedication to my own unmaking was bewildered by the insemination and conception of this new emotion. To hide my violently tilting apperception, I studied the can of meat I pried open. "You have no idea of the wisdom I possess that contradicts your assumptions of any treasure immortality offers."

"Then enlighten me, my wise new friend," she said. This second address of me as a "friend" stole back my full attention. Having never seen such an expression directed at me, I did not recognize the seduction in her smile. "While you regain your strength for travel, while I continue my personal war against Death, tell me your story. But if you'd kindly indulge a woman fighting for her life . . . Allow me to offer you a delirious bargain?"

My heart shook with yet another new and foreign feeling. It was all I could do to not choke on two words. "I'm listening."

"If, when your tale is done, I still live and am unconvinced of your conclusion to destroy yourself . . . and if you do hold in your lap the secrets of immortality, give me the chance to discover for myself the wisdom you claim to have. Gift to me the treasure you would throw away! Let me learn its worthlessness by my own devices." Her eyes shone with the brightness reserved for the most holy and unholy—and the sun upon a world of snow and ice.

In that moment, I understood why my creator broke his promise and destroyed my intended mate. Here was one who would be my equal, my partner, asking me to give her—to *gift* her—my wretchedness, and here was I, hesitating, balking at such an absurd opportunity.

She understood my silence with perfect clarity. With keen intellect, she tempted with an eloquence Satan, himself, would envy. "I see a loneliness in you that would make angels cry. I imagine the existence of one with no equal . . . might invite despair to trick him into believing relief lies only in his own destruction. You said you were returning to Orkney . . . to the body of one promised to you. Did you once share this life with another? I have watched a soldier wounded, but not mortally, surrender to death upon hearing his fiancée had died. Is that what drives you to seek your end?"

From beneath her skewed nurse's cap, disheveled golden curls haloed a face of unspoken promise rivaling anything a devil might offer a starving messiah in a desert. Her words alone unmade me in a way no science or unholy alchemy could ever do.

As she spoke, she'd reached not for the food I offered, but for me. Unflinchingly—eagerly, even!—she clasped her hand over mine and transferred a vitality my creator failed to instill.

In that small affection, two epiphanies struck me with the acuity of Divine Truth.

First, nothing I said would deter her desire for that which I so despised in myself.

Second, I would dedicate my existence no longer to my destruction but to the fulfillment of her deepest desire.

I was ignorant to the spectrum of consequence inherent in such flashes of omniscience.

* * *

It nears a century's passage since I met my Ingrid in that bombed out building. Yet the days we have spent together in sentient wakefulness comprise but a few months.

My time interacting with other humans, those who wish to reclaim our haven, has eclipsed the time shared with my beloved. Though undying, I am not immutable—beyond replacing injured appendages. Beyond even the conflicts, some of which have sparked unexpected esteem for our assailants. I devour every piece of literature scavenged from their invasions. I listen to their audio recordings. I deconstruct and reconstruct their technology that I might master it. I dissect and study the ever-diverse collection of corpses, seeking that eternal spark my creator gave but did not record: That evades me to this day, thwarting my shared immortality with she who I love above all.

I am no longer the being she met during her Great War against Death.

The stasis holding her captive for but a few days each year has preserved her *self* as well as her body. She *is* the same person I reclaimed from the threshold of death.

After we examine Ingrid's body, particularly her reproductive organs, and find nothing deformed or decayed, we sit upon a couch in a common room and share stories we have not yet told during our brief reunions.

"Did I ever tell you how I happened to be in that building when you found me?" She leans against me as she delicately sips coffee.

"You were trapped under a collapsed ceiling."

When she raises a brow at me, I smile—my death-black lips line perfect teeth.

Unrepulsed by my mismatched grin, Ingrid laughs, seeing only my jest. "I was interviewing for a job. I'd be caring for children—strong examples of the best in humanity—who had been liberated from inferior families. I was to be part of a team to ensure their health and retrain them for placement with families of superior heritage."

A discomfort twists my intestines; my mirth fades. Something I cannot define feels *wrong.*

"Perhaps," she says, "if we discover our immortality doesn't allow for my reproductive abilities—or if we require extended time to unlock the secret of natural reproduction for ones such as ourselves . . . Perhaps we could do similar."

"'We could . . . do similar'?"

"Venture from here . . . find superior children with inferior families, and bring them into our home. Once you've perfected the science of your immortality, we could make them like us."

"'Make them like us . . . '" I eliminate agreement or discord from my tone with surgical precision; I fail to hide the nausea her suggestion affects in me.

As she silently turns her coffee cup in her hands, the betrayal on her face knifes at my heart.

I tuck a curl behind her ear. "I much prefer the thought of us creating our own children. Your beauty while pregnant, I imagine, would make Venus jealous."

A smile returns to her lips and she kisses my caressing fingers.

We have been denied the time to grow and change together, and I am only now seeing the consequence of that reality.

* * *

1944

My beloved died when I removed her gangrenous leg.

Or so I thought.

I employed all the tools and knowledge I'd collected to replace it with that of the dead soldier preserved by the cold. She awoke a day after the surgery. A day after that, she had mastery over the replaced limb.

She told me her name was Ingrid Schulz, and she had, in fact, killed the soldier whose leg she now wore.

"He wears the clothes of your countrymen," I remarked.

"A lie. My true countryman would not have propositioned me as he did."

While she gave me her name, I did not give mine. I'd long decided none fit me. She asked if she could call me "friend." Later that name became "beloved."

Ingrid convinced me go with her to one of the facilities where her countrymen practiced the "natural philosophy" my creator studied. Though disgusted by the doctor who had worked upon me before an audience, I agreed; my desire for her company overruled all else.

A week into our travel, signs of decay resurfaced in her leg, a development I had never experienced. She theorized that despite halted breathing and heartbeat, she had not entirely crossed the threshold of death, and that prevented complete integration of the foreign flesh.

Rather than test that theory with her death, she proposed we try alterations to Frankenstein's chemical proportions with a fresh appendage.

I was searching for supplies on the other side of a slaughtered encampment when I heard Ingrid call out. I ran, anxious her limb had failed. Or worse, I had failed in staving off her mortality. I found her enthusiastically enrobed in gore, holding a bone saw and a freshly harvested leg. The leg's former owner, a woman in a different nursing uniform, consciously convulsed, bound to a wooden stretcher.

"Hurry," Ingrid said. "Perhaps since I still live, if you attach this while she also breathes, our flesh will better integrate."

* * *

Ingrid and I dance to a song she remembers from her youth, found on one of the devices collected from trespassing humans. Impossibility courts my every sense: the salty-alkaline taste of her recently-kissed skin, the vanilla-lavender scent of her freshly washed hair, the pressure and movement of her body against mine, the music of her laughter mixing with lyrics of love, and the admiration—the affection—on her face when she looks upon me. *Me*: a daemon of corpses whose existence has driven men to madness.

This moment should be nothing but perfection, but I am unsettled with the physiology of indigestion from the prior day's discussion of stealing children.

When the song ends, she asks yesterday's other disturbing question: "Have you ever studied my reproductive organs when . . . I was not awake?"

The heartache draws at my face more clearly than words can convey. I have failed; dread poisons the little time we have left before I must end this awakening.

Her expression shatters in mirrored sentiment. She turns away as if ashamed, and her voice trembles around her words. "I'm forgetting again, aren't I?"

I embrace her and rest my lips on her head. Forgetfulness signifies her sentience deteriorating despite my efforts. She is dying again. Tears sting my eyes and nose.

She wraps her arms around me, turns, and kisses up my arm. "It's happened just now, no? Well into evening on our second day together? Nearly a day's improvement from last time! You *will* discover the secret to our everlasting romance. Fret not, my beloved." She kisses my face. "What burden is patience for those of us who are eternal?"

I meant to comfort her with my affection, yet she comforts me. How could this not be a more perfect love?

*   *   *

1944

Ingrid's theory of a still-living replacement proved false. But rotting limbs became an inconsequential concern.

My beloved Ingrid unquestionably died during an air raid near the Russian border.

I found her buried in debris, missing the entirety of her left arm. Her angelic face sagged, bereft any life. Not even a trickle of blood fell from the gaping hole at her shoulder.

I laid her body and a fresh arm upon an altar within the crumbled remains of a church. I employed every note and tool and combination thereof I'd found or stolen. With each day I failed to bring her back, depression devoured my life, save for the tortured awareness of her absence.

In that darkest moment of existence, my contemptuous faith swayed further toward the existence of a most cruel Divine Creator. From nowhere coalesced a storm of epic proportion, a maelstrom dwarfing every tempest of myth and literature. A lightning bolt struck the fallen church steeple and sent its charge racing chaotically over the area. Over Ingrid's body. Even I was stricken, incapacitated as flames sprouted along wooden beams and tapestries.

Ingrid's gasp resonated louder than the electrified church bells. I sprung to my feet, gathered her body—her supple and breathing body!—and carried her to safety.

We had but precious hours, our rekindled love undampened by the torrents of rain that broke from the heavens, before her mind began to slip and a deep fear painted her countenance.

Ingrid clutched my collar as if it were her salvation. "You—in your history, you-you said you awoke with no memory of who-who you were . . . before." She cupped my face and tapped my temple. "No idea who this brain, this face belonged to."

I shook my head and kissed her hand, pulling her close. My personality may have held fragments of the person that once carried the head I was given, but my sense of self felt entirely my own, distinct from the pieces that made me.

"I'm-I'm forgetting who I am, who I was," she sobbed. "I am losing myself. To be reborn and to not be *me*, is that not still my death?"

I had not considered that distinction, that potential when I bestowed my creator's alchemy upon her body. Would what I brought to life still be the woman I loved?

Would she still love me?

"You must solve this new challenge, my beloved. Please," she begged. "Find a way to immortalize *me* as well as my body. Promise me this?"

"I promise." I would have sworn anything to ease her distress.

She gave me a kiss of deepest sanctity. And she vowed: "Then I promise I am yours for all of my existence."

Rain couldn't camouflage my tears. "And I am yours."

We kissed once more with the consecration of matrimony. Then she unsheathed the knife I kept on my belt and pressed its hilt into my palm. "End me now, while I still remember who I am. Preserve my body, and do whatever you must to make real our eternity together. End me and awaken me until we have solved this."

Knife in hand, I froze at the enormity of what she asked—of the pledge I made. But her eyes were a lake of perfect trust.

By any Divine Creator that may exist, I would honor *this* covenant.

* * *

It is just past the dawn of what would be our fourth day, but we have begun the month of darkness. Our last day together held but a fleeting, final glimpse of daylight through an overcast sky.

Under shimmering darkness, my beloved Ingrid lay naked in the snow beneath me, unbothered by the sharp cold as I. More practical than romantic, we spend our final hours together outside to maintain her body and keep her blood from soiling our home.

"It is time," she whispers, caressing away my iced tears.

Her trembling shifts from the afterwaves of orgasm to the fear she displays only in these final moments. Though she faces it bravely, she has not developed an immunity to this plunge into the unknown. Will I keep my promise to revive her? Will some new obstacle prevent my success?

Will my time without her companionship bring back thoughts of my own demise?

I know she wonders these things; I do.

"I love you," she states. "My Victor." She has taken to calling me that in the past few years. If she has forgotten my disgust for that name, if she wants to make it a mantle of greatness, or if she references unfaltering faith in my subjugation of death, I do not know.

Being so named frees my hand to lift my knife. Perhaps *that* is her intent; this act has gotten no easier for me either.

"I love you, my wife." I kiss her and plunge my blade into her heart. Its cut aligns with the same incision I made just days ago.

After that first resurrection, I learned her heart, unlike mine, did not regenerate from mortal damage. I give her a new heart with every awakening, each treated with a different formulation of my creator's chemistry.

I carry her, as a husband carries his bride, over our home's threshold and into her chamber. I clean her, preserve her, dress her. I do not dissect her or study her reproductive organs; my nod to her request was not a promise.

As I seal the chamber, her absence sucks at my life like a vampire of myth, and I press my hand over my heart.

My own heart.

Is that my answer? My own heart that has beat for only her these years?

My mind calculates how I might maintain consciousness to split my own heart, preserve it while I heal . . . Would the half removed from me regenerate for her? The science of the challenge intrigues my consciousness, stealing the space of depression, loneliness, and doubt in my skills.

But new questions infect my intellectual meditations.

Will the sharing of my own heart change who she is? Who *is* the person I vowed to preserve?

Will it change who *I* am?

As the Divine Creator laughs in perverse paradox, I call upon Him:

Will I keep my promise of eternity to my beloved?

There is no 23:38 Westbound

by J. Edwin Buja

Ben Williams stood alone on the Columbia Street station platform. He was very drunk and feeling sorry for himself. Three hours at that uptown bar, seventy-five bucks on drinks, and the bitch had had the nerve to tell him she wasn't *that* type of girl. He'd watched while she went off in a huff, got her coat and left the place. Ben followed her for a while, determined to get what he'd paid for. However, after a couple of blocks he'd turned and made his way to the station. He'd be home soon with a video and a box of tissues; the easiest solution.

Now, he was cold, frustrated, and on the only underground platform, waiting for the next westbound train. The 23:30 had gone whistling by and disappeared into the tunnel as he stepped onto the platform. The next train wasn't until midnight.

He needed to pee and the station bathrooms were closed.

Things couldn't get any worse. Ben stood there feeling sorry for himself.

Five minutes later, Ben paced the length of the platform, desperate and considering ducking behind a vending machine to relieve himself. The security cameras were broken, hanging by wires from the ceiling. He wouldn't be seen and given another ticket for public lewdness. When you had to go....

Stepping around the machine, he was startled to see a sleeping homeless person, unconscious from booze or drugs, stinking of stale piss. No matter. He unzipped. The sleeper didn't rouse despite the hot stream adding to his stench.

Ben shook off the last drops and heard the unmistakeable sound of the next train pulling into the station. Getting everything back in place, he rushed to the edge of the platform thanking the powers that be for sending the midnight train early.

Really early. Like twenty-two minutes early. That was entirely unheard of in this town. If anything, the train should be twenty-two minutes late.

Ben tried not to breathe as the train entered the station preceded by a stink that made him throw up a little in his mouth. It was worse than that pissy bum. He spat out the acidic muck, waiting for the train to stop.

There was an engine, blue and filthy, pulling only two cars. The cars didn't look much better than the engine, dripping slime, covered with soot, with grimy windows.

Ben shrugged, stepped forward when the door slid open with a terrific whine and a burst of hot, foul air. None of the others opened. Whatever was going on with this dilapidated train, Ben needed to get home. He'd complain to the transit authority in the morning when he felt better.

The car was uncomfortably hot and the floors beyond sticky. He almost lost a shoe in some brown sludge. The benches looked as if a thousand homeless people had used them as toilets. The walls were covered with scratches and some kind of fuzzy green stuff. Ben thought it was moss. Strewn about the floor and seats were piles of torn rags with an occasional shoe in the mix, and a couple backpacks.

From somewhere came a throbbing beat, like a bassline heard above everything else when someone has their music turned up too loudly.

Dragging his feet further in, Ben spotted something white in the corner by the door connecting the next car.

It was a skull. A human skull.

"What the fuck?"

Ben turned to get off as the door closed and the train lurched forward. His shoes were completely stuck. Unable to move, he bent to untie the laces and stepped out of them. The moment his stockinged feet touched the floor, he felt intense burning. He tried to get away from it, but wherever he stepped, there was more heat and even more of the sticky stuff trying to hold him in place.

The lights winked out. The train had entered the tunnel.

In the pitch black, the pounding bass grew louder, the heat and stink more intense.

Ben pulled out his lighter and flicked it on.

He screamed and tried to die faster, but it still took far too long.

* * *

Ben was the first on this circuit. There were many more as the months passed.

* * *

Nothing connected the disappearances. Some were reported missing within hours. A few spent days unnoticed due to expected trips or absences. Those who were alone in the world or cut off from society were forgotten; no one cared about them anyway. However, the disappearance of some prominent, high-powered men and women, including the Mayor's brother-in-law and his mistress, soon attracted police attention.

Deeper investigation to bring all the facts together would have taken effort and resources. The main detectives, Conroy and Jensen, were conscientious, did their best, but were too busy chasing after a mad bomber to bother with some rich assholes.

* * *

Conroy hung up the phone, trying to remain calm. Goddamn Mayor's brother-in-law, Gerald, disappeared two weeks ago and the police were nowhere near finding out what happened. There were no clues other than some vague security footage of Gerald walking down the street from his office at 11:30 p.m.

Five minutes later, he was picked up entering the Columbia Street subway station. The station's security cameras had been vandalized the previous year and never been repaired. A local burn-out named Sketchy told Conroy he had seen Gerald and some woman board a train though he couldn't pin down the time. There was no evidence that Gerald got off anywhere along the line. Sketchy was regarded as an unreliable witness. He was strung out, kept talking about a horrible stink, and claimed the train arrived with three cars but left with four. After drying out for the night, Sketchy couldn't remember anything. And he reeked of piss.

No matter how much the Mayor demanded action, circumstances refused to cooperate and provide answers.

One of the junior detectives, Conroy didn't remember his name, handed him a sheet of paper then hurried away. The paper disappeared into the inside pocket of his jacket. Conroy tried to stifle the little twitch he got at the corner of his mouth whenever he got excited.

"Come on, Jensen," he said, pulling on his overcoat. "We have to go to some hick town to see a severed arm and a piece of ass."

* * *

Conroy didn't catch the name of the state trooper sitting next to him, didn't care. Across the table two filthy hikers fidgeted, Plunkett and Blackstone—their names mattered—both covered in mud. They stank like a sewer gone bad. Given what they had tried to pass off as their story, it didn't surprise Conroy that they were jittery.

Yesterday, they were brought into the ranger station, incoherent, dishevelled, and scared out of their minds. In the backpack of one was a bloody arm that seemed to have been torn from a man. In the other's backpack was a chunk of flesh later determined to be a male buttock.

When shown the arm and buttock, the men fouled themselves then fell to the floor babbling about a train. The ranger on duty locked the pair in separate closets—he feared they might do each other harm—and called the state troopers. The troopers took the men back to their barracks where they promptly threw them in cells while whatever they were on could wear off.

Meanwhile, one of the troopers recognized a tattoo on the arm and called the city police.

Whatever the hikers had taken, it didn't wear off, but by the next morning the men were able to speak with some degree of clarity.

"Tell it again. One more time because I'm too stupid to understand." Conroy smiled.

"Saw this train go by. People inside, I think," said Plunkett.

"Pressed up against the windows," added Blackstone. "They weren't moving, more like shadows. Sort of looked unhappy, you know, like they knew they were done for."

"Yeah, kind of given up. Hopeless. Know what I mean?"

"Are you sure?" asked Conroy. "You saw the people?"

The men looked at each other, shrugged. "Maybe. Not really," said Plunkett. "More of an impression."

Jensen quietly said, "Fucking junkies." Plunkett glared at him but said nothing.

"It went by so fast," said Blackstone. "It came out of nowhere. We didn't even hear it coming."

"Can you show me on the map where you saw this train?" The trooper laid a survey map on the table. The two studied it, pointed at a couple of places near the U.S.-Canadian border. Blackstone traced a line roughly south between a couple of villages no one had ever heard of, across a river, through a state park, then up the valley overlooked by the ranger station. They had been picked up running along the bank of a dry creek, panicked because they couldn't figure out how to get across despite the absence of water and the bridge fifty feet down the way.

"Here," said Blackstone, rapping his knuckle on the map on a valley in the middle of a large green space. "I think."

"No, no, it was more like here," said Plunkett pointing to a spot further east.

"It doesn't matter, gentlemen," said the trooper. "There aren't any railroads up that way. Are you sure you weren't closer to the big river?" He tapped the large river to the west that emptied into the Atlantic.

"Yes," they both said.

"The engine was blue and it pulled four passenger coaches."

"Stank like fuck."

"Yeah," said Blackstone. "Made me barf."

"All right, then," said Conroy. "How do you explain this?" He held up the plastic evidence bag containing the arm. "And this?" The bag with the buttock.

The hikers stared at each other. A white-faced Plunkett said, "They fell off the train. We found them in a ditch once it was gone."

"By the tracks," said Blackstone. "Could he have been run over by the train?"

"No trains there," said the trooper. "Not even abandoned tracks. The closest line is twenty miles away. Just trees and bears there. Maybe you saw a bear."

"I know the difference between a train and a fucking bear," said Blackstone.

Conroy slapped his hand on the table, startling everyone in the room. "None of that matters. Bear, train, ocean liner for all I care." He waved the bag of arm in front of the hikers. "How did you get hold of Gerald Watson's arm? Where's the rest of him? Where have you kept him for the last two weeks?"

The detectives got nowhere and returned to the city in time for some startling security camera footage.

* * *

An accident Friday night closed down the eastern line so passengers were directed to the Columbia Street station where they could catch a westbound train then transfer further up the line to the eastbound. By now the security cameras had been fixed, enabling the detectives to see all that transpired.

Everything was normal. The 23:30 pulled into Columbia Street, loaded up, and was gone in two minutes. About twenty people, many from the roller rink up the road that just closed for the night, milled about waiting for the next train: the midnight.

At 23:38, a train pulled into the station. From the reaction of the people on the platform, Conroy could tell there were a couple of things wrong. The train was early, causing lots of them to check their watches. Many covered their noses indicating some horrible smell had wafted into the station, probably pushed in from the tunnel by the approaching train.

The train itself was wrong. Instead of the standard yellow and green paint scheme, this one was blue. In addition, there was an engine pulling it. The tracks were supposed to be electrified, so no engine was necessary, only a car at the front with a driver. From what Conroy saw, this train had a driver though he looked odd. Only his head was silhouetted in the tiny cabin window by a red glow from within. The shadow head turned slowly to watch the passengers board. As it did, a shade on the window was pulled down then quickly raised. This happened a couple more times. The train departed.

Of the five cars behind the engine, only three opened their doors for the waiting passengers standing directly in front of them. The cars were unusual, too. Rather than being covered with graffiti, these were relatively blank. That is, the paint scheme, again blue not yellow and green, was visible through trails of black stuff that ran down the sides from the roof. The windows were either opaque or covered with grime. There was no sign of movement within any of the cars. Even after the crowd boarded; nothing but vague shadows behind the windows.

The passengers rushed on board, though a few held back, no doubt due to the stink. However, they were suddenly drawn in. Conroy couldn't be sure, but when he watched the footage in slow-motion, it looked like shadowy arms reached out and pulled the reluctant passengers on board. The moment the platform was clear, the doors started to close. The train was already moving.

Just as the third car entered the tunnel, an arm reached through one of the not-quite-shut doors and tried to grasp at something.

Cameras at Division Road, the next station up the line, caught the train as it blasted past the empty platform. Somehow, it had gained another car. Upon its arrival at Ogden Towers, the penultimate stop on the line, the train let on six people waiting on the platform. Their reaction seemed to be the same as the other passengers: surprise and repulsion by an awful smell. It must have been bad because the station was at ground level, in the open air, rather than underground. Five people stepped forward to board. The sixth stayed back then turned to walk away. Something shadowy, like an arm, reached out, grabbed the retreating man and pulled him on board. As before, the train departed before the doors had closed all the way.

No one got off at the station. No one got off at the end of the line, Terminal Road.

The passage of the midnight train proceeded as normal.

Conroy and Jensen hurried down to the Columbia Street station to look for clues. They had screen captures of as many of the passengers as they could get from the footage. These were passed out to uniforms who had the job of doing a door knock at all the businesses and bars within a five block radius of the station.

Nothing at Columbia gave any hint that something unusual had occurred. Other than a residual smell that reminded Conroy of the meat-packing plant where he once investigated a murder, there was no indication that the strange train had passed through the previous night. Remembering the supposed arm that had reached out as the train entered the tunnel, Conroy sent Jensen down to the tracks to see if there was anything around.

Jensen didn't move. "Why me? Why not one of the uniforms?"

"Because I don't trust them to see what's important. They're uniforms, not trained detectives."

"Why don't you do it?"

"New suit," said Conroy though it was obvious the suit was anything but new.

"But there's a live track down there. I could get fried."

"Then step carefully," said Conroy as if he meant it. He didn't.

"Asshole," said Jensen as if he was joking. He wasn't.

Careful to avoid the live rail, Jensen crept towards the tunnel, clearly nervous about approaching the dark. He pulled out a flashlight. Immediately he saw something white next to the outer rail. Bending closer, he got startled and fell back, almost tripping and landing on the live rail.

"Did you find something?"

"You better get down here, Conroy. You're gonna wanna see this."

Careful not to get any station grime on his clothes, Conroy climbed down to the rails. When he saw what his partner had found, he said, "Son of a bitch. Another one. You coulda just told me."

"Thought you'd want to see it for yourself." Jensen shrugged then smiled like he was being friendly. He wasn't.

* * *

For five nights, Jensen drew the short straw that had him sitting on the Columbia Street platform from ten until one in the morning. Nothing unusual happened. The trains arrived on time—okay, that was unusual—no body parts were found, no one new was reported missing, though word on the street had it that some of the homeless from a nearby shelter hadn't been seen for weeks. Investigation revealed that they had disappeared around the time as Gerald Watson.

On the sixth night, one of the junior detectives drew surveillance duty. His backup was too slow to save him.

The backup had been in the station office watching the monitors. When the 23:38 pulled in, he watched his partner step up to the open door of the sixth car and peer in. He had been instructed to observe, not get on the train. Something pulled him on and the train departed before his backup arrived. At Ogden Towers, two stops up the line, a couple of drunken university students stumbled onto the train. Before the door closed, someone dove through and crashed to the platform floor. Something dark reached out from the door but couldn't find the escaped passenger. The train left the station.

Arriving at the scene, the police discovered that the escapee, now deceased, was burned beyond recognition. However, he did have a service pistol in a charred shoulder holster. Until the medical examiner could confirm it, it was assumed this was the detective from Columbia Street.

At the morgue, Conroy was not pleased when the M.E. assured him that the burned body was that of detective Wilberforce. As far as could be determined, he had been burned over his entire body by some kind of acid. Presumably, only his force of will enabled him to escape. Wilberforce was probably dead when he hit the concrete.

The next morning, the precinct briefing room was abuzz with talk about the deaths and the mysterious train. The crowd fell silent when Conroy entered the room. He didn't acknowledge any of those present.

"Now, last night, detective . . . " he looked down at the paper on the podium in front of him, "Wilberforce was killed on the 23:38 westbound train by a person or persons unknown. We know of at least two other people killed by these animals and there's no doubt that at least fifteen more people have gone missing after boarding that particular train."

"Is there any security footage showing the suspects?" asked someone from the back of the room.

Conroy shook his head. "No. The train doesn't appear on the footage of the station before Columbia, Preston Avenue. We do have footage of the train at the end of the line, but instead of stopping like all the regular trains, this one keeps going and vanishes into the tunnel out to the freight yards. Again, no cameras. The transit people seem to think the train joins the line somewhere before Columbia Street and exits somewhere further up the line on the old tracks. They haven't been able to find anything to indicate where or how this occurs."

"What about that arm found in the woods by those hikers?"

Scratching his neck, Conroy said, "Yeah. We still don't know how it got there and the hikers are sticking to their bullshit story about a train in the middle of nowhere." He pulled down a map then picked up a pointer. "Here's what's happening tonight. We'll have men on both sides of the platforms from Preston to Terminal. Except Columbia because the east- and west-bound tracks are in different tunnels." He traced the route on the map. "Extra cameras have been set up to give us a better view. A couple are positioned so we can see inside the cars and the engine cabin.

We've also got a chopper ready to follow the train if it exits the tunnel anywhere beyond Terminal Road, though we've had no reports of any train sightings out there."

"Where will you be?"

"I'll be watching at the Terminal Road office ready to go up in a chopper if necessary. Jensen will be boarding the train at Columbia."

"What? Since when?" Jensen stood. He looked horrified. "Why me? I got a wife."

Conroy raised an eyebrow, "I trust you to do the right thing. Don't worry. You'll be wired and have a bodycam. A SWAT team will board with you. If anything happens, we'll know about it."

"That makes me feel better. You'll know when I'm being killed."

Conroy said nothing but smiled at his partner as if he cared. He didn't. After instructions were handed out, he said, "Now, go home, get some rest, and be back here at nine-thirty. We'll be in our positions by ten."

* * *

Conroy sat in the Terminal Road station office, monitors arrayed before him. Four showed the Columbia Street station. Preston Street, Division Road, Ogden Towers, and Terminal Road had one each. There were also several with direct feeds from the police body cams. Sound had been set up for all the security cameras. A chopper waited in the Terminal parking lot to chase after the train if it didn't stop. There were also a couple of state cruisers out in the county where the tracks ended in the freight yards, about three miles past the tunnel exit. He didn't expect them to be needed.

Jensen and thirty members of the SWAT team paced about nervously on the Columbia platform. Jensen had tried to get reassigned, but Conroy wanted him there. If there was going to be any trouble, he knew he could rely on his partner to do the right thing. Plus, if anything went bad, Jensen's hot wife would need consoling.

The whistle of a train signalled its arrival at the station. Everyone froze. It was the 23:30 as had been reported by the men at Preston Avenue. The train stopped, a couple of passengers got off, were questioned by the police then let go. Nothing unusual. The train continued to Ogden Towers where it took a spur line into the nearby yard to await its next run in the morning.

At exactly 23:38, another train approached Columbia. This time there wasn't as much of a whistle from the air being pushed ahead. It was more of a heavy sigh backed by a steady pulsing boom. There had been no notification from Preston. Conroy wondered where the hell it joined the line. There were no branch lines between Preston and Columbia. The men on the platform tensed. The SWAT team pointed their guns at the spot where the train would stop, ready to blast anything that made a wrong move.

Jensen put a handkerchief to his nose to mask the stink as the train entered the station. This was the one. The train stopped and doors opened on all seven passenger cars. No one moved. On one of the monitors, Conroy watched the engineer behind the translucent cabin window. The more he stared at it, the more the window looked like an eye, with the engineer's shadow being the pupil. It appeared to be looking down at the men on the platform.

Something in Conroy's gut told him this was wrong and the men shouldn't board the train. Just let it go and stop it further down the line where no one could get hurt. Then he thought about Jensen's wife in that bikini she wore to the barbecue last summer.

With cries of, "Police, don't move!" Jensen and the SWAT team stormed the train. The moment the men set foot in the cars, they opened fire. As the last man boarded, the car doors began to close. One of the SWAT team guys dove for the platform and was caught half way by the doors. His upper torso and arms hit the platform and rolled away from the train in a spray of blood.

Body cam footage showed little more than confusion. Everything was tinted bright red. Conroy saw men running onto the train then stopping when their boots became mired in something. Most of them opened fire though it was impossible to see what they were trying to hit. All Conroy saw were vague shadows and several masses of matter that seemed to expand from the car walls. The gunfire muffled incoherent screams and shouts. A few of the men were engulfed by a black form that cut off their camera feeds.

Jensen's voice cut through the mayhem. "For fuck's sake, get us out of here . . . it burns! Oh, fuck, it hurts. Shoot it, shoot it. Run! Get out." He went silent for a few seconds as the train departed. The last thing Conroy heard from Jensen was, " . . . eating me!"

The moment the SWAT team had boarded, Conroy had ordered the men at the other stations to get ready. Once the train had fully left Columbia Street, he instructed the Division Road team to "Stop that fucking thing. Do whatever you have to." He had the pilot start up the chopper. At the very least, it would put some distance between him and…whatever this was.

All the body cams had gone dark. A few snippets of sound came through, but they were garbled. What he could hear was crunching and a kind of crackling, like bacon sizzling in a frying pan.

At Division Road, men waited on both the westbound and eastbound platforms. When the train pulled to a stop, doors on both sides of all eight cars slid open. Before anyone could move, black tendrils shot out, wrapped around the men, and pulled them screaming onto the train. Blood spurted everywhere. The train quickly left the station.

"Ogden Towers, stay the fuck back from the train if it stops. But blast the hell out of it if it does." Conroy stood watching the video feed from Ogden. His men were well-back from the edge of the platforms. The train blew through without stopping. Conroy could have sworn that supposed eye on the engine looked up at him and winked. He was hyped up and jazzed, letting his imagination run wild. Also, it looked like there were now nine cars. The tunnel speed monitors showed the train travelling far in excess of the allowed limit and getting faster. When it hit the curve before Terminal, it would likely jump the track.

"Cut the power to the third rail!"

The bureaucrat behind him said, "We can't. It'll shut down the whole system."

"Too bad. Stop that damned train." Conroy's hand went to his shoulder holster. He wouldn't really shoot if the man disobeyed him, but he wanted to scare him. At a signal from his superior, the engineer threw the switch. The monitors showed the train hadn't slowed.

"It's not going to stop," said Conroy. "I'll be on the chopper."

He ran out of the building, leapt aboard the chopper, buckled himself in, then felt his stomach flip as the machine lurched into the air. Through the mic, he said to the pilot, "Get me to the tunnel exit. I want to see where that thing goes."

A minute later, the chopper hovered over the highway that ran parallel to the tracks between the tunnel exit and the end of the line. Its spotlight lit up the black hole in the side of the hill. The train raced out of the tunnel without slowing in the slightest. At that speed, there was no way it would be able to stop before it ran out of track.

The chopper followed.

To Conroy, the train looked cleaner. The slime that had been oozing down from the roofs of the cars was gone. Even the engine seemed to shine in the spotlight. He tried to count the number of passengers cars, but he kept getting confused when the train passed under trees. At last count, he thought there were ten.

In the distance, Conroy spotted the flashing lights of the state cruisers. Things would get ugly now because the train would leave the tracks and crash into the trees or down one of the ravines nearby. The butterflies in his stomach flapped in anticipation of the carnage.

The chopper sped ahead of the train, so it was over the end of the tracks when the train hit them. The idiot state troopers had parked their cruisers just beyond the buffer stops. Conroy didn't think the buffers could possibly do their job and stop the train.

He was right. The train smashed through the buffers, careened off the tracks and shot through the cruisers, sending them and the troopers flying. Though it happened quickly, Conroy thought he saw a couple of shadows shoot out from the train and latch onto the airborne cops to pull them aboard.

The train didn't crash. Instead, it continued into the trees.

The chopper followed.

They lost the train for a few miles, though were able to follow its route due to the movement of the trees as it passed. When they caught up to the end of the train, Conroy couldn't believe his eyes. The thing was barrelling along tracks which seemed to curl up and flow into the end of the final car. Behind, there was no sign that they had ever existed. Swooping to the front of the train, it was clear it was not following any regular set of tracks. They spewed from front of the engine about thirty feet then hit the ground, allowing the train to move. As if on a conveyor belt of instant tracks that ran through the train. A way to travel wherever it wished. The sight of the silver rails and ties exiting the engine made Conroy think of a spider spinning silk.

Checking with the pilot, he knew they were getting close to where the two hikers had found Gerald Watson's arm.

The train broke through the trees into a small river valley. There were open fields on either side, so Conroy had a clear view of the train. It was blue, with an engine and ten passenger cars. There wasn't a spot of dirt or grime on it. The windows were now clear, but he could see no movement. There were silhouettes in the shape of people in some. It looked like a couple of SWAT helmets were halfway through the glass. Flying low near the engine, Conroy almost had a heart attack when one of the windows on the engine's cab looked up at him for a second. It blinked then stared ahead again.

At the far end of the valley, just visible in the light of the full moon was a large cave at the base of the mountain from which the river flowed. The train was heading straight for it, spewing track along the valley floor as it went.

"I'm going ahead, will hover near that cave," said the pilot. "I am seeing what's going on down there, right? No tracks?"

"Yeah. Don't ask me. I don't understand what the fuck is going on."

The chopper flew ahead then settled a little to the right of the cave, sixty feet in the air. The train charged ahead, aimed directly at the cave mouth. Fifty feet before the entrance, it veered off to the right and rode up the side of the mountain towards the chopper.

"Fuck," said the pilot. He tried to swing away.

Conroy looked down as the train left its track and flew into the air straight for them. The cabin's window eyes looked right at him. The front of the engine split apart to reveal a gaping maw lined with teeth dripping with red saliva. Steam poured out of a couple of vents on either side of the *mouth*.

The last thing Conroy felt was the burning sensation as the acidic saliva dissolved his flesh. He wished it didn't take so long to kill him.

* * *

On the other side of the mountain at 6:39 in the morning, seven minutes early, a blue school bus emerged from the forest where there was no road. It bounced across a field then found the dirt road that led to a farm down the way. In the distance, three children waited for their last ride to school.

The Thing in the Window
by D.E. Ladd

Protect me…

Dana Langstrom had long suspected that the object before her wasn't as lifeless as it appeared. A chilling sense of dread and danger flowed through her as she stared at it. She clutched herself as if a bitter arctic wind swept through the room. Chilled by the realization that she was a prisoner to this house, to her husband Bruce, and most of all, to the thing in the window. Despite the opulent surroundings that included Queen Anne furniture, sparkling crystal and silver, fine paintings, sculptures, oriental rugs, and all the other valuable items Bruce had collected over the years, Dana felt as though the house were a tomb that gave rent to snakes, spiders, and the restless souls of the dead.

The human-sized metal ornament hung over the window rigid in place. Like so many other valuables, it waited for one to notice it, to comment on how unique it was, how ancient, how intriguing. No one could possibly see beneath the deceptive veil that hid its true purpose. Even Dana could not see beneath it. She knew one didn't have to *see* evil to be aware of it. She wondered briefly what the victims saw, if anything, when it sprang upon them. The visions conjured of blood and madness were more disturbing than the thing itself. She turned away, hoping that when she turned back around again, it would be gone forever.

* * *

With Jimi Hendrix belting out "Purple Haze" over the radio to announce Janice Harper's arrival, her early-model Jeep CJ-7 pulled up to the house and came to a screeching halt inches from a jade-green Mercedes. Janice's long dark hair settled over her back and shoulders. Her round sunglasses reflected the four white pillars in front of her. Behind the mirrored lenses, her dark-brown eyes grew wide with disbelief. She stepped from the Jeep, pausing to take a long look at the house. She dug into her pocket and pulled out her phone to confirm the address.

"Seventy-One Fourteen White Brook. Shit. This is *it*?" Janice removed her glasses for an unobstructed view of the mansion. It looked more like a Roman palace with its high white columns and vaulted front porch.

She grabbed her camera and ambled along the driveway. Mouth agape, she clipped her sunglasses to her shirt pocket and approached the front steps.

"My god, Dana. You said you married well, but *this*..."

Janice felt out of place before the mammoth house, but it made her appreciate her simpler life, her strong bond with nature, and the open places where she felt most at home. She grinned and rang the doorbell, removing the lens cap from her Canon (which cost her more than her Jeep) and waited for the door to open. She wondered if a butler would answer.

The door opened, and Janice fired off a burst of five shots.

It was Dana, not a butler. Janice lowered her camera and blinked at her friend. "Dana? Oh my god. You look great!"

Dana smiled and the two old friends embraced for the first time in almost eight years, way back when they graduated from college. Her friend's embrace felt anxious—frightened. Dana was trembling ever so slightly, and Janice didn't think it had anything to do with joy. She had always been sensitive to such things in others. In Dana's case, she never missed.

After a few moments, Janice pulled away to give her friend a thorough going-over. Dana looked no different than she had eight years ago, except that her odd yet stylish chocolate-vanilla hair had grown to be shoulder length. But Janice saw fear in her eyes, a terrible storm of purplish-black clouds revealing a bitter tempest of dark secrets.

"What's wrong?"

"What?" Dana sounded defensive.

"I said, what's wrong?" Janice's face didn't flinch when she spoke.

Dana's face wrinkled into a more convincing smile.

Janice asked, "What? Why are you smiling?"

"Even after eight years, you still think you have this sixth sense about me." Dana grinned.

"So, what's wrong?" Janice persisted.

"Oh shit, Jan, it's...nothing, okay? Marital stuff, you know?"

"No, actually I don't." She rested a hand on Dana's shoulder and gave it a gentle squeeze.

"He's always out of the country, his job and all. I don't want to talk about that right now. Come on in, and tell me about *you*!"

Janice gave Dana a suspicious look and followed her inside, gazing about at the fancy décor all around. The inside looked as ancient and extravagant as the exterior, with tall white pillars, a floor of imported tile (off-white with a green border), large chandeliers with crystals that sent colored rays of afternoon sunlight flying about the room, and fancy furniture Janice had only ever seen in history books.

"I went to an attraction in Trieste last year, this huge castle, and it had these huge—" Janice stopped in midsentence as she rounded the corner.

Over one of the tall windows at the end of the hall hung something alluring yet repulsive, the likes of which she had never seen.

"Whoa!" Janice gasped and looked at Dana. "What is *that*?" She crept closer toward it as if stalking a wild animal, adjusting her camera to capture the exotic thing on film.

"Um, Jan—"

"This is incredible. It's like a giant rusty hood ornament." Janice aimed her camera at it.

"Janice, no! Please don't take any pictures of it." Dana forced a smile, and let out a nervous laugh.

Janice lowered her camera and faced her. "Why not?"

"It—it belongs to Bruce…and he doesn't like—"

"C'mon, Dana. It's not like I'm gonna duplicate it or anything," Janice said.

"I know, but…just *don't*," Dana whispered.

Dana stood transfixed on the thing in the window. She clutched at herself as if she were cold. A single tear ran down her puffy cheek.

Janice approached Dana the way a lioness approaches her cub. A spark of anger flickered within her deep brown eyes—an anger she had used before to protect her friend.

"Is he hitting you?" Janice's bottom lip flared outward, the way it did when she was angry.

Back when they were in college, a boy got Dana drunk and tried to rape her. Janice found out about it. She beat the attacker with such ferocity it took three campus guards to pull her off him.

Dana smiled. "No, it's not—"

"Is he fucking *hitting* you?" Janice's raised voice reverberated off the walls.

It was as if they were back in the dorm room, Dana's lip split open, her shirt torn, tears in her eyes…

"He's not hitting me. I wouldn't put up with that. Not after all you've taught me." Dana touched Janice on the arm.

Janice read Dana the way she did anyone when sniffing out the truth. They fell silent and Janice's piercing stare wandered around the room.

She noticed several small security cameras high on the walls, angled at different spots. When she looked back to Dana she was staring at the long window and the thing spread across it, fear and loathing in her soft blue eyes.

Janice followed Dana's gaze. The ornament she had found intriguing moments earlier became something else. Janice found herself blaming it, hating it, and not knowing why. Made from iron rods, rusted from moisture and time, bent at various angles to form the rough shape of a man. The arms were raised above its head and its legs were bowed outward as if it were riding an invisible horse. The hands resembled round, mitten-like things with four chubby fingers each. The feet were crude boots cut from thick plates of steel, and its head was a circular frame adorned with a crown of sharp fins. Another small group of fins sprouted on each hip like deformed little wings. Faint, ancient symbols had been etched into the flat bits of metal—the hands and feet, and the little wings. The thing appeared to be a more artistic alternative to security bars designed to keep burglars out. The presence of only one, on a single window might seem strange if her husband hadn't been a collector of antiques.

Janice cast a glance back toward Dana. Another tear rolled down the slope of her high cheek. Their eyes met.

"Let's go outside, okay?" Dana whispered.

Janice glanced up toward the ceiling at the small cameras pointed down at various parts of the room. Not surprising given the pricey furnishings. She took a step closer to Dana.

"Dana, what's the matter—"

"Outside. Please?"

She led Janice outside through a pair of French doors, onto a large deck, and then into a yard greener than a golf course and almost as big. A trail of white stones led to a pair of benches. Large maple trees swayed and hissed in the spring breeze. They each sat on a bench and faced each other. Dana's stare remained locked on the house.

Janice watched her with anticipation. "What's the matter, Dana?"

Dana flashed her a nervous smile.

"I'm sorry. We had to come out here. I didn't want it to hear us," Dana said.

Janice leaned forward with a dumbfounded look. She glanced at the house and bit at her bottom lip. "Didn't want…*what* to hear us, honey?"

"The thing. In the window. You saw it."

Janice smiled and nodded—Dana was playing a joke on her.

"Oh yeah, those *things* are notorious for eavesdropping. Gotta watch what you say around 'em. Yep, can never be too careful—"

"Jan, I'm serious. I didn't want it to hear us. It isn't safe."

Dana's expression gave no indication she was joking. A disheartening feeling clutched at Janice's heart. Her dear Dana, whom she loved for her innocence, compassion, and kindness, had become . . . *confused.* She steeled herself and drew a deep breath. The situation demanded her trademark levelheaded strength.

"What do you mean? It can *hear* you?" Her voice didn't come out strong—she sounded anxious and scared.

Dana sat up on the bench and looked Janice in the eyes. "That thing has murdered three people, Jan. Three people. Maybe more."

Janice had no idea how to respond. She knew Dana. She definitely wasn't joking. Janice looked at the ground then back up at her friend. There were no words for a conversation like this. To find them was madness itself.

"The first guy was a burglar—at least that's what he *seemed*," Dana said. She took out a cigarette from somewhere, placed it in her mouth, and lit it with a shiny silver lighter. She took a drag and exhaled. "Cops found him on the floor right beside it. Throat slashed. Christ, it was horrible. They said he was trying to escape after hearing Bruce coming down the stairs, which is bullshit. I heard that poor bastard being murdered. Feet scraping against the floor, gasping, and then a tiny yelp. I heard it all. But before that . . . Bruce whispered something. What the hell was it?" Dana flicked ash off her cigarette. A troubled smile drifted across her face.

Janice stared with wonder and confusion at the woman beside her, for she suddenly had no idea who she was.

Dana took another drag off her cigarette and exhaled. "Damn thing'll be after me next. It's got it in for me. I know it. I think it knows I suspect something." She dropped her cigarette and crushed it out with her foot.

Janice leaned over and pressed a hand over Dana's. "I think you should, you know, *talk* to someone about this." The insanity she'd just listened to rang in her ears.

"What do you think I'm *doing*? I'm talking to *you*." Dana scowled at her.

"No, honey, I mean someone who's . . . *qualified*."

Dana pulled her hands away and narrowed her eyes. "*Qualified*? What the fuck does *that* mean?"

"Well . . . like a doctor maybe—"

Dana jumped up from her seat. "Fuck that! Why do you think I asked *you* here, Jan? Why do you think *you're* here? Don't you think I know what a doctor would say? I'm not crazy, but if I stay here with that thing much longer..." Tears spilled from her eyes. She covered her mouth and sobbed. "I can't *leave*. It'll follow me."

Janice stood up, went over, and held Dana as she cried.

"Okay. Okay, honey. I'm sorry."

Dana wiped the tears from her eyes. "I'm all right." She sat back down, and Janice sat beside her. No matter how insane the whole thing was, how impossible Dana's claims, she had to listen.

"Go ahead, honey. I'm listening." Janice kept her tone down, as if too loud a voice might shatter what remained of her friend.

Dana snapped her fingers and pointed at Janice. "'*Protect me*,' that's what Bruce said."

"Protect me?"

"Yeah, before the *alleged* burglar was killed. That's what Bruce said. I remember now. He whispered it, and then he went downstairs. I'll never forget the look on that poor bastard's face—that icy stare as if..." Dana sniffled.

Janice said nothing.

Dana wiped her nose. "The next guy was an acquaintance of Bruce's. The minute they found his body among the wreckage of his car, I was suspicious. I hadn't really convinced myself of what had happened the first time, you know? The second guy's name was Ecker. Phil Ecker, I think. He was always on Bruce's mind. Ecker this, Ecker that. He'd toss in his sleep. He'd spit his name in anger all the time. He never said it, but I think Ecker had something on him. I guess Bruce decided life would be easier without the guy, so the thing got rid of him. The police came to ask me questions. Actually, they wanted Bruce, but he was in Germany at the time the guy was killed, so I guess he had a damn good alibi. Bruce had apparently threatened Ecker in front of others. The reason the cops came had something to do with the injuries Ecker sustained—far worse than those typically caused by an auto accident. They said they had to identify him by fingerprints since his face was so torn up."

Dana's gaze remained fixed on the house. Janice wondered if she really expected the thing to be peering around the corner, the faceless frame of a head looking at them and listening intently to her accusations.

"Bruce brought that damn thing back with him from South America. He bought it from an antique dealer who insisted it was a genuine Aztec relic. The guy called it Espixkitl." Dana spelled it out. "I can't remember what it means."

Janice's gaze remained fixed on her friend. "Espixkitl," she repeated.

"Yeah. The guy who sold it to him said it would protect him. I remember him telling me that much. He didn't tell me what he paid for it. I guess that doesn't really matter..."

Dana's voice flowed with a disturbing tranquility.

"Dana?"

No response. She had a glazed look of complete absence, staring at the window where the thing hung like a horrible iron spider.

"Dana!" Janice shook her.

Dana looked at Janice in a daze. "What?"

"You said there were three, right?"

"Three what? Oh, yeah. Three. Yeah, that's right."

"Who was the third?" Janice held Dana's hand, and she became more attentive.

"It was the saddest of the three, really. She was a student at NC State, studying to be a nurse. Pretty girl. That was the night I came home and found it gone. Bruce had left on business again. I came home from an art class I was taking, and the window was bare. I was so relieved. I thought, *Oh good, he took that ugly, cursed thing with him to sell it.* Then later that night, I was awakened by noises. I still don't know how it got back into the house, but I heard it walking across the floor. It sounded like squeaky hinges. I thought maybe it was the rainstorm outside, or I was overtired from entertaining all these crazy thoughts. I was too scared to investigate, so I pretended it was all in my head. I convinced myself of it.

"The next morning, I went downstairs to get a cup of coffee and . . . when I saw the thing hanging there, like it had been for the past two months, I felt a part of me escape. And I wanted to laugh. I felt as if . . . I had lost a battle in the war for reality. If this thing can walk around and murder people, I don't know where I fit in anymore…" Dana's voice trailed away. The same glazed-over look returned.

Janice squeezed Dana's hand and gave her a little shake. "It's okay, honey. I believe you. You hear me? I believe you." Janice forced Dana to look into her eyes before embracing her.

In truth, she actually believed Dana was mentally ill and needed serious help. At that moment, Janice suffered one of those rare occasions where she had no idea what to do. It wasn't enough to stop her from trying.

* * *

After doing her best to stabilize Dana, the two of them talked about their childhood and college days, how much fun they had had, how bad the music was today, how good it was then. They talked of Janice's photography, Dana's painting, and generally anything but what they had discussed earlier. After more than an hour, they headed back inside.

Dana had returned to her normal self. All Janice could do was force a smile and feel terrible about it. It was as if the two of them were playing a game—college buddies against the metal eyesore over the window. The objective was to see whether they could fool it.

A few minutes later, Dana dashed off up the stairs, wearing a strained smile that made Janice shudder.

"I'll be right back," she called from the halfway point on the stairs. "I have to get my sketches or my instructor will be *pissed*."

While Dana rummaged around upstairs, Janice remained below, peering up the staircase. With stealth and speed, she stepped over to the thing in the window and took aim with her camera.

"All right, you iron bastard…" She clicked off two shots. "I guess I'm going to have to get me a blowtorch"—she snapped off two more shots—"cut you up, and drop you into five different oceans so you'll leave my friend alone." Janice clicked off two more shots. She studied the rusty metallic figure and shook her head. "Jesus, Dana. What the hell am I gonna do with you?"

Hearing footsteps on the stairs, she stepped back to where she'd been before.

"Sorry I have to go to class tonight. We can get together later if you want. Bruce is leaving for New Orleans this evening, so maybe we can do something then." Her face still hinted at something terrible going on behind her eyes. She hid it well.

What about her husband? Janice wondered. Did he have any idea how delusional Dana was? Did he know she was walking around talking of strange things like moving window ornaments and murder? And now she was running off to an art class, as if nothing were out of the ordinary.

"Is that okay?" Dana asked as she moved toward the front door.

Janice followed her, suddenly noticing that the house even smelled old—like a private antique store in the twilight zone.

"Yeah, sure." Janice crossed the threshold. The warmth of the day tried to bring normalcy with its common sounds: cars passing by, a jet overhead, wind and birds, a buzzing lawn mower across the street . . . But a gray veil obstructed Janice's view of how she understood normalcy.

"Call me around eight-thirty, okay? We'll have all night together." Dana opened her arms. When they embraced, she whispered softly, "Don't tell anyone about what we talked about, okay?"

Janice had a terrifying thought: *Is Dana the one responsible for—*

"I promise." Janice pulled away and looked at her. "You gonna be okay?"

Dana nodded and smiled. "I don't know if I can stay here another night. I might stay with a friend in town."

"You wanna stay with me?" Janice asked. "You should stay with me. I want you to, really. I've got plenty of room."

Dana played with her hair. "Where are you staying?"

"Old Pond Road. I'm renting a cabin out there."

"That might be nice," Dana said.

"We'll talk about it later. I'll text you the directions, okay?"

Dana responded with a faint smile and a nod. "Okay."

After a few moments of heavy silence, Janice embraced her with more urgency than she had when she had first seen her. Although she never said it, she wanted Dana to know that after all the years of writing, of talking on the phone, and through those four years of college together, that deep down, Janice needed her just as much.

* * *

Janice drove on the twisting road back to the lake where she had rented a cabin for the week. She thought about her conversation with Dana, and it scared the hell out of her.

She turned off onto a dirt road, went up a steep grade between two tall pines, and came to a stop before the cabin. The front was mostly windows and faced the west, offering a clear view of the lake as the sun set. The water rippled like a sheet of undefined, sparkling color, stretched loosely over a restless pocket of air.

She entered the cabin, tossed her keys onto the table, and paused for a moment, thinking of how best to proceed. Her boss, Stewart Tristan, had found the cabin for her a week before she had arrived. Stewart was resourceful, and he always told her she could call if ever she needed anything.

Before talking herself out of it, Janice dug out her phone and dialed.

"Hello," a soft voice said on the other end.

"Stewart? It's Janice."

"Oh. Hi, Jan. How's everything at the cabin?"

"Great, I love it. Listen, I need a favor."

Janice explained her dilemma.

"Is she going to be all right, for the night I mean? Is she safe to be alone?" Stewart asked.

"She'll probably be staying with me for the night. After she's done with her art class. She's gonna call me later, so she won't be alone."

Stewart clucked his tongue. "Does her husband know about this?"

"Good question. He's not around much apparently, so I couldn't say."

"Did she actually *see* this thing move?" Stewart sounded worried.

"No, she didn't actually say she saw it move. It seems more like paranoia to me. *Extreme* paranoia, but still . . . I think she needs someone to unload on, and possibly some meds. I'm not really qualified to say."

"As long as she's not seeing things move, I think she'll be okay. A lot of times it's just a matter of proper medication," Stewart said.

"She didn't seem that bad to me. But I gotta tell you, it scared me to listen to her. And . . . she comes from an abusive family. She was almost raped in college. She's had a few rough spots in her life. That might be part of what's causing this." Janice picked up her camera and fiddled around with it.

"That makes sense. I'll make the call first thing in the morning and ask him to get in touch with you first."

"Thanks a lot, Stewart. Really." Janice exhaled with relief and hung up.

She checked her watch and headed for the basement.

Fishing nets decorated the walls. Rods and reels stood in the corners—a network of cobwebs strung between them. One small light dangled beneath a green metal shade, its faint orange glow barely enough for her to find her way around. Janice entered a smaller room she'd converted into a temporary studio. The radio was tuned to the only place on the dial it received worth a damn—an oldies station—and the main section of the basement echoed with "The Tracks of My Tears."

Janice popped the camera's SD card into her laptop and started processing the RAW files. There were over three hundred shots of several different landscapes, another hundred urban shots, a few of Dana, and finally, six of…*it.* She analyzed the digital negatives with a trained eye, squinting at the last one she had taken of the thing in the window.

"What the hell is *that*?" It didn't look like a smudge or a lens flare, which made her wonder if it could be a problem with her camera or the two-thousand-dollar lens. She magnified the first image of six, which only showed the metal ornament over the window. She looked at the second image and the next shots. Then it appeared—a reddish cloud encircling it. Janice remembered saying things to it. *Threats.* She looked at the last image again. The red cloud bent and twisted into sharp, barb-like fingers all over it.

She leaned away from her laptop and licked her bottom lip. The sixth image stared back at her, the burst of red ruining the shot. She looked down at her camera then back at the image on her screen.

"What is that shit?"

No explanation came to mind. She mentally backtracked to her conversation with Dana.

"Espixkitl…" she muttered. She opened a browser window on her laptop and searched for the word. Nothing came up. Until she found an Aztec-to-English translator. She typed the name in and—

"Blood guardian." Her gaze drifted up over the laptop screen and she stared at the wall. "The hell is that supposed to mean?" She searched the phrase and only found a single entry:

> In Aztec lore, a *blood guardian* refers to a wood or stone carving, a sculpture made of various loose materials, or a forged metal figurine created and blessed to protect the owner. It was believed that certain

rituals could animate these objects, allowing them to move on their own.

Janice read the paragraph three times before letting out a short laugh. She shook her head and sighed. "Christ, I need a drink."

She got up and headed for the stairs. Buddy Holly sang about something getting closer on the radio as she made her ascent.

As Janice neared the top of the stairs, she wondered if her camera's sensor was failing already. The thought enraged her, as the camera was only a few years old. Granted, she wasn't the gentlest person with her camera, but still. It was a Canon; they had a reputation for being tough.

She pushed the wooden basement door open and padded toward the kitchen. On the polished hardwood floor before her, a pinkish-orange glow radiated. The sun had begun its retreat into the lake, leaving behind a soft, reddish sky.

Janice figured if her camera wasn't broken there was no explanation for the red glow around the sixth image. Dirty sensors or lenses or lens flares didn't produce isolated artifacts like that. Even though she knew it wasn't, the sharp edges and subtle glow reminded her of an *aura.*

A noise from behind her.

The sound of creaking metal.

Janice froze. She didn't want to turn around.

There was a kind of leaden certainty in what she heard. Reaching for the shotgun in the corner to her left crossed her mind. Her skin broke out with tingles. She thought over and over again, *This isn't happening. This isn't happening. This isn't happening,* which quickly mutated into, *Oh my god! Oh my god! Oh my god!*

A familiar sound arose behind her.

Squeaky hinges. Metal rubbing metal. Metal bending. *Moving.* Right behind her. She heard a scream in her head to run. But her feet wouldn't budge.

A spiky shadow moved on the floor behind her.

Janice made a dash to her right, snatched the shotgun from the corner, and spun around.

Her entire body felt as if it were burning in icy flames.

It stood there in front of her—the thing from the window. It twitched ever so slightly, like a giant metal wasp deciding whether or not to attack.

Janice aimed the shotgun at it. It twitched again and took a creaking step toward her.

She let go with both barrels. Most of the pellets went through the frame. It staggered only slightly before starting toward her again.

"C'mon, you fucker." Janice dropped the shotgun and grabbed an old double-bitted axe from the wall. She swung hard and drove the iron thing into the wall. She tried to dart past it to the front door. One of its metal hands sprang out and knocked her backward. Janice hopped back up. Before she could make another dash for the exit, the thing sprang upright again. It squeaked its way across the floor toward her.

Janice's nostrils flared. She gripped the axe and stood her ground.

"C'mon!"

It charged her.

Janice swung the axe again and missed. She hit the kitchen cabinet instead, burying the blade deep. The thing knocked her to the floor with one of its chubby-looking hands. She staggered to her feet. A rusted-iron hand grabbed her face from behind and closed around her nose and mouth. The smell of metal choked her. As she flailed and tried to scream, it squeezed her face like a vise, crushing it. A coldness pierced her neck. She looked down and saw a metal fin protruding from her throat.

It was the last thing she saw.

The iron hands gave a twist. The sound of wet cracking bone rang out.

Janice's limp body fell to the floor.

* * *

Nighttime settled in, saturating the sky and the ground beneath with deepening shadows. Dana turned into the driveway, her headlights sweeping away the dark to reveal Bruce's Range Rover parked in its usual place. He was supposed to be gone to New Orleans by now. Dana calmed herself and took a few deep breaths. All she had to do was put together a small bag and leave. He wouldn't care. Staying with Jan, that's all she had to say. She composed herself and exited the car.

Poker face.

Upon entering the house, she saw a faint yellowish light around the corner. Bruce's whistling echoed off the walls.

Dana crept along the tile floor without making a sound. She passed all the familiar antiques, their shadows looking like silent spectators to a strange ceremony. As she rounded the corner and her eyes fell upon Bruce, her purse slipped out of her limp hand. The keys made a little *ching* sound as the bag hit the floor.

Crouched at the base of the thing in the window, Bruce turned and faced her with a smile. He held a bloody sponge in his right hand. A bucket of pink soapy water sat on the floor beside him. The thing was bloody in places. Pink soapsuds ran down its arms and right leg.

"Oh. Hi, honey." Bruce spoke as if he had been caught doing something relatively innocent—snitching a cookie before dinner. "I suppose you want an explanation."

His eyes fixed upon her and flashed like green gems, his features distorted and wrong in the dim light. The crooked smile he wore was like a flame beneath Dana's feet, bubbling a scream to the surface.

She backed away. It had happened again. She stared dumbly at Bruce, who stood there holding the bloody sponge.

"It's about time you knew. Or did you know already? You suspected something, didn't you?" He pointed at her and laughed. "Don't be afraid. It won't hurt you." He approached her with his hands out to his sides, as if to stop Dana from running away.

"It protects me." He said this as if it explained everything. His white teeth stood out in the heavy shadows. Several dark strands of his hair clung to his forehead, pasted there by the sweat of his labors. He was washing it off in the same manner one might wash their car or a dog. The thought lingered in Dana's mind, skipping like a damaged record each time she tried to make sense of it.

He's washing off the blood. Washing it off. Washing it off.

Dana stared at the thing's twisted iron curves, its jagged points, some of which remained crusted with blood.

"It couldn't be helped," Bruce said. "I'm sorry, Dana. I know she was your friend." He took another step toward her.

Dana's legs threatened to buckle beneath her. Shock muzzled her screams, though her lips quivered and tears flowed.

Janice. No. No. No-no-no-no…

Bruce pointed up at the security cameras near the ceiling. "Your friend said some nasty things. I'm not as good at reading lips as I used to be, but that doesn't matter. I *heard* what she said. Through *this*." He gestured toward the thing. "The espixkitl protects me. I guess it's a part of me now. It can protect you too."

Dana backed up against the stairs that led to the second floor. She couldn't take her eyes off the thing in the window. She expected to see it move. But it hung there motionless, rigid as a cemetery gate.

Bruce closed in on her. "Come here, Dana darling. Ask it to protect you and then watch what it does!" He reached for her.

Dana's scream erupted at last. Bruce grabbed her by the arms. She wrestled against him and slammed her left knee into his crotch. He bent over groaning as Dana raced up the stairs. He grabbed at her ankle and she kicked herself free.

Tears blurred her vision as she reached the top of the stairs.

She dashed into their bedroom, slammed and locked the door behind her. Eyes wide with terror, she backed away from the door and fell against the bed.

She dug her phone out of her back pocket and dialed 911. A female operator came on the line. "Nine-one-one emergency?"

"Help me! Please God, help me!"

"Calm down, ma'am. What's the problem?"

"My husband's gonna kill me! He's gonna kill me! Please God, help me!" Dana screamed.

A rapid series of thuds arose on the stairs—like a small, excited child running up them. The sound of bending, squeaking metal echoed between the walls. It stopped just outside the bedroom door.

Dana's mouth worked and her words came out in a jumbled scream. "Oh my god, it's here. Help me, God. It's outside the door! Help me. Help me!"

The door rattled. Heavy metallic thuds shook it in its frame. A twang of metal filled the room.

Dana dropped her phone and covered her ears as the bedroom door splintered and gave way to rusted metal blades. The door fell apart in large pieces. The thing tore an oblong hole out of the middle.

A round frame of a head with sharp fins along the top and no face peered in at her. The metallic arm tore at the wood until it could reach the knob.

Dana screamed as the 911 operator kept talking. "Ma'am? Ma'am, are you there?"

The thing burst through the door and charged at her. A strange *pong, pong, pong* noise echoed throughout the room—the vibration of the metal as it ran.

It *ran.*

And it looked funny running at her.

It must have been extremely funny because she was laughing hysterically as it closed in on her with its arms raised and then it lowered its head and the sharp fins were pointing right at her and it was coming and coming and coming and then a metal hand grabbed her throat and she couldn't breathe and then it lowered its head again like a bull and then it—

Rusty metal blades plunged into her chest.

Her eyes remained opened…

But the life in them faded…

Slowly and evenly…

Like a delicate snowflake…

Melting on warm human skin.

* * *

Inside the cramped interrogation room, Lieutenant Cribb loomed over Bruce like a grizzly. He leaned down and slammed his big palms on the table.

"Okay, Mr. Langstrom, you want to add anything to your bullshit story? Or are we supposed to believe that your ugly wall ornament is responsible for the mess we found at your place tonight?" Cribb stood up and rubbed the grayish-brown whiskers on his chin. He circled the table and raised his eyebrows as he looked down at Bruce. "Well?"

Bruce remained disturbingly calm. He looked up at Cribb's round face, grinned, and said nothing. He raised his hands, joined by handcuffs, rubbed his right eye, and shuffled his legs—joined by ankle chains. Two detectives stood by the door, a tall and thin black man in a dark-blue suit, and a slightly shorter man with blond hair in a tweed jacket with wire-rim glasses. They both scowled at Bruce as if he were a foul stench polluting the air.

Bruce smiled at them.

"I don't see what's so funny, asshole," the blond cop said. "Your sick ass is headin' for death row. Then *I'll* be the one doin' the laughing—me and the families of the people you butchered."

"I'm sure our boy knows exactly where he's headed." The black lieutenant gave Bruce a cold stare.

"So, what about it?" Cribb asked. "We got you at the crime scene with this . . . *thing* covered in blood, your wife's body, plus three other murders we think you had something to do with. The name Ecker ring a bell? How about Janice Harper? We found her body an hour ago. Janice was a good friend of Dana's, but you probably knew that." Cribb leaned in close to whisper, "Was she on to something? Hmm? The other murders maybe?"

Bruce ignored him.

"I think she was. Then there's the unsolved murder of Tracy Clemens, the student you had an affair with. She was found mangled almost a month ago. Just tell me this: How the hell did you wield that thing around?" Cribb stared at Bruce and rubbed his whiskers.

Bruce remained silent.

Cribb held his hands out to his sides. "You got nothin' to say? We got you pegged. We got that freaky metal thing in the evidence room down the hall, and we sure as hell—"

"Protect me," Bruce whispered.

The three detectives looked at each other. The two by the door started laughing.

"*Protect* you?" Cribb chuckled. "I don't think anyone could protect you now. I don't think anyone'll *want* to."

Half a minute later, a strange noise seeped in from the other side of the door. It grew louder and sounded as if it were getting closer.

It sounded a lot like squeaky hinges coming down the hall.

Keep On Trucking

by Daniel R. Robichaud

Devon led the way and the shivering little girl followed. They must've made quite a sight, a fifty-eight-year-old black man leading a four-year-old white girl along the snowy woods, following the roadside as it twisted across the Maine countryside. The snow was picking up again, winds howling around them, drawing the snowflakes round and round in tiny cyclones. The sub-freezing temperatures made exposed skin burn, of course, but it also wormed up sleeves and down necklines. Devon's furry hood served as one big collector, and he was grateful when the wind finally tugged it down. It had been dusk when the wreck happened, not that you could tell since the snow and sky bounced light around, casting everything in dull shades of twilight gloom. The child's sneakers shimmered with little lights at every step, tiny LEDs nested behind star shapes made dancing glows on the mounds of snow. Her arms shook every time the wind blew, but they shook harder when it didn't.

"I want my Mommy," she wailed, trying to pull her arm out of his grip.

"I'm sorry," Devon said. "But she gone. I'm all you got."

"I want my Daddy." Was she even four?

The girl was a slip of a thing, just over three feet tall and slim. Some bright red mittens kept her fingers safe from the cold, and a knit cap with dangling pink and red pom poms did the same for her crown. Otherwise she was not dressed for the weather, wearing only a sweatshirt and those damned sneakers. Should've had on snow boots and a heavy jacket. They might've been in the car, of course, cast aside because of a reliance on the vehicle's heater. Parents sometimes did dumb things from a place of love.

Devon, on the other hand, stood six foot even in his socks, so he was twice her size in his thick soled winter boots. His parka was not heavy, but it was insulated, bulky as hell. In another world, he might've passed it to her, keep the child from getting frostbit. This was not that world. "Move it, girl."

"Don't want to move."

He twisted her arm and she wailed, but he let up when she moved faster, her sneakers kicking through the fresh mounds of snow.

She sniffled. "You hurt me."

"I'm sorry," he said. "We got three, four miles to go. Can't be shuffling along." When he'd stopped off at the rest stop for a piss, there'd been some talk about closing it down early. He hoped that wasn't the case. Hoped they did not make it to the place just in time for the lights to dim and the last car gone.

No one was coming along the road, which was as good and bad. Devon knew what would happen if a squad car found them. He suspected what might happen if some civilian's car came along—they'd be on the horn to the Staties, and a cruiser would swing on by to harass under the guise of "ascertaining the situation."

"Mistah," she said, slowing down again. "Want my Mommy."

"I told you—"

"I cold. I tiiiired. Want Mommy. Want Daddy."

"Damn it, child. I'm cold too. We got to walk, though. So move your feet—"

"No." She jerked her hand both out of her mitten and out of his grip and slammed her fist and remaining glove against her waist, screaming, "Want Mommy!" just as shrill as she could.

"She dead," he snapped. "Your Daddy dead, too. If you don't want to be like them, then you move your little butt."

The wind howled around them, forcing a flurry of fresh snow into their faces, then something in the woods answered that howl.

"Shit," he muttered. "Damn it. *Shit.*" Devon looked at the little girl in her peach-colored sweatshirt, her snow pants, and her useless little sneakers. Dead weight. Thirty-nine pounds of anchor holding him back while that thing in the woods spirited after them.

When they snuck off, the humanoid creature with the red glowing eyes was glutting itself on the remains in the jackknifed sixteen-wheeler, and it would be heading toward the little SUV where the parents were dazed or dead in the front seat, and the little girl whispered their names in the back. Apparently, the truck driver and the couple were not enough to sate it, because it was coming this way.

"Shit. Damn it. *Shit.*"

She heard it, and shook all over again, pleading for Mommy or Daddy to come take her away, but they were dead. Had to be dead. It would have sniffed them out after it was done dipping its terrible snout in the truck driver's gut, done eating his sweetbreads. He could leave her alone out here, his mind told him, but in his heart he knew better.

Devon grabbed the girl's arm again and yanked her after him. She tried to keep up, and slipped on the slush and fell to the ground. Without thinking, he hefted her up by one arm and dragged her close to his chest. He moved as quickly as he dared, trying not to end up on his ass. If he did that, they would both be dead.

Devon Armbruster did not want to die in Maine. He wanted to die back in Florida, where it was nice and sunny. Sure, the Gold Coast saw hurricanes every year, but at least there weren't any weirdo monster motherfuckers eating traffic accident victims.

He made it a dozen steps before he stepped wrong and his foot twisted hard in one of the ways it should not have. Devon let out a shrill screech of pain and the girl screamed, too. The wind huffed around them, laughing. The thing in the woods laughed, too. It was closing in just as fast as you please. It was coming much faster than *Devon* pleased.

"Keep on," he muttered, finding his footing. Damn if the ankle didn't hurt, though. Nothing broken. Just a pull, a sprain. "Keep on trucking."

His drill sergeant, the copper-complexioned Anthony Jefferson, hammered those words into his skull at every formation, every forced march, every possible opportunity when Devon was young, fat bellied, fatter headed, and damned foolish enough to enlist in basic training.

"Keep on trucking, slim. Or you gonna to die in a combat zone." There weren't any combat zones in 1985, of course. Short of conflicts in areas few Americans could pronounce or even point to on a map, there wouldn't be any major action until Kuwait and Operation Desert Storm in 1990, almost nine months after he mustered out. Army service was not his deal. It gave him access to the GI Bill, though, and that made his years of service worth a little something more than three squares and modest paycheck. Still, that was the excuse Sgt. Jefferson offered him: "Life is short enough anyway. Don't lose yourself precious days, hours, or minutes for lack of hauling ass."

Even now, almost forty years on, he still found himself giving the expected servile response; was there such a thing as verbal muscle memory? If so, then *"Sir, yes, sir,"* was one of those phrases that got locked inside a former soldier's head. And yet, those words—*keep on trucking*—were a powerful and efficient mantra, perfect all those years back for keeping the young Devon on the trail with his fellow idiots and then focused on his college goals, later on. Those words even kept him on the straight and narrow marriage path when temptation reared its often slutty gorgeous head. Now, they guided him forward through the snow.

Keep on trucking. A damned silly phrase born out of the CB obsessed seventies, given major national play by stupid damned television and less than stellar movies. Nothing about the phrase made sense when a man was on his feet instead of behind the wheel, but there it was anyway. *Keep on trucking, Devon. Don't let yourself get dead for lack of hauling ass.*

In the trees, those howls grew closer. As they did, he could hear the scratching sounds and the shushing of branches bending under a sudden weight and then losing it. The sound of monkeys in trees, motion through brachiation. Whatever that funky little critter with the lambent eyes was, it was making time on them by skipping the overland route and moving through the branches. Relentless sucker.

The girl heard it and she murmured something that sounded like "when it go?" and he answered, "I hope it never gets here." She shook against him, huddled into a tight little ball. "When it go? Daddy say it was. When it go."

"*Wendigo*," he said. It was a name he knew from some show that was popular back when he was in college. *The X-files*, maybe. She shuddered and yeah, that was probably the name her Daddy used. So, he must've been coherent before Devon reached their SUV. Devon assumed they were rattled on impact. True, he wasn't thinking straight with the sight of that thing filling its belly with a dead man's sweetbreads. He saw the kid, and an old sense of duty kicked into gear, and he knew what he had to do. He left the service, but the service never left him, funny enough.

On he trucked, pushing through the snow. The howling turned into cackles, which sent shivers up and down his spine. This was what coyotes were supposed to do to you, right?

"I see him," the girl said, freaking out. "I see him!"

There was a sudden change in sounds. The tree limbs shushing turned brittle. A trio of gunshot-loud reports preceded the crash of something heavy into the nearby snowbanks. No more howling. Luck, it seemed, was on his side for a change. How often did that happen?

If this was a ton of good luck, then maybe the creature broke its damn neck. Most likely it was just dazed and would be along directly.

Devon stepped further from the roadside embankment into the middle of that space where the snow was thinner and the danger far greater from a speeding tourist who was riding without tire chains.

Some of his previous fears proved baseless. The rest stop's lights were not off. He saw them blazing through the Douglas firs in this stretch of the woods.

"We getting there, kiddo. We getting safe."

She was shaking, crying.

"Can you walk?"

She didn't want to, but he convinced her to try.

Getting closer. He praised Jesus, Mohammad, and the Buddha, too. Hoped the parking lot was not empty. It would be a hell of thing, making it this far to find no positive change to their situation. As they closed in, however, there was a situation he never counted on.

When he'd left this joint on his fateful way, the rest stop's windows weren't smashed in. There had been people finishing steaming cups of coffee or overpriced burgers and fries. There had been gentle bitching about the weather and honest concerns about what was to come.

Since then, everything changed. Now, there were busted windows. Snow heaped atop tables near the shattered panes. There were still sipping, munching shapes inside, but no gentle bitching, no concerns about travel or weather.

Devon realized he was a damned fool to think there was just the one cannibal monster motherfucker. There were more of them inside the rest stop, driven nuts by the wind and the snow and the heavenly disturbance. They were not sitting nice and neat at the tables, but they were still visible from the lot, their heads poking up as they chewed, thoughtfully gibbering to one another or howling like crazy demons.

Now, at least, he could see them better. Wished he didn't when he did.

The figures were humanoid. A head atop a rail-skinny body. Their skin was a mottled pale color, not dissimilar to week-old snow. Fine hairs covered them all over, darkest atop their heads and tending toward pale whites or grays elsewhere. All the better for tricking human prey into letting them get close enough to strike. Their mouths were a mess of teeth, and their eyes were not glowing all over, only where the whites should be. The irises and pupils were big and dark, reflecting the lights the way some nocturnal predators' eyes did. Eyeshine, he remembered that being called.

Shit, he thought. *Damn it. Shit.*

What were they supposed to do now? There was no safety here. This had been the goal, but it was just another disappointment.

The trucks. They had their own parking lot, of course, massive spaces designed for the big rigs hauling covered and uncovered cargo. This was the side they came into. One of those sixteen wheelers was making soft grumbling sounds in the night, engine running while its driver was off taking a leak or something. No way he (or she or they!) would be coming back now, not if one of those creepy little devils got hold of him (or her or them!).

But this could be the ticket one fifty-eight-year-old black man and one four-year-old white girl needed. Devon hustled toward the grumbling rig. The snow crunching under his feet was louder, now. Sound carried up to his ears as loud as gunshots. Any second, he expected a chorus of howls to erupt from the rest stop followed by a rush of shapes bursting through the broken windows in search of warmer prey.

Devon made it to the truck before that happened. The operator was not taking a leak. The blood along the side of the rig told him that much.

Someone might have been parking and getting ready to do so, maybe waiting for a passenger to come back, but they were gone now. The big goodbye-type gone. Dragged off toward the woods, from the look of things.

Devon hesitated before yanking on the door handle, wondering if one of those things might be inside, waiting to spring. Options were limited and fading fast. The girl was coughing, now, hand over her mouth to catch the bad germs. If it got any louder, their position would be blown. Now or never.

He pulled, and the door swung wide. Nothing came out at him but blessed warm air. A light mounted in the ceiling clicked on.

What the crunching of boots on snow had not accomplished, the light on the roof did. Howls erupted from the rest stop, followed by a flurry of movement. He shoved the girl in, ordering her to scoot over. He pulled himself up and slammed the door. The light turned out, but it was too late to stem the tide. Through the rig's windshield, he saw the horde coming, little shapes darting out and around the trucks in the way. He hit the lock on his door, leaned over to do the same for hers. She was already on it, though. Hitting the lock with those angry red fingers of hers.

He knew enough about trucks to know they would not drive like a car. Not quite. There were steps to get them going proper, multiple brakes to disengage. This one was hauling big tree trunks, and he really did not want those suckers to end up smashing their way into the cab.

Of course, he didn't want those creepy little suckers coming in, either.

He killed the brakes and jammed a foot on the gas and hoped for the best.

It was all he could do, what his drill sergeant told him: keep on trucking. Keep looking forward. He didn't want to die in a combat zone for lack of hauling ass. Win or lose, he would not lose precious days, hours or minutes for lack of trying. No sir, no thanks. He'd been fighting for every inch of ground he'd taken in his life. He didn't know anything *but* fighting.

He prayed whatever magic or weird science these creatures used to wreck that big rig back in the woods took too much time to employ right now. Devon prayed that he and the little girl could get just a little further down the line, far enough to live. What would happen then? No way to know. He grinned as they passed by the back of the restaurant, a little horde of shapes following after. Fast and relentless but neither as fast nor as unstoppable as this Detroit motor.

The wheels spun, then. Loud grinding sounds. Black ice or wendigo magic? Either way: *Shit. Damn it. Shit.*

"Don't let them eat meeeee," the little girl wailed. The scream that surrounded this was the perfect sound for either breaking concentration or making ears bleed.

Then, his truck's wheels found ice-free asphalt. *Thank you, Jesus, Mohammad, and the Buddha, too.* He considered giving the little fuckers a toot of the air horn, a final flip of the middle finger. Decided against it. No reason to tempt fate to flip him off back.

"Hold on, chile," he said before taking them along the next leg of their journey through a snowy Maine winter wonderland.

It Whispers in My Brain

by Peter N. Dudar

"Do you like it, Daddy?"

Brian Weaver was standing in front of the refrigerator, staring at the new artwork precariously held in place by alphabet magnets. The picture was bigger than her normal sketches, which she usually did on paper highjacked from the ink-jet printer in her mother's business office. All while his wife, Maggie, dealt with clients over her Bluetooth headset. The quarantine from the pandemic was in its eleventh month now, and Maggie was the only one bringing in money. Brian lost his job at the warehouse over the previous summer; another hapless victim of Covid-19 as Templeton-Andrews announced "aggressive restructuring" to mitigate the financial freefall the pandemic created. They didn't even fire him in person—instead sending a text message on a warm July morning that read, "Don't bother coming to work, Human Resources will be in touch to arrange your severance package."

Jeannie's artwork was the only cause for him to smile nowadays. And although he was pleased with her crayon rendition of their modest colonial on Booker Street—the lawn and the shrubs on either side of the door covered with new-fallen snow, with the strands of colored lights that they hadn't actually turned on since the first week of January—his eyes kept returning to the telephone pole the nine-year-old had included. The pole actually sat across the street, in front of the Crossman house, with a streetlamp arching out over Booker Street on an arm that made Brian think of an emperor in those old gladiator movies, giving the thumbs-down for a soldier not worthy of mercy. Jeannie had even gotten the lamp's arm right, and that *did* make Brian smile. It was the weird-looking *thing* perched on top of the pole that gave him pause. It looked like…a wounded crow, perhaps? Whatever it was, it was short and squat and looked almost paranoid, its beady red eyes laser-focused downward as if suspicious of what might be watching it. Rather than two legs protruding from its pelvis, there were *three*, only they weren't *really* legs—more like three snakes coiled around the top of the pole and the crossbeams where the power lines met their contact grounds leading to and from its sister poles up and down the block.

"Honey, is this supposed to be some kind of bird?"

"I don't know. I saw it when I was walking Brownie before my Zoom class started." Of course, along with his job being cut, the local elementary school was reduced to "remote learning," which meant home-schooling online, followed by a few hours of reading and ditto sheets printed off Maggie's computer before *Weaver's Insurance Company* officially opened office hours for the day. "It tried to talk to me."

"It . . . talked to you?"

Jeannie's cheeks flushed. "Not out loud with words or anything. It talked inside my head. It said it wanted us to be friends. I told it that I'm not allowed to talk to strangers. It gave me the creeps. Brownie barked at it and scratched at the pole, and I had to drag her back to the house and give her a treat to make her stop." *At least she's doing just like we told her,* he thought, wanting to dismiss this all as just part of his child's active imagination. And even if it were, he knew he'd still have to look at that wicked little creature every time he opened the fridge.

"Is it still there now?" Brian looked at his watch. It was pushing two o'clock in the afternoon. Maggie still had three more hours of answering calls and activating insurance claims before she could take off her headset and join them for dinner. It took some time after getting laid off for Brian to get used to the idea of helping get their daughter prepared for school, and handling the cooking and cleaning while his wife ran her business—her *successful* business—and kept them afloat. It seemed other families up and down their street were still suffering financial difficulties so Brian felt he shouldn't complain.

"I don't know," she answered, her cherubic face squinched tight as if trying hard to remember. "I think it goes away when the sun comes out."

"Well, let's go look!" Brian took his daughter by the hand and led her from the kitchen, through the dining and living rooms to the front door. He unlocked and threw it open, and both of them glanced across the street at the pole.

The crest was empty.

* * *

He'd forgotten all about the thing on the telephone pole by the time he'd set the dinner table and hollered up the stairs to where Maggie's office was situated, letting her know dinner was ready. She'd only come down once since he and Jeannie discussed her artwork; and that was to grab an apple to snack on and bump the thermostat up a few degrees. It was just one of the many conflicts in the Weaver house that he knew he was never going to win. Here it was, the first week of February and another snowstorm was about to blow in from the northwest. The house was a comfortable sixty-five degrees—comfy if she'd just relent and put on a sweater so the furnace wasn't kicking on every five minutes—but now, if he complained, she could retort that if it was a problem, he could find a temp job that paid a *little* more money than what he was getting from unemployment. Even when they bought the house, she'd had her petty squabbles that nearly drove him mad.

Maggie came downstairs and sauntered into the dining room, taking a moment to stop and sniff the aroma of their dinner as if she'd just entered the fanciest restaurant in the state.

"Oh, spaghetti and meatballs! It smells fantastic." She stood and watched silently as Jeannie slipped the napkins and silverware around each place setting, and then scooched into her seat. Brian watched his wife drag her chair out from the table and seat herself. She hadn't even bothered to remove her Bluetooth headset before leaving her office for the evening. It sat upon her long, golden hair like a cheap tin barrette, the microphone pulled upward along her cheek so that the tip nested just beside her left eye. It made her look like her lips were saluting, which rankled him. When she sat down, Brownie crept into the dining room and laid down beside her, waiting for her to secretly drop some scraps when Brian wasn't looking.

It occurred to him that things were no longer okay between them. Perhaps, being under quarantine and unemployed for this long was making him refocus on their relationship. Things were a lot worse between them than he'd originally thought. *We're together in the same house all the time, and yet we act like we're polite strangers rather than husband and wife.* The thought lingered as he watched her across the table from him, and he found himself wondering where it came from.

It felt like an alien voice was whispering inside his head, telling him these things. Exposing what should have been obvious.

"Has it started snowing yet?" Maggie picked up the bowl of spaghetti and meatballs and set it beside her plate. She used the pasta fork to scoop some onto her dish, and then placed the bowl back into the center of the table. "Oh, and do we have any merlot? Some red wine would go wonderful with dinner."

"It started snowing at three o'clock," Jeannie answered. "It's been coming down pretty steady. And I can't even get excited about a snow day because I'm stuck with this dumb *remote learning* shit."

"Jeannie, watch your mouth!" Brian glared at his daughter, shocked but fairly certain where she'd have picked up such colorful language. "We're at the dinner table, and if you can't mind your manners, you can be excused and march up to your room right now."

"Oh, calm down, Brian. She's absolutely right." Maggie pushed her chair back, stood up, and marched into the kitchen. When she returned, she had a bottle of red wine clutched in one hand and a bottle opener in the other. "This quarantine shit *is* getting old. And do you know who's to blame? The goddamn *libtards*! They're all communists, you know. Every single one of them worships Satan and eats babies. It's a goddamn conspiracy! Just look at that white-haired homo on CNN…what's his name? Do you know that he ritualistically drinks blood?"

"Maggie, *enough!* What the hell has gotten into you?" He threw his chair back and stood up. "First of all, we're at the goddamn dinner table, so take that fucking headset off and join us!"

His wife's chin dropped. She looked as if she'd been slapped in the face. She removed the Bluetooth unit immediately and set it on the table beside the bottle of merlot. When she did, her face changed. The irritation was immediately replaced by blushing cheeks and tears welling around her eyes. "Oh, my god…I'm so sorry. I don't know where that even came from." She took the corkscrew, opened the wine, and poured it into the empty glass until droplets of burgundy nearly spilled over the rim. "I've been wearing the headphones so much that I could swear I'm hearing conversations when I'm not even on the phone. And the craziest part is that sometimes…sometimes the voices are whispering inside my head."

Brian felt his blood run cold, and a wave of goosebumps flurried up and down his skin. *We're all going crazy,* he thought. *It's cabin fever or something.* He thought about the picture on the refrigerator, the one with that terrible little monster perched on top of the telephone pole across the street. Part of him almost, *almost* believed that his daughter had really seen it—she had a marvelous imagination, after all—but even now, here at the dinner table, Brian's mind was trying to name and categorize the thing as if it were a brand-new species. He could hear plain as day his old science teacher talking about *kingdom, phylum, chordata, genus, and species.* It had wings with plumage, but it also had reptilian legs. And those eyes…those glowing red eyes!

The lights from the chandelier above the table began to flicker. When they did, Brownie stood up and barked. She put her front paws on the table and glanced up at the light bulbs, her tail wagging furiously.

* * *

The thing had returned just after dusk. It flapped its wings through the falling snow and gloom until it found its perch—those glorious power cables emitting that low, healthy hum of electrical life. It perched, wrapping three snakelike tendrils around the top of the wooden beams, and squeezing as tight as it could. It was short, squat, with ebony reptilian skin that required the coldest of blood to survive, and long wings with plumage that protruded at terrible angles. On the inside of these wings were mounds of grotesque bumps which quivered like obscene eggs implanted just beneath its velvet skin before they could hatch. The thing's face was eyeless, relying instead on a long proboscis snout that performed all its sensory functions.

At first, that proboscis latched onto the telephone line, wrapping its dreadful lips around the cable—like earlier that morning—and letting its razor-sharp teeth gnaw through the rubber insulation until it reached the metal fibers. Once it attached, the thing could transmit its own thoughts and observations, based on millions of codes and algorithms it had previously feasted on during its earlier feeding.

The thing had no idea of what any of the information meant; it only understood that it must be shared in exchange for taking the thousands of volts it required to survive. So it did the only thing it instinctively knew how to do; it shared what lies it had already fed upon through the cables. Up and down Booker Street, and all across town, the citizens of Hetfield were slowly being brainwashed over their computers and cellphones and electronic devices.

* * *

"You don't think we'll lose power, do you?" Maggie asked as the lights continued to flicker. Brownie continued to bark and whine, the way she carried on when the mailman was walking up to their doorstep. Her barks were shrill, and Brian found himself getting angrier by the second.

He sighed and dropped his fork down onto his half-eaten meal. This was another battle they'd fought since buying the house. During the walk-through with their realtor, they were told the power grid that fed this house was less than half a mile away, just around the corner on Old Hetfield Road. With the town's fire department on Main Street sharing their same grid, if they were to lose power, theirs would be among the first homes restored in their community. Maggie still insisted they needed a generator; that if they *did* lose power, her business would demand its phone and internet remain intact. Her clients still needed twenty-four-hour access to their insurance policies.

Brownie was now barking louder; the same bark reserved for after everybody had gone to bed, and she then decided she *needed* to go outside and do her business, along with checking all around their property to make sure their home was safe. Brian thought of his child's sketch on the refrigerator, and of the *thing* perched up on the telephone pole with its bizarre plumage and the three long appendages wrapped around the top.

He thought of how it looked both sinister and predatorial.

"I'm gonna get her leash and walk her now. While I'm out, I'll check the lines around the house and make sure the snow hasn't caused a limb to come down."

* * *

The thing had suckled on the telephone line for a few minutes, but it still felt hungry, still felt like it hadn't been completely sated. It removed its proboscis from the line and redirected it toward one of the power cables closest to the street. Its long snout had tiny, needle-like teeth just beneath its ebon lips. When it clamped down on the outer cable on the post, it immediately felt the current passing just underneath its rubber surface. The tentacled legs squeezed tighter around the wooden shaft of the pole, and the monster started chewing its way through the cable. The black plumage on its spine fluttered outward in ecstasy. *This* was the power it craved, allowing it to send out its lies and sinister transmissions telepathically to anybody in town.

* * *

"Brownie, Jesus Christ, calm down!" Brian threw on his winter parka and knit hat, then snatched the retractable leash from the stand near the back door. Brownie was barking hysterically, her paws scratching at the kitchen door to get outside and stalk whatever was bothering her. It had occurred to Brian that some strange sound frequency was being emitted, like a dog whistle blowing at a range that humans would never be able to hear. Although it was entirely possible Maggie *could* hear it while her Bluetooth was still on, with the headphone still parked inside her ear. *What did she say back at the table? That she heard voices whispering inside her head?* Now, *all* the lights and lamps inside the Weaver house were flickering—threatening to go off completely—even though there was no sign of the growing snowstorm impeding on their power grid. Brian looked up and down Booker Street, at the lights inside his neighbors' homes were flickering as well. Even the Christmas lights on the trees outside the Sinclair house—the last in the neighborhood still displaying them were dwindling and about to go out. He kept thinking of his daughter's sketch, the strange lump of a thing atop the telephone pole across the street. But that was ridiculous. No nine-year-old was going to see a monster. No nine-year-old was going to see something that couldn't be dismissed as the whimsy of a child who spent her time watching cartoons after her classes were done for the day. Seemed like Jeannie had gone overnight from watching *Dragon Tales* and *My Little Pony* to those Japanese cartoons on NetFlix, where Caucasian girls her age had enormous eyes and oversexualized bodies. But Brian *couldn't* dismiss the crayon sketch on the refrigerator door. Something was entirely wrong. His daughter *knew* it, his wife *expressed* it, and their dog Brownie was now snarling as if something was trying to invade their home. Despite his winter jacket, Brian felt his blood run cold.

* * *

Brownie started growling the moment they stepped outside. Her long snout twisted into an angry snarl, and then she was pulling her lead toward the corner of Booker Street, facing the lamppost in front of his neighbor's house. Brian pulled back on the dog's leash, but once they reached the road, Brownie yanked so hard he lost his grasp on the plastic leash line. He watched helplessly as his dog raced full gallop into the road. Before he could reach her, Brownie was hit full-on by the snowplow that was clearing the road of the new-fallen snow. He watched as Jeannie's best friend in the world caught the plow's blade along the sinewy muscle of her hind legs, heard the devastating thump as her body went beneath the tires.

* * *

The thing at the top of the lamppost sensed all these things as its teeth pushed through the insulation of the powerline. Its tongue reached the metal wire beneath the surface, then electricity flowed gloriously through its monstrous body, sending waves of powerful impulses through its system. As it did, the lights up and down Booker Street quickly faded away. The neighborhood spiraled into darkness and the midwinter evening in Hetfield, Maine went completely black.

Brian Weaver screamed as his dog was crushed beneath the plow, then watched, terrified, as the monster on top of the telephone pole spread its wings, and those awful lumps on the insides of its wings began to glow; to light up the night sky with dozens of white-hot lightbulbs in horrid victory, calling its own kind forth. In his mind, he heard the screams of their response, telling the monster on top of the pole that they were coming. The snowplow never stopped. It barreled on down Booker Street, its driver stomping on the gas pedal as if he knew he'd made a mistake and wanted no part in stopping to sort it all out.

* * *

A few seconds after the lights in town went dark, the generator in his backyard roared to life, the one meant to keep Maggie's business communications up and running in the case of an emergency. Brian understood immediately that they had the only house on the block with a backup generator, or at least the only house that had the income during the pandemic to keep it gassed and ready. It occurred to him in the enveloping darkness that all his neighbors up and down the street would likely be panicking about losing power without even knowing about this monstrous threat holding watch above them. Or did they know, and were purposely barricading themselves inside, claiming they were just staying safe in quarantine?

More than that, he'd heard the screech of the thing's voice inside his head, calling out to its own to "come forth, brethren…there's food and life to be had in this place!" and understood what would happen next. Soon, dozens, possibly hundreds of those *things* would arrive, and plant their snakelike appendages around the utility poles in his neighborhood. Some would chew into the cables and spew their lies and obscene realities into them, perverting the understandings of reality to anybody too feeble-minded to understand what was happening. In the morning, the citizens in his own town would believe any blasphemy those things spilled into their brains, through whatever means or frequencies they could utilize.

Brian raced across the street to where his dog lay, her blood gushing onto the new-fallen snow and turning it crimson. Brownie's tongue poked out of her snout as she whimpered and panted and waited to be carried to safety. The snowplow had torn the poor dog's body open, spilling her guts into the white snow. Brownie could sense it. She looked up into the night sky, the snow steadily falling as the wind howled and the winter night grew tighter into anguish. She closed her eyes and howled as more of those monstrous beasts flapped their wings and landed on the wires along Booker Street.

Brian Weaver abandoned his dying dog and fled to the safety of his home.

* * *

"We have to kill the lights," Brian said as he stormed back into the kitchen and yanked his jacket off. "Now! They're out there and our house is the only one with power on."

"What are you talking about? Brian, there's nobody out there. And you're scaring Jeannie now." Maggie stood in the doorway of the dining room, their daughter clutched tightly in her arms. Jeannie was softly crying with her head buried against Maggie's neck and shoulders. Only Maggie was the one who looked terrified. Judging by how she was slurring, she'd probably finished the bottle of merlot. *Oh my god, I fucking* hate *her!* Brian thought. His own mind was racing, back to when he'd watched their dog—the one he'd protested buying because he never wanted the responsibility of cleaning up after it—torn apart in the middle of the street.

In his mind, he could already see those *things* swooping down from the sky and sinking their long proboscis snouts into Brownie's wounds, drinking the last of her life out of her as she whined and yapped in misery. *Vulgareans,* he thought with absolute clarity, as if the word had been whispered into his brain. *They're called vulgareans. They consume energy and replace it with lies and corruption.* Brian stormed across the kitchen and yanked Jeannie's drawing off the refrigerator door.

"*This!*" he shouted, holding the picture in front of her eyes. "*This* is what's outside, and *our* house is the only one on the block still with power because of *your* fucking generator!"

Jeannie pressed her face harder against her mother's shoulder and screamed.

"Stop it! You're scaring her!"

Brian shoved her aside, and then flicked the kitchen's light switch off. Then he was hurtling through the rest of the house, turning off light after light as he passed through each room.

* * *

The vulgareans knew *exactly* which house still had power. The original beast remained perched on the top of the pole, its serpentine tendrils still wrapped tight around its perch, the lights beneath the skin of its wings dark again. It didn't take long for others to arrive. Soon the snow-filled sky was eclipsed with beating wings and eyeless faces drawn by electromagnetic vibrations and sound frequencies. A *Central Maine Power* vehicle turned onto Booker Street, a floodlight attached to the driver's door craning toward the power lines up and down the block. When the driver noticed the dead dog pressed between the asphalt and sidewalk, he slammed on the brakes, shifted into park, and got out to investigate.

He never saw his monstrous assailants as they fell out of the sky and converged upon him. He never saw them, but he heard their cries inside his brain as they began tearing his flesh apart with the razor-sharp teeth inside their snouts.

* * *

At seven-fourteen p.m., the main power line that fed electricity directly into the Weaver house split apart and dropped onto the snowy earth. The livewire kicked and jumped as sparks flew out, and the vulgareans began to shriek in victory as they strutted around the dead man and dog in the road. There were dozens of them outside now. Brian could hear them screaming in his brain. Panic clamped down on his gut, making his bowels gurgle inside his belly.

He'd already shut off all the lights, but there were still live outlets in every room, feeding electricity into Maggie's office computer, the refrigerator, the televisions both in the living room and their bedroom upstairs. It had never occurred to him before how many appliances and gadgets they'd accrued over thirteen years of marriage, and how many consumed electricity whether they were being used or not. When the thermostat in the living room dipped below sixty-five degrees, the furnace in the basement roared to life. When it did, the vulgareans outside went silent and fixed their sightless faces toward his house.

* * *

The noise they made as they flapped their terrible wings against the aluminum siding would have driven Brownie crazy, and just thinking that made Brian nauseous. At one point, just as he was ushering his wife and daughter up to their bedroom to barricade themselves inside, Jeannie lifted her face off her mother's shoulder long enough to ask where the dog was. Normally, her question would have broken his heart, but Brian was terrified, distracted. The truth was that he could now imagine the CNN journalist Maggie mentioned at dinner sitting down at a banquet table and tearing the collie apart with his bare hands, holding a silver goblet out to collect its blood and raise a toast to Satan. At least, that's what the screams inside his brain were insisting, and it made all the sense in the world to him.

"Oh god…" Maggie whimpered. "What do they want? What do they *waaannnt?*"

"Shut up, goddamnit. They can hear us!"

The beating of wings against the aluminum siding grew louder, as if the monsters had homed in on their voices and were now hunting them down. There had to be at least a hundred of them outside. The beating of wings was now drowning out the frigid winds reigning down from the north, and the ice crystals that pelted nonstop against the roof and windows. Brian had closed the slats of the Venetian blinds, filling the bedroom with absolute darkness. The furnace in the basement finished its cycle, but the circulator pumps that ran the boiling water through the radiators were still going strong. From the attic, he could hear the sound of asphalt shingles being ripped away, followed by terrible scuttling sounds as they made their way to the attic door. From somewhere in the backyard, the generator was still thrumming, still sending current down to the electrical box in the basement. He heard all these things, but *that* wasn't what terrified him.

The screaming inside his head was now deafening, telling him that those monsters outside, the vulgareans, were still hungry.

He could no longer see his wife and daughter in the dark, but he could hear both of them moaning and weeping as Maggie rocked Jeannie in her arms at the foot of the bed. Maggie was whispering the Lord's Prayer into the darkness between sobs, and hearing her voice filled him with rage.

"Can you shut the fuck up, *please!* They can hear us."

"I hate you, Brian," she replied. "I hate you so fucking much. Look what you've done to our family."

She's a liar, the voice of the vulgareans insisted inside his head. *You know she is. Aren't you tired of her? Don't you think life would be so much better without her? Without them* both*?*

The generator in the back yard choked and sputtered for a few seconds, and then went silent. Immediately the circulator pumps pushing hot water through the pipes also went silent, as did the remaining ancillary electronics around the house. In his mind, he could picture the beasts yanking the power line off the generator so that they could take turns feasting off the remaining current. Seconds later, the silence was replaced by glass shattering and wings flapping as they entered the house.

Haven't you had enough *of them both?* the voices in his head cooed. Brian was surprised at just how friendly, how understanding they could sound when they wanted to.

The room was pitch black, but he could sense everything without using his eyes. *Echolocation,* the voice of his science teacher chimed in one last time. *Bats use it to hunt their prey. They make sounds, and then judge the distance between by the returning sound vibrations.* The vulgareans flapped their wings outside the bedroom door, their screams now deafening, their serpentine appendages whipping and slapping against the wooden door frame.

Brian crossed the bedroom in darkness to his wife and daughter. He placed his arms around them and gently lifted them to their feet. He could sense everything; the smell of Maggie's perfume—even though she hadn't left the house in months, she'd still insisted on smelling lovely—and the heat radiating off Jeannie's tear-stained face. He could feel their hearts racing, and the surge of power they radiated as their hearts pumped blood through their bodies. He felt their shivering and their goosebumps and their fear and unending sadness.

It amazed him how he'd been so blind to these things for so very, very long.

Give them to us, and we'll let you live!

It would be enough.

With all his might, he shoved his weight against his wife's torso, knocking her toward the bedroom window. Maggie toppled hard, knocking against the Venetian blinds, her hands fumbling in the darkness for something to grab onto. Brian's leg shot out, kicking her hard in the stomach, knocking the wind out of her lungs, and then the glass behind her shattered, her body flailing into the cold, then gravity took over and she was gone.

Jeannie followed directly after, and the vulgareans were waiting for them. They screamed in satisfaction as they swooped in to feast.

Brian could see their outlines as the beasts swarmed his wife and child. Then, dreadful sanity crept painfully back in and he realized what he'd done, realized that he'd been deceived, just as everybody else in Hetfield eventually would be. The vulgareans had robbed them of their power and replaced all their truths with lies.

Brian sobbed, whispered, "I'm sorry," to nobody in particular, and then leapt out the window to join his family.

Lavinia, The Traveler

by Patricia Gomes

She delights
in the slow English pronunciation
of names for red.
Luxuriates in pursing her full lips,
and the heady sensation
as her tongue
grazes her teeth
while reciting them aloud. Her lullaby:
scarlet
crimson
vermillion
cherry
magenta
cardinal
ruby
claret
flame

rage

fury.

The sky, a blazing pink
when she rises,
is put to rest
by the blanketing of full Night.
For a time, she staves off her appetite
by playing
with pretty things.

The past lovingly recollected
by crystal perfume decanters on vanities
draped in lace. Bottled lacquers, cuff links
left behind by an adulterous Carpathian lover.
Black sling-backs still buckled
and cast aside after the last curtain call.

Shiny, pretty things
that tinkle
and ding
and distract until

hunger

becomes undeniable, a living thing.
Hunger, no matter the language,
has a beating heart,
a coppery taste,
and a warm red name.

Kobold
by John C. Foster

The Methodist Ladies Organization was hanging lights on a picket fence with a stack of wreathes nearby. A wood-paneled station wagon idled with music from the holiday station gently filling the air.

The MLO waved and smiled when Sandy passed.

Sandy returned the smile and hurried on to see the tree before they could draw her into conversation. They were talkers, every one of them. Ville de Rasoir was known around the area for its tree lighting festival and she wanted to get there early to find a seat on the bandstand. It was a perfect winter day, dressed in December colors of red and green and blue and white. Sandy was glad she had a thermos of hot cider to keep her warm.

The street and sidewalks were crusty with salt, and piled snow along the curb made a fortress wall. A young boy wearing three layers of sweatshirts and no hat was making iceballs and throwing them at the swirling barber's pole. An occasional fragment struck the glass frontage of *Shave and a Haircut* but no one emerged to chase the kid off.

The boy turned abruptly toward Sandy. She was shocked by his eyes, so pale blue that for a split second they appeared completely white. Sandy thought he was going to throw a frozen missile at her, but he turned away and resumed his assault on the barber's pole.

She kicked a chunk of ice ahead of her as she passed an insurance office, the brick hulk of the municipal building, and the *Blue Jay Café* where they started playing Christmas music before Thanksgiving.

Sandy was already smiling when she arrived at the tree.

Cut from the surrounding forest, it stood tall and green against the snowy ground and blue sky. A beautiful pine that would shine with lights that very night.

It was then she noticed the two boys.

They were leaning against the bandstand and smoking. She lifted her hand in a reluctant wave and one boy waved back, inviting her to approach. The churned snow around their feet was spotted with cigarette butts and a fresh yellow patch against the bandstand suggested unsavory bathroom habits, but they were near enough to her age that it satisfied a need for normalcy.

And they had cigarettes.

"Hi," she said.

Their faces were spotted with acne and their acid washed jeans were a few years out of style. Rawboned types with narrow features, one with a mop of curly black hair. The other, who seemed in charge, had carefully feathered his own straw-colored hair.

They held themselves as if immune to the cold in the way that New Englanders do.

"Can I bum a cigarette?" Sandy asked.

"You smoke?" Straw Hair said.

"In Europe I smoked Gauloises."

The two townies exchanged looks, and the curly haired boy held out a pack of Camels. "Knock yourself out." She noticed that the skin below his right eye was a faded purple.

Sandy lipped a cigarette free and leaned in as the boy held out a lighter, hands cupped to protect the flame. She drew in smoke and let it trail from her nostrils with a sigh of relief.

"Thanks," she said.

"Pissoir ain't too big." Straw Hair grinned. "How come we haven't seen you around?"

"I was in private school in Groton. That's in Massachusetts."

"Did you go to the consolidated middle school?"

"I went to middle school in Vermont before we moved here."

"Why the fuck would anyone move here?" Black Hair wore bafflement like a familiar hat.

Straw Hair pushed off the peeling side of the bandstand. "My sidekick here is Ray Childers."

"Meetcha," Ray said, also straightening.

"I'm Sandy."

A rusty VW Bug puttered past, Prince blasting from half-opened windows. Party like it's 1999? Ville de Rasoir couldn't escape the eighties.

"You like Prince?" Sandy asked.

Childers coughed into his fist. "Gay."

His partner looked her up and down. "So, you wanna check out the bridge?"

"What bridge?"

"It's close."

"Okay." She fell in beside the two boys as they set off down the sidewalk and tapped Straw Hair on the shoulder.

"You didn't tell me your name."

He slid the cigarette to the corner of his mouth with a movement of his lips and grinned. "Dickie LaChaise."

* * *

An unplowed road made the walk harder. All three of them were huffing and puffing from the effort. They took turns crossing a rusty chain hanging across the road with a sign reading NO ENTRY. Dickie offered her a hand but she ignored it, flashing too much leg and feeling the chill as she crossed the barrier.

"I gotta go back." She spoke to the prematurely balding spot on the back of Dickie's head and he didn't bother to turn as he responded.

"It's right here," Dickie said.

"Don't be a wuss," Ray said.

She heard a car crackling over ice not far behind her and could smell wood smoke, so she knew she wasn't far off the main road. Still, she felt isolated amongst the trees, sounds muffled by the snow, breath steaming in the air. In the shade of the trees the cold became more pronounced, slipping fingers into every gap of her clothing. She wished she had a hat. She wished she had gloves. She wished she hadn't decided to follow two boys to a haunted bridge.

"So this bridge has been closed for like, fifteen years, right before we were born," Dickie said. "They were gonna make it into a historical thing—"

"Landmark," Ray added.

"Right," Dickie continued. "Then it happened."

"Fucked up the whole town."

"There was a big lawsuit but because they were drinking, it got thrown out."

They tossed dialogue back and forth like tennis players but Sandy wasn't sure she liked their game.

They trudged on until she picked up a chunk of snow and threw it past Dickie.

"What happened?"

Dickie turned around and one side of his mouth curled in a grin as he tossed his cigarette butt into the snow.

"Six kids disappeared."

"Zut alors." Sandy shivered.

"High school kids partying on the bridge then the bottom collapsed. That's what the cops said. They hit the river and went right through the ice. Not a single one made it out," Dickie said.

"They froze," Ray said.

"They drowned."

"No way," she said.

"Way. And it all happened right here." Dickie made a sweeping gesture with his arm and Sandy saw the long, covered bridge like something from a wall calendar. It was painted a faded red, with a cap of white frosting the gently peaked roof. The river gurgled over rocks twenty feet below, and while it wasn't terribly wide, it did look cold. A grim fascination tugged at her and she moved past the boys, pushing aside branches until she was close enough to see into the dark interior of the bridge and just make out the gaping wound in the floor.

"No way," she repeated.

"Totally way," Dickie shot back.

"Every kid in town has to go across it, like it's a secret rule," Ray said.

"A ritual." Dickie confirmed.

Sandy forced a laugh, shaking her head. "Count me out."

"Every kid does it." Dickie smirked and crossed his arms.

"I'm not doing—"

Something moved in the dark interior of the bridge.

"What's that?"

"What's what?" Dickie said.

"Something's on the bridge."

Ray Childers gave her a shove. "Stop stalling—"

He stopped speaking. Stopped moving. All three went as still as ice sculptures.

The eyes glowed a sickly green. Unblinking. Whatever shapeless thing it was wore the shadows like a concealing cloak, but the eyes were clearly staring at them.

"I have to go," Sandy said.

The surprise blow to the back of her skull felt oddly soft and she fell face down in the snow. Running steps thudded by and a snarling shadow swept over the teenagers.

"Hel—" A loud thud cut Dickie off mid word.

Sandy sat up to see a tall man in a Levi's jacket hot on Ray Childers' heels. The boy was caught before he could get into the trees and the two went down in an explosion of white powder. A big monkey wrench was lifted and brought down hard. The teenager stopped struggling.

Sandy rubbed the back of her head and fought back a wave of dizziness as the big Timberland boots of her rescuer thudded towards her. He dragged Childers behind him like a gutshot deer. Her rescuer was taller than any man had a right to be, and her gaze traveled up his blue jean length until—

Any thought of offering thanks was choked off in a scream.

The tall man had no face.

* * *

The axe split a length of stove wood with a single blow and the big man had to brace a boot on the stump before yanking the axe free. The work and a checked flannel shirt were enough to keep him warm.

It was a clear, cold night. Moonlight painted his property in silvers and grays, illuminating the small, snow-capped wooden cabin and a hand-painted sign proclaiming BEST TREES IN THE COUNTY. People called him Odd, though none were sure if that was a name or a nickname. His mailbox said DE FRONSAC but nobody ever called him that.

Odd fit well enough.

He stepped back from his work and glanced over the hillside and its forest of Christmas trees in carefully organized rows, poised like a phalanx of short evergreens ready to assault the forest beyond. They were coming in well, except for the Douglas firs. But he had a few nobles that topped eight feet, and the Frasers stood around six, which is where most of his customers wanted them. Claire Whitman at the Methodist Ladies Organization once suggested holding a tree cutting festival on de Fronsac's land but was quickly talked out of it. She was new in town, after all, and didn't know any better.

Soon enough the trees would belong to anyone with fifty dollars and a saw, but for now they were his, and he enjoyed their squat presence and the clean smell they lent to the air around his home.

Odd de Fronsac was a man built to be alone.

* * *

The dog started barking and Odd stood up from his chair beside the fireplace, already pissed. There was an ugly scrape of claws on glass and a blink of toxic green flashing beyond the window. The dog began to whine. He grabbed its collar. "Shush, boy!"

Odd dashed for the CB. He was reaching for the handset when it chirped.

"Odd, you there? Odd de Fronsac, come in."

"I'm here, over."

"Another one of them fuckers showed up." The voice crackled with static.

"Yeah, I just had a visit from you know what."

"You okay?"

"Yeah," Odd lied.

A high pitched whine sawed through the reply but Odd heard, "—the bridge."

"I'll be there in twenty."

*   *   *

Men stood in a ring, clouds of breath rising through gritted teeth. They knew electricity, these men. They knew flashlights and Coleman lanterns and walkie-talkies.

But they carried torches tipped with furious flame.

They knew guns, these men of Rasoir. All were hunters. Of their number, three had fought through the jungles of Vietnam.

But they carried small axes, hand forged of iron. Knives of the same metal rested in belt sheathes.

That which lived beneath the bridge demanded ritual and the men of Rasoir obliged.

They smeared their scalps with pinesap until hair stood in crazed ridges. Beards were likewise smeared and worked into forks, twigs woven through or stuck with the plentiful tree blood.

They, the Rasoir Men's Club, had once, no shit, fielded a softball team to compete with surrounding towns. The group was old, not as old as that which lived beneath the bridge, but old enough. It grew and shrank as men were born and died but always maintained a vigil.

Because strangers were drawn to Rasoir.

The strangers came and came until these men were grey and their sons replaced them on the watch.

"One of them bastards showed up today," Gerry Chance said, torchlight flickering off his steel rimmed glasses. "Ray Childers, Dickie LaChaise and Sandy DeLucca are missing."

"If we're quick, there's a chance they're still alive." George Scollins was a good man, but young. He would learn.

"Odd, you find his trail and take point," Gerry commanded. "George, you play Tail End Charlie."

George nodded but Gerry grabbed his arm. "You don't look behind you, no matter what you hear following. Understand?"

The younger man looked into the dark trees and swallowed his fear. He nodded in understanding.

Great clouds of angry steam jetted from Odd's lips as he left the group without a word, torch held high to study the mess of footprints in the snow.

The Rasoir Men's Club shifted and rustled and breathed until Odd crouched low, using his finger to trace the icy print left by a big Timberland boot.

"Here, boys."

They shook out into a ragged line behind him and marched into the forest.

*   *   *

Hilton Arthur Holley (the Third) operated under the misapprehension that he was the apex predator in whatever jurisdiction he found himself. He was not a sadist nor a murderer, but a mechanic who labored to fix the broken people in a sad world.

The village of Rasoir had drawn him as an infected tooth draws a tongue and he succumbed, putting in for vacation days and taking an elliptical, deceptive path to northern New Hampshire.

The trailer park was perfect, scattered across rough country and largely unoccupied. Snow-covered piles of junk decorated the few homes that held tenants. It wasn't hard for Hilton to discover an empty trailer shielded by a bony copse of birch trees.

Over the course of several days he had snuck in various pieces of gear beneath the cover of darkness, discovering that the trailer tilted enough on its foundation that objects set down had a tendency to slide. A great admirer of the absurd, Hilton found that this last detail added a soupcon of humor to his otherwise serious work.

The trailer park was entirely leeched of curiosity. No one noticed his arrival. The entire village was the same. He'd even risked a visit to the Blue Jay Café in the center of what they called town. No one cared about the tall stranger with red juice running from the corners of his mouth as he ate his hamburger. That his English wasn't as crudely clipped as theirs attracted no notice, nor the fact that to all intents and purposes, he was without a car.

They just didn't care.

The metallic tang of spilled blood recaptured his wandering attention. The odor distressed the boy and girl squirming in their restraints, though Hilton was generous enough to conceal the corpse of their friend in the cramped bathroom.

He brought the pliers to the kitchen sink and had to whack them against the metal basin to dislodge a tooth that clung with the stubborn tenacity of a barnacle.

The problem troubling the troglodytes of Rasoir did not seem to be located in the teeth, despite his early suspicions. Placing the pliers on the counter to dry, he crouched beside his toolbox and rummaged about until he lifted an awl.

"Perfect."

He plucked the nylon stocking from his head so they could see his grin, stuffing the disguise in his back pocket. *Look upon my face and despair.*

"I'm going to see if the trouble is in your nose."

He stretched to his full height, head nearly brushing the ceiling, awl dangling from one hand. The teens thrashed and grunted around loops of electrician's tape and even bonked their heads together for comedic effect. Hilton laughed, a good sport, then pointed with the awl.

"Eenie, meenie, miney, mo."

* * *

Odd waited at the entrance to the trailer park while the Rasoir Men's Club gathered around him. As each man arrived, his torchlight was added to the next, until they were bathed in a warm glow that gave life to the events ahead.

"Jim, you find us the occupied trailer that doesn't get mail," Odd said. Jim Miller was the postman and knew the what and where of everyone in town.

"This is that stranger was down to the Blue Jay." Jim blew his nose and stuffed the hanky back in a pocket. "Cocky bastard."

"They usually are," Gerry said. "Go on, Jimbo." He patted the bulky coat on the postman's shoulder. "We'll be right behind."

* * *

The trouble was not in the nose, fingernails or genitals and Hilton sat cross-legged beside the unmoving corpses, a goblin coated in gore, his white teeth grinning from the red slick of his face.

The leaking blood steamed as it slid away, following the downward slope towards the wall opposite the door. It was only because he tracked the red flow with his eyes that he noticed an outside light leaking in past the blinds.

Roiling torches were held above the heads of dark men ringing the trailer. All at once they shouted something that sounded like, "HO!"

A great blow struck the underside of the doublewide and it shuddered.

"HO!"

Another blow shook the trailer and Hilton darted across the narrow space to peer out, just as—

"HO!"

He heard a horrible crack beneath his feet when something gave way. The trailer lurched more and Hilton grabbed the counter for balance.

Hilton Arthur Holly (the Third) was a sadistic, murderous individual, but he was as smart as a whip. Almost before he had finished the calculation, he was scooting up the incline towards the door and exploding forth like an eagle taking flight.

Or would have, if the door hadn't been slammed in his face by the men outside. He sat hard and slid down the slope to bang against cabinets.

The floor fissured under another blow and then another. Pieces of metal and plastic flew up as if from an erupting volcano. Something pulled itself up into the doublewide.

Hilton giggled hysterically even as his bladder released. The light leaking from inhuman green eyes reminded him of a chemical spill. In its glow he made out dull, ruddy scales and stubby black horns jutting from the thing's forehead. It crouched in simian fashion; its chubby forearms ended in black clawed fingers.

It was two feet tall.

Hilton thought of the big window in the forward bedroom. He reared to his fill height and rushed at the toddler-sized nightmare as if to attack, but leaping high at the last moment.

Claws raked his foot, ripping the boot off and nearly taking the foot with it.

The serial killer landed hard on his chin, biting his tongue. He rolled onto his back as the creature approached.

A strangled laugh escaped his lips. The goddamned thing even had a clumsy toddler's walk.

Hilton Arthur Holly (the Third) scrambled on hands and knees for the immediate safety of the bathroom, climbing over the first body and tucking his long frame into the cramped space and slamming the door shut behind him. He dragged himself upright. The window was too small to escape through.

The bathroom door cracked as a clawed hand punched through at knee height.

This time he screamed.

* * *

Hilton flew through the air and landed in the snow outside the trailer.

He struggled up to his hands and knees, watching his own blood rain onto the snow beneath. A boot kicked him in the ribs, flipping him onto his back. Cruel faces studied him, smoky breath steaming from their mouths like from a locomotive.

Hilton struggled to prop his elbows beneath him but Odd stomped him back down into the ice and slush. "Never should've come to Rasoir, asshole."

And because this was the first time for the younger man, Odd let George say it. "Welcome to Razor Town."

The Kobold leaped down from the crippled doublewide and landed in the snow. Torchlight glinted off of fresh blood on its ruddy scales. Scales that resembled iron ore when seen in daylight.

It looked up at the towering men and planted fists on its hips, the familiar gesture drawing greater attention to its overlong arms. Potbellied and belligerent, it waited.

Gerry Chance gathered himself before taking a step forward. That horrible head snapped around to fix him with a poisonous stare.

"May we deliver him?" His voice was forced but casual.

The Kobold placed a finger alongside its nose and blew hard to clear the opposite nostril. Snot struck the snow and steamed like a fallen meteor.

It nodded and crunched away through the snow on stubby legs, vanishing as soon as it left the glow of their torchlight.

Headlights approached and Odd stepped forward to meet the car, detouring around the serial killer. He threw an arm over his eyes.

"Turn off your goddamned lights," he said. The Chevy station wagon ground to a halt and the lights snapped off.

A moment later the driver's door opened and Odd recognized the scarf-draped form of Marie Vlack, president of the Methodist Ladies Organization.

"There's no cause for that language, Odd de Fronsac," she said, stumping forward so she could speak in a normal tone of voice. More women of the MLO emerged from the car behind her.

"Are they inside? The little ones?"

"I think so."

"We'll take it from here," Marie Vlack said. "This part is ours."

Six women marched past, hats pulled low against the cold. Six plus Marie to make seven. Though the Men's Club dispatched varying numbers every time this happened, the MLO always fielded seven members, a number of great significance. After six high school students were taken, it was the MLO that made a new bargain with the Kobold living beneath the bridge. Since then, it had taken no more townsfolk.

"You okay?" Gerry asked. Odd said, "Yeah," though soon enough his hand would swell to the size of a catcher's mitt.

"Let's bring this asshole to the bridge."

"Why didn't it just eat him here?" George said, still learning.

"It likes to eat at home," Gerry said.

George imagined it sitting at a small kitchen table in a tiny monster's kitchen and suppressed a madman's giggle.

"Why doesn't it just carry him home?"

"The Kobold is two feet tall," Jim Miller said. "It's a matter of leverage."

* * *

Walking was a part of it, the bloodied killer herded through the snowy woods by torch-bearing townsmen. They talked about Larry Byrd and Magic Johnson and argued about the rumor of mandatory facemasks in hockey. Jim Miller noticed deer tracks and said he planned to come back and bag himself a buck. Occasionally they shoved the killer and laughed when he tripped over roots and fallen branches, his face red and wet from planting in the snow, his hands bound behind him.

Jim Chute plucked the nylon stocking from Hilton's back pocket after one such fall, with Hilton's face still stuck in the icy crust and his ass high in the air.

"Not even original." Chute dropped the stocking.

"Nothing about this guy is original." Odd's boot slammed hard into the back of Hilton's thigh and he squealed like a pig before staggering upright.

"I can pay," Hilton gasped. Then the group had to wait several minutes as the shock of a broken nose wore off and he could be prodded back to his feet.

"Say that again and we pull out your tongue." Gerry Chance rubbed snow on his knuckles. He was getting older and the doc said arthritis was a sure bet.

Eventually they reached the covered bridge and the site of Hilton's attack on the three teenagers. In the uneven torchlight the yawning mouth of the bridge seemed to flex as if eager to snap shut, the red sides were the brown of dried blood and the white cap of snow was the orange of hot metal.

"Hand okay?" Gerry Chance asked.

"Good enough," Odd replied.

"George, you go with him."

George Scollins nodded, having not yet been Under Bridge. Under Bridge didn't refer to the covered bridge, that relic of New England post cards.

Under Bridge meant the old bridge.

"Off we go, Sunny Jim," George said to demonstrate his lack of fear. Odd dragged Hilton to the sloping bank of the river and shoved him over. The former Georgetown Law student made quite a racket as he tumbled down the slope, coming to rest against a dead tree near the water. The two townsmen followed, slipping and sliding despite their care.

Lifting their torches over his twitching form, Odd said, "The worst is yet to come, fucker."

Unsurprisingly, this didn't motivate Hilton to leap to his feet and

Odd had to lay the tip of his burning torch on Hilton's thigh to get him moving.

Up above, Gerry Chance heard the shriek of pain while fishing a new pack of Marlboro's from his pocket. He peeled off the cellophane and let it fall.

Down along the riverbank travel was difficult and it took them an hour to cover a mile. The mournful wail of a coyote drifted through the trees.

"Holy shit," George said.

"Yep," Odd replied, remembering the first time he laid eyes on it.

Ahead was an old stone bridge hidden in the woods. No roads led to it and all but necessary townsfolk had forgotten it. Above the bridge the woods thickened into old growth, nearly impassable. Refrigerated air pushed its way out of the dark archway to ruffle their hair where the pinesap was weakening its hold, as if the bridge itself were breathing.

"Time to get wet."

The river was narrower and deeper under the bridge. Chill water slopped over the tops of Odd's boots and froze his thighs, a cold so cruel it burned. Soon enough it sent his balls climbing for warmth and crested his belt. He bit back sounds of pain, starting a countdown in his head to gauge the onset of hypothermia.

George Scollins' breath was reduced to shallow sips of air as he watched Odd survey the ominous hulk of the bridge. A deadfall of branches and thorns crowned it in a burlesque of madman's hair, and the arch below yawned like a gaping, black mouth to inhale the river.

"Get in." George's voice was thick with tension and he prodded the killer forward until Hilton splashed in up to his knees. George followed with his torch held high to protect the flame.

"I don't want to go in there," Hilton mewled, as honest a sentence as he'd uttered in years.

"I don't care." George pointed with his blazing torch.

Hilton went under at one point and Odd grabbed a fistful of hair to yank the taller man to his feet. The killer was bunched in fear and shame, head drooping as if to avoid regard, and never managed to straighten to his full height in what remained of his life.

"Keep your torch dry," Odd whispered and his words stuck to the wet walls as if glued. "It's not safe to lose the light in here."

Dank things hung from the slimy stone arch above and caressed their cheeks with rotting fingers even as sharp claws raked and jabbed at them. The wooden branches cracked like bones as Odd kicked his way through.

The Under Bridge had a voice, a tubercular awfulness that urged them to go back.

It was quick when it happened. Fingers parted a beaver dam of sticks and small hands shot forward. George had only a moment to notice the plump, childlike arms coated with dull scales and fingers tipped with black claws.

Hilton Arthur Holly (the Third) was snatched away. That was the word. Snatched. One second he slumped between the two torch bearing men and then he was gone, pulled into the beaver dam in an explosion of sticks, vanished before George could squawk in surprise.

"Quickly now," Odd urged his younger companion and they sloshed back the way they came, torches sputtering and spitting in the damp, their breathing ragged with effort.

The emerged into a bright moonlit night. Odd ignored his own sense of relief, pushing George Scollins ahead onto the bank and fighting the urge to look back at the bridge.

There was always a chance it was still hungry.

High on the ridge above a line of torches marked their goal and shouts of encouragement gave their tired muscles the strength to climb, dropping their own torches now to hiss and die. Hands reached down to pull them up the last few feet and then they were off at a run through the winter woods. Torches fell from fists and their tight bunch straggled out as the fleet of foot outdistanced their slower comrades. Fear filled their wings with wind and gave them unnatural speed over the snow.

Thirty minutes later Fitzy opened the bar for them and the men warmed themselves with whiskey, every light in the place blazing as the two who ventured Under Bridge borrowed sweatpants from the bar owner. Gerry Chance cranked up Bing Crosby on the jukebox loud enough to wake the entire town and the men sang carols in ragged chorus, pretending not to notice when George Scollins broke down in tears.

Odd's hand did indeed balloon up to the size of a catcher's mitt and Fitzy fetched him a bucket full of ice. The taciturn man flexed his fist inside the bucket and everyone allowed that his shivering was from the icy treatment and not relief. Odd took time to pour George Scollins a backbreaking shot of tequila and even smiled as they slammed the drinks back in unison. This was possibly the friendliest gesture anyone in town had seen from Odd de Fronsac.

The Men's Club drank until dawn had taken solid hold and staggered drunkenly to their trucks and cars.

The bargain with that which lived beneath the bridge had been kept, as it had before, as it would be again.

This was Ville de Rasoir.

This was Razor Town.

Fifteen Years From Now
by Howard Odentz

The three of us run quickly through the Springfield night because there are sirens in the distance, and they are for us.

Jimmy, Muni and I have stolen food—two cans of asparagus tips and some moldy bread. Our ribs have begun sticking out of our sides like fish gills and our stomachs are round and distended. What choice do we have but to take what we need?

I suspect that the Magistrate knows that we must resort to theft. We are fed weekly out of slop-filled stable bins at Forest Park Zoo. There is never enough.

Besides, feeding us only once a week is like not feeding us at all.

It's a reason to round us up.

The Magistrate is crafty. They have declared stealing food of any kind an MPO—a Maximum Penalty Offense. Those caught committing such a crime are punished in front of cheering crowds at The Quadrangle.

The crumbling buildings that surround that place are museums from The Before. No one speaks of The Before. No one wants to acknowledge a life thrown away. Instead, those in power want to pretend that our world has always been like this.

So, the normies gather on Wednesday evenings to see our pain. They cheer and scream at this century's bread and circus where lions and gladiators have been replaced with creatures like us, born with spots, or webbing between our toes, or even extra bits.

Tusks and tentacles and tails, oh my.

Is our misery fun for them? Who knows? I think it's all designed to hide the plague apathy that has turned many of their children into monsters.

Maybe the normies will wear masks next time. Maybe they won't. It doesn't matter anyway. We'll be long dead before a *next time* comes.

'This time' is all about starvation, so we steal and we run.

We run to keep our hands attached to our bodies. We run to keep our feet from being chopped off or our eyes plucked out. We run for any number of Magistrate penalties, each worse than the last.

"Oomph," mutters nine-year-old Muni as she trips and falls on the ruined sidewalk behind me. Her sad, vestigial wings which are no more than wet leather flaps, struggle uselessly against her back. I stop long enough to grab the collar of her filthy shirt and drag her to her feet. She has no tears in her black eyes. None of us cry anymore. What's the use?

"Move," I growl. We must get off the street. Our lives weigh in the balance.

In the distance the sirens echo against the tall, grey buildings of the dilapidated city. They squeal inside my head like the howls of punished children who no longer have tongues or are missing other parts. They squeal like my brothers and sisters who weep in pain from their phantom limbs because the real ones have been taken as punishment, or entertainment.

This is what we have become.

Slap, slap, slap go our feet against the cracked and jagged sidewalk. Jimmy runs faster than Muni and me with his extra-long antelope legs. He is almost a full block ahead of us. His sinewy appendages, dressed in shredded jeans, propel him forward into the night.

Jimmy has always been fast like that. He's always been reckless. That's why he is hit by an armored transport as he dashes across State Street without looking.

One second he's alive; the next he's gone.

If the sun were out, I would bear witness to Jimmy flying apart in spectacular detail with fountains of blood and shreds of skin. Since darkness shrouds the city, all I see are a few shadows leaving him in different directions.

Muni is behind me. She sees nothing.

"Damn", I whisper with my forked tongue. He was holding the asparagus tips and the moldy bread we stole.

Damn. Damn Damn Damn.

As Jimmy leaves this life for a different one, I grab Muni by one thin arm and thrust her down an alley between a burned-out storefront and a long-gone toy store with a locked metal grate covering its window. Muni knows nothing of toys, except from the stories that older kids tell.

Even the concept of playing is foreign to her.

"Cade," she hisses, trying to pull away from me. "What about Jimmy?"

There is no more Jimmy. Like I said, one second alive, the next gone.

I blow cool mist into the autumn night. "Gone," I tell her. She takes the news like it's no news at all. She's dead inside, just like me. "We need to leave. Now."

A minute later the two of us are squeezing through a slice in the chained link fence at the back of the alley.

As we wriggle through the opening, Muni looks over her shoulder and sees the head of the alley grow bright with flashing lights. The cars with the sirens on them are passing. They've come to see what's left of Jimmy and to retrieve asparagus tips and moldy bread.

Someone will be feasting tonight.

We both freeze and hold our breath. As the lights and the sirens recede, she turns to me and says, "We can't go back with nothing."

"I know," I say as my mind churns—always thinking—always planning.

There's a trashcan next to us. Muni opens the lid with no real expectation of finding anything inside, save for a feral cat or raccoon.

Nothing.

She looks up at me. I stare into her grimy face because I know what she's thinking. She doesn't have to say a word or utter a sound. I know what she's thinking but I want to find another way. Even with Jimmy in pieces and our stolen food under city tires, there has to be another way.

I'm fooling nobody but myself.

"There are three of them," she whispers as she turns into something more dangerous than just a hungry little girl with broken bat wings. "I counted."

"So you said." I bite my lip so hard that I almost taste copper.

"Easy peasy," she shrugs and I realize that we are living in Hell.

I nod my head and turn away because if she keeps looking at me I might lose any humanity I have left. "Okay," I say to her. "Whatever."

Minutes later we are following well-worn paths in the city that nobody uses except for monsters like us. The trails go over the tops of buildings and sometimes into the sewers, but they are safe from the sirens and the people who would harm children, only for the act of being deformed and hungry.

Shortly, we are climbing a metal ladder on the side of a building that is no longer in use. Three stories up, we enter an abandoned apartment through a broken window. The dank rooms have long ago been picked clean of food. That still doesn't stop me from opening up broken cabinet doors and peering inside an ice box that hasn't held ice in it since before I was born.

"Come," Muni says as she scrambles between upended furniture, out an interior door, and through another that leads to a flight of stairs. Together we scale the broken steps to the rooftop. The door there isn't locked. As a matter of fact, there is no more door handle. It's been removed so that others like us can move swiftly through it with ease.

On top of the building we scurry across the black tar. I stop for a moment to look out over the city. The lights are still on over State Street where they are using shovels to clean up the bits of my friend with the antelope legs. His name will leave my head within a week. The thought of him will disappear completely in another.

"Cade," Muni says again and grabs for my hand with little sharpened claws.

"Okay," I tell her as I allow her to pull me to the edge of the roof, barely even stopping at the long planks that reach over to the roof next door.

Like circus performers from The Before, we dash across the wood, pretending that there isn't a chance we could ever fall.

This is how we move through the city, rooftop after rooftop, silent through the night. Eventually, we find a great gash on the top of a building, and lower ourselves into its dark, foreboding bowels. We hear muffled voices far down a hallway but ignore the danger.

After all, we're dangerous, too.

We reach the basement and a broken wall of bricks that leads into the sewers.

The air is so foul that I stop and retch, but there is nothing in my stomach to let free. Instead, acid burns the inside of my throat, and my eyes water.

A lifetime later—enough for the Moon to move partially across the sky, we surface on Pearl Street. There are warehouses here, block after block of them, with their internal mazes of rooms within rooms.

My throat is raw because of the acid and our pace. I don't know how Muni can keep up, but she does. She has become only one step away from feral. I see it in her eyes. Moreover, I hear it in her words because she is the one who has decided what we are going to do next.

There are only three of them.

She's right. Three is easy enough, if you have the stomach for it. Three is cake.

We creep along a cracked sidewalk, hugging the scarred facade of a building riddled with bullet holes until we are where we need to be.

The door, once glass, is nothing but a frame.

"Fourth floor," says Muni. "At least the last time I checked."

I really don't want to do this, but there's no other way.

The center staircase is littered with debris, but that doesn't matter to us. We scuttle up the broken stone and cracked wood like cockroaches, with only the faintest whisper of our legs rubbing together or our phantom mandibles *click, click clicking.*

On the fourth floor landing we hear crying. I close my eyes and swallow. Part of me wishes that we would only find silence, but then where would we be?

Crying, unfortunately, is good news.

"See?" whispers Muni. "There." She points down an internal hallway to a faint glow.

"How stupid," I say. "Fire can be seen."

She nods and slips past me down the hallway and toward the reddish bloom.

Thirty seconds later we are in a doorway to an old bathroom. There are no windows and the fire is small.

The girl on the floor looks up at me. In the light of the flames I can see that she's a normie. Still, there are circles under her eyes. Her dull orbs are filled with nothing but apathy. In her arms are bundles wrapped in rags.

Three of them.

"No one helped me," she says. She can't be more than thirteen, but I don't know for sure. Hunger stunts everyone's growth.

One of the bundles starts making noise and a flipper hand slips free from the filth. The girl actually rolls her eyes.

"Do you have food?" she asks. There is nothing to her voice. It's been sewn together with spider silk,

Muni steps forward. The babies, so tiny and fragile, squirm in their mother's arms.

"Not here," Muni tells her as her stomach growls and her deformed wings rustle against her back.

"Out there," I blurt out in a half-hearted attempt to cover the noise. I tilt my head sideways. "Not too far from here."

Muni takes another step forward. I can see her thoughts in her body language. I can taste her instinct on my split tongue. She's so far away from being a child that it's hard to believe that she was ever supposed to be human.

"Can I hold one?" Muni asks the girl with her arms outstretched and her little clawed hands curling and flexing. The girl shrugs and jostles the bundles in her arm. Muni gently picks up the closest baby, the one with the flippers, and cradles it like a porcelain plaything. Seconds later her face brightens just one shade as some sort of child-induced fantasy claims her.

She looks up at me and smiles. Then she looks down at the girl. "Have you named it?" she asks.

It. We've been reduced to calling babies "it."

The girl shakes her head. "What's the point?" She's right. There is no point.

Suddenly, Muni whirls on her feet. I expect her to run with the little half-dead thing in her arms, but that's not what she does. Instead, she holds the baby up to me—this stinking, filthy bag of weak flesh. "Look," she says. "It's a dolly."

"Sure, whatever," says the weak thing's mother. "The *dolly* needs food."

I take a deep breath and repeat my empty offer. "Like I said, we have food not far from here."

Muni jostles the infant in her arms and coos at it.

Every last shred of my humanity circles a drain and disappears.

One of the other babies has stripes across its face, beautiful like a tiger. I reach for its tiny hand and scrape my fingers against sharp claws. This one could grow to be dangerous. This one could even be as monstrous as the ones who cheer in the Quadrangle.

The third baby is the weakest. There are no stripes and no flipper hands. Instead, its tiny head is oblong instead of round. Once, a long time ago, I saw a book from The Before that had a picture of ancient Egyptian royalty with heads shaped like that. I can't tell if there's more wrong with the baby or not. I suppose I don't want to know, anyway.

In the end, we take them all with us.

After stomping out the fire until there is only smoke choking us and burning our eyes, we each take one of the babies and slowly descend the staircase to the third floor, then the second and the first.

"Who are you?" I ask the girl who should still be fat from pregnancy and filled with milk, but is wearing bony skin instead.

"Ida," she says.

"Ida?" I give her a funny look.

"Yeah," the girl says in a voice of someone who has all but given up. "Ida Know."

I don't suppose it makes a difference what her name is. Ida Know is probably as good as any.

At least it's honest.

"I'm Cade," I tell her. "This is Muni."

She doesn't nod or smile. Instead, Ida Know says, "Whatever," again.

I get it. I really do.

Outside, the three of us hold the babies tightly to our chests and make our way alongside the building then run across the street to where junkyard tires are stacked in a maze. We weave through them, round and round, until we come out the other side near a row of old brownstones that are as seemingly void of life as the warehouses on Pearl.

The babies don't make a sound, which is good. Maybe they already know what's going to happen. Maybe it's written in their DNA because some humans are different creatures than we were in The Before.

We're now something starving and dark.

Three brownstones in, we duck underneath broken cement stairs to a basement apartment door and gently wrap on the faded wood.

Tap. Tap. Tap.

Tap. Tap. Tap.

Tap. Tap. Tap.

Then I carefully twist the nob and the three of us with our infant cargo melt into the darkness.

The others are inside—the children who we cleave to as family because nobody else cares.

There is a single candle lit in an inside room. My found family is crouched around the scarce light, some with hands outstretched as though the tiny flame can give warmth.

Their hunger is a living thing. I can feel it scratching at my insides.

"Whatcha got there?" asks one of the older girls. Her name is Plumtree because once upon a time she lived with her family on Plumtree Road and had a room of her own and maybe a puppy dog.

"Dollies," says Muni as she holds up the baby she clutches for all to see. The little thing is barely even visible in the candlelight but everybody takes notice of its flipper.

The thing that I'm holding in my hands makes a little burping sound, like the last gasp of something that is about to pass on, then somehow finds the strength to kick its legs.

Another little girl about Muni's age but missing a hand, stands and comes up to me. She doesn't say a word. She just holds out a spotted palm and a stump and I gladly give her the bundle that I'm carrying.

Just like Muni, her eyes light up.

"Dolly," she whispers. "Dolly."

Then Ida Know comes into the candlelight and sighs. "Is there food?" she asks. "If there isn't, I already had my own place."

Plumtree steps forward and reaches for the last of the three bundles—the one with the bean-shaped head. Ida freely hands the baby to her.

"There's food," Plumtree says as she looks around at all of us with our hungry faces and our hollowed-out eyes before gently smiling down at the monster baby in her arms.

"Where?" says Ida Know with the tone-deaf voice of someone from The Before. "Where is there food?"

It's an ignorant question.

While Plumtree cradles the thing in her arms that may just live to see another apocalyptic day, and Muni and the other girl play with their dolls, the rest of us, including me, curl our bony fingers into claws and bare our teeth.

The funny thing is, when Ida Know finally realizes what is going to happen to her, she doesn't even scream.

Not a sound.

Not even once.

Flutter

by John Grover

December 1967

To repeat, the Silver Bridge between Ohio and West Virginia has collapsed. Over thirty vehicles plunged into the frigid Ohio River. Witnesses recall hearing a horrible metallic screeching sound mixed with something indescribable as the cars fell like dominoes, flashing taillights vanished into the….

"Will you please turn that off?" Lucy turned and glared at her boyfriend. "I don't want to hear it. Today has been awful enough."

Sam reached over and switched the car radio off, letting awkward silence fill the car again. "How long are you going to stay mad at me?"

Lucy didn't answer right away. She focused on the road in front of her as it bent sharply and stretched into a thickly wooded area. The only sound she was interested in was the roar of the engine joined by the hiss of the warm air vents.

She crossed an old rickety bridge. The straining wood clattered beneath the car, and Lucy immediately thought of the Silver Bridge. She held her breath and prayed to God that the small timbered bridge held.

"Lucy…?"

"Do you know how long you spent talking to her?" Lucy didn't look at him. "You were flirting. Right in front of me."

"I was being polite."

"Like hell you were."

Sam rolled his eyes. "Christ, Lucy. It was a Christmas party. It was supposed to be fun, remember?"

"Yeah, I saw how much fun you two were having. She touched your shoulder more than once."

"I can't help it if I'm irresistible."

"You were encouraging it."

"That's bullshit and you know it."

She turned to look at him, anger brewing in her chest, her hands clutching the steering wheel tighter.

"That's real nice, Sam. I'm sure your mother would be so proud of the way you talk to me."

"Keep her out of this," Sam snapped. "You always bring her up when we're fighting."

"You fight your way, I'll fight mine."

"Just drive, Lucy. We can talk about this at home."

"I want to talk about it now."

She was about to unload a lot more when a chill ran down her spine. Lucy glanced at the dashboard and reached over to turn the heat up.

"Jesus," Sam said. "You're gonna roast us."

"I'm cold," she said as snow dusted the windshield. Lucy turned on her high beams. The falling snow was making her nervous. There was plenty of it nestled along the sides of the road, wrapped around skeletal trees like soft, plush blankets, but this was fresh and she detested driving in it.

She slowed as the road became slick and a strange sound caught her attention. At first she thought it was the wind but it sounded more like flapping or…a flutter. Lucy dismissed it and turned her defroster on higher.

"Why are you driving so slow?" Sam asked in a huff, his arms folded.

"Do you see the snow?"

She inhaled, trying to relax. As soon she exhaled, she spotted a pair of bright headlights in her rearview mirror, coming fast.

White light flooded the inside of the car. Sam turned around to look out the back, squinting, putting his hand over his eyes.

"What's this guy's problem?"

"I don't know. He's going really fast in this weather . . . he's almost on top of me."

The pair of glowing orbs rushed up behind their car and stayed there. Between the snow and the darkness she couldn't tell what kind of vehicle it was. Her pulse raced and her heart thumped in her ears. The mirror was engulfed in light.

"Sam…?"

"Jesus, what an asshole. Don't let him get to you."

"I can't go any faster or I'll slide all over the road. What is wrong with him?"

"If he doesn't like how you drive, he can just pass. To Hell with him."

Snow piled up quickly on the road, becoming slippery as an eel. The car windows continued to fog up but now a thin layer of frost crackled over them.

Lucy turned the heat to max. It didn't work. Behind her the pair of headlights bore down on them, looking as if they would crash through the back window at any moment. She huffed again and again as panic surged through her.

"Calm down, Lucy."

"God, Sam. I can't help it. He-he's getting too close…. He's…"

The lights suddenly veered to the left, off the road, and vanished. Lucy gasped and nearly hit her brakes but kept on driving, slowing more as they approached another bend in the road.

"Did you see that?" She glanced at Sam and then into her rearview. "Where did he go?"

"Who cares? He's gone. Let's get home."

Lucy took some deep breaths and tried to get her heart to slow down. She didn't know why the car or truck behind them had gotten under her skin the way it did.

"Music," she said. "Let's listen to some music." She turned the radio back on and switched from news to something instrumental. Sam said nothing more to her, only stared outside his window watching the snow come down faster.

Another mile and Lucy could barely see the road. The wipers battled to keep up with the snowstorm's assault.

Where is our turn off? We should have come up to it by now.

That strange sound she'd heard earlier reverberated outside of the driver's side window again. Lucy swore it was like a . . . flutter. Flapping wings somewhere deep inside of her head. The sound grew louder and louder, rising above the sounds of the storm.

"Sam do you hear that? Sam….Sa—

Headlights appeared in front of them, blazing bright and hot. Lucy screamed and turned the wheel sharply. "Sam!"

"Oh my God!" Sam braced himself against the dashboard.

The car skidded across the road, crossed lanes and swerved. Lucy fought to keep control, her palms slick with sweat, body jerking violently around her seat. A loud screech then the fluttering sound poured out of the radio.

"What's going on!" she screamed. The spinning car came to a stop inches before a gnarled tree, the holes in its trunk resembling a face leering in at her. Hands trembling uncontrollably, Lucy looked out the windshield. Red lights on the road glowed through the falling snow, moving closer and closer.

"What is that?" she whispered.

Sam turned, his face pale white. "Is it the cops?"

She shook her head. "That's not the cops . . . it's . . . something else .

. . it's not even a car . . . it's a. . ."

The red lights streaked toward the windshield. Both of them screamed as the lights shot up into the sky.

"Get the fuck outta here!" Sam yelled.

Lucy grabbed the wheel and hit the gas, tearing from the side of the road and skidding down the street. Her tires kicked up snow and ice. Fluttering resounded all around them. It seemed to be the only sound Lucy could hear.

Flutter.

"Sam, what the hell is that?"

Flutter

"God, make it go away!"

Flutter.

A screech rose above the flutter, tore through the sky then something hit the roof of the car. A scraping sound clattered across it.

Lucy screamed.

The car spun out of her control again, and into a ditch. The car sputtered and died, the radio silenced. The heat melted away into the icy cold. Lucy checked the clutch and turned the key again and again but nothing happened.

"Are you all right?" Sam asked, reaching over to touch her arm.

She jumped. "Oh my God . . . what are we going to do?"

He looked around, searching through every window as they quickly covered with sheets of powdery snow. "I see a light through the trees." He pointed out his window. "There's a house back there. We'll ask to use their phone and call for help." He reached for the door.

"Sam wait!" Lucy grabbed his arm with both hands. "Something's out there."

"We can't stay here, we'll freeze."

She listened closely but didn't hear the flutter, then stared past Sam through the window and watched the trees thrashing in the wind.

Sam reached his hand out to her. "C'mon. The house is just through the trees. We can't stay here. We need help."

Lucy crawled to his side of the car and let him curl his arm around her. She clung to his warmth and held her breath. He pushed open his door and climbed out, helping her along.

"Be careful," he said. "It's slippery."

She pulled her coat tight and glanced at the sky. Her dress rippled in the wind and her legs were already starting to feel numb. She wasn't prepared to be out in this weather. Thank God she'd worn flats instead of heels. All Lucy could think of right now was home and listening to The Beatles on her record player. Why did she ever accept that invite to the damn party?

Sam led her into the thicket, their feet sinking ankle-deep in the snow, biting wind lashing at their faces. A glimpse of amber gold light glinted through the trees.

Flutter.

It resounded somewhere above them. Lucy nearly stopped in her tracks but Sam pulled her along, snow beating down on them. They finally stumbled up to a two-story white house with green shutters. The two of them dashed up the front steps. Sam knocked on the door.

"Hello!" he shouted. "We need help! Our car broke down! Hello!"

There was no answer.

Lucy checked her wristwatch and noticed it too was dead.

"Hello!" Sam grabbed the doorknob and eased the door open.

"Sam no, it's someone's home…"

"We don't have a choice. We just need to use their phone."

Sam pushed his way into the house. Lucy followed behind him, shutting the door and leaving the storm outside.

A strong musty scent permeated the home. The air was damp and mold bled down the walls, their floral-patterned wallpaper curling with age. The couple stood in a living room that looked as if it hadn't been used in fifty years. The light above them flickered. Lucy glanced around for a phone but didn't see one.

"The kitchen," she said to Sam. "There has to be one in there on the wall or something."

"Okay."

She trotted ahead of him, through the living room into a dining room where she noticed large scorch marks on the wall in the shape of a face, bulbous eyes drooping all the way to a gaping mouth locked in an eternal, tormented scream.

Lucy shook it off and pushed her way through a swinging door into a dilapidated kitchen. Cupboard doors dangled from hinges, a rusted sink dripped with water. The floor was covered with dead leaves and dirt. She spotted a phone on the wall next to the backdoor. Sam stepped up beside her. The light in the kitchen flickered as she picked the phone up.

She stared at Sam and hung up the receiver. "It's dead."

"Maybe we should stay here and wait out the storm," Sam said.

Lucy looked around and shivered. "I don't like it here."

"Well, what else are we going to do?"

"I don't know."

"We're staying here."

"Sam . . . look at this place. Something's not right. Where's the owner? What if they come back and find us here and…"

A thump rolled across the ceiling. Both of them looked up.

"That must be the owners," Sam said. "Let's go find them. We'll tell them what's going on and ask to stay here."

"I don't know…"

"Lucy, c'mon. We're not going back out there." He pointed vaguely out of the kitchen. "This is our only option."

Another thump, chased by a creaking sound. Sam moved quickly out of the kitchen. Lucy followed him reluctantly as he weaved around the dining room table and into the living room. There was a staircase beside the front door.

Sam started up the stairs and gestured for Lucy to follow. She hesitated on the first few steps, discovering another scorched face on the stairway wall. She dry swallowed and looked past Sam at the second floor hallway, the light at the top flickered, but she followed. Upstairs they discovered several bedrooms and a bathroom. Lucy followed Sam to one of the bedrooms. He knocked.

"Hello?" he called. "We're sorry we let ourselves in but we need some help."

There was no reply.

He opened the door and stepped inside. Lucy huddled behind him. The bedroom was sparse with a dresser, a lamp on a single nightstand and a large bed. The bed was soiled with leaves and dirt.

"Something's not right here."

"Lucy, just stop it. C'mon." He stepped back into the hall, ushering Lucy with him.

THUMP.

They turned towards the door at the end of the hall. Lucy took Sam's hand. It was sweaty. The two started toward the last door. It seemed to take an eternity to reach it.

When Sam reached up to knock, the door slipped open with a creak. Lucy followed him inside. It looked like the master bedroom with the biggest bed Lucy had ever seen and an ornate headboard. It had been positioned against the back wall but was a mess, its covers balled up and musty. The light above them flickered on and off and the stench of decay rose in the room. A shuffling caught their attention.

Both of them made their way around the bed to the corner of the room. The fluttering sound returned, and it was everywhere. It was all Lucy could hear but suddenly stopped when they spotted the rotting corpse sitting on the floor. Vacant eyes leered at them, tattered clothes festered with moss, and a crumbled hand was frozen in a longing reach.

A scream died in Lucy's throat as the corpse's bloated body rippled and its flesh bubbled. The jaw opened and unhinged, falling into its lap. Thousands of moths burst from the mouth, battering Lucy and Sam. The fluttering sound swallowed the room, buzzing and screaming inside Lucy's head.

Her scream finally escaped as she grabbed hold of Sam. He folded his arms around her while the moths assaulted them, streamed through their hair, fluttered over their faces, against their lips. Sam turned them both around to shelter them and….

The moths soared to the foot of the bed and gathered in a massive swarm, slowly shifting, coiling, and forming a humanoid figure. It stood impossibly tall, head nearly meeting the ceiling. Scorched flesh writhed across its body and prickly mandibles stretched from its face. Gossamer wings unfurled from its back, stretching seven feet wide. It stared at the couple.

Lucy screamed as the lights went out, plunging the house into darkness. Red eyes pierced the black, blinking across the room.

"Sam!" Lucy screamed. "We gotta get out of here!" She reached for him but grasped nothing but air. "Sam! *Sam*!" She waved both hands in front of her, struggling to find him.

Sam was gone.

She collided with the bedroom wall, pressed herself against it and struggled to find the door. Her heart raced, sweat dampened her face despite the icy cold rippling through her body.

"Oh God . . . Sam! Help! Somebody help!"

Red eyes floated across the room toward her. She thrashed against the walls and tripped across the floor into the hallway. She threw herself against the nearest wall and pushed forward, afraid to look back, afraid to know if the thing was following her.

Running into the banister she tumbled down the stairs, ripping her dress, nose bouncing off the floor. Pain washed over as she rolled around to see the red eyes coming down the stairs for her, the fluttering all around, growing louder and louder, consuming every thought. She opened her mouth to scream but moths vomited out. The red eyes closed in.

* * *

"A shame, a goddamn shame," Officer Andrews said. "As if we haven't had enough tragedy." He climbed over the snow and away from the car.

"Are we too late?" His partner held blankets and supplies in his arms.

Andrews bowed his head. "I'm afraid so. Poor kids froze to death. The car must've broken down in the storm last night and without any heat…." He let out a heavy sigh. "I'll call the ambulance and the coroner."

"God . . . I wish one of the plows had spotted them."

"Me too." Officer Andrews pulled his radio from his dash and radioed back to the station. He stared at the small car and its frosted windows, his gaze drifting into the woods and through the trees. He caught a glimpse of an old, abandoned house and saw . . . something . . . with large wings skim past it and into the trees. He closed his eyes and shook his head before returning to his call.

* * *

July 1997

Anthony, his sister Gina and their pal Leo climbed through the broken window of the old house.

"Are you sure you want to do this?" Leo asked, last to climb into the living room. He nearly fell on his ass and crashed into the coffee table beside him.

"Hell yeah." Anthony turned and held back his laugh. "It's my eighteenth birthday. I've been wanting to do this all year. Hurry up, the sun is going down. We need to get upstairs."

Gina checked on Leo before following her brother into the foyer. "You really think we're gonna see anything tonight?"

Anthony nodded, taking some candles out of his shorts' pocket. "You know the stories. This places is *so* haunted."

"It's old and smelly, not sure it's haunted."

"C'mon, Gina." Anthony stopped at the foot of the stairs. "You promised. It's gonna be cool."

"It better be."

"It will," Leo called from behind them.

Gina turned. "Now you're on his side again?"

"The stories are true," Leo said. "My grandfather told me that story about Lucy and Sam. I just don't know if the house is safe."

"It's fine." Anthony started up the stairs, taking one step at a time, slowly, relishing every creak and every puff of dust. A fluttering vibrated somewhere inside the wall beside him. He hoped the sound would help creep out his sister and best bud. Although so far they seemed not to notice.

Anthony climbed to the top of the stairs and stood in the hallway. He looked to his right, glimpsed the open door to the bathroom with its stained, cracked toilet and broken vanity mirror, then looked left. The door at the end of the hall was half open. He sucked in some air, turned to the others and started toward the door.

"Here it is…"

Gina and Leo had reached the landing and followed behind him, their steps creaking in the hallway. Anthony felt the floor vibrate slightly beneath him but didn't give it much thought. Dust rose from the edge of the bedroom doorway. The frame was blanketed in a tapestry of cobwebs.

The master bedroom was shrouded in shadows. The last of the dying light was no match for the oppressive dark that bled into the room. A smidge of excitement mixed with unease surged through him. He walked over to the foot of the old bed, rotting pieces of headboard scattered across its mattress, holes in the blankets. He sat on the floor and propped up two candles, lit them with a lighter.

"For Lucy and Sam."

Gina snatched the lighter from Anthony's hand and lit a cigarette.

"What are you doing?"

"What's it look like?"

"You're being disrespectful." He took the lighter back as he watched the smoke circle her head then drift to the ceiling. "Mom know you smoke?"

"I'm twenty. I don't need her permission."

"Whatever. Put it out."

Gina rolled her eyes.

"I mean it. We're here to see if Lucy or Sam will show up."

"Or *it*," Leo said.

"It what?" Gina turned to him as she crushed her cigarette out on the wooden floor.

"The Mothman."

Anthony met Leo's gaze but didn't say anything.

"Cut the shit," Gina said.

"It's true," Leo said.

Gina looked over at her brother. "That is what this is really about?"

Anthony shrugged.

"I thought we were here to see if this place was haunted?"

"We are," Anthony replied. "And to see if it…comes back."

"You two are idiots," she said. "You really think a giant moth thing killed two lovers in the middle of nowhere? Then what…? Moved them from this big, old house into their car to make it look like they froze to death?"

"It happened," Leo said. "My grandfather saw it. It flew through the forest that night before the bridge collapsed. It was huge and had red eyes. It was seen the year before that too, on the roof of the munitions plant."

"O—kay." Gina looked back at Anthony. "So what now?"

"Let's just see what happens," he said. "Let's all be quiet and think of Lucy and Sam. How cold it was that night, the snow, this place and…"

A thump rattled across the ceiling. All three of them looked up and followed the thump as it rolled down the back wall. An icy chill caressed

Anthony's arms and neck despite the summer heat. Cold sweat broke out on his forehead right before the thumping stopped.

Fluttering rose from the walls around the room, growing louder and louder, buzzing inside of Anthony's head, filling his ears, vibrating through his teeth. He clasped his hands over his ears.

"God . . . you guys hear that?"

"I don't hear anything now," Gina said.

"You can't hear that?"

"What is it?" Leo asked.

"It's—it's like a thousand wings flapping all at once. It's so loud…I can't…" Anthony closed his eyes.

When he opened them, the candles blew out. The flapping continued outside. He jumped to his feet, shaking and turning slowly to look out the bedroom window.

Two red orbs pierced the pitch-black outside. Anthony's mouth dropped open. His hands twitched.

"Anthony?" Gina's voice called, but he couldn't move. "Anthony!" She grabbed his arm and the window shattered.

Glass exploded inward. The three of them screamed and bolted for the hallway. Gina and Leo raced down the hall, stumbling blindly over each other, clawing to escape. Anthony fell behind, cold air blasting his back before a loud creak echoed through the hallway.

"Gina! Leo!" He cried in panic. Cracks splintered the floor as it opened beneath them like the maw of a giant beast. Wood shredded, the banister crumpled. In an instant Gina and Leo were gone.

"*No!*" Anthony dropped to his knees. As the dust cleared he looked down into the chasm. The bodies of his sister and best friend lay in a sea of wooden shards and debris. Tears rolled down his cheeks. He put out a desperate hand, as if he could actually touch them.

The fluttering sound whispered to him again. Anthony looked up. On the other side of the chasm stood a tall figure. Giant red eyes dominated most of its shadowy face. Huge wings stretched to either side of the hall, scraping its walls.

Anthony screamed with rage and pain as the Mothman lifted into the air. It floated across the cavernous hole in the floor toward him.

Unable to get to his feet, unable to shake the grief and pain, he turned and crawled back toward the bedroom, through the door, over broken glass and dirt. Fluttering vibrated all around him.

He rolled onto his back to see the towering hybrid of man and insect, of darkness and writhing flesh, float through the doorway toward him, wings stretching further and further, consuming the room as it descended.

Anthony tried to scream but only the fluttering sound came out.

* * *

October 2017

Malcolm strung the last of the orange pumpkin lights and checked the homemade ghosts he'd propped up with PVC piping. They looked cool. So did the zombie he made with one of Jake's flannel shirts, and the old crone with one of his mom's old black dresses and a broomstick. Not that he was expecting many trick-or-treaters at the new house. The property had just been rebuilt this year and a new driveway finally met the main road. Probably no one knew they were tucked back here within the thicket of trees. At least not this year.

He headed back inside and was met by their energetic Boston Terrier, Sammy. Wondering what Jake was getting into upstairs, Malcolm followed the hallway, past the side table adorned with a lighted haunted house and pumpkin, to the master bedroom. It was empty. No husband.

"Jake?"

"In here." The voice came from the room next door.

Malcolm stepped into their makeshift office. Jake sat at a desk at the back of the room, browsing his laptop.

"What are you doing? Thought you wanted to take a nap?'

"I couldn't sleep. I kept hearing this weird noise."

"What noise?"

"I don't know, like a flutter or something. In the walls." He didn't turn around, gaze was fixed on the screen. "It got me thinking about this old house. I just found something. You're not going to believe it."

Malcolm shook his head. "*Now* you do this? We've been here three weeks. You couldn't have looked this up before we bought the house?"

"You know me, Mal. I love a good mystery."

"Don't I know it." He walked over to Jake, put his hands on his shoulders and slowly rubbed them. "So, what is it?"

"Look at this....a couple of people died here thirty years ago. They fell into the basement when the floor collapsed. There were rumors that the girl's younger brother pushed them because he was jealous."

"Jealous?"

Jake shrugged. "Says here he didn't like that his best friend was trying to put the moves on his sister and he flew into a rage."

"Really?" Malcolm glanced at the screen.

"Yeah." Jake's voice had an air of excitement about it. "But . . . it gets better. Brother says a monster called The Mothman did it. They put him in an institution because he kept saying it was real and following him everywhere. Hear that Mal? The Mothman!"

"Here we go," Malcolm sighed. "I knew you'd start talking about monsters and legends, not the fact that some disturbed guy killed his sister."

"Or they really did meet the Mothman before they fell through the floor."

"Jake…"

"I'm not saying anything, really. But, it's kinda creepy that people died here."

"Yeah it is. Surprised the realtor didn't tell us. I thought they had to reveal things like this."

"It was over thirty years ago and it was an abandoned property. We were probably the only saps that showed interest in it and they didn't want to jinx it."

"Guess you're right." Malcolm turned from the computer and started back toward the door. "C'mon, let's order some takeout."

Jake was shockingly quiet. He scanned the articles and stories about the Mothman and the Silver Bridge. "Huh . . . yeah sure." He looked over his shoulder at Mal then around the room.

Malcolm looked back, asked, "What?"

"The house *is* sound, right?"

"Of course. Don't worry. Everything has been replaced. I walked the house with the inspector myself. Everything is solid. Nothing is going to collapse."

Jake smiled. "Okay. Let's get pizza."

Malcolm grinned back. "You got it."

* * *

It was the cold that woke Malcolm. Discovering the other side of the bed empty was what concerned him. He sat up and looked around the darkened room, letting his eyes adjust. Sammy slept soundlessly at the end of the bed as usual.

"Jake?" Malcolm eased his covers aside and a chill hit him. He shivered but continued into the hall, peering into the office but Jake wasn't there. The computer was off.

He strolled down the other end of the hall and checked the bathroom. Not there, either. He checked the spare bedroom. Nope. Malcolm cocked his head then went downstairs.

Maybe he's getting a midnight snack. The kitchen was dim and quiet. The refrigerator hummed softly, the nightlight above the counters lent a shallow green light to the space. A ghost gawked from the windowsill above the pumpkin cookie jar.

"Jake?" The basement door was ajar. He walked over and heard a shuffling sound from the other side. Malcolm eased the door open the rest of the way and switched on the light, hurrying down the stairs.

Jake paced across the stone floor, dragging dirt and leaves with him, a dazed look on his face. Malcolm stood for a moment, his heart beating faster now.

"What are you doing down here?" Malcolm stepped toward him and reached out his hand. "Are you okay?"

Jake flinched and stopped. He looked at Malcolm with tears rolling down his cheeks. "This is its den…"

"What? What are you talking about?"

"Lucy told me . . . and Gina . . . and…." Jake started to tremble.

Malcolm grabbed hold of him. "You're having a dream. It's okay…. I'm here. Let's go back to bed. C'mon…"

"No!" He grabbed hold of Malcolm, eyes wide. "We have to get out of here. Mal . . . we need to go. We're not safe!"

"Jake, stop! You had a nightmare. That's it. Let's go back upstairs."

"Don't you hear it?"

"What?"

"That flutter? It's everywhere. All around us. In the walls. It's coming for us, Mal. It's coming."

"Jake…" Malcolm curled his arm around him. "Let's go up and talk. Please. Everything will be all right." As he ushered Jake to the stairs, he could feel him shaking .

Jake stopped and looked back into the basement, his head jerking from left to right. "It's coming…"

"C'mon. Let's get you back to bed."

The two of them crept into the kitchen. Malcolm nudged the cellar door closed behind them while Jake stared at the walls, looked up at the ceiling and shuffled across the floor.

Both of them jumped when their Terrier let out a terrified bark. The dog stood at the front door, his hair bristling, teeth showing and barked with a rage unseen before.

"Sammy!" Malcolm called, rushing over to calm him down.

Jake slowly walked up behind them, shivering as the dog barked louder.

"My God, Sammy. What is it?" Malcolm stood up and grabbed the front door's handle.

"Mal, no!" Jake said. "Don't open the…"

"I have to make sure nothing's out there. Calm down!" His patience had worn thin. "It'll be fine."

He swung the door open and stared out into the yard. The orange pumpkin lights illuminated the ghoulish faces of the Halloween props, but there was one that stood taller than the others. Its red eyes glowed in the hazy light as shadows slithered through the yard

"That's not funny, Mal!" Jake cried, sidling up next to him to gaze outside, his voice laced with panic. "When did you put that up?"

Malcolm shook his head, and slowly backed into Jake. "That's not one of mine…"

Great wings flapped and the creature crashed through the Halloween decorations.

"Run!" Malcolm screamed and slammed the front door.

Jake scooped up Sammy and raced toward the dining room. Malcolm followed. The sound of the front door bursting off its hinges pealed through the house, chasing them room to room, vibrating through the floors, rattling the walls.

Malcolm's heart thumped in his ears as they tore through the kitchen and through the backdoor, chasing after Jake. His feet crunched on a sea of dead leaves. A flapping sound (or what is it a flutter?) rose behind him, growing closer and closer. Icy tendrils squeezed him, the air thickening, sweat soaking his face and hair.

A long, deafening screech filled the air as a gust of wind hit him like a tidal wave. He stumbled forward, trying to keep his footing, trying to keep his eyes on Jake and Sammy. Lightning-scarred trees reached with long, spindly arms, lashing at his face, snagging his hair and shirt.

He nearly lost sight of Jake as the woods closed in around him. Finally, as if hurling through wave after wave of earthly blockades, he reached his husband and wrapped his arms around him.

"Get down!" Malcolm screamed as he forced Jake and Sammy to the ground and covered them with his body.

A whirlwind roared over them. Something scraped Malcolm's back and he dared to peer upward, just catching the huge shadowy form lift above the treetops.

When the wind subsided, Malcolm slipped off of Jake and Sammy. Jake looked up at him, his face pale, his eyes wide with terror. He opened his mouth but couldn't find the words.

Malcolm nodded and hugged him. "I know….I know…let's get the hell out of here."

They turned back toward the house, running past without bothering to stop. They jumped into their SUV, leaving everything behind, barreling down the driveway and into the road.

Eventually they crossed into Ohio. Malcolm glanced into his rearview mirror and saw a tall, dark figure with wings and glowing red eyes standing on the bridge behind them. He blinked and the figure was gone. He looked over at Jake cradling Sammy in his arms, and let out a sigh of relief.

The Ookie Birds
by Paul McMahon

Richard Chambers turned up Heritage Hill, still annoyed his secretary refused to handle this for him. He couldn't force her to, didn't have a legal leg to stand on, but he'd have given her almost anything to spare him having to face his Mom's deterioration again. Seeing her frailty at Belinda's funereal had shaken him badly, but he told himself burying her daughter, so soon after losing her husband, made her seem worse than she really was.

He steered his Lincoln MKS to the wrong side of the street and parked nose-up along the crumbling, frost-heaved sidewalk. He'd promised Mom he'd arrive at ten o'clock. That gave him twelve minutes until he had to leave this fine new car smell.

Just like that, he felt her standing above him, watching him from the second-floor apartment. He refused to look up. If their eyes met, he'd have to go inside before he was ready.

He resisted the urge to re-check his briefcase for the assisted-living brochures he wanted to show her. He'd checked twice before he left home. They'd been there then; they'd be here now. As would all the legal documents he needed, including Mom's silly Literary Executor form, which he'd brought despite knowing why she wanted it.

Weeks before her accident, Belinda had told him Mom's declining sanity grew especially pronounced around the subject of Dad's old scripts. He'd had no reason to doubt her. She'd been Mom's sole caretaker for years, driving her to doctor appointments, ensuring she took her medications, handling the bills and all the other duties a human life required.

When Belinda died unexpectedly, all those chores and responsibilities fell to him. No way could he incorporate so much into his busy life. His only option was to coax Mom into a long-term care facility where he could pay other people to handle it. It'd be better for her, too. She'd have people her age to befriend and interact with. A huge step up from this ghost-town.

A shadow moved up the street. For a moment, it looked like some kind of animal was digging through the trash a few houses up. Though he stared for a solid minute, he didn't see anything move again. Must have been a shifting shadow as the sun slipped behind a cloud.

Richard sighed. He turned his attention to the opposite side of the street. A lot of these houses stood empty now. Mom was the only one who remained from his childhood days.

He glanced at his watch, then opened the car door and started wriggling his body out from under the steering wheel. Briefcase in hand, he stood, slammed the door, and leaned on the side of the car while he caught his breath. A gym membership might do him some good.

Richard started the long walk to the back entrance of the old three-decker, then spun and glared at the house across the street. For just a wink, he'd seen a very tall man approaching him across the yard. Nothing there, though. Another shifting shadow.

He took his time climbing the back hall stairs to Mom's apartment. Even so, by the time he reached the second-floor landing, he needed a few moments to compose himself. Mom was standing in her kitchen, both main doors wide open, watching him through the screen door with a look of horror.

"I'm not going to drop dead on you, Mother."

She lowered her head slightly.

"No," she said.

"Are you going to let me in?"

She nodded, slowly, and made no move to come open the screen door. Finally, she said, "It's open."

He sighed, pulled on the screen door, and stepped through, letting it bang shut behind him. Mom didn't look quite as frail as she had at Belinda's funeral, she even had more color to her. She started to smile, but her expression froze.

Richard stepped forward, thinking his mother was about to faint. She blinked, her posture straightening.

"Are you feeling okay?" he asked.

"Fine, fine."

"I don't believe you."

"Don't give me any static."

He watched her face, and for a moment it didn't look like she knew he was there. Then her eyelids fluttered and she focused on him.

"You shouldn't have come."

"Mom, I *had* to come. We've talked about this."

"We could have met someplace."

"In order to do that, I'd still have to come here to get you. We might as well sit at the table and enjoy the privacy."

"Ain't no privacy here."

Shaking his head, Richard slapped the briefcase on the kitchen table harder than he intended. On the wall, between the two windows, hung a mediocre painting of a lilac bush in the sunlight. A Belinda original.

"Mom, it's all privacy here. We're the only two people."

Mom shook her head. He looked at her, wondering how so much age could have appeared in her face over the years.

"It's just us, Mom."

"It isn't. They're here."

Richard sighed. "No one's here, Mom. There's barely anyone in the houses around us, either, because they're at work or school or . . . deceased."

"No. *They're* here. Right here in this room with us."

He didn't have to ask the next question. He knew the answer already. He couldn't help himself, though.

"*Who's* here, Mom?"

"The Ookie Birds."

"The Ookie Birds. You mean Dad's cartoon characters?"

"You *know* that's who I mean."

"Mom--"

She cut him off. "They're not real, right? I don't need your static, Richard. Belinda said the same thing to me about a thousand times."

"Mom. Belinda's . . . "

She shook her head and looked away from him.

"You don't have to tell me," she said. Looking back at him, her expression was intense. "They don't want you here, Richard."

He saw such belief in her eyes that for an instant, he could feel the things surrounding him. Movement on the ceiling caught his attention, and he blocked his mind from imagining a bird hovering up there. He'd only seen a shifting reflection of light, maybe a car passing on the street. He wouldn't allow himself to look, though. There was nothing there, not by the trash cans earlier, and certainly not coming across the street toward him. The sooner he got Mom into a place that would look after her, the better off he'd be.

"They're not real," Richard said, more for his own benefit than Mom's. Her kitchen chair looked rickety, and he said a quick prayer it would hold his weight as he settled onto it.

"Mum, sit down over here please." He indicated a chair across the table, but she didn't glance at it. Instead, she pulled out the chair closest to him, sat down, and leaned against him.

Richard sighed and pulled his briefcase closer. The latches didn't flip up when he hit the release buttons.

"This would be a lot easier to do if you weren't so close, Mom." He looked at her and realized she wasn't seeing him. She was looking at something over his shoulder. She reached up and passed her hand in the air behind his head, as if shooing a fly.

"Mom?"

"Yes, Richard?"

"Can you please go sit on the other side of the table?"

"You know I can't."

"I know no such thing. Let's just take a look through the brochures I brought, see if anything strikes your fancy."

"No. I don't think so."

Richard closed his eyes and kept his fists from clenching. "What do you mean, you don't think so? The whole reason I came here today was so we can find a place and get you somewhere you'll be safe and well-cared for."

"The Ookies will follow me."

"The Ookies don't exist, Mom."

"They'll kill everyone there."

"They'll--" Richard looked at her. She met his gaze full-on and he looked away quickly, unnerved. It was his own fault. He should have gotten Mom into a home right after Dad died. He'd been so wrapped up in his own life he'd avoided Belinda's phone calls and only responded when something financial came up. Something he could help with. If he'd just taken the time to get involved earlier, Mom might not be this far gone. Or at least, not alone and fending for herself.

Time to fix this.

Richard tripped the latch releases again. Nothing happened.

"Do you know what your father once told me?"

He sighed, ignoring her as she waved her hand behind his head again.

"He told me the Ookies were angry. He said they wanted to be on TV."

Richard held the releases in the open position, but the latches still didn't let go. He wedged a fingernail under one but couldn't budge it. It felt glued in place.

"They think he failed them for not selling them to a TV network. Even though he tried."

"Mom, can we--"

"He *tried*, Richard. They rejected him. All of them, even the little public stations."

"And with good reason."

She pulled away from him. "What are you saying?"

"I'm saying, Mom, that Dad's scripts needed a lot of work."

"He knew that Richard. He hyped the idea more than the actual scripts."

"Dad let me read them after I finished law school."

"No, he didn't. He never let anyone read them."

"He thought I could figure out where he went wrong. Said I was always criticizing Belinda's art, so he hoped I could tell him something useful." In complete honesty, he hadn't paid much attention to the scripts when he'd read them. Dad had insisted on sitting right there, watching every second. The man's stare had put him off.

Mom's expression grew hurt as she realized he was telling her the truth. "He never let me . . . "

"I couldn't help him," Richard said.

A twist of pain ratcheted up through his stomach. He ignored it.

"You know they want to kill you, right?" Mom said.

Richard shook his head. "Shouldn't have had hash for breakfast. And I don't want to talk about the Ookie Birds anymore. I came here to find you a new home."

She nodded, but the anger stayed in her stare. "So, show me something," she said.

"Okay."

He flipped the releases on the briefcase once again, but nothing happened. "I seem to be having some--"

She reached up and made the fly-shooing movement over the briefcase, and the latches popped up. He took a moment to process that, then opened the case.

"It was the green one, in case you're interested."

"I'm not."

"It was sitting on your case, holding the thingies down."

"I'm sure." He reached into the front pocket on the inside of the lid and pulled the first brochure free. Holtzman Home Estates, the most expensive option available. Paying for it would hurt. He was betting Mom would reject his first offer out of hand. "This is a very nice place--"

The lid of the briefcase slammed shut. He jerked back just in time. Doing so re-aggravated the pain in his gut.

"I'm not looking at anything until we sign the Literary Executor papers."

He started to ask her why, but the pain in his gut expanded suddenly, making him lean away from her to find comfort. "I think I need to use your restroom."

"Stop it," she said as she waved her hand at his side. The pain ebbed. "That's the red one. He's mean."

"Seriously, Mom," he said through slow, careful breaths. The pain was gone, but who knew when it might return.

"It keeps stabbing its beak into your side."

He gaped at her.

"Bet it hurts."

"I just . . . I just have to go to the--" he hissed as the pain came back, stronger than ever.

"I told you, they want to kill you." She stood up and moved behind him, and immediately the pain stopped.

"What the hell is going on, Mom?"

"What do you care? The Ookie Birds aren't real, right?" She leaned over him, put her hands on each side of the briefcase and opened it. "Get the paperwork, Richard. I intend to sign ownership of your father's scripts to you. Then I'll be happy to look at any brochures you want."

"But . . . but I don't want Dad's scripts."

"No more static, Richard. It's the only way."

Richard sighed. "This is ridiculous," he said, as he leaned forward and slid the papers out anyway. "What am I supposed to do with a bunch of clunky old scripts?"

"Sell them. It's the only way they'll be happy."

"By all means, Mom. Let's make the Ookie Birds happy."

It took only a few moments. Richard signed, then directed Mom where to sign.

"Is that it?"

"That's it."

Mom sat back in her chair, a big grin on her face. Richard placed the completed forms inside the briefcase. "Now, in the event of your death, I'll inherit possession of Dad's work."

"What? I have to die?"

Richard looked at her. "That's what the form is for, yes."

She looked around the kitchen and her smile melted into a look of pure anguish. "I can still see them, Richard."

"I don't doubt it," he said. He prided himself on not rolling his eyes.

"Will they kill me now?"

"Mom, as long as we're signing paperwork, this is a Power of Attorney. It'll give me access to your money and assets, and leaves me in charge of your bills, including board at whatever retirement home we decide on."

"Don't look at me like that."

"I'm not looking at you."

"Don't."

Richard turned his head. Mom had gone pale.

"Maybe we should sign the Health Care Proxy as well."

"Do it quickly," Mom said.

Richard talked her through it, condensing his usual speech as much as he dared, and still Mom was impatient to get to the signing. They finished the Health Care Proxy first, and then he started his spiel on the Power of Attorney.

"Forget all that. Where do I sign?"

"I've got to go over all this."

"The green one is drooling and staring at me."

She snagged the pen out of his hand and leaned closer to the table. Seconds later, she'd signed the paper, putting him officially and legally in charge of her life.

She surprised him by standing up. "While I still can," she said. He thought she was heading for the bathroom, but at the last moment she turned and walked into her bedroom. Richard decided to forge ahead.

"This first brochure's from Holtzman Home Estates," he called out. "It's the biggest, which means there will be lots of other people there for you to mingle with."

He glanced toward her room, recognized another of Belinda's landscapes, this one far too red for his taste, but Mom was rifling through a drawer.

"You'll get your own two-room apartment, and it boasts all the amenities of everyday life on the property."

"Found them," Mom said.

The scripts, he thought. *That's what she's after.* "Mom, you don't have to do that."

"I don't want them here anymore. Whatever it takes, I want to be rid of them."

Richard watched her shuffling back to him clutching a roll of papers like something you'd whack a dog with to make it behave. Maybe Holtzman Home Estates offered psychiatric counseling. He'd have to look into it.

She reached the table and held the scripts out. Richard swallowed and took them.

"I can't believe you kept these," he said.

"Your father wanted to keep them in the family. He thought someone might be able to salvage them some day."

Richard snorted. Even skimming them while Dad watched, he could tell the scripts were awful. He hadn't said as much, though. He'd given the old man a line about them being "not quite there," but offered no suggestions on how to fix them.

Richard pulled the elastic off the rolled paper.

"Richard?"

There were four scripts in all, each eight pages, the stories unfinished. The top one was titled "The Ookie Birds: Mardis-Gras Madness."

"Richard? I can't see them anymore."

In it, the three Ookie Birds bumbled around a colorful parade, breaking things and making life difficult for everyone. Nobody in the script could catch them. In fact, nobody in the script even seemed to know they were there. The Ookies had clear sailing to do whatever they wanted.

"Richard?"

"What, Mom?" he said. He looked up and yelped when he saw the round, red face grinning at him from Mom's side.

It was definitely bird-like in appearance. Far bigger than an actual bird, though. Its eyes were perfectly round but the pupils didn't line up. Atop its head rose a strand of what might be hair except it sported three perfectly formed red feathers at the tip.

"What the . . . hell?"

The Ookie raised a stubby red wing and waggled its feathers at him. "Mom?"

"You see them, don't you?"

In front of the bathroom, sitting on the floor, the purple Ookie bird towered to the ceiling. It was scrawny as only a cartoon character could be, its neck long and striped red and white like a barber pole. Its feet jutted out in front of it, three oblong yellow toes sticking up while feathers on the strand of hair atop its head brushed the ceiling.

"I love you, Richard," Mom was saying. "I'm so sorry I had to do this to you, but I just can't take any more."

The purple Ookie Bird smiled, its beak stretching at the sides like rubber, its narrow red tongue wiggling in its mouth like a spasming worm.

"This can't be--" Richard looked at the scripts in his hand and yelped as a black maw opened in front of his eyes. It snapped closed millimeters from his nose. The green one. It sat on the briefcase, which was closed again. The bird's stubby wings covered the latches. Instead of waving at him, it lurched forward and snapped its cartoon jaws in front of his face again. When Richard jerked back, it lowered its head and snickered.

"This hurts," Mom said.

He looked to his left, saw the red Ookie, the mean one, poking its beak into Mom's chest. Its feathers were the color of boiled lobster, and the single black eyebrow over its bulbous eyes crooked down in a "V." The purple one leaned forward, watching intently. Its toes wiggled with glee.

"Just do it," Mom said.

She was begging the Ookies for death. They were here, they were real, and he'd put her off for weeks. Her own son. She must have felt abandoned. Shunned. Richard could barely comprehend that he'd made his own mother feel so deserted and alone.

The red Ookie Bird pulled its beak out of Mom's chest. It smiled at him, though its grin looked more like a grimace. It turned to Mom and its eyes narrowed even further.

Richard leaned over, tried to catch the thing's beak as it stabbed toward Mom's heart. He felt nothing, as the bird pixilated into a mass of blurry lines, and then resolved again a few feet away. He remembered Mom passing her hand behind his head earlier. She'd been keeping it away from him. The way it had disappeared in a mess of jagged lines reminded him of the old horizontal and vertical knobs on the TV set they'd had growing up.

He'd watched such great cartoons on that thing back in the day. Cats chasing mice, dogs chasing cats, coyotes chasing birds.

Richard picked up the pen again.

"I've got it, Mom. Give me a minute."

He unrolled the first of Dad's scripts and started writing.

* * *

Richard managed not to beat himself up while Mom was in surgery. Heart attack, they said. When they asked how long she'd been suffering, it had taken all his self-control not to laugh.

Sitting beside her, waiting for her to wake up, proved more than he could take. He'd put her off too long. If he'd acted sooner, heeded any of Belinda's concerns, hell, if he'd given Mom the benefit of the doubt earlier today . . . .

By the time she started to come around, Richard had convinced himself she'd die in front of him.

"Richard?" Mom said.

"Mother." His voice was strong, all his pain, failure, relief hidden away, like a good lawyer.

"If you're here, I'm sure I'm not in heaven."

"Thanks, Mom."

"No, no, no. I mean I'm not dead. I'm alive. With you. That's what I meant."

"I'm sure."

She sighed and closed her eyes. He should get a nurse, but they had Mom's monitors hooked up out there. They'd know she was awake.

Mom opened her eyes again. "You did something," she said. "To the Ookie Birds."

"Let's keep it to ourselves."

"What did you do?"

Richard sighed. He wanted to go to the door and ensure medical staff were not on their way, but Mom had a hold of his hand and he wasn't ready to let go yet.

"I remembered the cartoons I used to watch as a kid."

She looked at him, waiting.

"They all had enemies. An antagonist to stop them. Dad's Ookie Birds were unchecked."

"You added *more* of them?"

"A cat. A gray and white striped housecat, big round face, twitchy tail. I scribbled it into the character list on each script."

He fell silent, but she didn't look away from him. She wanted all the details. He sighed. Glanced at the empty doorway.

"It showed up. It walked into the kitchen from your bedroom and swiped at the purple one. Then they ran, feathers everywhere. The cat chased after them."

"Have you . . . ?"

He kept his eyes on her face. "Nope. Haven't seen them since. Want to know what I named it? The cat?"

Mom looked at him out of the corner of her eye, waiting for the end of the story.

"Static."

She laughed, a quick snort of breath, and her face scrunched. A machine beeped, voices in the hall approached, and Richard held his breath until Mom winked at him. Casually, he brushed a purple cartoon feather off the bed by her feet.

"You're such a good boy."

His chest filled with pride. He decided he wouldn't make Mom look at his brochures after all. He'd call Holtzman Home Estates before the end of the day. Paying for it would hurt, but this was his Mom. Little boys were supposed to take care of their mom.

She squeezed his hand. "You've been crying," she said, and then he was.

The Sick and the Cursed

by Timothy P Flynn

tainted in their darkness
they found each other, hiding
an insatiable bloodlust, a secret
so monstrous, only the damned
can share

that first night—their beginning
him, the hunter unaware he is prey
her, savoring the moonlight air
when he stole her off the street to play
but she liked games, too

his knife dropped as she shifted
her binds tore away, his eyes twitch
contorting muscles, dark brown fur
filled in her naked body, guttural
growls escaped the elongated snout
monster versus creature

the jagged scars from her claws
healed, she spared his life—sadist or
psychopath—she was cursed, alone
he was sick with insatiable urges
but he idolized his unkillable pet
as he learned her lunar cycle

she obliged to his underground
playroom, his work, the unnamed faces
her moonlight runs became ritual, cleaned
with a precise eye for detail, untraceable
these monsters, the sick and cursed
found each other, tainted in darkness

Ulcinium
by F. R. Michaels

"Rider!" the lookout called down to the centurion.

The centurion scaled the ladder to the battlement and peered into the gathering dark across the Illyrian landscape.

"That has to be one of Stylian's detachment," he said.

"We sent ten men, sir. Where are the others?" the lookout asked.

The centurion narrowed his eyes. "What's wrong with him?"

The horse trotted up to the fortress, limping on its off foreleg, its rider lolling lifelessly on its back.

"Open the gate," the centurion commanded.

The soldiers opened the gate and the horse, foaming and whinnying, stumbled through. The corpse of a soldier sat lashed to the saddle, wreathed in a cloud of buzzing flies. Ragged gashes zigzagged down his face and neck, his eyes empty sockets, his torso encrusted with days-old blood.

The centurion climbed down and studied the man's mauled face.

"It is Stylian himself," he said.

"What could have done this to him?" one of the soldiers breathed.

"Ulcinium," whispered another.

The men gathered around the dead rider. Their fear hung in the air like a leaden mist. The centurion turned on them.

"Who among us are cowards?" he demanded. "You are soldiers, comport yourselves like soldiers! Back to your posts!" He pointed to a soldier who looked as though he was about to piss himself. "You, inform the commander!"

The soldier ran off. The centurion scratched the scar on his chin.

"Get this horse to the stables, we'll cut him down there," he said. "Bishop Fat-Ass is due from the capital any time now, and the last thing we need is for him to see *this*."

"To see what, exactly?" spoke a sonorous voice behind him.

The centurion bit his lip and turned.

Behind him stood a heavyset white-haired man wearing rich but well-worn travel clothes. A red sash with black crosses hung from his shoulders.

"Your Grace," the centurion said, his voice cracking.

"Your name, Centurion?"

"Leontius, Your Grace."

"Well met, Centurion Leontius," the white-haired man said. "I trust you were told of my visit?"

"Yes, Your Grace. We were concerned when you didn't arrive this afternoon as expected. Travel in this summer heat must be exhausting for . . ."

The bishop raised a bushy white eyebrow. "A man of my girth?"

Leontius swallowed. "Your horse, Your Grace. I meant to say, your horse."

"Quite so. Brutal weather. I arrived through the East Gate just now. I came to question why my mount was not being attended." The bishop looked past the centurion to the dead man. "But I can see you have greater concerns at the moment."

"Paulus, see to the Bishop's horse," Leontius commanded.

"Sir!" A soldier peeled his gaze away from Stylian's mutilated corpse and ran to the East Gate.

"And by the way, Centurion," the bishop said, "my name is pronounced 'Bonifatius,' as in 'Bishop Bonifatius of Scythia, special envoy of the Holy Father and our Emperor,' long may he reign. Or Boniface, if you prefer."

A bead of sweat trickled down the side of Leontius' face.

"I meant no disrespect, Your Grace."

"That is reassuring," Bishop Boniface murmured, his eyes back on the dead man. "Now, let us have a look at what has happened here. Centurion, bring me a torch."

"Your Grace?"

"A torch," the Bishop repeated slowly. "A stick with fire at one end of it, one of those. Bring me one."

Leontius nodded to an underling, who fetched one from a nearby sconce. Boniface took it and stepped up to the corpse, studying the dead man, bringing the flame close to see.

"Dead two or three days, I would say," he muttered, shooing away flies. He leaned in and sniffed. "Three. It looks as though he lashed himself to his horse, see how the knots are close by his hands, tightly bound so he could not untie them easily. Yet the welts on his wrists tell us he struggled against them. Curious. And these wounds, here on the head, neck, and torso, these are not sword cuts. Regard how the flesh is torn. Claws and teeth. These gashes, here on the neck, from these this poor man bled to death."

He closed his eyes, muttered a short prayer, made the sign of the cross, and handed the torch back to the soldier.

"Summon your surgeon and have him do a full examination of the body," Boniface said to Leontius. "This man may have tied his own ropes, but he did not maul himself to death."

"As you say, Your Grace."

"Now if you would be so kind as to escort me to the man in charge of this fortress, I have urgent business. Who commands here?" Bishop Boniface nodded back to the dead man. "Please tell me it's not him."

* * *

"Commander Ionnes!"

"What is it, Urban?" Ionnes demanded.

The door opened and a young man peeped around the portal.

"Bishop Boniface, sir," Urban said. "He has arrived from Constantinople and is demanding immediate–"

The bishop pushed his way into the room, not troubling to await introduction, nearly knocking Urban to the floor.

"You must be Ionnes," he said.

The man behind the desk stood up straight and cleared his throat. "I am Commander Ionnes." He gestured to a grizzled soldier who stood beside him. "This is Corvinus Opilio, my second-in-command."

Boniface held out his ring; Ionnes and Opilio each gave it a grudging kiss.

No two men could have been more different to Boniface's eye, the blunt heel and the sharp blade at either end of a spear. Ionnes, impeccably groomed, soft running to fat, a man boosted up the ranks through politics and family connections. Opilio, in contrast, stood scarred and hard, tough as weathered stone; a rough-edged plebian who'd earned his command by stubbornly remaining alive and upright at the end of every violent engagement.

"What news from the capital, Your Grace?" Ionnes asked.

"Justinian is dead," Boniface said. "His successor, Justinian II, long live the Emperor, refuses to pay the Persian tribute, so our eastern borders prepare for war. But, you would already know all this. And you would also know that this is not the reason I am here."

"Please, Your Grace, have a seat. Opilio, stay. Urban, bring wine and figs for our guest."

"I am afraid my timing is inopportune," Boniface said, sitting. "I arrived around the same time as a deceased soldier who rode in tied to his horse."

"So I have been informed," Ionnes said.

"Truly, I am sorry for the loss of your man. May God's mercy shine upon his soul." Boniface smoothed his clothes. "Now that that has been said, allow me to broach the reason both the Holy Father and the Emperor himself sent me in this ungodly summer heat to some backwater Illyrian garrison."

The two soldiers sat, Ionnes looking chastened and Opilio looking angry. The bishop surmised Opilio's face always looked angry.

"I am here about Ulcinium," Bishop Boniface said. "Specifically, your failure to determine why there has been no communication in or out of the town or harbor for a month. Your dispatches are spectacularly uninformative."

Ionnes paled and pressed his lips together. Opilio shrugged in frustration.

"We know nothing, Your Grace," Opilio said. "There's been no word from the garrison or the town itself. No travelers or trade have come out in more than a month, and those who go in, do not return."

"There is concern at the capital that it may be plague." The bishop studied both men's faces, but they gave away nothing. "Is it plague? Or pirates? The town has a history."

"Unknown," Ionnes answered. "Six days ago Opilio sent a detachment of men to the garrison. Ten men, all veterans, all volunteers. They have not returned, save the one you saw tonight."

Boniface leaned forward in his chair, causing Ionnes to lean back in his. "Constantinople has concern for Ulcinium, of course, and the Holy Father has an especial interest in the monastery outside the town. I have come for answers and will not go back to the Holy Father and our new emperor empty-handed."

"Understood, your Grace," Ionnes replied.

Boniface stood. "Well, late is the hour and I have traveled far and need rest before I solve your Ulcinium problem for you. Please have the young man bring the wine and figs to my quarters. We will reconvene in the morning."

* * *

In spite of the long day of travel, Boniface found himself restless. The commander had offered him the quarters that the regional officers and politicians used when they visited, nearby to Ionnes' own housing. Boniface opted for a small bunk by the men. He unrolled his travel bag, and took the note out from the Holy Father, a few short lines of Greek outlining the true purpose of his visit.

He heard soft footsteps in the hallway outside his door. Boniface tucked the Pope's message away and crept up, listening. As the footsteps passed, he opened the door. He tried to do it quietly and winced at the loud creak; he froze, but the footsteps did not pause.

Boniface poked his head out and saw a young woman walking away. He scowled. Women were not permitted in the soldiers' barracks, and this one appeared to be sneaking out.

"Young lady, are you lost?" the bishop called out. The figure ignored him and left through a side door.

Bishop Boniface followed, but when he stepped through the door, the hallway beyond stretched dark and empty to either side. Vanished? Curious, though he had seen stranger things during his time working as an envoy to the Holy Father. Investigating barefoot in his nightclothes had never turned out productive in the past, however, so Boniface shook his head and retreated to his room. He had a bigger mystery to solve at Ulcinium.

* * *

"I understand the surgeon returned an unusual report on your man's body," Boniface said as they broke their fast at the following daybreak.

Commander Ionnes cleared his throat. "Yes, Your Grace. It appears that apart from the mauling, Stylian had, ah, made a mess in his underclothes."

Boniface noted the delicate wording and obvious uneasiness in the Commander's voice.

"It is not unusual for a man to release his bladder and bowels at the point of death, Commander. Surely you know this."

"Not that, Your Grace. He had expressed several, ah, manly emissions into his *subligaculum*." Ionnes' face turned bright red.

"He had ejaculated into his underwear?" Boniface asked.

"Yes," Ionnes replied brusquely, then cleared his throat. "More than once, and, um, copiously."

Boniface scowled at that, thinking. "That is unusual."

"And hardly a topic to be discussed at breakfast with a bishop, I am certain."

The table was laid with a curious amalgam of basic army rations and sumptuous delicacies: Hard *paximadion* bread with a fine lemon marmalade, *mizithra* cheese and salted *botargo* mullet roe, *piston* porridge flavored with minced figs and walnuts, and rough soldiers' wine sweetened with honey and served hot.

"Tell me, did you sleep well, Your Grace?" Ionnes asked, changing the subject.

"I do believe I may have seen a ghost last night, Commander,"

Boniface said.

Commander Ionnes glanced up from his food. "A ghost? Surely, Your Grace, a man of God would not believe in the shades of the dead?"

"I spotted a young woman walking the corridor past my quarters. When I went to look for her she had disappeared."

Commander Ionnes appeared puzzled then smiled. "Ah, Your Grace, you must have seen my daughter, Helena."

"Your daughter? You quarter with your wife and children here at the fort?"

Ionnes waved Boniface's statement away with a soft hand bedecked with rings. "It is only temporary. I am having a new villa built in Scodra. My wife is there, overseeing the work. Helena is here, with me."

Boniface blinked at him. "With all due respect, Commander, a Roman fortress is no place for a young girl. What if you were attacked? What could she do but be a distraction?"

"Illyricum is hardly the frontier, Your Grace. Helena has, ah, special needs; I like to keep her close. And what safer place can there be for my princess than a fortress full of hardened professional soldiers?"

Boniface stared at the other man for a while before saying, "Are you sure you thought that statement all the way through before you uttered it, Commander?"

Ionnes glanced up from his food. "Mm?"

A centurion burst in, fear on his face. He ran over to the commander and whispered in his ear. Ionnes froze and went white as if he'd been stabbed.

"Commander . . . ?" Boniface prompted, concerned.

Ionnes' mouth worked a few times before the words could escape. "Summon Opilio!"

He'd no sooner spoken the words when Opilio appeared at the door.

"She's gone, sir!"

"What?" Boniface asked. "Your daughter?"

Ionnes stood, shaking. "Are you sure? Have you checked the baths and stables?"

"I've had every man searching since her servant found her room empty at breakfast," Opilio replied. "She left during the night, as best we can tell. She took her horse and some provisions, and snuck out through a side door. The centurion on duty claims he saw no one leave, but fresh hoof prints lead away from the North Gate."

Bishop Boniface stood, blinking. "That must have been her I saw last night, sneaking out."

"And you did not stop her?" Ionnes squealed.

"I called out but she ignored me. When I went to look she had already gone."

"No one is blaming you, Your Grace," Opilio said, his hard eyes fixed on his commander. "Helena may have gotten, well, *close* to one of the missing men in Stylian's detachment. And she is a headstrong girl."

Ionnes spoke to the centurion. "Summon the legion. I want every man out there, I will personally lead . . . "

Opilio interrupted with a calming gesture. "Sir, it will take too much time to muster the men. And you, Commander, should stay here, in case she comes back. I will go. One man and one horse can move faster than a century of soldiers on foot."

Opilio paused while his commander digested the words.

"Besides," he added. "I know where she's going."

Ionnes went even paler. "Ulcinium?"

"That is my fear."

"How far is it to the town from here?" Boniface asked.

"Not far," Opilio answered. "Three days' ride at most, less for a single man riding hard."

"Two men," Boniface said, standing. "Have your soldiers ready my horse. We can leave immediately and intercept her, and bring her back together."

"With due respect, Your Grace, time is critical and I've no provision for a passenger."

"I will not slow you down, Opilio," Boniface assured him. "Despite my bulk, I travel fast and light. And wherever you seek Helena, it would not hurt to have God on your side."

Ionnes gave them both a tight nod, his eyes wet with tears.

"Go, Opilio, and take the bishop with you. If he slows you down even a single stride, leave him behind. Bring my daughter back, whatever it takes. And Opilio . . . "

Opilio paused at the door. "Yes, Commander?"

"Don't *you* vanish on me."

"You'd never be that lucky, sir."

Boniface also paused at the door. "I will look after him, Commander."

* * *

Opilio rode hard across the rough terrain, pushing himself and his horse. Boniface, as promised, kept up without complaint. Early summer rains had given way to baking afternoon heat, solidifying the mud and preserving the tracks. The two men followed the hoof prints, but spotted no sign of Helena. As morning hardened into stifling afternoon, they stopped briefly under a boll of trees to rest the horses in the shade.

Opilio sat on the ground and pulled out provisions of cheese and hard bread, and a skin of watered vinegar.

"We should eat something now," he said, handing a slab of cheese and bread to Boniface. "There may not be time later."

Boniface took the coarse meal, and shared some of his own provisions of dried meat and fruit. "May I ask you something, Opilio?"

Opilio grunted around his food. Boniface took the sound as a yes.

"The commander. With all due deference, he does seem a bit, well . . . "

"Soft?" Opilio supplied.

"Your word. But yes, a bit, to hold such a position out here in Illyricum. Yet Ionnes has the respect of a man like you, even friendship. Why is that?"

Opilio glanced over at the bishop. "Ionnes is a good administrator. He's smart, well-connected, and keeps the men fed, armed, and paid. It is a not job I could do. But the Commander does it, and well. Ionnes is a hardworking and prudent man."

"And his daughter? Having her at the fort, is that prudent?"

"Helena is . . . "

Opilio stopped speaking and suddenly jumped to his feet, sword out, listening. Boniface was startled at the swift grace with which he'd moved.

"Opilio?" Boniface whispered.

Opilio put a hand out for silence.

Boniface heard hooves approaching, and stood.

A cart mule appeared from the road ahead and ran through their camp in a stumbling gallop, its harness cut and leads trailing in the dirt. Opilio and Boniface watched it go.

"That was . . . odd," Boniface muttered.

"I do not like 'odd,'" Opilio said. "Let's go find what that mule was running from."

* * *

Evening had fallen by the time the two came upon the abandoned cart. Without its mule or driver, it had rolled down a hill and overturned in a ditch. Trade goods, ropes and rough cloth, spilled on the ground. There were several cakes of coarse salt as well.

"I do not like the look of this," Opilio murmured. "These ropes and bolts are poor quality, but salt is valuable. Even if the owner left it, scavengers and thieves should have claimed it."

Boniface mopped the sweat off his face and neck with a damp handkerchief, and studied the scene in the waning light.

"Harness cut with a sharp knife, but only partway through the last lead. The mule breaks free and runs off, through our camp. Man continues on foot in," he pointed, "that direction."

"Toward Ulcinium."

"What now?"

"The light is fading. We cannot track in the dark. We camp here for the night."

"Here?" the bishop asked. "But what if whoever attacked the rope merchant shows up again?"

"Then pray for their souls, Your Grace," Opilio said, hand on his gladius, "because I am not in a merciful state of mind."

* * *

At first light they remounted and rode on, but the ground had grown hard and the tracks faint. Opilio paused at a fork in the path, Boniface behind him.

"There are two routes to the garrison from here," Opilio said. "One uses the eastern road and the other is a path along the river. The river path is shorter, we'll take that one. If we do not find Helena perhaps we can find whoever attacked the rope merchant."

"Would that be wise, Opilio?"

"I fear no man, Bishop."

Opilio rode down the river path, his horse cantering at a brisk trot. Boniface spurred his own horse to catch up.

"I do not for a moment doubt your valor," he said. "However, has it occurred to you that what may have killed your man Stylian and may have hold of the commander's daughter even as we speak, that it may not be human?"

"I don't believe in ghosts," Opilio said.

"There are greater things to fear in this world than the shades of the dead," Boniface said. "Before I became a bishop, I was sent to Syria to treat with a pride of sphinxes. Curious creatures. They have the bodies of lions but the face and speech of men. It was the Holy Father's idea that they could be converted. He was wrong. For all their human aspects they proved to be treacherous and conniving beasts."

"That sounds human enough to me," Opilio quipped.

Boniface grunted. "My attempts were futile, and I barely escaped with my life. There is still a question if such creatures may have souls. Perhaps if I had had more time . . . "

"I fought the Ostrogoths, under Belisarius, Your Grace," Opilio said. "I helped drive the barbarians off of the Italian peninsula, regaining part of what was lost in the west. One thing I learned during that campaign is there are creatures walking this earth that may be human in outer form, but within they are as soulless as beasts."

"You speak of the barbarians?"

"I speak of Belisarius."

Boniface looked at Opilio a long time before answering.

"You malign the man," Boniface grunted. "He was a hero of the Empire, second only to Justinian himself, may they both rest in peace."

"I was in Constantinople when he suppressed the Nika riots," Opilio muttered. "Were you, Eminence?"

"I was not in the capital at the time," Boniface said. "But I know what happened at the Hippodrome."

"The Emperor's version? Or the truth? The warring Greens and Blues invited to the stadium for the chariot race?"

"The Greens were a violent gang of thugs and criminals," Boniface said.

"So were the Blues. And yet Justinian paid them off, and let them leave. Then Belisarius and his soldiers came in, blocked off all the exits, and murdered every single person in the Hippodrome."

Boniface shifted uncomfortably in his saddle. "The Greens had crowned Hypatius as emperor right under Justinian's nose. What was he to do, flee and accept exile?"

"He would have. I understand his wife talked him out of it. He decided instead to unleash his beast of a general."

"It is the Emperor's duty to maintain the peace; it was Belisarius' duty to enforce that peace."

"Peace?" Opilio snorted. "That is a very different definition of the word peace, Your Grace, than I am familiar with. I was only eight years old when it happened, but I remember. The screams. Relatives weeping. Soldiers returning from the Hippodrome covered in blood from head to toe. Thirty thousand people. None were spared. All on Belisarius' orders. Explain to me, Your Grace, how such a man finds his way to the Kingdom of God . . . "

"Joshua killed at least that many at Jericho, on God's order. Belisarius was, at his core, a soldier. As are you, dear Opilio. Soldiers are often called upon to do terrible things. If I may ask, how many men have you killed?"

"By my own blade, forty," Opilio answered. "Thirty-two during the Italia campaigns, six were prisoners I was ordered to execute, one was a madman run amok when I was on garrison duty in Thracia. And one was a friend I killed in a drunken argument over a whore in Corinth."

"I am sorry."

"So am I. She wasn't worth it."

Opilio held up his arm to stop. They had arrived at the riverbank. A litter of armor and weapons lay scattered along the ground. Of the men, no trace remained. Opilio dismounted and studied the ground.

Boniface slid off his horse and ambled up behind him. "This does not look like the scene of a battle."

Opilio lifted up the eagle standard of the legion, thrown along the ground with the rest of the gear. "No. I've never seen a battlefield without a murder of crows to feast on the dead. No crows, no blood, no bodies, and the ground isn't churned up nearly enough."

On second look, the discarded armor and weapons did not lay exactly randomly. They formed a hurried trail in a direct line to a specific destination.

"The footprints all lead in one direction," Opilio said. "They dropped their weapons, peeled off their armor, and ran. There are no other traces, nowhere enemy troops or insurrectionists could stage an ambush. And Stylian had time to lash himself to his horse . . . but why would he do that?"

Boniface used the opportunity to soak his handkerchief in the river water and wipe his red, sweating face.

"Too hot for an ambush," he muttered. "Where do the footprints lead?"

"Where else? Ulcinium."

Boniface turned, a question poised on his lips.

Then they heard the song.

The tone wafted on the wind, growing stronger, a chorus of voices, a song of such piercing sweetness and ferocious longing that quickened the blood and ensnared the mind . . .

"That song!" Opilio barked. "Use the mud! Plug your ears!"

He fell to his hands and knees, scooping mud from the riverbank and stuffing it into his ears, but he had moved too late. Opilio rocked back onto his knees, a scoop of mud in both hands, the mask of anger he wore on his face falling away and leaving a docile longing in its place.

The song held no words, but tones cycled through a series of cascading perfect fourths in a repeating round, like an arpeggio both discordant and overpowering, with an entwined meandering melody. The sound of it overthrew the men's minds, grounding itself in the basest depths of desire, sparking and inflaming an uncontrollable lust. Sense and judgment burned away, replaced by an irresistible desire to find the source of the sound, to fulfill the promise of gratification and quench the flame of need.

Boniface quivered, holding on desperately to his reason. He rooted through his travel bag with frantic speed. His fingers came out slick with melted wax. He cursed, then prayed in shouted sobs, trying to drown out the sound.

"Pater hêmôn ho en toes ouranoes . . . hagiasthêtô to onoma sou . . . " Our Father, who art in Heaven . . . hallowed be thy name . . .

He tried in vain to focus his will on his words. He felt his determination wilting under the song's spreading shadow.

"*Kae mê eisenenkês hêmas eis peirasmon*," he whispered, *lead me not into temptation*, and the walls of his faith fell.

Boniface, trembling, clambered to his feet, and followed Opilio in a stumbling race to the source of the song: the monastery at Ulcinium.

* * *

When Boniface awoke, his first sight was of the body of Christ, hanging from a wooden crucifix high on a stone wall across from where he lay. The inside of his head felt as muddy as a churned pond. His feet bled from the run up the rocky hillside. Boniface remembered the song, and despaired. He knew these walls, had walked these floors, had visited this place in his younger days: he lay in the monastery at Ulcinium, though it no longer functioned as a monastery.

He was in a nest of *seirenes*.

It all made sense now: The disappearing men, Stylian lashing himself to his horse, even the rope merchant. They had heard the song, and were lost. Stylian had known the danger and bound himself, and although he strained against the ropes, and even ejaculated in his underclothes from the lust ignited by their song, he could not free himself. Denied their prize, the sirens had swarmed and mauled him to death.

With its torches extinguished, the monastery had the aspect of a crypt: Stone corridors lay dark and silent, but for the low scraping of claws, the occasional soft flutter of wings. An abhorrent smell assaulted his senses, a miasma of rotting meat and feces and unwashed animals and the musty scent of sex, like the filthiest of brothels combined with an untended farmyard.

Boniface drifted at the edge of consciousness, despairing. They had failed. Opilio was nowhere to be seen, and if Helena had fallen victim to the sirens' song, she too was lost. Scuffling sounds drew his attention, and he craned his neck to see.

Small figures scuttled among the shadows, no more than waist high, creatures out of a nightmare: a woman's head with lank, scraggly hair, the shining eyes black throughout, with ragged sharp teeth lining its mouth. The head sat upon a slender neck attached to a feathered body, with human-like breasts protruding from the pouting chest. The wings spanned outward with clawed fingers extending from the second joint, which they used to crawl among the broken stones of the monastery floor, and to pick and pull at flesh or small objects that grabbed their attention. Raptor feet, thick and sharply clawed, scrabbled over the stone floors and debris and clutched at their victims. The stench of the beasts nauseated him.

To his right, half-eaten corpses, men and women both, littered the floor. The sound of weeping came from his left. A young man wearing the tattered shreds of military garb, evidently one of the men from the detachment, cried and pleaded as a siren scrabbled up his legs. His manhood bled, raw and torn, and yet the siren sang into his face, and the man's desire responded. Even Boniface, weakened and sprawled along the floor, yearned for the touch of that creature, the promise the song instilled. The siren mounted the soldier and ground against him in bestial movements, her claws buried cruelly into his hips, while the man shrieked and shuddered. Boniface watched his struggle and realized the soldier was spent and could no longer continue.

The siren screeched at him, unable to draw any more seed. She called to her sisters, and a flock of the filthy beasts fluttered over on their dark wings, covering him. The man screamed weakly as their teeth tore at his flesh. He squirmed and wept, with breathless sobs, as they devoured him alive.

One of the sirens left the feast and scuttled clumsily over half-eaten corpses and debris toward Boniface. His travel bag still hung tangled over his shoulder, but there was naught therein he could use for a weapon. He groped around, his hand closing over a thighbone, sticky with congealed blood and strings of meat still attached. His fingers clutched at it, but could gain no grip.

All sirens are female, he remembered from his meeting with the Emperor's advisors. *Their song attracts men and women alike, but they need human males to breed.* Boniface wondered, as his death approached him, what abhorrent act had first bred these hideous creatures, back in the murky reaches of history.

The siren stepped over his body, straddling him, tearing open his clothes with her jaws and clawed feet. She would take his seed, and when his seed was spent, devour his flesh with her sisters.

Boniface wanted to weep with terror, but he had no more breath. He tried to pray, but his lips could not form the words. Instead, a nugget of clear thinking at the core of his mind begged to God that his heart would give out before this abomination violated him.

The siren crooned into his face, that melody of madness and desire, and Boniface responded against his will. The creature mounted him, its claws hooked into his skin and muscle; she impaled herself and hunched against him with violent motions. The small dissolving remnant of Boniface that remained sane despaired. Disgust and loathing filled his mind and heart, terror rang in his gut, and grief for the Commander's lost daughter tore his soul. Throughout, the siren's song trumpeted its false promises of joy.

As the act ground on, Boniface thought he heard a woman weeping. He turned to look, and spotted a distant figure crouched over a dead soldier. She pulled something from the dead soldier's belt, wiped at her eyes with an angry swipe of her forearm, and strode away silently, like a ghost. Through the murky clouds of insanity, Boniface thought he must have imagined the whole scene.

Then he heard a low boom in the near distance, like the slam of a heavy wooden door, echoing through the dead halls. The sound startled the sirens. Their heads snapped up, birdlike, following the noise. The siren that had mounted Boniface likewise jumped, the motion causing her feathers to ruffle and her breasts to wobble. She paused, wary.

In that brief respite of clarity, Boniface's groping fingers closed over the wet thighbone and he swung it with the remains of his strength. It was an awkward blow, weak and hampered by the remnants of the leg still attached. The bone cracked across the siren's head and sent it sprawling with a screech.

Before the creature could recover, another low boom echoed within the monastery. The sirens clustered together, hissing and whipping their heads about in concern. Another boom, shortly after from elsewhere, another portal shut.

Through the clearing fog in the Bishop's brain, a single clear thought shone: *Someone is closing all the exits . . .*

One more booming slam, close by, and all the sirens fluttered and screeched. Their attention was hooked by something he couldn't see.

And then he heard the scream: A woman's scream, distorted, like the yowl of an animal. Not of terror, nor of grief, nor of despair: A scream of white-hot rage.

She fell upon the sirens like a storm, the young woman from Boniface's half-seen vision, swinging a sword in ferocious swipes. Four of the foul beasts fell with her first slash. The remaining sirens regrouped to extend their necks and sing at her. Boniface heard the tones and felt the lust and longing saw through his nerves, but the young woman charged into the sound, unmoved, unstoppable, cutting down the creatures like a fury.

When their song failed, they swarmed her. The lightly-built sirens found only steel and death. When swarming failed, they fled, clumsily fluttering and flapping away in the confined corridors.

Something hot and wet fell onto Boniface's torso: the siren that had mounted him, cleaved nearly in half. She flopped about feebly, squalling, and died.

Repulsed, Boniface found his strength and shoved the carcass off of him, then rolled over and crawled away from the sounds of violence. His progress was impeded by exhaustion and, incongruously, his painfully erect manhood dragging against the stone floor and debris. The bishop crawled through bones and rotted flesh, feces and scattered feathers, and gluey fluids the composition of which he desperately tried not to contemplate.

"Heavenly Father, if you get me out of this alive, I will bathe for a week," he grunted to himself as he crawled on.

Behind him, the young woman – enraged, methodical, relentless – hunted down the remaining sirens. She drove those who'd reached higher perches into corners by pelting them with loose rocks, stoning them until they fell, and dispatching them with a thrust of her sword.

Boniface found a storage room with an open door. Sweating, panting, grunting with pain, he dragged himself inside. The stench of this room surpassed even the miasma from before, and Boniface retched, but his stomach held nothing to give. As his eyes adjusted from the dimness of the corridor to this greater darkness, he saw the nests, the eggs, and the brood mothers staring at him.

They were larger than their sisters, grotesquely fat, flightless, sitting on their clutches. At the sight of Boniface crawling toward their nests they stood as one, hissing, and lumbered toward him with bared teeth.

Boniface wept, squeezed his eyes shut and commended his soul to God.

But instead of razor teeth biting into his flesh he felt a foot stomp on his back, squeezing the air out of his lungs in a grunted "oof!" as the young woman ran over his prone form into the nest room. He heard the susurrus of swinging steel, the screeching and the slaughter of the brood mothers, the smashing of eggs, and then silence.

Footfalls approached, walking up to Boniface as he lay among the matted straw and filthy bloodied rags of the nest room. He rolled onto his back and heard the clang of a dropped sword. His head clear of the siren's spell, he looked into the face of a beautiful young woman, spattered with the blood of monsters.

"Miss Helena, I presume?" he asked.

She made no response. Boniface felt his strength failing, saw his vision graying out at the edges. A veil fell over his sight as his consciousness left him.

* * *

Boniface awoke again, somewhat surprised to be alive. He lay upon a low couch, with clean bandages over his wounds. His manhood throbbed and stung, raw, as did the myriad scratches and punctures on his chest and hips, and his feet ached abominably. His head, however, was clear, free of the snares of the sirens' song. He sat up gingerly.

Opilio stood by the door in earnest conversation with the commander and the young woman from the monastery, the girl who had run such a ferocious massacre among the sirens.

"He is awake!"

Commander Ionnes broke away from the group and knelt beside Boniface, grasping his hand earnestly.

"You did it, Your Grace, you brought my Helena back to me!"

Boniface opened his mouth to protest, but his tongue and throat were too parched for speech. Not that it would have mattered, Ionnes was hardly listening.

"Whatever it is you would have as a reward, you need only name it! I have great friends in the capital, Your Grace, and the story of your and Opilio's heroism will ring throughout the Empire, I swear it!"

He rejoined his daughter, who gave Opilio and Boniface a sad little shrug before leaving with her father.

Opilio closed the door and walked over. He too sported fresh bandages but seemed strong and alert as ever. He poured watered wine from a pottery decanter into a wooden cup and placed it on the table beside Boniface's couch. The bishop took the cup and drained it in a draft. The two men shared a look.

"Are you going to tell him?" Boniface said, holding his cup out for more wine.

"I will," Opilio said. "As soon as I can push a word in."

Opilio refilled the wine, then pulled up a stool and sat, staring down at the older man. His face grew hard.

"You knew," he said.

Boniface looked into the cup of wine, and gulped it down.

"Speak to me," Opilio said. It was not a request.

"I *suspected*," Boniface replied. "I was under orders from the Holy Father himself. My mission was to identify, and if verified, attempt to convert the sirens. Failing that, I was to capture one alive to be brought back to Constantinople. The Emperor himself wanted to see if they could be trained to sing on command, or if their song could be replicated by human singers or instruments."

"To be used in war," Opilio said, "against the Persians."

"Yes. And in the West, to regain the rest of what was lost. Restore the Empire."

"You had come prepared, with wax earplugs in your pack, but they'd melted in the summer heat." Opilio refilled the goblet. "Tell me of the Holy Father's interest."

"He wanted their song used to help convert the pagans."

"But the song is a snare. It leads men and women to destruction, not salvation."

Boniface closed his eyes briefly and nodded. "I know that now. I thought I was prepared, that my reason would guide me, and my faith would shield me. I was weak. And a fool."

Opilio considered this. "We both were foolish. But wiser today, now that we've lived to see it. It's how I've learned most of what I know."

"That young woman just now, that must be Helena," Boniface said. "I saw her, at the monastery. She was weeping over a dead soldier, and took his sword."

"That is she. We had unknowingly overtaken her in our search. She had taken the east road rather than following the river, and we were riding hard. I'd say her arrival at the monastery was well-timed."

"I watched her wreak a devastating slaughter among the sirens."

"She did, and thoroughly. Not one survived, not even the eggs."

Boniface looked away, studying a random spot on the tiled floor. "The spell of the sirens ensnares men and women alike. Yet, their songs had no power over her." He looked back up at Opilio. "Is she so strong in her faith? In her will?"

Opilio stood.

"Yes, in a manner of speaking," he answered. "Helena has been deaf since childhood."

Boniface grunted in brief surprise, then nodded to himself.

"Obvious, now that you say it," he muttered. "Scripture teaches us that God made the weak things in this world to shame the strong. But truly, who are the strong? That young woman, what we would consider a weakness, dear Opilio, was instead her strength, and our salvation."

"Rest now," Opilio walked out, pausing at the door. "The sooner you're healed the sooner we're rid of you."

The Bishop watched him leave. He found his travel bag hanging from a corner of his couch, and discreetly felt around for its cargo hidden in the secret pocket. He lay back and closed his eyes, reprising in his head the events of the past few days, debating with himself if he should deliver the siren's egg he'd taken from the nest to Constantinople, or smash it.

The Weatherman and the Monk

by Nick A. Zaino III

Martin reveled in the sunrise as his first weather balloon of the day rose into a clear blue sky. The North Pacific was a place of almost unspeakable beauty, but that vista could be broken at any moment by enemy warships. Especially so close to Japan. Martin had yet to see one with his own eyes. He'd heard the crew talk about close calls. Some of his fellow observers who drew assignments in the Atlantic hadn't been so lucky. Whole ships were lost, presumably to German submarine attacks, even with protective escorts. Hundreds of men at a time, swallowed into the sea, observers and combatants alike.

The two destroyer escorts that accompanied his cutter didn't make Martin feel safe as much as they reminded him there was still a war going on. Not so long ago, he was happily stationed with the Coast Guard in Hawaii, with his wife and newborn daughter, keeping the skies safe for an increasing number of overseas commercial flights. His knowledge and experience monitoring atmospheric conditions was now a tactical advantage. The Germans had been defeated, but Japan was still unbowed. Something was being planned to end it, and whatever it was involved every bit of information about safe routes through the Northwest Pacific the Navy could muster.

Martin moved back to his theodolite viewfinder to track the balloon as it drifted further away. It should have floated up into the windless sky, but sped quickly out to sea as if driven by a propeller. The equipment had been acting up the past several days. The weather was clear and dry for June, but the transmitters were showing wild swings in pressure and humidity. The volatility made his findings almost useless to his Navy bosses. Nothing made sense.

"How's it looking, Marty?"

Martin looked over his shoulder at Specialist Gary De Luca watching the balloon drift out of sight.

"Another beautiful day," Martin said. "It shouldn't be, according to the transmitter, but here we are."

"I'll take it," said De Luca. "Never question a sunny day."

"Shouldn't you be somewhere, checking guns?" said Martin. "Being a gunner and all?"

De Luca laughed. "Don't you worry about it," he said. "We're about as set as you can be on this old tank. We've got two destroyers full of good men who can handle anything you throw at them."

"You're a better man than me," Martin said.

The balloon drifted out of view. Martin looked through his viewfinder. As he scanned upward, he caught a glimpse of something on the horizon. He moved his sites back down to the water and refocused.

"De Luca," he said, "if there was a ship anywhere in sight, we'd be able to track it, right?"

"Sure. We'd see it on the radar, miles before it got to us."

"Then what's that?" Martin motioned De Luca over to the theodolite.

De Luca leaned into the lens. "Where'm I looking, doc?"

"To the left, near the horizon."

It took only a second for De Luca to find what Martin had seen. His face went slack under the viewfinder. "That's . . . the broadside of a Japanese battle cruiser!"

The destroyers had apparently already spotted the enemy ship. They were circling into position between it and the cutter.

"It's not headed for us," said De Luca.

"Then where's it headed?"

De Luca watched for almost a full minute. Martin could barely see the ship with the naked eye, but it was getting bigger.

"Going full speed a bit to our west."

"Attacking?" Martin said.

"I don't think so. There's no other ships with it." De Luca scanned the horizon. "And no planes. I'm not entirely sure it sees us. But we're ready if it does." He tossed the theodolite back to Martin and hurried off to get the crew in place.

Martin couldn't help but look at the cruiser again. He noticed the water around it starting to rise, a strange wave in calm waters. His heart jolted. He could see men leaping over the railing and into the water. The guns were firing, but not at the Americans. They fired behind them, at the water.

As the battle cruiser approached, the destroyers started firing. The cruiser kept coming; kept firing into the water. They didn't notice they were taking fire, still less than half a mile away.

A wave rose up and obscured Martin's view of the cruiser. When the water settled, the cruiser had stopped cold. Martin froze. He forced himself to take in a long breath then release it calmly as he refocused through the lens.

A shadow emerged from the water around the middle of the ship. It climbed up the hull, a deep, matte black that absorbed the sunlight. Martin blinked, wiped his eyes, and held up the binoculars once again. The shadow-object wrapped around one side of the battle cruiser looked like a giant human thumb.

The destroyers were halfway between the cutter and the battle cruiser. Their guns had stopped firing – they were watching, too. Everything quieted. The air was getting slippery. Martin wiped his brow, fixated.

The thumb began to pinch the cruiser. The center of the steel ship raised as it began to break. The ends drooped. Sailors jumped from deck, trying to escape whatever was on the other side of that boat. There were flashes of light and sounds of guns firing. The metal tore as the cruiser snapped in half. Each severed half took on water and sank out of view revealing giant black fingers on the opposite side.

Beyond the fingers, a black dome rose from the water, an oddly perfect island. It was growing, making waves. The cutter rocked and the destroyers swayed.

One destroyer circled back to the cutter, but the other, further out, remained within striking distance of the black hand. Two orange pools of light glowed in the water as the black dome continued to rise. It must have been twenty feet high at that point. A few seconds later, the orange lights emerged. They were eyes.

The orange eyes watched as the last bits of the cruiser sink. A humanoid head and neck were now visible, towering over the roiling water. Only the eyes held any color, the rest of its features indistinguishable in the bright morning sun. Its head was smooth, like the shaven heads of the Buddhist monks in San Francisco.

The first destroyer moved closer to Martin's cutter. The other was headed toward the monk when its guns began to roar. The monk's eyes shifted from the spot where the cruiser had sunk. Its fingers submerged.

Martin noticed the monk's head didn't bob and move the way a man's might treading water. The bottom of the Pacific was thousands of feet down. *It couldn't be standing on the bottom,* Martin thought. What was it? It wasn't mechanical, some new weapon. It didn't look like some giant sea animal. It looked human.

Martin felt detached, as if he were watching a movie. When he'd volunteered for this mission, he'd contemplated every way he could die at sea. He had convinced himself it was inevitable. Some poor sap would have to explain this to his wife, Rita.

The monk was unfazed by the shelling. It stared at the attacking destroyer, unblinking.

A hand on his shoulder spun Martin around. It was De Luca.

"Doc! Inside, now!" De Luca dragged Martin up the metal stairs to the bridge while Martin kept looking over his shoulder, terrified to look away.

The captain and several crew members were on the bridge, watching. Martin picked up his theodolite. His view was less clear from inside the bridge, but he didn't need much magnification to see what was happening.

The monk's chest and sloping shoulders were now visible. It stared down at the deck of the destroyer. The big guns ceased. The destroyer no longer rocked with the waves. It was still as the monk, waiting.

"They're not responding to our messages," said the radioman. "It's just . . . quiet."

"Get ready to move," said Captain Behan.

Martin went back outside to get a better view. Through his lens, he could see the two hundred person crew of the destroyer lined up in formation on the deck, as if submitting to inspection. One seaman stood out from the others, hands behind his back, looking up at the monk. Were they having a conversation? Martin noticed a metal barrel. The seaman swiftly climbed in and the monk covered it with a tip of its finger. After several silent minutes, the monk emptied the barrel, dumping the limp body of the seaman on the deck in a splash of water. The monk then refilled the barrel with seawater and carefully placed it on the deck as the next man stepped up. The process kept repeating.

The men on the deck stood in neat rows keeping their eyes forward, never flinching. Martin noticed a few other bodies sprawled on the deck.

Then the remaining destroyer pulled up beside the cutter and obscured Martin's view of all but the top of the monk's head. He contemplated what he'd been watching: two hundred men being drowned one-by-one while the others waited their turn.

The cutter began to rock violently. High above the ship in front of him, Martin saw the doomed destroyer raised up into the sky at the end of the monk's long, smooth arm. It dangled there for a moment, men and debris raining into the deep water below. Then it was hurtling toward Martin, flying over the cutter and destroyer and hitting the water somewhere past them with an enormous splash, nearly tossing Martin off the stairs as the cutter lurched.

The two remaining ships turned to escape the monk at top speed. Martin looked back. Much of the creature's torso was now protruding from the water, and yet it remained still as the waves lapped around it. It followed the escaping ships with its fiery eyes. Martin swore the monk was staring into his soul.

* * *

Martin fixed a radiosonde to a balloon, which was white enough to see in the ship's lights against the darkening sky. He still had a job to do. Even if the ship's radios and radar were malfunctioning and Captain Behan was navigating somewhat blind, the data Martin collected might get him and every other man on the ship home. He was still getting readings from some of the balloons he'd sent out. If nothing else, the ritual was a distraction, and the promise of actionable data gave him a small sense of control.

He'd never been more desperate for dry land. But the cutter and the destroyer were headed west, away from the strange monk and the carnage. The closest place they could find refuge that way was the base on the Northern Mariana Islands. That was a lot of open water.

Captain Behan tried to act like the monk was just another obstacle the crew had to face, like a sudden storm or a surprise attack from a submarine. The crew followed suit, plotting their course and getting their equipment back on-line, but they were spooked. De Luca, his only friend on the ship, was usually a talker. He sometimes liked to sneak away and watch what Martin was doing and shoot the breeze. Now, he was checking the battlements, counting ammunition, and making sure the gunners were ready. The destroyer was on alert too.

Martin went back to the bridge to monitor readings.

Captain Behan looked over Martin's shoulder. "Your equipment still working, Wright?" he said.

Martin nodded. "Not sure I trust the readings, but yeah," he said. "Pressure keeps spiking, but it's nothing but clear skies out there."

"To what do you attribute that?"

Martin hesitated. "The erratic readings started before yesterday."

Captain Behan was terse as ever. "The readings you're seeing now, they're consistent with the conditions we've been experiencing?"

"I don't know what to say," Martin said. "Nothing makes sense."

"It is our job to make sense out of what doesn't," Captain Behan said. "Today, I saw something I have never seen before. Do you know how often that happens, Wright?"

"I would think--"

"It never happens, Wright," the Captain continued. "Not since my first detail. And if I've never seen it, the Navy hasn't seen it, and we need every last scrap of information on what happened today to make sure the

Navy is never surprised again. There is too much at stake. Fear is a luxury. Understood?"

"Understood, Captain." Martin took a deep breath and straightened his spine.

"Good. Back to work."

Captain Behan returned his attention to the radiomen. This was the part of the service Martin could never reckon with. He was a civilian at heart. As soon as he could, he would return to the National Weather Service and revel in a simple, boring, domestic life. He had come here willingly. Someone had to. Martin couldn't have lived with himself if he'd stayed home and done nothing. He would do his part to end this madness once and for all.

Martin concentrated on his readings from the last balloon. There should have been storm clouds and unbearable humidity. There should have been lightning and driving rain. It had been a dry, clear night when he came inside, and on the other side of the glass, it looked like nothing had changed.

There was a line of pink and yellow still visible below the dark blue and black. Martin hunched his shoulders and heard his back crack as he settled in for a long night.

* * *

Martin wasn't sure how long he'd been asleep at his station when he was jolted out of his chair and onto the cold steel floor. It took him a few seconds to reorient himself. Captain Behan was standing straight as a rail on the bridge, his hands clasped behind his back. At some point, he had changed into his full dress blues. Martin blinked the spots out of his eyes as he looked beyond the glass.

Two perfect bright orange circles loomed in the darkness a hundred yards ahead of the cutter. Martin couldn't exhale. He blinked again, clearing his vision more. He called out to Captain Behan. No answer. Behan stared into the monk's eyes. He didn't notice when Martin got up and patted him on the back. Something in his periphery made every muscle in his body clench. There was more than one set of orange eyes blazing outside. He could see four sets from his place on the bridge.

Martin raced out to the main deck. The monks had the ships surrounded. A light rain sprayed down, and when lightning flashed in the distance, Martin clearly saw the outline of the monks' heads in the water, still unmovable as a mountain range, the fire in their eyes swirling in synchronicity.

The destroyer was alongside the cutter, dangerously close. It rose higher in the water, but Martin could make out the silhouettes of men moving slowly and deliberately, no sense of urgency.

On the cutter, men emerged from below deck in their service whites and fell into formation. Martin ran to De Luca.

"De Luca!" he yelled. "What's happening?"

The Specialist seemed like a sleepwalker, solemn, expressionless.

"De Luca!" Martin yelled again. "There's something wrong with Behan."

Frustrated, he punched him in the shoulder. De Luca continued to march his predetermined course. It was the same with every one of the men. Martin's shouting had no effect. The rain didn't wake them. They formed lines with choreographed precision as they filled the deck.

Martin started back toward the bridge as every light on the ship flicked on at once. The same happened on the destroyer.

A set of cannons on the destroyer began to roar. Martin could see the shells burst into light as they made impact with the monks' faces and then disappear harmlessly. The monks made no move to stop the barrage, and Martin was suddenly worried for the gunners.

The fire lasted for several minutes while all else on and around the ships remained still. When the guns stopped, Martin steeled himself. He thought he heard shrieking from the direction of the destroyer. It frayed Martin's nerves, but it was mercifully short-lived, and then all was silent again.

Behan moved from his spot on the bridge and made his way down to the rear deck. Martin shouted again, trying in vain to break whatever spell he was under. Behan took his place in front of the rows of men and waited.

Martin ran onto the bridge and tried to call for help on the radios. Nothing, not even static. He considered trying for one of the battlements, but thought better of it. He walked around the ship, looking for shelter or some way to fight. All decks were filled with silent, staring men, nearly a hundred and fifty crew members. He made his way through their ranks looking for any flicker of life on their faces. He found none.

Whatever the monks were doing, they had started with the destroyer. Martin thought he heard voices but couldn't understand the language.

That limbo dragged on for what seemed like hours until he began to pray the monks would sink the cutter and get it over with. All the while, Behan and his men stood on the deck without shifting. Martin knew they weren't acting of their own accord.

Finally, the ceremony on the destroyer ended. Martin's breath quickened. Between the two ships, giant black fingers slowly rise from the water and grasped the middle of the destroyer. The metal groaned and crumpled, and then screeched as it began to tear. Martin pushed his hands against his ears but it did little to muffle the sound of the destroyer breaking up, thick steel tearing easy as aluminum foil.

The once mighty ship displaced tons of ocean water just a few feet from the cutter, but the cutter didn't move. Once it slipped completely under the dark water, Martin was able to see the full ring of monks surrounding them. They closed the ranks and blotted out the moon so just the small space between two heads allowed any trace of light to show through.

The monk directly behind the boat rose, looking down at Behan. Three men who had been hiding below deck sprang out from the shadows with machine guns blazing towards the monk's eyes. Martin allowed himself a brief hope that this last-ditch effort would have some effect. The monk trained its gaze on them and waited for the trio to expend their ammunition. One by one, the guns ceased.

Two of the men stared into the eyes of the monk. Their expressions turned and they took their place in formation with the rest. The remaining man screamed and wailed himself into a frenzy. "I'll kill you!" he cried. "I'll kill you all!"

The monk reached out, delicately, and took the man between its thumb and index finger and lifted him over the formation of sailors. With the slightest of pressure, he crushed him, sending his blood spraying over the tidy white suits of those below. Not one of the men moved.

The monk returned its attention to Behan. The captain began to speak, but not in any language Martin recognized. It was guttural, all squashed phrasing and harsh vowels. When he was done, he removed his coat, then shirt and stood stripped to the waist. He curled his fingers into the flesh of his stomach and began to pull, face twitching. The skin tore. Behan kept pulling until he had opened his skin to his ribcage. His innards slumped forward but didn't fall completely out with the rush of blood. The captain stood trembling on the deck for nearly a full minute before he collapsed.

Three of the men fell out of formation, disappeared momentarily, and returned with a metal barrel. The monk took the barrel and dipped it into the ocean, filling it with saltwater. The first man broke formation and stood next to Behan's body. He began the same process, speaking in the same rough language. When finished, he stripped completely and lowered himself into the barrel. The monk covered the top with its finger until the barrel shook with the involuntary spasms of life leaving a body. When the shaking stopped, the monk emptied the barrel with the lifeless body of the sailor back onto the deck.

Another man walked calmly from formation and took his place. It continued like that, orderly and formal, as each sailor received his end. The monks were in no hurry. They dispatched man after man, leaving their husks steaming in piles.

Without realizing it, Martin had taken his place in the very back of the formation. An aneurysm blossomed deep in his skull as he struggled but he could no longer force himself to move. His body would not obey his impulses. The rain had gotten stronger but made no sound, and there was no thunder paired with the sporadic lightning. The only thing Martin could hear was the explosive muttering of each individual sailor standing for their judgment.

Martin wanted to weep. He had lost track of time, but the line was getting shorter. As he got closer he could feel a hum emanating from the monks, an inscrutable conversation. De Luca was only a few spots ahead. Martin tried to make eye contact but couldn't get his attention. De Luca was placid. Peaceful.

The piles of extinguished sailors now took up most of the deck, and the smell of bile and seawater was overwhelming. Under different circumstances, it would have made Martin wretch uncontrollably. He was too numb for that. All he could feel was a dull pressure all over his body, as if he were slowly sinking into the crushing depth of the ocean. He began to feel something like calm.

When it was De Luca's turn, he didn't speak. He stripped down like the others and approached the barrel. As he climbed up to take his final dip, he turned and found Martin in the crowd. He smiled though sad eyes. De Luca then let himself drop, and in a few minutes, it was over, and he lay on the deck with the rest.

De Luca's smile broke Martin. He wanted to scream, to cry, to pull De Luca's body away, but he was trapped inside of himself. He knew his death was inevitable and became impatient for it. Nearly a hundred and fifty dead. Just a few more to go. Martin would be the last one to die, the only witness to the carnage of the past twenty-four hours.

The sky was clearing, and the first stretch of red defined the border between the ocean and sky behind the monks. Martin was relieved to know it was finally his turn, until the monks turned their eyes to him. The pressure increased dramatically. The monks began to buzz. For the first time, he could see their mouths as they opened in unison, emitting the same orange, swirling light.

Martin felt thoughts invading his head that weren't his own. They didn't come from his rational mind. Life is inevitable. Death is inevitable. We are given both. To navigate them, we are given love and fear.

The hum from the monks grew louder. Everything Martin feared flickered through his mind. The bodies in front of him. The men he had seen in newsreels going off to war. The ships the monks had destroyed. The *Dorchester*, which had been lost in the Atlantic earlier in the war. Japanese planes diving into ships. Bombs falling on the house where Rita and his daughter were living, their bodies in the wreckage. A storm overtook a fleet, sinking the ships and bombers. The war was lost. It was his fault. Tears wet his cheeks as the images sped by. He felt himself losing consciousness.

Then he saw Rita. As she might be at that very moment, radiant in a blue dress, tending to their daughter in her cradle. He saw them on their first date, laughing over dinner in an expensive restaurant. He'd tried to impress her, but she'd said she hated the food there, so he'd paid the check and they wound up at a diner, enjoying each other's company until the place closed down. He saw the birth of his daughter, the exhausted smile on Rita's face. He saw his parents and grandparents and aunts and uncles gathered around a table at Christmas dinner when he was eight. He saw soldiers and pilots and seamen returning from the European campaign to be with their loved ones again. His body expanded, taller than buildings, over the cities and towns, then larger than the cosmos, where he could see stars and planets and all of creation. Everything began to retreat as he shrank, smaller and smaller, until he was an insignificant piece of dust in a meaningless universe.

"Yes," he said. Martin's small, broken voice startled him. His breath was his own again. His will was his own. "Yes!" he shouted again, drawing it out with the last breath in his lungs.

Martin opened his eyes. The monks were gone. The sea was calm, and the cutter was once again rocking gently with the waves.

Alone on the ship, he went to his equipment locker and retrieved his first balloon of the day. He inflated it, fixed it with its radiosonde, and let it go and watched it with his naked eye as it floated into a clear blue, orange, and yellow sky of unspeakable beauty.

About the Cover Artist

"I shine a light in the darkness so you can look your fears in the eye."

Ogmios has a passion for creativity and a flare for the dynamic. An artist, author, game designer and the publisher for OTB Comics & Games, Ogmios is also art director and co-founder of Rising Phoenix Game Con, manages the art show for Camp NECON Writers Conference and was the Artist Guest of Honor at TotalCon 2020, the largest game convention in New England. Art by Ogmios can be seen on many published book covers and interior illustrations including prior releases by the New England Horror Writers. He has a strong background in graphic design, has run his own multimedia company, and was an art director for a memorabilia company working directly with clients like Disney, the NFL, Macy's and NASA. In addition to book covers and illustrations, he has created comics, game art, software graphics, poster art, band CD covers and art, tattoos, t-shirts, broadcast animations, video graphics and much more. Ogmios works primarily with pencil, ink and digital paint to bring to life subjects like fantasy, sci-fi, myth, and especially monsters and creepy things. Current projects include his table-top game, *Lightning RPG* and several comic projects through OTB Comics & Games, book illustrations for two-time, best-selling author Lisa Campion and a children's book with Bram Stoker Award finalist Meghan Arcuri and Haverhill House Publishing.

About the Authors

K. H. Vaughan is a refugee from academia with a Ph.D. in clinical psychology. In his other life he taught, published, and practiced in various settings, with particular interest in decision theory, forensic psychology, psychopathology, and methodology and philosophy of science. He writes and edits dark speculative fiction including horror, science fiction, and fantasy.

James A. Moore is the author of over twenty novels, including the critically acclaimed *Serenity Falls* trilogy (featuring his recurring anti-hero, Jonathan Crowley) and his most recent novels, *The Godless* and *Boomtown* He has twice been nominated for the Bram Stoker Award and spent three years as an officer in the Horror Writers Association, first as Secretary and later as Vice President.

The author cut his teeth in the industry writing for Marvel Comics and authoring over twenty role-playing supplements for White Wolf Games, including *Berlin by Night, Land of 1,000,000 Dreams* and *The Get of Fenris* tribe book for *Vampire: The Masquerade* and *Werewolf: The Apocalypse,* among others. He also penned the White Wolf novels *Vampire: House of Secrets* and *Werewolf: Hellstorm.* Moore's first short story collection, *Slices,* sold out before ever seeing print. He recently finished his latest novel, *The Warborn*, and is currently editing *Halloween Nights*, an anthology of new stories for Halloween.

Kristi Petersen Schoonover grew up in the woods but has always felt her home was by the sea. Her stories have appeared in many magazines and anthologies, and more are forthcoming in *Angela's Recurring Nightmares*, *Gen-Xed*, and *Crow& Cross Keys*; her books include a story collection, *The Shadows Behind.* She is founding editor of the dark literary journal *34 Orchard*, part-time co-host of the *Dark Discussions* podcast, and co-chair of the Horror Writers Association's Connecticut Chapter. She lives in Connecticut with her husband, Nathan, where she still sleeps with the lights on. Follow her adventures at kristipetersenschoonover.com.

Cindy O'Quinn is a two-time Bram Stoker Award-Nominated writer. Author of "Lydia", from the Shirley Jackson Award winning anthology: The Twisted Book of Shadows, and "The Thing I Found Along a Dirt Patch Road". She is an Appalachian writer from the mountains of West Virginia. Steeped in folklore at an early age. Cindy now lives in the woods of northern Maine. The old Tessier Homestead is the ideal backdrop for writing her dark stories and poetry.
Her work has been published or forthcoming in The Bad Book, HWA Poetry Showcase Vol V, Northern Frights, Eerie Christmas Anthology, Under Her Skin, Were Tales: A Shapeshifter Anthology, Space & Time Magazine, Chiral Mad 5, and others. Follow Cindy for updates: Facebook @CindyOQuinnWriter, Twitter @COQuinnWrites, and Instagram cindy.oquinn.

David Bernard is a native New Englander who now lives (albeit under protest) in South Florida, a paradoxical place where, when temperatures drop below 60°, locals break out parkas to wear over their plaid shorts and sandals. He also doesn't understand why they call it "snowbird season" if you're not allowed to shoot them. His work regularly appears in Pulp Adventures magazine. He can be found in such anthologies as Alternative Apocalypses (B Cubed Press), Legacy of the Reanimator (Chaosium), and The Chromatic Court (18th Wall Productions).

When asked what he does, **Rob Smales** tends to answer "I write words." When feeling particularly full of himself, he may go so far as "I write the words that occur to me at the time." Groupings of these words, often referred to as *stories*, have appeared in over three dozen publications and anthologies, been nominated for three Pushcart Prizes, won a couple of readers' choice awards, and thrice appeared in Ellen Datlow's honorable mentions list regarding her *Best Horror Of the Year* anthologies. Most recently, a story of his appeared in *Totally Tubular Terrors* ("Stardust"), and he has an upcoming release in *34 Orchard* ("Letter to the Other Side"). Facebook lists him as *Dad, writer, editor, postal worker—in that order,* and he hails from Salem, Massachusetts, where he works, writes, and, occasionally, sleeps.

Victoria Dalpe is an artist and writer based out of Providence, RI. Her dark short fiction has appeared in over twenty-five anthologies and her first novel, *Parasite Life* came out in 2018 through ChiZIne Publications and will be re-released in 2021 through Nightscape Press. Her short story collection, *Les Femmes Grotesques*, will be out with Clash Books in 2022. She is a member of the HWA and the New England Horror Writers. Victoria also co-edited the Necronomicon 2019 Memento Book with Justin Steele.

Katherine Silva is a Maine author of dark fiction, a connoisseur of coffee, and victim of cat shenanigans. She is a two-time Maine Literary Award finalist for speculative fiction and a member of the Horror Writers of Maine, Maine Writers and Publishers Alliance, and New England Horror Writers Association. Katherine is also a founder of Strange Wilds Press, Dark Taiga Creative Writing Consultations, and The Kat at Night Blog. Her latest book, *The Wild Dark*, is due out October 12th. You can find more info about Katherine at katherinesilvaauthor.com.

Errick Nunnally was born and raised in Boston, Massachusetts, and served one tour in the Marine Corps before deciding art school was a safer pursuit. He enjoys art, comics, and genre novels. A graphic designer, he has trained in Krav Maga and Muay Thai kickboxing. His work has appeared in several anthologies and is best described as "dark pulp." His work can be found in APEX MAGAZINE, FIYAH MAGAZINE, GALAXY'S EDGE, LAMPLIGHT, NIGHTLIGHT PODCAST, and the novels, LIGHTNING WEARS A RED CAPE, BLOOD FOR THE SUN, and ALL THE DEAD MEN. Visit erricknunnally.us to learn more about his work.

Richard Alan Scott's work has appeared in Premiere, Shroud, and

Albedo One, Ireland's #1 Genre magazine, as well as the Walls and Bridges Anthology. He is part of the Labyrinth Creators Journal of New Orleans and is featured in a CD/Book, The Black Stone: Stories for Lovecraftian Summonings, from Eighth Tower Records in Italy. He has been a Guest Writer for Crystal Lake Publishing's Still Water Bay and Shallow Waters series. He has finished two novels that are being queried and lives in rural Rhode Island near Lovecraft and Eddy's Great Dark Swamp. Visit him at richardalanscott.com

Morgan Sylvia is a metalhead, an Aquarius, a coffee addict, and a work in progress. A former obituarist, she is now a full-time freelance writer. Her fiction and poetry have appeared in several places, including *Coming Through In Waves: Crime Fiction Based On The Work Of Pink Floyd; Pseudopod; Wicked Witches; Wicked Weird; Haunted House Short Stories,* and *Endless Apocalypse.* She is also the author a horror novel, *Abode*; a fantasy novel, *Dawn*, which is the first of a trilogy; and two poetry collections. The most recent collection, *As The Seas Turn Red,* was nominated for an Elgin Award. She lives in Maine with her boyfriend, two cats, and a chubby goldfish, the cutest rescue dog ever, and several murders of crows. She is currently working on a novel and a short story collection. You can follow her at www.morgansylvia.com

Trisha J. Wooldridge writes novels, short fiction, non-fiction articles, and poetry that occasionally win awards—child-friendly ones are penned under T.J. Wooldridge. She's edited over a hundred novels and seven anthologies, including NEHW's *Wicked Women.* Her work can be found in all of the NEHW anthologies she hasn't edited; the Shirley Jackson Award-winning *The Twisted Book of Shadows*; *HWA Poetry Showcase 5, 6* and *8*; *More Tales from the Mythos Volume 2*; *34 Orchard* journal; *Paranormal Encounters*; and *Don't Turn Out the Lights, A Tribute to Alvin Schwartz's Scary Stories to Tell in the Dark.* www.anovelfriend.com.

J. Edwin Buja is a retired technical writer who lives in a village in Ontario, Canada. His first novel, The Wood Book One: The King of the Wood, was released in 2019. The second novel, The Wood Book Two: The Consort, is being released in 2021. He has published several short horror stories and is currently working on two ghost novels. A history major at university, he enjoys doing research for stories and has a special affinity for World War One.

D.E. Ladd has written short stories, novels, and screenplays in multiple genres, including fantasy, action, horror, thriller, science fiction, and drama. Derek is a PAGE Awards winner whose work has been featured in *Four Hundred Words* magazine and the *Stories of Oregon* audiobook. His chilling true story, The Penny Ghost, will appear in an upcoming issue of Scary Monsters Magazine. He spent over thirteen years working with clients as a professional content editor and story consultant, and when he's not writing he spends a great deal of time preparing for an alien-zombie-ninja warrior invasion.

Daniel R. Robichaud lives and writes in Humble, Texas though he dearly misses Worcester, Massachusetts. His work has appeared in *Sick Cruising, G is for Genies, H is for Hell, J is for Jack-'o'-Lantern, Infernal Clock: Inferno*, the May 2021 issue of the Flame Tree Press Newsletter, *Haunts and Hellions, Shark Week: Ocean Animals, The Periodical, Forlorn,* and *parABnormal* magazine. Forthcoming appearances include *The Devil's Doorbell 2, The Howling Dead, Attack of the Killer ____,* and *Wicked Creatures* anthologies. His fiction has been collected in *Hauntings & Happenstances: Autumn Stories* as well as the *Gathered Flowers, Stones, and Bones: Fabulist Tales,* both from Twice Told Tales Press. He writes weekly reviews of film and fiction at the Considering Stories (https://consideringstories.wordpress.com/) website. Keep up with him on Twitter (@DarkTowhead) or Facebook (https://www.facebook.com/daniel.r.robichaud).

Peter N. Dudar is an essential worker who helped keep our country running during the pandemic. Dudar has been writing and publishing fiction for over two decades, and shows no sign of slowing down. He is a proud member of the New England Horror Writers, with this being his sixth appearance in their anthology series. Learn more about him at www.PeterNDudar.com.

Former two-term Poet Laureate of New Bedford, Massachusetts (2014 – 2021), **Patricia Gomes** has been published in numerous literary journals and anthologies, most recently in *Sledgehammer, Pink Plastic House, Wicked Women, an Anthology of New England Horror Writers, Speculations, Alien Buddha Press, Star*Line, Bay State Echo, and Abyss & Apex.* Twice nominated for The Pushcart Prize, Gomes is the author of four chapbooks. Performing her work extensively throughout the New England area, she also conducts workshops for adults, students, and children. Ms. Gomes is the co-founder of the GNB Writers Block, and has been nominated for a 2021 Rhysling Award.

John C. Foster's novel *Dead Men* was published by Perpetual Motion Machine Publishing in 2015 and his second novel, *Mister White,* was published by Grey Matter Press in April of 2016. His debut collection of short stories, *Baby Powder and Other Terrifying Substances*, was published by Perpetual Motion Machine Publishing in January 2017. His short stories have appeared in numerous magazines and anthologies including *Shock Totem*, *Dark Moon Digest* and *Dread – the Best of Grey Matter Press* among others. He lives in Brooklyn with the actress Linda Jones.

Author and playwright **Howard Odentz** is a lifelong resident of the gray area between Western Massachusetts and North Central Connecticut. His love of the region is evident in his writing as he often incorporates the foothills of the Berkshires and the small towns of the Bay and Nutmeg states into his work. Howard's works include the young adult zombie romps Dead (a Lot), Wicked Dead and Dead End, the thrillers Bloody Bloody Apple, What We Kill, and Bottle Toss, the creepy anthology Little Killers A to Z, and the horror shorts Snow and Bones, both of which have been translated for the Italian market. The mysterious has always played a major role in Howard's writing. He is endlessly fascinated by the psychological aspects of those who are thrown into thrilling or otherworldly circumstances.

John Grover is a fiction author residing in Massachusetts. He completed a creative writing course at Boston's Fisher College and is a member of the New England Horror Writers Association. Some of his more recent credits include stories in The Heart of a Devil Anthology by Fantasia Divinity and The Ancient Ones II Anthology by Deadman's Tome. He is the author the new zombie apocalypse trilogy Underground and several collections, including his best of collection: Best of Shadow Tales—featuring reprinted works. Please visit his website www.shadowtales.com

Paul McMahon finally has an office and is writing like crazy, which is ironic because writing keeps him from losing his mind. His work has most recently appeared in the NEHW anthologies Wicked Tales, Wicked Witches and Wicked Haunted, as well as the superhero anthology Caped and the werewolf anthology Flesh Like Smoke. For years he'd maintained a regular movie review column on the much missed Cinema Knife Fight, where he was known as The Distracted Critic. His first standalone novella, Chilopodophobia, is available at most online book retailers. He is hard at work on a mosaic novel tenta9tively titled Bower's Cloud.

Timothy P. Flynn is a dark poet from Massachusetts. His previous poetry resides in Space and Time magazine, Anthocon's book collections: Anthology Years 1-3, Wicked Tales, Scifaikuest, haikuniverse, Haiku Journal and the HWA Poetry Showcase Vol 5 & Vol 6. He is a member of the New England Horror Writers and recipient of the 2021 HWA Dark Poetry Scholarship. Follow him on Twitter: @TimothyPFlynn or on Instagram: instagram.com/timothypflynnwriter

F. R. Michaels is a bipedal hominid who happens to like weird and scary stories. Seriously. His work has appeared in Alfred Hitchcock's Mystery Magazine and Haunts (as Frank Michaels) as well as the anthologies Strangely Funny II, Mysterion, and Wicked Weird. He dwells on the Northern Hemisphere of Earth and writes horror and dark fantasy.

Nick A. Zaino III is going to keep doing all of the things until he gets one of them right. In June of 2021, he celebrated twenty years of covering comedy for the Boston Globe as a freelance writer. He also released a new EP of original folk called Hardcover Fiction and season two of his podcast The Department of Tangents, which features interview with notable creators in comedy, music, and horror. His horror fiction has appeared in One Buck Horror and *Rom Zom Com: A Romantic Zombie Comedy Anthology*. He continues to write, record, and broadcast via social media from his basement bunker office in Lynn, Ma. Despite its third person nature, he is also the author of this bio, perhaps his greatest work.

About the Editors

Scott T. Goudsward: By day Scott is a slave to the cubicle world, by night to the voices in his head. He writes primarily horror but has branched out to sci-fi and fantasy. Scott is one of the coordinators of the New England Horror Writers. His short fiction has most recently appeared in *Fright Train.* His latest novel Fountain of the Dead has been re-released through Crossroad Press. The new co-written non-fiction book Horror Guide to Northern New England is out now from Post Mortem Press. Anthology projects include the new books Wicked Creatures from NEHW Press and Fright Train from Haverhill House Press (Co-edited with Tony Tremblay and Charles R. Rutledge. Scott is currently working on a YA novel and looking for homes for new anthology possibilities.

Daniel G. Keohane is the Bram Stoker-nominated author of *Solomon's Grave*, *Margaret's Ark* and *Plague of Darkness* and recently released a middle grade YA novel *The Photograph* written with David Hilman. Writing as G. Daniel Gunn he's released the horror novel *Destroyer of Worlds* and novella

Nightmare in Greasepaint (with L.L. Soares). His short fiction has been published in dozens of magazines and anthologies over the years, including *On Spec*, *Cemetery Dance*, *Borderlands 6, Apex Digest* and many more. You can visit Dan and keep up-to-date with prior and future work at www.dankeohane.com

David Price is a writer and editor who lives in Woburn, Massachusetts and has worked as a hardwood floor contractor for more than thirty years. He is a member of the New England Horror Writers, the Science Fiction & Fantasy Writers of America, the Horror Writers of Maine and the Horror Writers Association. David is author of the paranormal suspense novella, *Dead in the USA*, and the weird fantasy novel, *Lightbringers*. He has edited the anthologies *Wicked Tales, Wicked Witches, Wicked Haunted*, and *Northern Frights 1 & 2.* @_David_Price_ davidpriceauthor.com facebook.com/priceiswriter/

The New England Horror Writers (NEHW) provides peer support and networking for authors of horror and dark fantasy in the New England Area. NEHW is primarily a writer's organization, focusing on authors of horror and dark fiction in all mediums (novels, short stories, screenplays, poetry, etc) in the New England area. We are also open to professional editors, artists & illustrators, agents and publishers of horror and dark fiction. NEHW activities include book signings, readings, panel discussions at conventions, and social gatherings. With members ranging from Maine to Connecticut, NEHW events take place in varying locations in an effort to provide support for our members throughout New England. Find us on Facebook or at www.newenglandhorror.org.

www.ingramcontent.com/pod-product-compliance
Lightning Source LLC
LaVergne TN
LVHW091037080826
845145LV00002B/532

* 9 7 8 0 9 9 8 1 8 5 4 5 3 *